THE FATE OF THE REALM

THE FATE OF THE REALM

Rose Marie Machario

Cover art: Randy Humphrey

Editor: Holly Marie Phillippe

Published by Seventh Star Press, LLC.

ISBN Number: 979-8-9861185-1-2

Seventh Star Press

www.seventhstarpress.com

info@seventhstarpress.com

Publisher's Note:

The Fate of the Realm is a work of fiction. All names, characters, and places are the product of the author's imagination, used in fictitious manner. Any resemblances to actual persons, places, locales, events, etc. are purely coincidental.

Printed in the United States of America

First Edition

Dedication

This book is dedicated to those in my life who have never given up on me, even during my darkest days, and for bringing me back to the light…

A special thanks goes out to two of the most creative people I know, that helped to bring my vision of the book's new cover to life. Ashley Burt, who created the pendant of Yggdrasill, seen on the beautiful cover, that Randy Humphrey so skillfully designed. And to Stephen and Holly, the best publisher and editor, that an author could ever ask for…

For all of my dearest readers and fans, this sequel is for you…

And to all of my Pagan sisters and brothers, Blessed Be…

PROLOGUE

Princess Ellyria Rose was sitting at her white vanity, combing out her waist-length black hair, in front of the large oval mirror. Staring back at her was the reflection of a girl, that was still not yet a woman. She did not look a year older. She did not feel a year older. Her skin was porcelain white, all but her sun-kissed cheeks. Her bee-stung lips were the same hue as of a spring rose. Her almond-shaped eyes were the perfect shade of sparkling sapphires, which could change to the color of emeralds if she became angered. Although the reflection of her, had not changed and it was soon replaced by images of her past. Princess Ellyria's adventures within the past year came into play within the reflection of her enchanted mirror, as she recalled the events in her mind. Events that changed her life forever…

In the race to find The Amulet of Elements, Princess Ellyria had set out on a most adventurous quest to find the necklace before the wizard did. Upon reaching the place where her visions had shown the amulet to be, she was captured upon arrival by the Vikings. After finding the amulet, they set out to trade with the gypsies, in the land of Inamor. The Viking, Rob the Red, sold the amulet to a gypsy and decided to take Princess Ellyria with him, to their ship that was docked in Regnuom. Princess Ellyria thought that she would never be rescued so far out at sea, until fate reunited her with Lord Brom, who had joined his brother, Captain Jake, on the very ship that she was on. Her joy was short-lived when a marauding battleship full of Vikings attacked. It was Princess Ellyria's quick wit that saved the merchant ship Draki, and all of their lives. The vessel had minor damages, but it still had to dock in Inamor for repairs. Lord Brom and Princess Ellyria returned to the gypsy market in search of the amulet, where they met the bandolier of the gypsies, Vadoma, who informed her of her new destiny. With only three days, before she was to receive the Power of Litha, Princess Ellyria had to learn to harness its majick, but they were not prepared for the wizard, Raul, to make his appearance during the quickening. Princess Ellyria had not had the skills to save her mentor, but she managed to fight off the wizard until he retreated. Lord Brom and Princess Ellyria said farewell to Vadoma, before heading back home to Toledya, without the amulet…

Princess Ellyria saw the images of the past fade from sight. Over the past year, she had worked hard to prepare herself for the impending battle with the wizard. Having only just mastered her power of telekinesis, she still lacked the power of empathy and the ability to communicate with animals. Vadoma had said they would come when needed, once the other powers had been mastered. She smiled to herself. One down, and two to go…

"What is to come? Show me," she said, to the enchanted mirror.

The mirror became clouded, her image vanished, and darkness took over completely. She could see nothing. What did that mean? The Princess peered deeper into the large mirror. The darkness lifted, revealing a forest filled with bright light, then it grew dark again. Princess Ellyria's reflection returned. She had yet to master the mirror's majick. Perhaps one day, she might learn to control it. She stood up, then looked over to her oversized wolf Isis, who was sleeping in her favorite spot by her bed. She was suddenly tired. It had been a long day of spell work, and it was time to retire for the night. It was nearing the Summer Solstice, the anniversary of becoming the Chosen One, and she had finally embraced her destiny. It was only a week away and she had planned a return trip to Inamor, to study with the gypsies' new bandolier. She crawled into her four-poster canopy bed, before she knew it, she had drifted off to sleep…

Sweat trickled down her body underneath her nightgown. She could not get the images out of her head of the visions, that had just invaded her sleep. The cries of the innocent were protesting their entrapment, and the evil presence she felt, made her heart beat faster with fear. She could only recall images of tiny dancing lights and a giant tree in a forest of darkness. It was the fear and the great sadness that had awakened her.

Princess Ellyria leaned over clutching her head, a few moments passed before the room had finally stopped spinning. She looked up, curious as to the hour, then with a wave of her hand revealed the darkness outside her window. When she lowered her hand, the curtain covered the window again...

Princess Ellyria closed her eyes, after returning to her pillow, her head embraced by the down feathers that were stuffed inside…

PART ONE: THE CURSE OF THE BLACK FOREST

Tiny voices screamed as they were caught in butterfly nets. Unable to fly out, their light of life grew dimmer, lacking enough air to breathe. The tiny creatures were being jostled about, in the dark sack they had been shoved inside. Only two were inside, a male and a female, they were siblings. After having been taken while in mid-flight, it had damaged the young male's tiny wing. His sister tried to console him, but he was slowly drifting in and out of consciousness. She too could barely keep her eyes open…

A young man entered the meager cottage carrying a small brown sack. He set it down on the wooden table, then stepped back waiting for his mistress to give further instructions.

"How many were you able to find for me this time?" a sensual voice questioned the young man.

The young apprentice knew his mistress would be displeased with him, so his long hesitation only seemed to irritate her.

"Well?" the woman asked, growing increasingly agitated.

When he finally spoke up, he prepared himself for the lashing that he was sure he would receive.

"I was only able to find two this time," he confessed, looking at the floor.

The older woman rose from her wooden rocking chair and went to the wall, where a whip hung from its hook.

"You know the punishment. Turn around and take off your tunic. I have told you now several times, that I require no less than three of those filthy creatures, yet you have only brought two," she scolded, in a calm voice.

The boy screamed out in pain with the first lash, that sliced open his dark ashy skin. Blood trickled slowly down his back when the second blow from the whip came. He clenched his teeth awaiting the next attack, which seemed to penetrate harder, cutting open the tender flesh between his shoulder blades. Bracing his body up against the table, he received several other lashes, by now he had lost count. He could not take any more pain, and his knees buckled underneath his own weight. The last crack of the whip made him scream again, as tears soaked the young man's cheeks.

"Mother, please stop! I am sorry! I will go back out, and find more! Please, I promise!" he pleaded, then heard her hang the whip back up on the wall. His back burned, and the stickiness of the blood had already begun to clot, tugging on his skin as he stood up. After he wiped the tears from his face, he flinched as his mother began to wipe the blood from his back.

"You know that I hate having to punish you, do you not?" she scoffed, while dipping the blood-soaked cloth back into the basin of cool water. After wringing out the cloth, she continued to cleanse his skin. "I only meant for you to learn that it is of grave importance that you listen, and do as I say. Is that understood?" His mother scolded, then returned the cloth to the water and helped him to put his tunic back on. "Now go, and finish what you set out to do the first time. Do not come back until you have at least two more."

The older woman peered into the brown sack after the young man had left the cottage into the darkness. Reaching inside, she tried to grab one of the tiny creatures, and quickly retracted her hand back from inside the bag, placing a finger inside her mouth.

"You vile little sprite!" she cried out, then turned the bag upside down, and two tiny winged creatures fell out onto the table. One lay motionless, while the other quickly went to it and cradled its tiny body in its lap. She leaned down to get a closer look. She saw that one of them was not breathing and picked it up by its wings. It was dead. "Uh, oh, this will not do. Here, kitty, kitty."

A solid black Skogkatt jumped down from its perch on the cabinet and rubbed its body up against her mistress.

"Here, Kisa, how about a nice treat for you?" she called, dangling the dead sprite over the forest cat's head.

The tiny, winged waif on the table was crying and jumping up and down, saying something in her native tongue.

"Oh, what is the matter little one?" she asked, leaning down to face the three-inch person. She saw tiny tears glisten in the light, on the half-naked sprite girl's face.

The sprite's body was that of an adolescent and only covered by leaves, that were held together by the thread of a silkworm. The male, most likely her brother, was dressed in the same fashion, only a leaf covered the lower half of him. He lay there limp, from the wings she held him by.

"I suppose that you do not want me to give him to my cat, huh?"

The girl shook her head no, pressing her hands together, with an urgent look about her face.

"Ah, that is too bad," she said, then tossed the lifeless body into Kisa's open jaws.

The tiny girl sprite fell to the table, bringing her little legs up in front of her. She wrapped her arms around her knees and began to rock back and forth. Miniature tears made small puddles on either side of her. She looked up at this giant white-haired monster before her. She tried to get up, but the woman caught her just in time before she could take flight. The sprite was helpless, as her captor began to rip off her tiny wings from her body, then placed them in a jar. Blood spilled from empty wing sockets and the tiny female neared the point of fainting, before being shoved inside a gaping mouth.

Well, she went down fairly easy. She did not even kick on the way down," she mused, to Kisa while laughing. The large cat purred and stretched after she finished playing with her meal; tiny wings were all that remained on the floor by her paws. "Was he good, my precious?" she questioned, then lowered herself back down in her rocker, and watched as the few liver spots on her hands began to disappear. Kisa jumped into her mistress's lap, causing the woman to wince uncomfortably under the weight of her heavy cat. After Kisa settled in her lap, she purred to the wondrous sensation of soft hands stroking the length of her body. "Now, we only have to wait for our next meal to be brought to us."

The woman continued to rock in the chair, lulling herself and her familiar into a little nap…

Chapter 1

Princess Ellyria Rose had awakened, to the warmth of the sun pouring in from the window of her bedchamber. She lay there in bed, too comfortable to leave, and wished to linger just a little while longer. The open window let in a cool morning breeze, that blew the light material hanging from her four-poster canopy bed. Such tranquil serenity caused her to drift off to sleep once again…

Flashes of bright light came to her in the darkness, and she could feel great sorrow coming from the trees. The forest was shrouded with an evil presence, that held its own occupant's prisoner. The cries were getting shriller, they were no longer coming from the trees, but from something else. The heaviness in her chest returned, she could not move, could barely breathe, and the dull ache in her head was deafening. The cries had become screams. The dancing lights were growing dim, leaving nothing to see but the darkness. She heard a distant voice calling to her. She walked through the forest trying to find where it was coming from. Without being able to see in the near distance, she had to be cautious in unfamiliar surroundings. All of a sudden, a glowing being came to her, reaching their hands out to her.

"Princess, we need you! Please, help us!" The woman in front of her shouted before she vanished into thin air…

Princess Ellyria woke up barely able to her catch her breath. She placed her hands to her head and looked about her room. It appeared unchanged, but something was different somehow. Shrugging it off, Princess Ellyria got up from the cozy bed and began to get ready for the day. She brushed her hair, washed her face, and put on a light, pale pink, cotton gown.

Once she stepped out into the hall, she braced herself up against her door. Once the feeling had passed, she headed downstairs. By the time she reached the bottom of the stairs, the dull ache in her head had returned. She placed her hands on either side of her temples and closed her eyes…

"Ellyria, Ellyria!" Queen Anna shouted, when she found her daughter unconscious, on the floor at the foot of the stairs. "Please, someone help!" she screamed, trying to get anyone's attention.

Prince Anthony heard his mother and ran to her side.

"Let us get her to the parlor, and lay her on the chaise," she told her eldest son.

He picked up his sister in his arms and carried her into the parlor, gently setting her down on the chaise.

Prince Dakota had heard the commotion and ran in to join his mother and brother. After he entered the room, he saw his younger sister lying motionless on the chaise.

"What happened?" Prince Dakota asked. He knelt beside her and retrieved the smelling salts, from the pouch that he always wore on his belt. He waved them under Princess Ellyria's nose, and slowly she started coming around.

"Oh, are you alright, my dear?" her mother asked, wiping her hair from her face.

Princess Ellyria blinked a few times, then opened her eyes fully to reveal Prince Anthony, Prince Dakota, and her mother standing over her.

"What happened? Where am I?"

"I was going to ask you the same thing," Prince Anthony said.

"Do you feel unwell?" Prince Dakota questioned, as he checked his sister for a fever, thinking perhaps she was becoming ill.

"Not really, but earlier I felt incredibly - lightheaded, then I had a horrible pain in both sides of my head," she answered, shaking her head no. "I feel better now."

They all looked at her strangely. Princess Ellyria slowly sat up, clutched her head immediately, then laid back down.

"Why are all of you feeling so worried right now? I am fine, it will pass like it did earlier this morning," she confessed. "Anthony, if you are in a hurry to meet with your men, just go on. I will be fine."

"Wait a minute. How did you know that?" Prince Anthony queried, looking confused.

"I do not know really. It is rather strange," Princess Ellyria winced, then grabbed the sides of her head again, rolled to her side, crying from the sudden pain.

"Let us get her some chamomile tea please," her mother called out to Nan, who was standing by the entryway of the parlor.

"Yes, your Highness," said Nan, who left quickly to the kitchen to fetch the tea.

Princess Ellyria let out a sigh of relief, as the pain subsided.

"So, you were saying this happened earlier? Was that the first time?" Prince Dakota questioned.

"No, actually. It happened before I went to bed, once in the night, and twice this morning," she answered, rubbing her temples.

"Can you think of anything that might have triggered these episodes?" Prince Dakota asked, then waited for her to take a few sips of the tea that Nan had brought in for her.

" I hope you feel better soon sister, but I am afraid that I can not wait any longer. I am being sent to Regnuom this morning, to see how things are holding up without a king present to protect the throne. I shall return soon," Prince Anthony promised, then bent down to place a kiss on his sister's forehead before leaving the room.

Princess Ellyria was sitting up now, taking slow sips of the hot liquid.

"I had a dream, or a premonition of sorts, I believe," she answered, looking at her brother, and mother. "It was very strange, and it did not make any sense to me."

"What was it? Do you remember any of it?" her mother asked.

Princess Ellyria cradled her cup in her hands and tried to recall the images again.

"There was darkness and tiny dancing lights. I heard their cries, and I felt their pain. I am not quite sure what it was, or how I was feeling, or what they were. Then a lady that was surrounded by a glowing light called out to me in a forest. She needed my help, but she disappeared, then I woke up. I had also seen strange images of darkness, and the dancing lights in my mirror, before I had gone to sleep. What do you think it means?"

Her mother and Prince Dakota looked at one another, then back to Princess Ellyria.

"Why are you concerned and nervous, mother?"

Queen Anna lowered her gaze to the floor, then to her daughter again.

"Sister, I do believe that you have gotten your second power, the power of empathy. Somehow, it has been triggered by this new event," Prince Dakota said.

"The premonition that you had, of whomever, is obviously powerful enough to call to you for help; it would make perfect sense. Do you have any idea where this is taking place?" Queen Anna agreed, nodding her head.

"I could only see a forest. Although, I know for certain it is not the Dark Forest of Woe. Perhaps the gypsies could help me?"

"I understand that it is your destiny to defeat the wizard, and to help those in the realm. I just wish that you could stay here and remain safe, until it is time to face the wizard. I know that you are not quite ready yet," her mother chided, then reached out to hold her daughter's hand.

"I shall be fine, and I will not be going after the wizard. We have not heard anything of him since I managed to get away. That was a year ago, mother. Have faith in me, please. I shall only be going to Inamor, and I can leave when Prince Ian leaves to secure the throne in Regnuom for father," she proposed, then squeezed her mother's hand in return and smiled.

"How did you know about Ian?" Prince Dakota questioned.

"It was what Anthony was thinking, but somehow I felt how he felt about it," she answered, feeling strange with having such knowledge. "Mother, will you speak to father for me?" The eagerness was written all over her face.

"I suppose I could," Queen Anna smiled at her daughter. She embraced the girl, as she had practically leapt off the chaise towards her.

"Oh, thank you, mother. I promise to stay out of trouble and remain with the gypsies the entire time that I am there," she swore.

Princess Ellyria finished her tea, then left to go find Isis, who was probably already out in their favorite wading spot…

Chapter 2

Raul was pacing back and forth angrily. He had tried so many different variations of the power-stripping potion, but it just was not coming together the way he desired. After trying to come up with a solution for nearly a year now, he had decided to try another route. Perhaps instead of trying to get the Princess to drink the potion, he could put it into something to eat. This he would have to ponder further...

"Come here, boy."

Toby stopped scrubbing the floors and went to see what his master wanted.

"Yes, sire?" Toby stood waiting for orders.

Raul looked at the boy in front of him; he had grown so much in such little time.

"How old are you now, boy?"

"I just turned twelve, sire," Toby said, then began to fidget with the string holding up his trousers.

"How are your lessons coming?"

"Fine, sire. My tutor says that I am doing well and that I can read just as well as her," the boy replied proudly.

Raul decided this was as good a time as any, to tell him his good fortune.

"Well then, that is good to hear. You do read rather well now," he responded, studying the boy's face. He looked rather worried, then thought it best to give him something to smile about. "I have decided to take you on as my apprentice. What do you have to say about that?"

Toby could not hide the disappointment in his face, because he was hoping he would be released from his service.

"Why do you look as though I just killed your pet?"

"Well, sire."

"Speak up. You may speak freely."

"I, I just assumed that you were going to let me go see my father, sire," the boy said timidly.

Raul was amused by the boy's innocence. He placed an arm around him and led him to the window.

"I will give you some sound advice, young one. Assuming makes an arse out of you, and me. However, I will let it slide just this once. Do not let it happen again. Do you understand?" he chided, looking down at the boy.

"Yes, sire," he said, staring out the window.

"I think you should come with me," the wizard said, patting him on the back, before he grabbed the boy, then they disappeared...

Raul had brought Toby to the last place that he could have never imagined. Home...

Toby looked up at Raul, with disbelief in his eyes.

"Why did we come here, sire?"

Raul looked down at the boy and pointed off into the distance. Toby's eyes widened as he started to run off, but the wizard caught him by his shirt.

"Not so fast, boy."

The boy lowered his gaze to the dirt road. He was so close to his father, yet so far away.

"I did not bring you here to return you to your father. I brought you back to say goodbye. If you are to become my apprentice, then you must cut the ties that bind. There is no other way," the wizard advised, before disappearing.

Toby looked all around him. Where did he go?

All of a sudden, Raul reappeared at the blacksmith's workshop. Toby saw him, and his heart beat faster than he had ever felt before. He saw Raul speaking with his father, but he was too far away to hear what was being said. He saw his father looking over in his direction, and without thinking started running to him. He was not sure what was driving him to be exact, but it was completely on impulse. He did not stop though, he ran through the middle of town, even knocking into people walking by. Only a few feet from reaching his destination, he stopped dead in his tracks. Toby fell to his knees and screamed. He covered his face with his hands, unable to look upon the terrible sight in front of him…

Raul snatched the boy and returned to the cottage. He had told the boy it had to be done, and to stop his blubbering. This was his new path, not the path of a soot covered, poor blacksmith, like his father. He allowed the boy to retire to his bedroom, but he would expect him to continue with his chores as if nothing had happened.

Toby lay on his small straw bed and cried himself to sleep shortly after. In his sleep, he was haunted by images of the wizard and his father. Running as fast as he could to get to his father, pushing past the passerby, dodging in and out of the crowd; he had even seen his father try to run to him. The wizard prevented him from going, his father grabbed his hot iron from the fire and tried to stab the wizard with it. Raul became quite angered and caused the poker to burn his father's hand. When the poker was dropped, Raul seized his father, ripped out his heart, then let him fall face-first into the fire. The wizard saw that the boy had seen what had happened, took a bite of his father's heart, then just for show, threw it into the fire.

Toby woke up from the nightmare, his clothes were soaked with sweat. He had also wet his bed, something he had not done since he was a little tyke. He was hurt beyond reason. First from his mother's passing shortly after he was born, which left his father to raise him alone, to then being taken away from his father; only to see him one more time, before he was murdered mercilessly in front of him. He would avenge his father right now if he could. Without knowledge he was powerless, and he had no one else that could save him from the wizard.

Toby vowed that night, to learn everything he could from Raul, to become his apprentice. Then one day, he would have his revenge in honor of his father…

Chapter 3

A few days had passed and Prince Anthony had returned to Toledya, with news from Regnuom. He went straight to his father's study to inform him of his findings.

"You may enter," the King announced, motioning his eldest son to come in and sat down.

"Father, I have just found out that none of the Lords are willing to assume the throne in Regnuom. I am guessing they do not want the responsibilities. It is such a peaceful kingdom," Prince Anthony informed him.

"Are you positive? I do not want to send your brother Ian into a mob of angry Lords over the throne," King Jason replied, rubbing his chin.

"I am positive, sir. Lord Thomas led a meeting with the few Lords that remain, and none of them wanted the position," he assured. "Are you sure Ian is ready to sit on a throne?"

"I think it will be a good experience for him. It will also help me to see what kind of ruler he will make," he replied. "Besides, it will only be an acting king position, since I am technically the King of their realm by the treaty your great grandfather, King Charles, had made."

Prince Anthony understood and would not dare challenge his father's authority.

"Would you like me to fetch Ian for you?"

"Yes, thank you, son," King Jason replied, then watched his eldest son leave the room. He would have been so proud if Prince

Anthony had shown interest in the crown, but he insisted that he become a knight. He understood his son wanting to be right in the action, and not at a desk all day like he was. The only time he was able to be in the excitement was during a great battle, but in a peaceful kingdom, war is seldom seen.

Prince Anthony returned with Prince Ian, but had to leave to settle his affairs and rest a while, from his hasty journey back home earlier.

"You wanted to see me, father?" Prince Ian asked.

"Yes, please come in my son. I would like you to be the acting King, in the kingdom of Regnuom," he announced.

"I would be proud to serve you on this matter, father," Prince Ian said, beaming inwardly with excitement.

King Jason knew that his son would be excited. He could see it all over his face, even though he was trying hard to keep it from him.

"That is good to hear. Right now they are accepting of you stepping in, as the acting King of their realm, so make sure you do not do anything to cause them to feel otherwise. Understand?"

"Oh, yes sir. I understand completely. I will not disappoint you, I promise," he reassured his father.

"Very well then. You will also be escorting your sister to the gypsy kingdom of Inamor, on your way to Regnuom. I am not too comfortable with this, but she will be under the gypsies' protection, and she is quite powerful enough to take care of herself. She is not, however, ready to go up against the wizard from what your brother Dakota tells me, but she has mastered her telekinesis," King Jason addressed, then stood up to walk out of the study with Prince Ian. "Make sure that you get her there safely, and send word to me the moment that you reach Regnuom."

"Of course, father. I will," he promised. Prince Ian left to bid farewell to his giant lion, Migata, and to inform his sister that she was going as well. They would leave at first light…

Princess Ellyria Rose rode in the carriage alongside her brother Prince Ian, at her father's insistence. She would have preferred to simply ride on horseback, calling less attention to their persons. The royal flag of Toledya was flying proudly in the air; a personal escort by six of her father's guards would carry on with her brother to Regnuom. Surprisingly, she was not being left with a personal guard while in Inamor. Her father had reluctantly decided to let her be on her own, once she arrived in the gypsy camp. It was three days until Midsummer, and she was excited to join in the celebration with her new family. Even though her mother was a full-blooded gypsy, she no longer practiced all of their customs since becoming queen. Though she still honored the culture and was incredibly proud of where she came from. The last time Princess Ellyria was in Inamor, she had received the Power of Litha, and become Vadoma's student. She thought of the woman who had given her own life for hers, and she missed her greatly. Returning there would bring back some of those horrible memories of her death, and how Raul had killed her.

Princess Ellyria looked out of the window of the carriage. It was a much slower trip than on horseback, even at a faster pace, and the journey was taking way too long.

"So sister, are you excited to go on an adventure that does not involve an abduction this time?"

Princess Ellyria flashed him a dirty look, from her glaring green eyes.

"I am sorry. I suppose that was not very funny, was it?"

"I shall let your inadequacy for being considerate slide this time, brother," she said coldly, but all those years of torment from him as a child made her quite bitter. Yes, of course, she loved him, he was still her brother, but she had to put him in his place. She was not that little girl he used to pick on anymore.

"I am sorry, Ellyria. I swear it. I cried the first time that you were captured, and the second time when you ran away. I was worried sick for you. I do love you, little sister."

"Well then, you could show it more often, instead of teasing me all of the time."

"Teasing you is my way of showing affection, you know that. Do you not?"

She just looked at her brother seated across from her in the carriage. It made sense since he had always been the jester, not the rebel like Prince Rowan, or the leader like Prince Anthony, or even the thinker like Prince Dakota. In a way, she was a little like all of her brothers, whom she used to envy so much growing up. Only within the past year, had she finally put her green monster to rest.

"Yes, I do love you too, brother. Even though you are a jerk at times," she teased.

Princess Ellyria looked back to the window, out in the distance she could see the large Oak Tree, where she and Lord Brom had rested once. There, just over the hill, was the elusive lake they had had an incredible experience in. Lilies and patches of thick clover surrounded the perfectly clear water. She closed her eyes and began to blush, from the feelings which stirred within her. She masked her face with her hand, so her brother did not inquire about the state of her cheeks, for she knew they were hot with color. She cleared the arousing images from her mind, but could not free the vision of Lord Brom. He had not sent any word to her since their parting. Maybe it was for the best, but she did miss him considerably. Her mother had told her to move on, saying if they were meant to be together they would be reunited one day. She could not foresee herself being in love with another, not like she loved Lord Brom, nor could she begin to fathom being with another man either. Right now her focus could not stray, she had to focus on her spell work, and learn more from the gypsies.

No more fantasizing about Lord Brom, Princess Ellyria swore to herself. Even though she was curious if he ever fantasized about her...

Chapter 4

After a year out at sea, Lord Brom had learned everything there was about working on his brother's ship, the Draki. He could do just about anything, from fishing, to the requirements of the first mate; Captain Jake had even taught him captain's duties as well. At the end of the day, they pulled in their nets, and were now heading to port to sell what they had caught to the fishmongers, then return to the sea. They would head north past Regnuom, to the colder waters, to catch the larger fish...

Lord Brom had stayed on the ship, with the first mate, Rob the Red, and some of the crew. They unloaded the crates to the eager merchants, who were ready to buy up all the fish for resale. Afterward, Lord Brom had returned to his cabin to clean up, and to wash the smell of the ocean off of him. When he had the bath drawn for him, he could not help but think of his Princess. When she had required the bath to make her accommodations better, while on this ship; he could not help but laugh, at the very idea of such a thing. He immediately shut up when some of the crew carried this tub up the stairs. Lord Brom had asked his brother where they had even gotten that large of a tub, or how they stored it on the ship. The porcelain tub with the gold claw feet he had gotten as a gift from a sheik in the desert, for the trade of some silks he had come across in the gypsy market. How she smelled like roses, as the wind blew through her hair, sending it straight to his nostrils. Her skin was so incredibly soft to the touch, her hands so innocent, as they touched him with feather-like strokes. He loved to run his fingers through her long black hair, so silky smooth, with the hidden aroma of roses. He adjusted himself at the very thought of having her. He was so close, when they were together at the lake if her father's guardsmen had not rudely interrupted them. His loins ached with need. He had not been with a woman in a year now, not since that little blonde barmaid he had turned into a woman. She was a real piece of work, once he had unleashed her desires, and her father was the only real problem that he had encountered. Right after he spilled his life into the girl, her father busted in the door before he had the chance to pull out. What a mess the rest of the night had been. He had the worst luck, after getting so inebriated he thought some toothless, uncomely whore was his Princess and went up to her room. He did not remember much of what exactly happened, or what he prayed did not happen with her. The angry father brought the master-at-arms to arrest him, for raping his daughter. It was definitely not rape; she was just as eager as him for their little romp. All of these memories of fornication had him so hard that it hurt. He reached down and grabbed his swelled manhood to ease his pain. It did not take long for him to quell the savage beast of his loins. After he finished his bath, he rose out of the tub. His statuesque body glistened from the little sunlight coming in through the porthole, as the water reflected it. Even the best sculptor in the world could not have replicated his rippled muscles, that stood out all over his body. Water dripped from his golden, mid-length hair, down his broad back, to his perfectly round buttocks and powerfully lean, long legs. He grabbed the large drying cloth and stepped out of the tub, before wrapping the towel around his chiseled waistline. Standing tall at a striking six foot four, his head nearly reached the ceiling of the cabin and he had to duck slightly going in and out of the doorway. He looked out of the port window to the ocean; his light blue eyes usually matched perfectly with the sky, but not today. Dark clouds were forming in the distance. The wind was on their side and would carry the ship to her destination with haste, with luck from the Gods, they would out-sail the impending storm...

Thunder clapped and lightning struck out, into a sky of blackness. The Draki rose up and down, as the waves crashed over her deck. Men frantically tried to keep her on course, but the oars broke against their futile attempts. The large sail was being held in place by several men trying to tie it down tighter. The wind caught the sail, lifting three of the surly men up off of their feet. Captain Jake tried to steer the ship, but too many odds were against trying to get the rudder to turn her back on course. Lord Brom grabbed the ropes, to help the others that were now flying through midair halfway up the mast. He managed to bring them back down; the three men and Lord Brom were joined by two more crewmembers, to help tie down the sail. They paused only for a moment, to catch their breath, when lightning struck the mast and started a blaze. Frantically the crew grabbed the buckets. One by one they worked as a team, bringing up the water, then passing the buckets down to those on the end, who threw the water up onto the sail to prevent it from catching fire as well. Then the rain came down hard and the wind blew it sideways, making it difficult to see. The rain was a blessing, putting out the fire on the mast. With the fire extinguished, they attended to their biggest worry. The storm had blown them off course. In the night with the starless, black sky, they could not get their bearings to know where they were now. Captain Jake looked down at his compass, but the rain came down too hard to see and the ocean stung his eyes, as waves lashed at his ship with its fury. The compass fell and was washed off the deck, he tried to grab it in time, but he could not let go of the wheel. The storm raged on, the ocean fought back against the ship with equal force, nearly sending some of the crew overboard. Only the moments when bolts of the deadly light illuminated the sky, were they able to see. The lantern had been blown out by the wind hours before, leaving the ship's upper deck in total darkness. Lord Brom fought hard just to walk against the elements, to see what else needed to be done now that the sail had been tied back down.

"We have tied the sail back down, the men can not row anymore, they have already broken too many oars. What do we do now?" Lord Brom shouted.

"We can only hang on and pray to the Gods, that she does not flip us over!" the Captain shouted, then steered the ship as best as he could, trying not to break the rudder. "Just keep an eye out on the sail, if the wind catches the wrong way, it may break the mast," Captain Jake ordered, shaking his head; there was nothing left to do, but try to keep the ship from capsizing.

With no signs of the storm passing, they braced themselves waiting until the worst of the storm was over. The rumble of the skies was deafening, and it vibrated throughout the ship. The crewmen continued a watchful eye on the sail, as they stood guard at the bottom of the mast.

A horrible groan was heard, yet it was not the familiar sound of thunder. The ship began to teeter sideways, as the waves towered over her, making her look miniature in comparison. The deep groan became louder, and the crew grew fearsome. Rob the Red went to his Captain with a dreaded idea of what it could be.

"Captain, sir. Did you hear that?" Rob shouted, over the storm and crashing waves.

"No, I can not hear much of anything over this storm," Captain Jake exclaimed, raising a hand to his ear.

The sound came again, from the side of the bough.

"Never mind, I heard it that time," Captain Jake confessed, pointing in the direction it came from.

Rob the Red braved getting close to the edge, which was a dangerous place to be right now. He turned around to face the Captain and saw him frantically waving his arms.

"Rob! Get away from there now! Run!" Captain Jake shouted.

The bellow from the monster shook the ship; the men turned

to see what it was, then stopped dead in their tracks frozen with fear. Lord Brom looked up and saw the hideous serpent rising up from the depths of the ocean and lurking over the bough of the ship.

"Tis' the Jörmungandr!" Rob the Red shouted, then ran as fast as he could from the side of the ship.

"Run! Run for your lives!" the other men screamed.

The giant serpent wrapped its body around the front of the ship, as the giant tail came crashing down onto the deck. One of the men screamed as he was trapped underneath the serpent's tail. The crew rushed to his aid, grabbing axes and swords to cut him free from the monster. While the head of the Jörmungandr was busy fighting off its attackers, its powerful jaws clamped shut on one of the men, biting him in half. The man's legs fell from the monster's mouth into the ocean, as it pulled back its head from the long spears that threatened to kill it. The sea monster roared in pain, as the crewmen hacked at the heavy tail like an ancient tree, still trying to free the man from underneath. Even with its tail, bloody and frail, it flung the men away with wretched force. The men flew back across the deck and hurried to get back up to fight the serpent. Axes were sent down into the beast's tail in unison until it was severed; blood spurted out onto the men and all over the deck.

The Jörmungandr bellowed at the remaining stub of its once long and mighty tail, sending it into a blind rage. The ship began to teeter to one side, as the serpent pushed it over with all its might. Men grabbed anything they could to hold onto, so they were not sent over the edge.

Lord Brom and Captain Jake threw spears at the monster's head, many missed their target, but a few of the spears found their mark. The monster reared back its head in pain, as spears dangled from its massive neck. The brothers waited patiently for the beast to come for them, but a massive wave hit the ship and water crashed into them. When they got up the monster was nowhere in sight. The men looked at one another, then looked all around the perimeter of the ship, with still no sign of the monster anywhere.

Suddenly it reappeared, surprising them from behind. The massive jaws came down hard, crashing into the deck and missing its target, as the men got away just in time. Lord Brom and Captain Jake, with spears in hand, plunged them deep into the monster's neck. The serpent raised its head up before the brothers had a chance to let go. Lord Brom twisted the spear shoving it in deeper, blood squirting all over him. Captain Jake let go before the serpent rose up any higher, leaving Lord Brom alone in mid-air. Holding onto the spear with one hand, he grabbed the knife from his side holster and reached over to slit its throat before letting go. Lord Brom was so disoriented, that he failed to notice the monster coming down on top of him.

"Brom, get out of the way!" Captain Jake shouted, before he ran toward him and knocked him out of the way. Both men tumbled over one another just in time, before the massive head hit the deck. The beast was slain and men struggled to push it over the edge of the ship, before the weight of it tipped them over. When they had shoved the rest of the monster over the side, it was too late to notice where they were headed.

"Captain Jake, look!" Rob the Red shouted, over the storm.

Captain Jake and Lord Brom both looked up in time to see they were heading straight for a rocky shoreline. Frantically, the men tried to fight against the storm, several tried to untie the sail, while others grabbed oars to help the Captain turn the ship away from disaster...

CHAPTER 5

Hidden within the canopy of the forest was an entirely different world, a lush green sanctuary hidden from prying eyes. Once protected by the Elder Queen, it now has become a prison without walls, cursed by an evil force, keeping all inhabitants from ever leaving, and magical folks from entering the forest. Only the Elvin Halfling, Alfar, has the power to come and go as he pleases. His blood from his human half allows him to be unaffected by the curse's power. Mortals are the only ones that could enter the forest, but they rarely managed to escape. Before the curse, humans that did enter the forest fell in love with the hidden realm, and would never want to return to their own world. Now that this once beautiful, enchanted forest was cursed, they either feared the forest or had been caught by the darkest evil that never allowed them to leave…

In the middle of a clearing and sitting on a thick bed of clover, up against the largest tree in the forest, was Alfar. The sun was making its way up over the horizon, casting down its radiant beams and reflecting on the tiny drops of dew upon the clover. He loved the dawn, with its fragrant smells, and the peaceful serenity of silence. All of the forest creatures were still fast asleep, as Alfar enjoyed watching the sunrise; every day the sky had shown a different variation of colors that it painted. This was his soul's pleasance. He did not wish to return home to his mother. He did not think that she would even care if it were not the fact she was waiting for what he was sent out after. His back was still very sore, but there was something about this Elder Tree when he was near, it comforted him somehow.

Reluctantly, he stood up from his quiet place of solitude and leaned over to pick up his brown sack. He looked upon the giant tree and placed a hand on its massive trunk. He felt such great energy from it, that it was hard for him to leave…

Alfar opened the door to the cottage, where his mother was waiting. She was quite angry with him. Hastily taking the sack from him, she reached in and removed what she had been waiting all night for. The tiny creatures were barely alive, from being trapped inside for most of the night. The young man looked away, he could not stomach watching his mother's daily ritual. When she finished, she placed the tiny wings in a jar with the rest of them. She turned around to face her son, and her demeanor towards him changed.

"Get to work on your chores now. I shall have your breakfast for you if you get them all finished in time," his mother spat the first rule of the day.

"Yes, mother," he replied, before he began his chores. If he did not finish his chores by the time breakfast was served, he missed his chance to eat. He had to sweep the floors, scrub them, chop wood, then bring it in for the fire, fetch water from the well, tidy up the rest of the cottage, all before breakfast was made ready.

Most days, he was able to get all of his chores done because he woke up before dawn to start them, while his mother slept. Some days though, if he had been whipped the night before, he was usually in too much pain to even get out of bed. A sound lashing seemed to come almost once a week; no matter how hard that he tried to please his mother and she always found a reason to take her anger out on him. Breakfast was nearly ready and he could smell the porridge from outside, as he brought in the last of the firewood. He had already lugged in the water, cleaned the floors, and tidied up around the place, but he had to make sure that it was near perfection.

"Alfar, breakfast!"

"Is everything to your liking, mother?" he asked, then sat down at the table, while his mother looked around the room

"It will do," she said, with her blue eyes fixed on his, then joined him at the table and waited for him to serve her.

He had to be very careful with the hot porridge. If any were spilled, it was a lash from the whip, if he accidentally spilled it upon her, he would be lashed so bad, that he would be in bed for nearly a week. That happened only once, and he learned not to spill the porridge. While they were eating, he was not allowed to speak unless she spoke to him first; if he spoke without permission, it was a lashing. He was mute unless instructed further.

"I want you to go to the gypsy village, stay low and out of sight. They are expecting the one that I have been waiting centuries for, the one that can save us all. Find her and bring her back to me before Midsummer's Eve. If you fail, we all will perish.

"Yes, mother," he replied, with his head held low.

Alfar set out after breakfast, on his long journey to the gypsy village. It was only a few hours on foot to get there, but he brought some sweet bread and biscuits, along with a pouch he filled with water from the small pool of water that dripped from the Elder Tree. He was excited to finally be away from his mother, for the first time in his seventeen years.

Without having ever left the forest before, it would be an entirely new experience for him indeed…

Chapter 6

The arrival to Inamor was followed by a warm reception. Upon seeing the royal flags of Toledya, Mala was the first to greet Princess Ellyria. She was the gypsies' new bandolier and also an Awenyddion, like Vadoma had been. Mala eagerly awaited the Princess, she was going to be her tutor, since Vadoma had passed. Even though the gypsies did not pass down the teachings of magic to outsiders, Princess Ellyria was the exception. She was born half gypsy, and her grandmother had been raised within this clan, so that still made her familia...

Princess Ellyria barely made it out of the carriage, when Vadoma's predecessor came to greet her.

"Welcome, Princess Ellyria," Mala said, embracing her.

"Thank you, Mala. I am so happy to be here. This is my brother, Prince Ian."

"A Prince. It is a pleasure to meet you, Sire." Mala blushed, she found him to be very handsome with dark hair and dark brown eyes. He had a nice smile, quite tall, and she imagined him to be very strong.

"No, please, the pleasure is all mine," Prince Ian said, smiling at the pretty woman, as he took her hand and placed a gentle kiss upon it.

"So, brother, do you not need to be heading on to Regnuom before midday?" Princess Ellyria interrupted, rolling her eyes at her brother's dramatic introduction.

Prince Ian turned away from his present distraction, then turned to his sister.

"Oh, yes. Yes, I suppose I do," he answered. He looked back to Mala and flashed her his best smile. "I do hope that we meet again someday," he declared, before kissing her hand one last time.

"Be careful the rest of the way to Regnuom, brother," Princess Ellyria instructed, then embraced her brother to bid him farewell.

"Me? It is you that I am worried about. Mala, please watch over my sister. She is the only sister that I have," he said, before he kissed her on the forehead, then let her go.

Princess Ellyria and Mala stood and watched, as Prince Ian climbed back into the carriage. He was gone before they knew it, with the knights as his escort.

"I apologize for my brother's behavior. He is usually not so bold," Princess Ellyria said, trying to make excuses for him.

"That is quite alright. If he only knew how old I was, then he might not have been so 'bold', as you put it," she giggled, feeling like a young girl again.

"How old are you, if I may ask?"

"I am nearing my third cycle in life, almost a crone, by gypsy standards," Mala answered.

Princess Ellyria looked at this very pretty woman, who appeared as though she was her mother's age, and she was surprised indeed. Mala had smooth skin, very little silver in her hair, except for a single strand in front, and her brown eyes only showed great wisdom.

"You can not even tell. You are beautiful."

"Thank you for your kindness. I will show you the way to your tent, we have arranged for your comfort, befitting a Princess of course," she said, then led Princess Ellyria into the camp.

The tent held more expectations than she even had in mind. It was quite large in size, with a small bed in the corner, a small claw foot bathtub in the opposite corner, and a small table for writing, or scrying; she was sure there was a crystal ball underneath that black cloth.

"Oh, Mala, this is too much. You did not have to go through all this trouble just for me. I would not have ordered all of these things. I do not know how to thank you," Princess Ellyria responded graciously. She was not a demanding princess and had only requested to have such luxuries when she was on the Viking ship because they had kidnapped her. It was only by Lord Brom's brother, since he was the Captain, that her requests had been met.

"No, please do not feel that way. You are the Chosen One after all. Vadoma would have wanted me to make sure that you were as comfortable as possible. Besides, you are still a gypsy, one of our own."

The two women embraced. Princess Ellyria had never felt so welcome.

"I will leave you to rest, you need your sleep. If you need anything at all, someone will do their best to get you whatever you like," Mala added sweetly.

"Thank you again for everything. I will take a long nap I think."

Mala nodded her head and left Princess Ellyria alone in the tent.

The few trunks that had traveled with her, had already been brought to her tent earlier. She did not pack lightly, if she went anywhere of her own accord, she liked having some of her personal things, as well as extra clothes. For this trip, she had only two small trunks with her, one for clothes, one for her books, and other personal items. Without having a wardrobe to unpack her clothes, she just left them in her trunk, until she might be able to find one. After the long journey of constant sitting, her backside was sore, she laid down on her side, so she would be able to rest easier. She was not sleepy as much as she was simply tired, but slowly she succumbed to slumber…

"Princess Ellyria, Princess Ellyria. Please, you must help us. We are trapped. You must find us. Help us," the voices whispered. She tried to find out where the voices were coming from, but it was too dark to see that far ahead of her. The forest was thick and lush, as she slowly made her way through it. She came to a clearing in the middle of the woods, and there in front of her was a giant tree. The voices seemed to have vanished. All was quiet, except for the sound of water droplets. The tree appeared to be crying, as she had never seen water fall from a tree. A small pool formed at its trunk and created a small brook. She wanted to see where it led. The little stream led further into the forest, but no matter the obstacles, fallen trees, rocks, and or inclining hills, the water still overcame them. The water stopped, as she looked up to see where she was. The light from the moon over the clearing was the only light she had, to make out a small cottage before her. She began to hear the cries again, not only did she hear them, but she felt them also. Her heart ached for them. The heaviness in her chest was like a dead weight pressing down upon her. Then she heard shouting, someone was inside, so she stayed back in the cover of the woods. She had never felt such anger before, as she did now. She put her hands over her face and fell down to her knees. What was happening to her? There was more than one person in the cottage, someone else was there, and they were in wretched pain. Suddenly her back felt like it was on fire; the pain became so intense, that she had heard herself scream…

Princess Ellyria was drenched in sweat and could barely breathe, she kept her eyes closed and her hands covering them, to keep out the light. Mala had heard her screaming and ran in.

"Are you alright? I heard you screaming. I came as fast as I could," Mala said, then reached out to embrace the Princess, but when she did, Princess Ellyria pulled away and cried out. "What is wrong?"

"I do not know, my skin feels like it is burning."

"May I?" Mala pulled down the back of Princess Ellyria's day gown. She gasped at the sight.

"What is it? What do you see?"

"Your back. It looks like you have been whipped, but there is no blood, just bright red lash marks."

"What? I do not understand. How did that happen?"

"What were you doing?"

"I was sleeping and had a vision. I felt all of their pain, their anger, and their fear."

"Whose pain and anger?"

"I do not know."

Princess Ellyria wished that she knew...

Chapter 7

Nightfall came and the stars lit up the night sky; reflections of silvery light shone brightly through the window in King Jason's study. He usually did not work so late in the evening, but he was getting a few loose ends tied up, while waiting for word of his children's safe arrival to their destinations. He was not worried as much for his son's welfare, since he was accompanied by several guards. His daughter, however, was without an escort at all. Even though she was quite safe in the gypsy camp, the wizard could easily conquer even the best of their shamans. He rubbed his eyes before his hands covered his face, then he ran his fingers through the remainder of his light brown hair. He let out a sigh, followed by a yawn, and then leaned back in his chair reaching his long arms to either side of him, as he brought them up over his head, before he let them fall to the arms of his chair. All of a sudden, he was startled by the flutter of wings and the sound of cooing. He turned to the window, and there on the sill was a carrier pigeon. He got up slowly to not frighten it, since they were such flighty birds and walked over to the window. He wrapped a large hand over the bird's back and picked it up gently, turning it over to reveal the message rolled up on its tiny leg. After he had retrieved the message, he set the bird back on the sill and read the message. He let out a sigh of relief. The message was from Prince Ian. He said all was well, and that he and Princess Ellyria had made it to their destinations safely. He was quite relieved; now maybe he could finally go upstairs to his sleeping wife. Perhaps he was not too tired after all, and he could wake her up. Smiling to himself, at such an enticing thought, he went on upstairs to his bedchamber…

The castle was quiet, no sounds, no stirrings. However, in the tower, a light flickered in the window. Prince Dakota was still wide-awake working on his latest problem, and Isis was keeping him company. He was diligently trying to figure out what potion Raul had tried to get his sister to drink. He had searched through all of his books for the past part of the year, and there were so many different potions that one could use, that it seemed to be taking forever. He had to go through each potion, to find out which one exactly would have served his purposes. Finally, this had to be it.

"Isis, I do believe I have found the very potion the wizard was bent on your mistress to drink," Prince Dakota exclaimed. Isis barely looked at him, then laid her head back down to continue sleeping. This made perfect sense to him, a power-stripping potion. Too bad this could not be used on the wizard. Or could it? It might be worth a shot anyway. The formula would have to be wrought just for him. Unfortunately, there would be no way to trick the wizard into drinking it. He could mimic it to work if it were thrown at him, like how most of his other potions worked. This would take time to get the formula just right, but he would work day and night if he had to, to make this formula…

The castle remained dark and quiet. The flickering light from the tower was the only light that could be seen by the sky. A raven perched itself to rest on the large stone flower, on top of the fountain in the courtyard. Its eyes took in all the wonder of the gardens and looked up to the light from the tower. It flew up and perched itself this time, just outside the window. Looking in, the raven spied a man with a wolf sleeping in the far corner of the large room. Many vials were laid out, and he had been mixing several different colors of liquids. The man would go back and forth from reading in the large book, then writing everything he had read onto some parchment. The black bird hopped a little closer to the open window, to get a better look inside. The man diligently worked, pouring each of the formulas into the glass vials, then writing more notes onto the parchment. He seemed to have had an idea come to mind, as he went over to the bookshelf and brought back yet another book, then set it on the table that he was working from. After mixing another ingredient, the liquid in the vial began to smoke from the top, as the vapors formed from this combination.

"Yes, finally. I have mimicked the power-stripping potion into a formula. Only one more item and it should work if it is thrown onto the person, that you want it to work on. I truly amaze myself, even if I am the only one listening," he said, looking over to a sleeping Isis, then went to the bookcase.

When he returned to write down the last ingredient to make the power-stripping potion work, the parchment was not there. He looked all over, moved everything out of the way, and searched the entire table. He got down on his hands and knees, thinking the wind may have carried it to the floor, but it was not there. He stood back up. This was bad, he could not remember everything that he had written down, but he would try. He grabbed another piece of parchment and quickly wrote down everything from memory that he could. This had to work, if not, he would have to start all over…

The raven flew, as hard as his little wings could carry him back to his master, with the parchment of paper tightly clutched in his claws…

Chapter 8

The Draki had smashed up against the rocks at the bottom of a cliff and had suffered extensive damage. After a full day's work put in by the entire crew to repair the ship, they were getting short with one another and restless. It was the middle of the night, they now worked with only the light from their lanterns, and the light from a most beautiful sphere in the sky...

"Captain, the men are beginning to fight amongst themselves. I have personally set several of them apart, just to keep them from killing one another," informed Rob the Red.

Captain Jake ran his fingers through his hair, as he stood overlooking the crew from his place at the wheel he was trying to repair.

"Gather up the men, I have an announcement to make. Find my brother too while you are at it, and send him to me first," Captain Jake replied. He knew that his men had been working nonstop since the Jörmungandr attacked them, and the storm they had been caught in had done extensive damage to the ship. Most of the major repairs had been completed, but the deck remained a mess, and the mainsail had been torn. He decided that he needed to let some of the men go off and take a much-needed break, while the remainder stayed back to sew the sail and finish making repairs to the deck. Luckily, and to his surprise, the rudder was not nearly as damaged as the side of the hull, which had been the first thing that was repaired, to prevent any more water from seeping through. The small boats were set out to try and pull the large ship out from the rocks after the repairs were made, so they were able to set the anchor away from the rocky shore.

Lord Brom arrived at his brother's side before the rest of the crew was gathered for the meeting.

"You wanted to see me?"

"I am going to release some of the men in your care, to go and get into something, so they can relieve tension between them. I will stay back with a few that had rested earlier by my order after the hull was finished. Take Rob with you, he has not only been working on the repairs, but also having to play as referee to all those blokes too."

"Is that why you are calling a meeting?"

"Yes, exactly."

The entire crew gathered below the crow's nest, waiting for word from their Captain.

"I want to first thank you for all of your hard work to get this ship back on course. After the fretful nightmare, we had to endure the night before, it is a wonder that we are not all insane by now. However, we are in unknown territory. I try to avoid the Rhine, for the simple reason that this ship is too large to get in and out of this mighty river unscathed. We have successfully repositioned the ship to face the ocean, and hopefully, by the first light of dawn, we can set sail again, back to our homeland as planned. I am letting the majority of you get off this ship to enjoy yourselves for a while. However, I want you back here before dawn, so we can set sail. Is that understood?" Captain Jake made a motion to the men that he wished to remain with him. "You men stay here with me, we have a sail to sew back up. The rest of you are to go with Rob and my brother, they are in charge. If you do anything out of line, you will answer to them first. Depending on your insubordination, will be how I will deal with you upon your return. Is that understood?"

"Aye, aye, Captain," the crew replied.

"Well, off with you now," Captain Jake ordered, waving his arm in the air.

The crew lowered themselves into the small boats that were tied to the ship. This was unfamiliar territory indeed. How were they going to scale that cliff?

Lord Brom and Rob the Red set out for the shore. With several men in each boat, they were able to paddle rather quickly.

"How do you suppose we will be able to climb that cliff?" asked Rob.

"There, look! There are torches lit," Lord Brom said, as they approached the small rocky shoreline.

"I do not recall those being lit up the other night, do you?"

"No, but I suppose we will be able to see now," Lord Brom said, before assisting the others to pull the boat up onto the beach.

The men gathered around the lit-up path leading to steps, that had been carved out of the side off the cliff.

"Well, is that not convenient," Rob stated.

"Maybe a little too convenient I might add," Lord Brom chuckled. "Well, let us find out where it leads."

They set out on the path of steps that seemed to take forever to climb. When they reached the top, they could see miles all around them. At the top of the mountain was a brightly lit-up tavern. As they came closer to it they began to hear music, it was soft and sweet, very pleasant to their ears, and they were unable to shake the strange feeling of being drawn to it. The tavern was nearly a good twenty feet from the rocky steps that led back to the beach, and the torches that had led the way suddenly went out as they approached the door. A sign on the side of the two-story building had the name, 'The Nixen,' above the sign that read, 'open.'

"What a strange name for a tavern," Rob voiced his opinion.

The door opened before Lord Brom had even laid a hand on it. The soft sound of music had become louder, as they cautiously stepped inside. The large room was filled with brightly colored lanterns, and a magnificent array of exotic objects, from a glass water fountain in the center of the room, to many different sizes and shapes of seashells, and fishing nets that were used as decor. The place was strange indeed, especially since there was no one in sight. The men had finally all gathered into the building, as the door shut on its own from behind them. Lord Brom quickly turned to the thud it made upon slamming shut.

"This is quite an establishment. Do you not think, Brom?"

Lord Brom did not answer Rob. He was too distracted by the alluring beauty that was descending down the staircase. This tall slender woman with blood-red hair dressed in a pale blue, transparent dress that left nothing to the imagination. Her large perky breasts stood out from the material, and the silhouette of her slender shape was accentuated by the way the empire waistline of the dress displayed her ample curves. The men could not take their eyes off of her and found themselves entranced by her unique beauty. Especially, Lord Brom. He could not move a muscle, he could not speak, and it was like he had been put under a powerful spell. Then her words spilled like honey, as she began to speak.

"I am Lorelei, I own this establishment, and you gentleman are trespassing," she purred.

Lord Brom felt himself smacked by Rob. He heard him whisper to say something, but words did not come.

"I do not care for unwanted guests. Speak now as to why you are here."

"Madam, please forgive our intrusion, your sign said that you were open, and we were taking a break from repairing our ship when we saw your lights. We can leave if that is your wish," Lord Brom managed to say.

The woman was now standing at the bottom of the stairs facing them.

"Well, why did you not say so?" she smiled like an angry cat. "Ladies, it is safe, you may come down now."

At least a dozen women came from upstairs, enough for each man to practically have two women at a time. Lord Brom noticed by the way the women were barely clothed, as to what kind of establishment this was. The women danced all around the men, with scented veils they paraded around with. They wrapped their scarves around each man, as they pranced like nymphs, and hummed a lively tune. Desires began to awaken, as the men were lured into another hidden room downstairs.

The doors were opened, revealing a large array of small pallets of pillows, that were elaborately decorated with bright beads and sequins. The same see-through material of all colors draped from the ceiling and cascaded down over the many pallets on the floor. The entire room was sweet-smelling, with the familiar aromas of lilies, and the strong scent of a woman's arousal.

After the men were led into the room, the women began to disrobe them, leaving their excitement for such beautiful women in plain view for all to see. The raging beauties took turns undressing each other in between lustful kisses. They writhed their bodies close, rubbing each other with soft hands, and kissing each other's secret places.

The crew looked on as if they were in a dream. Rob the Red wasted no time, as he grabbed two of the kissing women and found his pallet. As did the others as they broke off in pairs. Two women joined some men while others only had one. Rob was watching, as the two women before him were enticing him with their heavy petting, kissing, and fondling. He could barely contain his desire a moment longer, as he interrupted their play. He entered one of them with ardent fervor, as the other female kissed him deeply, then took care to stroke the sensitive spot that was being plundered by Rob's huge member. The sounds of pleasure were echoing throughout the room, as bodies writhed and entwined in ecstasy. Rob withdrew himself from the fair-haired woman, to push himself into the brunette, but not before both women grabbed his swollen manhood to savor the flavor left behind. The brunette cried out as the heavily endowed man thrust himself deep into the wet depths of her, as the lustful fornications raged on from within the hidden room...

Lord Brom had followed the red-headed beauty to her privy

chambers upstairs. Lorelei wasted no time in undressing this golden god before her. Never had she seen such statuesque perfection in a man. She could not wait to have him. She lay him down upon her huge four-poster canopy bed; the sweet smell of dew-covered honeysuckles and morning glories filled his nostrils, with such intoxicating aromas. She had removed the thin material of a dress that she wore, then let it fall to the floor beside the bed.

Lord Brom rolled his eyes to the back of his head, as her hot breath fell upon him, and her mouth seemed to have swallowed him whole. He could not hardly control the sudden urge of his body's flinching. She placed a hand on his hip to settle him, as she continued her attack on his large member with her tongue, which felt as if it wrapped around his entire shaft. He let out a moan, as he had never experienced such carnal pleasure before, that had made him want to lose all control. She stopped her abuse upon him and crawled on top of him, she kissed him on the mouth exploring him fully. He returned her ardency and began to cascade kisses from her mouth to her neck, as he grabbed her ample breasts in his hands. She arched up with pleasure, as his mouth clamped down on one of her nipples, then he did the same for the other one. She swelled with anticipation and moisture, between her long slender legs. She grabbed his member when he let go of her breasts, pulling him to her, as she settled herself down onto his hips. She felt completely filled with his massive size. He arched his body into her, as he grabbed her hips pulling her down, so he could fill her deeper. She began to ride him easily at first but soon found her own rhythm, building up to speed to catch up with the intense first wave of pleasure, that hit her full force. She fell on top of him and kissed him deeply again. The taste of her mouth had become intoxicating, and his senses were on overdrive, as the dam of her pleasure broke all over him. She never stopped the sway of her hips, as she kept in time with the beat from their hearts. Her pace quickened, as Lord Brom was no longer able to contain himself. He arched up, grabbed her mouth again, and then her breasts that were teasingly in front of his face. She pulled herself away from him and began to ride him harder, grinding him into her deeper, sending him into a chaotic spin. He felt himself building, then let out a loud moan that managed to escape from his lips, as he spilled his life into her. She did not slow down, as she too released her pleasure.

All of the sudden, Lord Brom heard screams from down below. When he turned his head in the direction of the door, she grabbed his face with her hand and turned it back towards her. She smiled before opening her mouth wide, to expose several razor-sharp teeth and a serpent's tongue…

Chapter 9

Raul turned from his books to the sound of pecking at the window. He opened the shutters to reveal the raven that he had conjured with the Amulet of Elements.

"What have you brought back to me?" he asked, taking the parchment from the raven's claws. The raven squawked, then flew inside to perch onto a shelf. The wizard read the ingredients that were written down, everything made sense to him, but something was missing. Yes, one of the ingredients was indeed missing. "Stupid foul bird! You took this too soon, the final ingredient was never written down!" the wizard screamed at the raven. "You must return and see what information you can get. Now, go!"

The raven flew out of the cottage and headed back to Toledya.

Toby entered the room to see what all the commotion was about.

"Remind me the next time that I conjure another animal, to give it some actual brains," he said to the boy.

Toby just nodded his head and went on to do his chores.

"Oh, wait, boy. I need you to fetch me some fruit. I need them for a potion. This can be your first test. Pick three different types of fruit that would be best suited to use to poison someone. Make haste, and do not come back without it," he ordered.

Toby grabbed an empty brown sack, before he headed out the door.

Raul began to start work on the new formula. At least he would have the potion ready for the fruit to soak in, while he waited for the raven to bring back the information on the final ingredient for the potion. Once the boy returned, he would prepare the fruit, and then try to find a way to get it to the Princess…

Toby thought while he was out he would go and see his tutor, Azil. She had helped him so much over the past year, that he wanted to do something nice for her. His sack was full of all kinds of delicious fruit, so he wanted to share some with her. When he went to her tent, he was shocked to see her appearance. He had always seen her with her veil on, and just assumed it was a fashion choice. He would have never thought it was because she looked like a hideous monster. After deciding he would just leave, since she had not seen him, he tripped on a stone and made a significant thud right beside her tent. The older woman came out from the tent to see what the noise was.

"Oh, Toby. Are you alright, dearie?" she asked, kindly helping the boy to his feet.

"Yes, ma'am," Toby replied, and was glad she had put her veil back on.

"What are you doing here? Your lessons are finished now."

"I know, but I wanted to bring you something," he offered, then reached deep into the brown sack and felt around. After finding what he wanted, he pulled it out and presented it to her.

"An apple. Thank you, dearie," Azil said, and reached out to embrace the boy, but Toby stepped back.

"I have to get the rest of this fruit to my master. I shall come back and visit you soon," he said, while backing away from the tent, the old woman grabbed his arm.

"Tell me, dear boy. What does your master want with this fruit?"

Toby knew better than to relinquish any information to her, but something in her eyes made him wonder if she would indeed make a good ally.

"Can I trust you to keep a secret?"

"Yes, of course. You can trust me. I would never harm you, you are my favorite pupil," she said, with a wink of her eye and a hidden flash of a wicked smile.

Toby began to tell her how he had come to be with his benefactor, and how he was a powerful wizard. Azil listened intently, hanging on to every word the boy said. When he got to the part where Raul had killed his father, she reached out and gave a reassuring pat on his hand.

"I am so sorry to hear about your father, dearie. That must have been horrifying for you," she offered her condolences. "If there is anything I can do to help you get away from that monster, you let me know."

"Thank you, but I do not think there is anything you can do. He is much too powerful, and when he gets the Princess's powers he will be invincible," he muttered suddenly, then covered his mouth with his hands.

"What is the matter? I told you, that I could keep a secret. Do you not worry about a thing young man," the old crone reassured. With a smile, she pulled his chin up to look at him. "I can help you. You just have to tell me what you want me to do, and I will do it," she added.

"I want revenge."

"Well, dearie, revenge is my specialty."

The old woman told him many things, to help the boy in his predicament. He listened to her, after she had finished, he had a pretty good idea of what he needed to do…

Toby returned to the cottage with the requested fruit. Raul was finishing up the final touches to make the potion ready.

"Did you bring me what I had asked for?"

"Yes, sire."

"Well, let us see what you have brought me, shall we?" Raul inquired, turning over the bag, allowing the fruit to spill out onto the table. "First we shall have our lesson. Which of these three fruits will be the best suited for the potion?"

Toby picked the three.

Are you sure?"

"Yes, sire."

"Very well then. First up is an orange, it will never work, the peel will not allow for good absorption. Next, we have an apple," Raul paused, and could not contain his laughter. He was quite amused by the boy's naivety, "Do you know why an apple would never work? Only an idiot would use an apple to poison someone. Apples are a form of good majick, the fruit when you cut it open like this," taking his athame he cut the apple from stem to end, "here it shows the pentacle, a symbol used in good majick. It is useless to use a good magical item for evil. Do you know why?"

Toby shook his head and waited for the answer.

"Using a good magical object for evil is redundant, when you are trying to poison someone, it has to be from a neutral object, or an evil one. Using this apple is a contradiction in itself, for good majick will always try to cancel out evil. So if we use this apple it will cause our spell to backfire. Understand?"

"Yes, sire."

"Good, let us continue. Lastly, we have a peach, a very good choice. The skin is soft and will absorb the potion quite easily. It is a neutral object, therefore not causing our spell to backfire. You have done well for your first time, young Toby."

Toby was almost in shock, that was the first time the wizard had actually called him by his name. He always had just called him 'boy' before. Why the sudden change?

"Come now, let us soak this peach, then you can help me to decide how we shall entice the Princess to eat it. First I need to find out where she is," he said, then called to the remaining two guards he had at the cottage. "Go find out where the little Princess is. Do not come back until you know where she is, and then report back to me immediately. Do not fumble this up. Do you understand?"

The guards nodded their heads and left the cottage.

"Now, back to the peach," the wizard said. He placed the peach in a wide-mouthed bowl, poured the warm potion over it, then covered it with another bowl, the bottom side in to create a vacuum. "There, that must soak for several hours. Make sure you do not take off this bowl. The potion must soak inside the peach completely, for the spell to work properly. Understand?"

"Yes, sire. I do," Toby responded, nodding his head.

"Good. I am going to get some sleep before the sun comes up. There is more work to be done in the morning," he informed the boy, before retiring to his bedroom.

Toby looked at the bowls that were stacked together. Not yet. He would wait until those two buffoons returned, then he would find a way to pin the blame on them. He too then retired to his room for a much needed nap.

His plan would begin in the morning before the wizard awoke…

Chapter 10

Alfar remained hidden at the edge of the camp, watching the one he was waiting for. She was so beautiful, with her long black hair and porcelain skin, she looked like a dream. He only wished that he could see her eyes, he bet they were as beautiful as the rest of her…

Princess Ellyria met with Mala at dawn to learn about herbs. She had told her about the many different species and their usage, as well as the common names, and the majickal names that were often intermittently used. After the lesson, Mala told her to go and collect all the herbs she had taught her about, but to stay away from the forest.

"What is wrong with going into the forest?"

"The Black Forest is cursed, you do not want to go in there," Mala warned the Princess.

"I am not afraid. I have been in way worse forests before," Princess Ellyria replied bravely.

"It is not a matter of being unafraid. You may not be able to get out of the forest if you enter. Many have gone missing without explanation."

Oh, well. I will stay away then. I do not want to end up

missing," she teased.

"This is no time for foolery, you must heed my warning of the forest. Oh, and stay away from the Urmen."

"What are Urmen?"

"Faeries."

"Faeries? Really? I did not know they actually exist. This is so amazing."

"No, they are not. Faeries are tricky creatures. Not all are bad, but most are, just be careful," Mala warned.

"Alright, I shall be careful, I will not go into the forest, and I will not go near any faeries. Got it," she reluctantly agreed. She wanted to have at least a little adventure while she was here…

Princess Ellyria walked through a meadow that had a wealth of many different species of herbs. She had brought with her a basket, intricately woven by the women of the clan, and used it to gently place the collected herbs. The meadow was so peaceful. The village was always busy with people bustling around, too much sometimes for her. She missed the tranquil solitude of her bedchamber, back home in the castle, and the quiet of the summerhouse, but most of all she missed the large fountain in the courtyard. It had been so hot lately, and with Midsummer being tomorrow, it would only get hotter with summer's official arrival. She would give anything for a nice swim to cool off. A lake would be wonderful to find, or a stream would do, even if just to splash about in.

Princess Ellyria continued her walk through the field, paying little attention to the nagging feeling in her gut. She had wandered farther away, from the safety of the village, and could see the outline of the forest in the distance. Then much to her delight, she saw a small river appearing to come straight out of the forest and down the hill, to the far right side from where she stood. She picked up the hem of her dress, then ran towards it.

The little river was almost the size of a large stream upon a closer view, but that would still do nicely, for she just wanted to splash about and cool off. She set down her basket full of herbs and kicked off her shoes. The water sent chills up her spine, and goosebumps covered her arms and legs. She was not expecting the water to be so cold, but it was very refreshing, nonetheless. As she was playing in the water, she had this overwhelming feeling she was being watched. Suddenly, she was nervous, almost jittery. She looked around her surroundings, seeing nothing to alarm her, she went back to splashing about. After a few moments, she decided to sit on the bank and dangle her feet into the crystal clear stream. She leaned over to peer into the water, when she had that strange feeling again, almost like a pull, that she could not describe. Then she heard a noise from the surrounding bushes. She shrugged it off thinking it must have been an animal, until she heard it again.

"Who goes there? Show yourself!" she declared. There was no answer, and the rustling in the bushes had ceased. Perhaps it was an animal after all? All of the sudden, she knew that she was not alone. She stood up and walked slowly towards the bushes. Careful to not make any noise, she had stayed barefoot and crept around to the far side of the bush, to sneak up upon whatever it was. When she arrived at the side of the bush, she peeked around it slowly, and let out a sigh of relief. It was nothing. At least nothing was there now, perhaps it had been a squirrel or a mouse. When she turned back around toward the stream, it was already occupied.

There standing along the embankment was a tall, slender, young man, who appeared to be about her age, with dark hair, and oddly colored skin. She walked toward him, and he immediately stepped back.

"It is alright, I promise that I will not hurt you. My name is Ellyria Rose. What is your name?" she asked, as she slowly walked closer to him. From his dark looks, he did not appear completely human, and she was positive in her observation when she saw his ears protruding from underneath his shoulder-length black hair.

He made no move to step away from her, for he was too intoxicated by her beauty to move. When she was standing in front of him, he looked at her sapphire blue eyes, and they were exactly the way he had imagined. She was equally fascinated by him and had become strangely excited. His deep forest green colored eyes held such incredible wisdom, for a young man such as he.

"I am called Alfar, I live nearby. I often come here to relax. You have discovered its tranquility, have you not?" he questioned.

"Yes, it is quite peaceful. I am from Toledya and am on holiday, visiting with the gypsies across the meadow. Have you been there before?"

"No, I am afraid. I only come as far as the stream."

"Where is it that you live?"

"I live in the forest with my mother in a cottage," he replied, unsure if he had said something to frighten her, by the look on her face.

"Was it something I said?"

"No, not really. I had just heard some bad things about it, is all."

"Like what?"

"The forest is cursed. If anyone goes in, they do not come out," Princess Ellyria said. She was not sure how to feel about him, even though she was quite attracted to him. Something about him drew her in.

"I can assure you, the forest is not cursed. Although, mortals do have a tendency to want to stay once they venture inside. The forest is enchanted, full of faery folk, and exotic creatures," he informed her. He smiled at her: he could not help it.

"Well, thank you for opening my eyes to that fact," she teased. He was so handsome, with his dark grayish skin and black hair; made him look all the more alluring to her.

"Shall we?" he offered, then motioned to the forest.

"I am not sure. We have only just met, and I am afraid that I am going to have to decline. I actually need to be getting back with these herbs. My apologies to you," she offered.

"No, that is alright, I understand," he said, lowering his head, then turned to walk away.

"Wait, Alfar. Would you like to meet here this time tomorrow?"

"Yes. Yes, I would."
"Good. I shall see you then."

Princess Ellyria picked up her shoes and her basket, then set out for the village; smiling with anticipation for tomorrow...

Chapter 11

Prince Ian sat alone in the large, quiet study. He had only been here two days and had done absolutely nothing. Only endless hours of sitting, pacing, more sitting, and more pacing. When he signed on for the job, he was trying to prove to his father, he could be a king one day. Now, he was not so sure. He understood that he was just the 'acting' King, but he did not realize it would be so boring. He was used to adventure, non-stop excitement, and the freedom of doing what he wished, on a moment's whim. His days here were filled with glorious amounts of nothing. It was the worst torture ever. He should suggest to his father for it to be used as a form of punishment in his dungeon. He was not sure how much more of this he could take, and just when he was about to fall asleep, one of his personal guardsmen entered the room.

"Sire, there is a gentleman here to see you."

"What is it that he wants?"

"He said that he has a problem he wished you to address, your Highness."

"Alright, show him in. I shall hear what he has to say," the Prince agreed half-heartedly. At least it would give him something to do.

"Your Highness," the man addressed, then bowed properly before him. "Thank you for seeing me."

"What may I help you with?" Prince Ian questioned, with a regal tone.

"Sire, my neighbor's pigs got out of their pen and stomped all over my spring harvest, well, of what they did not eat anyway. What can you do about it?"

"I am afraid that is not my place. You need to take it up with your Lord of the province. Good luck to you."

The man bowed again and left the room. Prince Ian got up to look out the window. He saw the man in the courtyard, now standing beside a woman that appeared to be crying. He saw the man wrap his arm around her, trying to console her. Prince Ian walked back to his desk and sat down. Leaning back in his chair he looked up at the ceiling. There was absolutely nothing special about the ceiling. He began teetering on the back legs of the chair, trying to balance himself. His hands were stretched out on either side of him, and his legs kicked out in front of him. While he was enjoying the effortlessness of his balancing act, the guard opened the door and startled him. The guard had difficulty containing his laughter, as he watched feet fly overhead, as the Prince flipped over and landed on his royal arse. The guard cleared his throat as Prince Ian scrambled back to his feet, collecting the chair and setting it upright.

"Yes. What is it now?" a flushed Prince Ian asked.

"Some people here to see you, Sire."

"Very well, show them in."

A young couple entered the room, in a not so pleasant state, Prince Ian had observed.

"How may I help you?"

Both the man and woman began shouting at him, at the same time. He was surprised by their lack of common courtesy.

"Wait! What is this? I did not ask to see a shouting match. What is the problem?"

They started arguing again. Prince Ian gave a loud whistle, and the young couple stopped bickering, with shocked looks upon their faces.

"I want only one at a time to speak. Do not raise your voices to me, ever again. I am the acting King of this realm, I will be respected and addressed as such. Do I make myself clear?" he declared, beyond annoyed already, and he had not even heard their problem yet. Not that he wanted to, but he had to, unfortunately.

The couple shook their heads.

"I apologize for my wife, Sire. She does not know how to act in public."

She gave him such a look, that Prince Ian was expecting the man to fall over dead at any minute.

"Your Highness, 'tis I who should be apologizing for my barbaric husband. He is void of all common courtesy, and that is why I am here to ask for you to dissolve our marriage."

Prince Ian was beginning to feel a terrible headache coming on.

"I find both of you to be exasperating. So tell me, how long have you two been married?"

"A little over a month now," the man replied. His wife kicked him in the leg. "See what I have to put up with? It is abuse, it is."

"My husband is the abusive one, Sire. He leaves me alone all day, then comes home to ravage me, and eats his supper without so much as a thank you. Then during the night, after I have worked hard all day, he takes me again, only to roll over, and continually keep me awake with his loud snoring. Now, if that is not abuse I do not know what is," the man's wife complained, rolling her eyes.

Prince Ian watched the couple fight amongst themselves again.

"Young man, what do you do that has you gone all day?"

"Sire, I work. I am a merchantman and a farmer. I go to market and sell crops. I am only gone, so I can provide for this ungrateful…" He was then cut off, by her shrill screams.

"Ungrateful! I cook, clean, and wash your smelly clothes all day, and then I perform my wifely duties come nightfall. You are the one that is ungrateful, not me!" she shouted.

Prince Ian was finally fed up with this nonsense.

"Listen, I have grown tired of your needless complaining," he said, then pointed to the woman. "You, wife, need to curb your tongue. Your husband is a nobleman, that seems to be working hard to please you. He must love you, to put up with you," he added, then pointed now to the man. "You should at least show some kind of restraint when taking her, try to at least ask her permission first, woo her, make her want it too. Try to thank her for what she has done. Women work hard as well and should be rewarded for what they do also. I will not grant you separation. You two richly deserve one another. Go home, and do not come back unless you have killed one another."

The couple turned toward one another, they both looked confused.

"I said go, off with you now," the Prince demanded, then pointed to the door.

The couple left the room without another word.

Prince Ian got up and stretched. Curious, he went to the window. The couple emerged out into the courtyard, he saw them kiss, then they walked away, hand in hand. Oh, how nice for them. He was so glad, that he could help. He was even more grateful for them to be gone. He could now continue his important duties, as acting ruler of the kingdom. He found himself sitting once again in his chair at his desk. Yes, very important duties indeed. The day seemed to be going by so slowly. He had been up since dawn, and the sun was only now at the center of the sky. It would be several hours before nightfall. What would he do with himself now? Suddenly, two of his guards came rushing in.

"Sire, we have captured two men from Narruc, and they were asking questions about the Princess."

"Bring them to me."

The two men were brought in before him.

"What are you doing here?"

The men stood there in silence.

"I asked you a question. Why are you here?" Prince Ian asked again, then walked over to them and grabbed one by the ear. It always got him to talk, when the nanny did it to him as a child.

"We were sent to find the Princess of Toledya," the man winced.

"Who sent you, and why?"

"The wizard Raul did, Sire."

Prince Ian let go of the man's ear, then walked a few paces away. He ran his fingers through his hair, then looked over at the two men.

"I want you to go back to your wizard and tell him, that she could not be found. Do you understand? Go straight back to Narruc, and do not ever come here again!" he warned, breathing so heavily, that his cheeks burned. "I do not believe that I stuttered. Take them out of here, and make sure to give them a warning."

The guards accompanied the two men out. Prince Ian was curious and went to the window. After a few moments, the guards dragged the two men into the courtyard and gave them their warning. Beaten and bloody, the men were given back their horses, and they rode out of the courtyard.

"I need this message to go straight to my father, at once, use your fastest bird," Prince Ian said to the messenger, that he had called to him.

The young man exited the room with haste and the rolled-up parchment. Prince Ian knew that if the wizard were looking for his sister, he would not stop until he found her. He must get a message to Princess Ellyria as well. She must know at once, to be prepared. With his orders to remain in Regnuom, he would have to send one of his men to her for protection as well. He called in his best man, and sent him to Inamor to warn his sister, and watch over her.

Prince Ian was at odds with himself, his new responsibilities, and the need to protect his sister. He wanted to please his father and prove to him that he was responsible enough to take charge of any circumstances, that may present difficulties. The fight between a brother's love and a king's son was lost to duty and privilege.

Princess Ellyria would have to make it without him, and he wished that his man would find her, before the wizard did…

Chapter 12

The sound of cooing alerted King Jason to turn towards the window, a carrier pigeon had landed on the windowsill. He rose from his chair to see what information the bird had brought, and from where. He gently picked it up, then retrieved the parchment from its leg. After setting the bird free, he called for an important meeting with his sons.

Prince Anthony, Prince Rowan, and Prince Dakota, all gathered in their father's study, curious as to why they had been called upon.

"I have just received word from Ian, that Raul is searching for your sister's whereabouts. He sent one of his personal guards to warn her, and to protect her as best as possible. Anthony, Rowan, and I need you both to create diversions, set a false trail for the wizard to sniff, but keep any tracks, far away from Inamor. Dakota, have you finished the power-stripping potion yet?"

"No, father, not yet. Although, I am very close," Prince Dakota informed him.

"Good, you go on and finish. Let me know when it is completed," King Jason replied.

Prince Dakota left the room for the tower, set on his own mission.

"Where should we start, father?" Prince Anthony inquired.

"You shall start here. We want him to think the Princess, is here at home. It will pose too much of a problem for him to try, and storm the castle, and hopefully, it will give Dakota enough time to finish the potion," the King added.

Prince Dakota was working diligently to prepare the potion, for the final ingredient. Since he lost the original formula he had written down, it was a painstaking experience to start all over again. He was finally ready to add the final ingredient, that would make this potion work upon impact. The formula would be greatly coveted by the wizard, so he had to keep a watchful eye out.

In fact, a watchful eye was indeed keeping a lookout. Luna stood guard in the nearby Oak Tree, that was overlooking the tower window. The giant white owl rotated her head to see a raven fly by, then perch itself on the windowsill. She watched, as the unusual black bird seemed to be peeping in on her master. Silently, she flew down lower to a nearby branch. The raven was unaware of her presence.

"Yes! Finally! I did it! The potion is now complete!" he shouted excitedly. He wrote down the final ingredient, on the parchment that he would soon add to his Book of Shadows. He went to retrieve it from the shelf, leaving the formula on the table. When the raven saw the opportunity, it darted inside to grab the parchment. Prince Dakota wasted no time when he spied the raven on the table grabbing the formula.

"No! Stop!" the Prince shouted, running to the table and startling the bird, who then dropped the parchment back onto the table. Luna heard her master's cries and flew down to the next branch to see in the window, but the raven was already fleeing the scene of the crime.

"Luna, stop that bird!" Prince Dakota shouted out the window. He was so grateful the thieving fowl did not make off with his potion. He heard the raven squawk, then looked out the window again. He saw Luna with the dead black bird in her mighty talons, as she flew back to the window. She dropped the corpse on the windowsill for Prince Dakota to examine. A few moments after he started to look over the raven for any indicator as to whom it may have belonged to, as it slowly began to fade away. He knew exactly who the conjurer had been, the wizard. That would explain the mystery of where his first formula went. It had to have been the raven that had stolen it, not the wind carrying it away. It made the situation all the more dangerous now. The wizard had the main formula, it would not be long before he figured out the final ingredient. Unless it was proving too difficult, and that is why he sent the raven out again. Prince Dakota took the formula, transferred it to his book, and burned the parchment to ashes. He must tell his father, not only that it was completed, but also the wizard had it all, except the final ingredient of the formula…

King Jason was standing at the window of the study, waiting for any news from his sons, when his second eldest son came running in out of breath.

"Father, I, finished, it," he said, between gasps of air. He had run all the way, as fast as he could from the tower.

"Good work, son."

"Wait, there is more," Prince Dakota said, after he was finally able to catch his breath. "The other night, when I had thought I had lost the original formula, I was wrong, it was stolen from me. I caught a raven today trying to steal the parchment, that I had written the formula on, luckily I scared it into dropping the paper. When it flew out the window, Luna grabbed it and broke its neck. After she brought me the dead bird, it vanished within moments. It was a conjured spy, sent by the wizard," he added.

"Are you saying that Raul will try to finish this formula, to use on your sister? Am I following so far?"

Yes, exactly. So that is why I am going to take the potion and find the wizard first, before he even has a chance to figure out the last ingredient he needs to make this potion work. He must be stumped of course, or he would not have sent the raven to try and steal the formula again," he said.

"What are you thinking? You can not go up against him!"

"One, he will not recognize me. Two, I will throw the potion, before he has a chance to know that I am even a threat to him. I shall have Luna with me, she will fly me out of harm's way, before he can conjure any spell," he told his father.

"Alright, but be careful," King Jason said, before his son hastily left the room...

Luna arrived in the city of Narruc, and landed on the outskirts of town, so as to not alert any of the wizard's men to their whereabouts. Prince Dakota had the potion safely tucked away in his side pouch, and he patted his giant owl.

"Keep watch over me. I shall whistle if I need you," he said, before he motioned for her to fly off. Luna perched herself in a tree to stay close by, but out of sight. Prince Dakota made it into town, remembering the last time he was here. It was when Liza had abducted his sister and he had rescued her from the dungeon, with a diversion he had created with his black powder. Now he was walking right into the belly of the beast, in his search for the wizard.

As he was walking through town, an old woman shrouded in veils motioned for him to come into her tent.

"I am unsure why you have led me in here madam, but I am on a quest and need to be leaving if this is not of importance," he explained to the old crone.

"I know who you are. I am a friend. We share a common enemy, and I can help you defeat him if you let me," she pleaded.

"I know you not as a friend, but as a strangely covered woman, who I met only moments ago. How is it you think that you can help me?"

"I know the wizard is after your sister's powers. He must be stopped. He will become omnipotent, and then no one will be able to stop him. Not even the Chosen One, if he consumes her powers. I know where he is, he will not suspect an old woman to be a threat, but he will see you as a threat. I am right, do not deny it. I am your only hope. You charging in will only leave you dead. What say you?" questioned the old woman.

Prince Dakota was not sure that he could trust her. Who was she really?

"What do you have to gain in all of this?"

"My son. The wizard has my son, and he will kill him if I do not get him out of there. Please, let me help you, then we both will win."

Prince Dakota pondered. What did he have to lose really?

"I have to go. I have a potion that can stop him, well at least should remove his powers," he informed her.

"You are not sure that it will?"

"Well, no. There is no real way to test the formula without someone that has powers to remove, so I am basing my formula on a theory."

"Then you should let me take it. If it does not work, then at least my son has a chance to run away, and I will be enough distraction for the wizard. So long as my son is away from him. I do not care what he does with me," she argued.

"Very well then. I trust that you will be able to hit your mark. Throw it straight at him, do not miss. You will have the upper hand since he will not see you as a threat. Go, and get your son back," Prince Dakota said, then passed her the potion vial. He had no other choice, but to trust her. If she failed, then he could make another. "Be careful," he added, then started to leave the tent, but turned back to her. "I never caught your name?"

"It is Azil, dearie."

"Well, good luck, Azil," he said, as he walked out of the tent. He could not shake this feeling of familiarity about her, but she was a peasant, and he never noticed her before. He wished for her to be reunited with her son. He could only imagine how painful it must have been for her, to have lost him to the wizard. When he lost his sister, it was all he could think about until he got her back. He would return home and make more potions.

In the worst-case scenario, if the old woman failed, he wanted to be prepared...

Chapter 13

Princess Ellyria could not contain her excitement. She ran through the meadow as fast as her feet would carry her. She had finished her lessons for the morning and said that she would return later, for the Midsummer festivities. Mala had given a troubled look, but she told her not to worry, she would not get into any trouble. After all, it was not like she could not take care of herself. She had gotten out of several situations that were bleak before, that was without her new powers, prior to becoming the Chosen One…

When Alfar had finished with his morning chores, his mother piled on more for him to do. He tried so hard to please her, but nothing seemed to make her happy, no matter what he did. The cottage he kept was so clean; someone could eat right off of the floor. The laundry was always washed and put away neatly. Oftentimes, his mother did the cooking, to prevent him from eating it, if she became displeased with him. On very rare occasions, she would have him prepare the meals. He had asked himself over and over again, why he remained here with her…

Princess Ellyria was the first to arrive at the river, where she promised to meet Alfar. She wore her favorite long, white cotton gown with the empire waistline, short sleeves gathered together with tiny bows, and a low square neckline, that accentuated her breasts. She wore her long black hair down, the front and sides were braided together, rolled in a bun, and pinned to the back of her head with metal combs. The water was clear and she used it to look at her reflection; everything was still neatly in place, then her image vanished by the flowing river. A few moments passed, when she saw the faint outline of a woman's face that was not hers. A beautiful woman, with hair the color of sunshine, appeared before her in the water. The woman was crying, her tears flowed into the river, then the image of her vanished. Princess Ellyria sat back on her legs. Her heart ached with loss; her mind was trapped. Why was she sent the image of a woman, and how could she feel what she was feeling? She looked into the water, waiting to see if the woman's image would return, but it did not. Princess Ellyria rose to her feet, then looked around. She began to think about Alfar. Where was he? He should have been here by now…

Alfar's mother was waiting patiently for him to return with her mid-morning snack. Kisa was asleep in her lap purring deeply and twitching her tail, as if she were dreaming. When the boy returned, the brown sack in his hands was quite full of sleeping little folk. He had stumbled upon a nest in a tree and carefully took them out, while they were in their peaceful slumber.

"How many did you capture this time?" his mother inquired, while gently caressing her familiar.

"I managed to collect five for you. Are you not proud?" he asked, hating what he had done, but wanting to make her happy.

The white haired woman looked at her son, who was practically beaming.

"Lay them out on the table."

Alfar did as requested, one by one, he gently pulled out the sleepy sprites. They varied in size and age, but all were just tiny children. One by one, the crone reached over and grabbed a sprite, pulled off its wings, then popped it into her mouth. Kisa had awakened from her nap from the smell of food, and right away began to beg. The last and tiniest sprite woke up to rub her bright eyes. She started to panic after seeing her surroundings and led by instinct flew away. Kisa leapt into the air and caught her between her claws. The cat waited for further instructions from her master. The little sprite scratched up and bruised cried in her hands, awaiting her fate.

"That is a good kitty. I will take that," said her mistress. She picked up the crying faery and held her in the palm of her hand. "Whatever is the matter little one?"

The miniature girl looked up at the giant white haired woman. Tears shined brightly, reflecting the sunshine that was coming into the window, that dripped from her cherub cheeks.

"Alfar, put this one in the cage. She needs to grow a little more. See to it that she is fed. Oh, and clip the end of her wings, so she can not fly away."

"Yes, mother," he responded, with his head hung low. He carefully took the sprite from her hands. Her wings were already damaged from Kisa's attack, so he did not feel the need to clip them. He peaked at the girl slumped over in between his large hands. She was such a pretty, little thing. He placed her in the cage that hung from the ceiling. The metal bars were so close together, that even the tiniest of sprites such as her, would not be able to fit through. He shut and placed the lock on the door, so she could not get out. His mother kept the key around her neck on a ribbon, so no matter how badly he wanted to help his tiny cousin escape, he could not. When he finished, he wiped the tear from his eye before his mother saw him.

"Will you need anything else before I go, mother?" he offered. Alfar was already late in meeting the Princess by the river, and he wanted her to still be there when he arrived.

She looked him up and down. He wore a strange amount of enthusiasm, more than she had ever seen.

"Where are you running off to?"

He was afraid to tell her, but she would beat it out of him if he refused.

"I am going to meet with the Princess," Alfar replied, almost afraid to tell her, but she would beat it out of him if he refused. He was surprised when his mother looked as though she would burst with pride, a rare sight indeed.

"Well done. I am impressed. Does she seem to like you?"

"Yes."

"Good. Now, I want you to bring her back here. I would like to meet the girl, that has my son's heart."

Alfar's cheeks began to warm.

"Make sure you bring her here before the sun sets. She can help us, save us. She is our only hope, my son," his mother urged.

"Yes, mother. I promise that I shall bring her back with me before sunset."

He left the cottage. His mother never told him of this great threat, other than there was an evil wizard who had killed her only sister when she was still a young girl. Her sister was nearly nineteen years her senior, but still, they were very close. She taught his mother everything she knew before she was murdered. His mother's revenge was the only thing that seemed to keep her going. As he walked through the woods to join Princess Ellyria at the river, his heart seemed to skip a beat. With quickened pace, his feet carried his anticipation and excitement every step closer to her...

Princess Ellyria sat on the riverbank waiting patiently for her new friend to join her. She was unaware that he had made it to the edge of the woods and was watching her. To him she was a vision of loveliness, that was captivating and made him want to do foolish things. It was like someone had paused the world and only this moment remained, as he looked upon her from afar. She felt as if time had slowed, to the point of her becoming impatient. He could wait and admire her from the canopy of the woods no longer, so he burst through the trees. She knew he was near; incredible desire filled her heart, as she saw him coming straight for her. She quickly got up and ran towards him; meeting each other halfway, they stopped within inches of each other.

"I thought you were not going to make it?" she breathed. She felt her cheeks growing hot, and a pull that seemed to command her to step closer. His exotic good looks and free spirit intrigued her.

"I had some extra things to do for my mother before I was able to leave," Alfar informed her. He saw the sunlight dance on her rosy, pink cheeks; wondering what it would be like to kiss her.

Princess Ellyria was growing hot and blaming the midday sun, but in actuality, it was desire, an almost uncontrollable urge to… She grabbed Alfar without even the ability to control her own actions and then kissed him passionately. Alfar was completely taken aback by her kiss and was hesitant at first, due to his inexperience, but he followed her lead and let himself be drawn in by her. The world did seem to pause for the moment, as they both were swept away by their kiss…

Entering the opposite side of the forest, coming in from Regnuom, was Ian's personal guard; coming to warn the Princess about the wizard, to protect her. He decided by taking a shortcut; he would be able to arrive in Inamor faster than by traveling the main road. Once the guard found the trail, he was stopped dead in his tracks by a lovely vision. He dismounted from the horse while being drawn to the white haired woman in front of him.

"You are forbidden to enter into this forest. What is your business here?" she questioned the strange man, wearing the royal colors of Toledya.

"I come here with orders from the King. I apologize, but I knew it to be a shortcut from Regnuom to Inamor. I truly meant no harm," he replied sincerely.

"Strange how your colors say you are from Toledya," the woman stated.

"Yes, madam."

"So why were you in Regnuom?"

"I am sorry madam, I can not divulge the King's orders to a commoner."

"You find me common!" she exclaimed, while slowly and deliberately approaching him with catlike prowess. She ran her fingers down the front of his chest plate and over the royal insignia.

He looked at her unique, frosty blue eyes, with a gaze as cold as ice.

"No madam, I do not find you to be uncomely at all; however I still can not discuss my mission with you," he informed her and was growing weary of this argument. He turned around to get back on his horse, but she was already standing in front of him.

"Wait. How did you?" the guard remarked.

She stopped his wagging tongue, by thrusting hers into his mouth. She paused her attack on him for a moment.

"Pray tell me, what was your mission?" the woman asked.

"The wizard is after the Princess; I was sent to warn her and protect her," he blurted out, unable to stop the words from spilling out of his traitorous mouth, which was then silenced, as she kissed him once more.

"Good boy, you are going to turn around and come with me. Is that understood?"

"Yes, madam," he replied. The guard obediently followed her into the cottage.

She took one of her carrier pigeons from its cage, pressed a note to its leg, then carried the bird to the window.

"You know where to go, now fly!" she said, then released it out the window sending it on its way. She turned back to her new pet while trying to decide if she should have a little fun with him before she ate his heart. He followed her to her bedroom; where she led him to her lonely bed. She had him stay there, while she gathered her supplies for the spell. He would prove to be not only a vessel, but a sacrifice as well. It would take everything she had to go up against the wizard by herself, but if her son was able to lead the Chosen One here, then she could have her fight alongside her as an ally.

"I need you to remove your clothes," she instructed the man on her bed.

He obeyed, then began to remove his armor and clothes. She set all the ingredients on the table beside the bed; meanwhile, in a medium-size bowl, she mashed together the herbs, oils, and faery wings. She disrobed, standing naked in front of him. Her pale skin seemed to glow, as he squinted his eyes to see if it was his imagination. His eyes feasted upon her, as his gaze fell to her exquisite, petite shape. Her breasts were that of a young woman's, small but round, her nipples stuck straight out teasing him, and her flat stomach led his gaze to the white patch of hair that covered her womanhood. Long slender legs carried her over to the side of the bed, where he met her in a passionate embrace. Hungry mouths covered one another with ardency, as angry tongues lashed about. She laid him down on the flat of his back, never ceasing her attack upon his lips.

He cupped her supple, firm breasts in his hands, as his arousal grew with intensity. She straddled him, letting him enter her with equal eagerness. He kissed her breasts that he held in his hands, while tugging each nipple between his fingers, until he trapped one in his mouth. She arched her back in pleasure and rode him with vigor. He grabbed her hips and pushed himself deeper within her wet embrace. He was not a small man, so she let out a cry as his hard endowment reached her deep within. She watched as he closed his eyes, surrendering himself to the motion of her hips. Their passions soon intensified, as she knew that he was close to spilling himself into her, thus she was also nearing her bliss.

While his eyes were still closed, she pulled the athame out from under the folds of the quilt, that she had secretly placed it under. She held it behind her, then began to ride him harder, until the intense wave spilled over her. He was so close to letting himself go, that he had not paid attention to what she was whispering, nor the fact that she was chanting. He opened his eyes for a moment, to see her slice the palm of her hand, then saw her clench her fist to squeeze the blood flow down into the bowl. Next, she placed her bloodied hand to his heart.

"We are one," she whispered.

He could not stop as he freed his pleasure and felt her release as well. She watched him press his head back, with his eyes closed, as she rode on waves of pleasure, while they both were letting themselves go. She recited the final words before she plunged the athame into his chest, then removed his still-beating heart. While he was still hard inside her, she drank the blood from his main artery and let it fall all around her. She continued to slowly ride the still warm body and took a bite from the quivering heart. She set the heart into the bowl and lowered it beside her; she rubbed the warm blood all over her naked flesh, while never losing rhythm. She hastened her speed, as she let herself lose control.

"Rise! Awaken!" she cried out, as the wave of pleasure carried her away once again. Breathless, she waited until the man opened his eyes. The window to his soul was empty, but he could still see her. She carefully placed his heart back into his chest and placed her hand over the wound. Light surrounded the hole in his chest, sealing it closed.

He looked up at her, she was covered in blood, riding his manhood, and he could not remember how he had even arrived there. When she tired of him, she dismounted. He lay in the bed covered in his own blood and hers. He could not move.

"What has happened to me? Who are you? Where am I?" he asked in confusion.

She did not bother to dress, then turned to him in all her blood covered glory and smiled.

"My name is, Vala. You are in my cottage. You are also dead. Any more questions?" she replied, then watched the shocked expression wash over his face.

"What? How am I dead? We just finished making love. How is it that I can not move?" he proclaimed.

She began to laugh, as her blood soaked breasts bounced playfully.

"Yes, I just had you, before and after I killed you. You can not move because I did not permit you to do so. Does that satisfy your curiosity?" she answered, then walked over to the side of the bed.

"No. You still did not answer me, as to why I can not move," he asked again, then felt the warmth of her hand on his cold leg and felt it tingle.

"I am a necromancer, among other things. I can control you," she stated, then moved her hand over to his placid manhood.

He watched in amazement, as he became aroused through no desire of his own. Then as she waved her hand over the rest of him; he was able to move entirely on his own. He only felt tingling, but no warmth or free will. She allowed him to stand up, his manhood still standing by her will alone. She bent over the bed using her will and commanded him to take her from behind. Vala enjoyed her new pet; he would serve her well, in the bedroom and out…

Princess Ellyria and Alfar found themselves being more alike than they had ever imagined. They had talked for hours about their childhood, which was completely different in comparison, but they were the same age and shared similar interests.

"I will let you in on a secret," Alfar stated. He looked into her deep, sapphire blue eyes; he could get lost in them and would not care if he never returned.

"Tell me," she urged. The feelings that were erupting within her, were unlike what she felt when she was with Lord Brom, who made her feel brazen and yet weak around him, at the same time. However, she could feel a real connection with Alfar. She could see her being with him, not just joined by desire and lust, but a bond that she could not explain.

"You are the first girl that I have ever kissed, but I am sure that you noticed," he confessed, as his head lowered almost in embarrassment.

Princess Ellyria giggled, then leaned over to kiss him again. Alfar returned her kiss with such tenderness, that they both grew weak. She gently pulled away from him and he looked confused. His desire for her was too hard to ignore. She felt her empathic powers growing and could not control the feelings she was absorbing from him. She could feel his deep down his arousal for her without even touching him, and the intensity of the heat between them caused her cheeks to burn.

"Come, I want to show you something," Alfar called out, as he motioned to the meadow.

After Alfar helped Princess Ellyria to her feet, she gave him a curious glance and tilted her head to the side.

"What is it?" she asked, clasping her hand in his, then followed his lead.

They went to the center of the meadow, where some of the flowers had not yet bloomed. He sat her down and he knelt beside her.

"Watch," he said, then slowly waved his hand over the flower. It opened and revealed a beautiful red poppy.

"That was incredible! How did you do that?" Princess Ellyria exclaimed.

He enjoyed her smile and making her happy.

"There is something about me that I think you should know. I do not want you to feel frightened or change how you feel about me. Can I trust you?" he questioned, then searched her face for some kind of reassurance.

"Yes, but you are scaring me a little. What is it, Alfar?" she asked, then tried to get a premonition from him, but there was nothing.

"I am not human, at least not all the way," Alfar confessed, as he watched her become uneasy.

"What are you, if you are not human?" Princess Ellyria wondered, pulling her hand from his, and why did it seem that she attracts all the bad ones?

"I am half-human and half Elvin," Alfar admitted, pushing his black hair away from his irregular shaped ears.

She leaned in closer to examine them. His ears were not completely pointed, as Elvin folk; Alfar's ears were slightly more rounded, with a less defined point. He could easily pass for a human if he kept his hair over them. His dark ashy skin would make one curious though.

"What makes your skin so dark?" she inquired, taking his hand in hers once more.

"I am half Dark Elf, at least that is what my mother says," he told her, then dropped his gaze from hers and let it fall to their entwined hands. Her skin appeared to be even paler in comparison to his. Hers was like freshly fallen snow on the first winter's morn, and his was like the night that consumed the day.

"Is your mother an Elf as well?"

"No, she is... She is complicated."

Princess Ellyria was slightly confused by his vagueness. Alfar was so elusive, which made him all the more attractive to her. She really did not care how he became the way he was, she only found herself caring even more about him.

"What of your father? Is he like you?"

"She never mentioned my father, so I am guessing he is. Many different species of faery folk will seek out humans to lay with, so their offspring can live among them."

"You come from such a wonderful place," she admitted, fascinated by his heritage and could not wait to explore his world.

"Why do you not come to see it for yourself? I will be with you, and you will be my guest. My mother is also looking forward to meeting you," he offered, knowing that this was the perfect moment for an invitation.

"Have you mentioned to her about me?" she asked puzzled. Why would his mother want to meet her?

"Only just this morning. My mother questioned where I was going and I told her that I was meeting with you. She thought it was wonderful that I had finally met someone that I had shown interest in. She asked to meet the girl that had stolen her son's heart," he answered, uncertain of what she was thinking, but the look on her face was carefully masking her feelings. "Do you still want to visit my world?"

Princess Ellyria did not think it could hurt, since Alfar would be with her. His mother seemed to be interesting enough. She kissed him on his cheek and smiled.

"Yes, I do. Show me your world, Alfar."

Hand in hand Alfar led the Princess into the place he called home…

Meanwhile, Vala had since bathed after her afternoon romp with her new pet, who she now called Gagarr. She had cleaned him up as well and put him into peasant clothes, so the Princess could not recognize him. She burned his clothes, then threw his armor into the fire so it could melt down to nothing. Her pet was placed outside to guard the cottage and she would reward him later. First, she would check up on her son. She poured the black liquid into a bowl and peered inside.

The images slowly revealed that her son was heading to the cottage, with the Princess. Her son was not a complete failure after all. She must tidy up around the cottage, so she appeared to be like a normal mother. She would not want to frighten the girl, with all the blood and faery wings lying all over the floor. Once the Princess arrived, Vala would be the perfect hostess and make sure that the

Princess felt right at home…

Alfar had led Princess Ellyria deep into the forest, where the largest tree stood. A pool of water formed from the branches, giving the appearance of tears cascading down into the river on the right side, and a large patch of thick clover grew to the left. She was amazed at the sheer size of the tree and its beauty. The trunk of the massive tree was wide enough for nearly ten men to lock hands and wrap themselves around it. The branches were heavy, with their abundance of green leaves. Vines cascaded down the backside of the tree, giving it the appearance of a woman's long, flowing locks of hair.

"This tree is so beautiful. What is it called?" she inquired.

"This is the Elder Tree. It is sacred amongst the Vikings. It is forbidden to cut it down," he informed her.

Princess Ellyria looked up at its mighty branches that almost blocked out the sky, only allowing for tiny rays of dancing light to shine through.

"May I touch it?" she asked, drawn to its life force. She could not help wanting to touch it.

"I think it would be permissible," he giggled, watching her walk over to the tree that seemed to have her so entranced.

Princess Ellyria reached out her hand to the massive trunk, when she touched it the energy coursed through her entire being. Images began to flood her mind like the impact of a storm. Her knees buckled out from under her, but she braced herself up against the tree for support. The woman from the river appeared, she was trying to tell her something, but the Princess could not understand her native tongue.

"Please, I do not understand. What is it you are trying to tell me?" asked Princess Ellyria.

"What is the matter? Whom are you talking to?" questioned Alfar.

Princess Ellyria ignored him. The woman was speaking to her again, this time she could understand what she was saying. She appeared to be glowing and asked for help, stating that she and all of her kind were trapped. The Princess closed her eyes, then fell to her knees, yet still had her palms placed on the trunk of the tree, while she entered a deeper state of consciousness. The secrets of the past had been released from its inhabitant deep within this prison. A white haired woman of alluring beauty cursed and imprisoned the protector of this very tree and the entire forest. Not one magical creature or being could escape these woods; only humans were immune to the Seither's curse. Within the hollow of the tree, which was majickally protected, was a half Elven and half human infant that was swaddled in green leaves. Once the infant's mother had been trapped within the tree, the white haired witch stole the baby and took him with her deep into the forest. Time had not passed during the Elvin Queen's entrapment, for she was still crying for her infant son to be returned to her. A wave of emptiness washed over the Princess as she had never felt before, as she wept. That is why the tree appears to shed tears, because it is crying since the Queen and the tree was fused into one being. Everything made sense to Princess Ellyria now. She looked over at Alfar, who was beside himself with worry. She must warn him about who he thinks his mother really is and try to get him away from here. If she took him back to the gypsy camp, she could help find a way to break the curse. When she tried to stand up, she collapsed to the ground, then Alfar rushed to her side.

"What happened? Are you alright?"

Princess Ellyria tried to speak, but words could not pass her trembling lips.

"Do not try to speak. I shall take you home to my mother. She is a healer, and can help you," he told her, then picked her up into his arms, carrying her to his cottage.

Princess Ellyria shook her head no at him, but her movements were so slow that he did not notice; she was too weak to stop him. He had a pure heart and could feel his desire was only to make her well, but he was also naïve to the fact that the one he called mother, was not his real one…

Vala sent Gagarr to her room and made him wait there in silence, until she called for him. The cottage was warm and inviting, because of the fire that was lit in the hearth and the aroma of fresh-baked bread, that permeated through the home from the stone oven above. She placed a kettle over the fire to have ready, in case the Princess wanted some tea. To her surprise, when Alfar brought in the girl, she was not expecting that he would be carrying her.

"Oh my, Alfar. What has happened to her?" his mother asked.

"I do not know. Can you help her?" he pleaded.

"I could, if I knew what she was doing to have caused this," Vala replied, seeing the dried tear stains upon his dark cheeks.

"She was touching the Elder Tree, speaking to herself, and then she just collapsed," he informed her, unaware that he had already said too much. His mother had darkness in her eyes that he had never seen before, which frightened him.

"Help me get her into the chair and grab some rope," she ordered, giving him a concerned look, the anger finally leaving her eyes.

"Why? What is wrong? I thought that you were going to help her?" he questioned frantically.

"She has been consumed with the darkness, my son. Do not worry, I can save her," she proclaimed, while placing a hand on the boy's shoulder.

"What do you need the rope for?" asked Alfar.

"Do not question my actions, just do as you are told!" she called out, watching the boy drag his feet. "I'll need your help to restrain her. If she gets use of her hands, she could kill us both," she added.

"What do you mean? She would not harm anything," Alfar said, reluctantly bringing the rope, then dropping it to the floor.

"You do not know, do you? She has not told you?" questioned Vala, seeing the depression on her son's face.

"Told me what? What is it that you know that I do not know?" pleaded Alfar.

"She is the Chosen One. She possesses great powers, but if she is swayed, she can use them for evil. The wizard could have gotten to her. If he has, it will be up to us to turn her back toward our side. Do you understand? You must help me convince her that we can help," she explained.

Alfar aversely did as he was told and tied the ropes tight behind the Princess's back, so that she could not escape or use her hands. He really thought that he knew her and let out a sigh…

After a few hours, Princess Ellyria woke up finding herself bound and gagged in a chair. She tried to move, but the ropes were too tight. She was not blindfolded, so she looked around the cottage and saw that it was empty, until she saw Alfar. She moaned into the gag until he came to her.

"I am sorry Princess, but this is for your own good. My mother says that you have been swayed by the wizard and will try to kill us if you are free," he informed her.

She shook her head frantically, knowing that she had somehow tricked him into thinking this. Tears stung her eyes, as they threatened to make an appearance.

"Please do not cry, it will not work. Mother says that you would try to use your feminine wiles on me, to get me to untie you. I am sorry, but she is very wise, and I need to listen to her," he said, then walked away to tell his mother that Princess Ellyria had finally awakened.

A very attractive older woman, with long. white, wavy hair approached her.

"My name is Vala, I am Alfar's mother. You must be Princess Ellyria Rose. I have heard many things about you. I also know many things about you. I know that you are the Chosen One, and I know that you are the only one that can kill the wizard Raul," she stated, then turned to her son. "Alfar, go and fetch more firewood, so that our guest does not catch a chill," she added affectionately, then pulled down the Princess's gag from her mouth.

"I also know who you are. I know that you are not Alfar's real mother and I know what you truly are. You are a Seither, are you not?"

Vala smiled and walked around to the back of the chair, placing her hands on the girl's shoulders, then leaned down beside the Princess.

"Are you not a smart one?" she whispered, with a heavy breath into the Princess's ear, then walked around until she was standing in front of her. The older woman then knelt at her feet, while placing her very warm hands on the Princess's knees, looking up into the girl's deep, emerald green eyes.

"What is it that you want from me?" Princess Ellyria

questioned, as she glared into the woman's ice blue eyes with disdain.

"I need you to fulfill your destiny, a little earlier than you had planned. I can teach you everything that I know if you agree to help me," Vala explained.

"Why would I help you when you have tied me up and held me here against my will?" the Princess asked. The anger she felt from Vala was mixed with an unusual desire that she had never felt before and it was alarming. What did this woman want from her?

Vala softly ran her hands up Princess Ellyria's thighs and flashed her a wicked grin. The woman was incredibly aroused, the Princess could feel it mirroring within her loins, confusing her. When her dress was lifted to expose her soft thighs, she understood what the white haired woman was about to do.

Vala stood up, and gently kissed Princess Ellyria right on the mouth. Without really knowing how to react, the Princess was swept away by this woman's seduction of her. The Princess did not kiss her back at first, as Vala's moist tongue explored her mouth. If she could only control her empathy power, because she did not think she would feel as equally as aroused as she currently was.

Vala grabbed the sides of the girl's face, and became more ardent with her kisses, Princess Ellyria submitted uncontrollably to her and kissed her back. Helpless in her binds, the Princess was made to endure the exploration of her body by Vala's gentle touch. The woman's hands trailed down from the Princess's blushing, soft cheeks, to the nape of her neck covered in long black hair, and then down to the bold neckline of her dress.

Princess Ellyria's ample breasts quivered, as her breathing became heavy, with the soft touch of fingers caressing them. Vala stopped her assault on the girl's full mouth and leaned down to place soft kisses on the Princess's young firm breasts. Her hands cupped them and awakened the nipples trying to escape the confines of her dress. Fingers explored the taut nipples through the material and Princess Ellyria sucked in her breath, as Vala bit one through the fabric. The witch returned to her knees in front of Princess Ellyria and pushed her dress up further, to expose the satin undergarments the Princess wore. Carefully Vala spread apart clenched knees, to touch the very spot that would weaken the girl further, so she would do as the Seither commanded and fall under her spell. Princess Ellyria threw back her head in the chair, as she felt the satin material being pulled away from her body and down over her legs. Hands made their way slowly up the inside of her thighs discovering the heat within.

Vala looked up at her captive and watched, as her effect on the girl was working, it would not be much longer until she would have total control of her will. She had proved to be much harder to sway than her pet had been, but her pet was a man with no powers and Princess Ellyria was very powerful. She also knew it was a premonition that the Princess must have had when she touched the tree, a premonition that she would soon forget. Vala needed Princess Ellyria to become her ally, and what better way for her to do that was to make the girl her lover. Sweet kisses fell to creamy thighs trailing slowly up to an even sweeter spot. Princess Ellyria was helpless to fight her, she could only succumb to the gentle kisses that had matched even Lord Brom's. Pressed tightly into the chair, with the ropes that bound her, she was powerless against her own desire and arched herself into the pleasure that held her prisoner.

Footsteps approached the door. It was Alfar returning. Vala rose quickly, pulled down Princess Ellyria's dress, and wiped her mouth before her son came in. The seduction spell would wear off soon, before Vala ever had the chance to accomplish what she had set out to do…

Chapter 14

Toby rose early before the wizard and proceeded to do his daily chores. When he went outside, Azil was waiting for him.

"How are you, dearie? Is everything in place for our plan to succeed?" she questioned the boy.

"Yes, sort of. The two men Raul set after to find the Princess have not returned. How are you going to escape him, once I get away from here?" he inquired, worried for his mentor.

"I happened upon the Princess's brother, the alchemist. He gave me this potion that will strip him of his powers rendering him a mortal man. It will be easy to escape him without his powers," she informed him of her good fortune.

Toby beamed with anticipation of freedom, that would come in just a few short hours. He would not be able to avenge his father yet, but he knew who could and he trusted her to do it for him.

"What should I do now?"

"Go back inside, do what you usually do. Try not to attract attention to yourself and wait for me to come. I will not let you down, you have my word."

The tutor and her pupil both paused upon hearing a noise coming from the woods, then the sound of footsteps.

"Quick, go inside, someone is coming," she hurried the boy along. She turned away herself and ran into the cover of the gnarled trees.

Toby ran back into the cottage without looking behind him,

to see who was headed for the cottage.

The two minions Raul had sent out in search of the Princess had returned. Quickly, right before they opened the door Toby knocked over the bowls, leaving the peach out on the table. Raul heard the commotion and came out in time to see one of the hungry men eating the peach...

"No! You blundering idiot! Toby!" the wizard screamed. The boy came running in from his room, to not look suspicious.

"Yes, sire?"

"Boy, where was this peach when you saw it last?"

"You put it in between those two bowls, sire."

"Would it not seem strange to you, if you happened to see bowls purposely stacked together, that you would not bother them? Am I correct in this scenario?" Raul directed the question to the man still shoving his face into a peach. The man continued to eat and never caught on to the question directed to him. Raul quickly smacked his only chance at getting the Princess's powers out of the man's hand. It fell to the floor and began to rot before his eyes.

"What was that for? I was only hungry," the man complained.

"Are you that daft? No one told you to eat that peach did they?" Raul scolded the man.

"Well, no. I just helped myself," replied the minion.

"So, not only are you an idiot, but a thief as well. Do you know what the punishment is for thievery?"

"No, sire," the man gulped.

Raul walked over to the table and picked up his athame, then turned back to the one that foiled his plans.

"The crime is usually the removal of one's thieving hands I believe," he smirked.

"No sire, please have mercy. I was only hungry and did not know the purpose of the peach. I would not have eaten it, had I only been told," he pleaded.

"Toby were you out here when this man took the peach?"

"No sire," the boy lied. "I was in my room cleaning up, after I had finished my chores. I came out when you called for me," he claimed.

"Even though no one was here to tell you to not eat the forbidden fruit, you did it anyway. That is what makes you a thief, and you will be punished!" the wizard screamed. Raul grabbed the man's hand, stretched it out on the table, then began to saw the man's hand off at the wrist with the athame.

"No! Please! Ahh! No! Sire, please! Owe, mercy!" the man cried, as his hand was slowly being sliced through to the bone.

Raul paused for a moment, blood covered the front of his robes and was spewing forth from the nearly amputated hand. He lifted the athame to speak and flung the warm blood into the face of the other minion standing frozen in fear, from the sight before him.

"You want mercy, you say?" Sorry, I do not do mercy," he announced, as he brought the blade down into the man's wrist to try and sever the bone, but the blade became stuck. "Drat! I love this knife. Someone go and fetch me the axe," he ordered. Raul tried to wriggle free the knife, but it would not budge.

Toby dragged in the axe and passed it to the wizard. In one fluid motion, the axe came down on the man's arm, just below where the athame had become stuck. Blood spurted all over the place and the panicky man began to run around screaming, while holding his blood soaked, hand-free arm. Raul grinned from ear to ear, as he finally freed his athame, holding it into the air like a trophy. He then took notice of the crazed man, who was now getting on his last nerve. He walked over to the man quickly and slit his throat with his prize.

"Now, that is mercy. No one should ever have to listen to that kind of unnecessary racket," he spoke, as the body on the floor twitched. "Finally, some peace and quiet," he smirked, then turned to his other personal guard and smiled. "So, what did you learn about the Princess?"

"Nothing, sire. We searched the entire realm, all the way to the kingdom of Regnuom. Even when the King captured us, he told us that she was not there, and to tell you that we could not find her," he confessed, letting out a nervous sigh.

"You are a complete idiot!" Raul exclaimed, throwing his

head back in maniacal laughter at the humiliated man. "Did you not just hear yourself?" he continued to laugh, unable to contain himself.

"Well, sire. I am not quite sure what you mean." the guard replied.

"Of course you would not, would you? Did you gather any information concerning the Princess's whereabouts at all?" Raul inquired, finally able to calm himself.

"There was a rumor that she was ill and was being looked after, while she remained at home, sire."

Raul scratched his head with the bloody athame. This posed a problem indeed. Who was this new king in Regnuom anyway?

"Anything else that you would like to add?" questioned the wizard.

"Sire?"

"Is there anything else that you would like to add? I do not believe that I stuttered."

"No, sire," responded the guard.

"I am so tired of your incompetence. Go back to town and take that with you," Raul ordered, pointing to the dead man on the floor. "See what you can find out about this new king and where the Princess is. I do not believe this illness shite. Someone is protecting her," he queried, rubbing his chin, then motioned for the guard to leave. "Do not just stand there, go already!"

The surly man dragged out the corpse and left the cottage.

"Toby, take that hand and bottle it. One never knows when a potion calls for a dead man's hand," Raul informed his apprentice.

Toby took the severed hand and went to find a large enough jar to put it in. Waiting patiently for the next phase of his plan, he went on with his work as if nothing were going on…

Azil waited patiently for the man to drag the dead body from the cottage, before she came out from the cover of the woods. She watched as he hoisted the corpse into the wagon before he climbed on himself, and then rode off out of sight. After a few moments, she slipped to the side of the cottage and peered into the window to see if she could see the wizard. He seemed to be absorbed in his work and it would be a good time as any to surprise him. Although she did not see the boy, she was positive all the commotion that was fixing to take place would get his attention. Azil had not yet figured out how she was going to make her grand entrance, so she decided to simply knock on the door. She took in a deep breath and let it out before her hand reached out for the handle.

The wizard's concentration was broken by the sound of knocking on the door and he could not stop what he was doing to see who it was.

"Toby, see who that is beating on the door. I am trying to focus, send whoever it is away. I can not be bothered right now," Raul told the boy.

Toby obediently went to the door knowing exactly who it was outside. He let out a sigh and opened the front door.

"I can not believe that you knocked on the door. I thought you were going to bust it down or something?" he whispered.

"Just play along," Azil quietly replied.

"Who is that at the door Toby? Send them away, tell them we do not want any of whatever it is that they are peddling," Raul grumbled.

"It is my tutor, sire. She came to bring me a new book to read."

"That is fine. Go outside and leave me alone. I have work to do."

"Yes, sire," Toby replied.

Azil sent the boy out the door and he ran for the woods. This would have been an excellent time for her to come with him, but instead, she wanted vengeance.

Raul flinched as the door slammed shut. He tried to teach the boy some manners and all of a sudden he forgets them?

The old woman walked only a few feet, when she stepped on a worn beam in the wood floor, alerting the wizard to her presence. He could not yet see her, since the wizard was in the next room.

"Who is there? Toby, is that you?" he questioned. No reply was made, only the sound of silence echoed through the cottage. Then the sound was heard again. "What the...?" Raul was beginning to become unnerved and got up to see who it was in the cottage other than himself.

Azil was standing by the fire; her veil covered her face, leaving only her penetrating grey stare visible.

"Who are you? What are you doing here?" Raul questioned irritably.

"I am Toby's tutor," a familiar voice muttered, from under the protection of their veil, smiling. This was going to be fun.

"Where is the boy now?" the wizard wondered, suddenly vexed.

"He left. I am sure that he will be back, never," Azil mused.

Raul was growing impatient with this woman, who sounded so vaguely familiar to him. Perhaps it was from the boy, talking about all the time spent on their lessons. Azil could not help but laugh at the bewildered look on the wizard's face, since she had never seen him in such a state.

"What is so blasted funny? Who are you really?" he interrogated the stranger.

Azil removed her headscarf, slowly revealing the monster that was hidden underneath. Raul sucked in his breath in horror. Such gruesome sights never took him aback, but this was a bit much to take in, even for him. The entire side of the woman's head was void of what resembled any remnants of human appearance. The hair was gone, and the skin was so marred that one could not even make out where her face had once been. Her nose was completely missing and half of her mouth had been burned away, leaving her jawbone exposed. Even though her neck was covered by the scarf, one could see the wrinkled charred remains of her flesh. The other half of her head had grey hair, that mingled with a rough shade of brown; her grey eyes were the only recognizable characteristic of her remaining feminine features. The wrinkled, pale skin of her left cheek and the corner of her mouth was all that had not been burned away. He still could not believe who it was and he stood there motionless, at the dreadful image before him.

"What is the matter? Do you not recognize me?" Azil asked. She had her arms crossed in front of her, as she patiently waited for him to answer.

"Liza? You are supposed to be dead? How did you escape the fire?"

"I crawled to the trapdoor after I had finally come to. I had passed out from the great pain you inflicted on my body. I was so badly burned, as you can see, but I managed to getaway. I left the eunuch guard in my stead to make it look as if he were I, in case someone stumbled upon the body, so they would assume that I had died. By not removing the dead guard, you left me with the perfect alibi. It took me months to heal from broken ribs and burns. I have returned to pay you back for what you have done to me," Liza declared, as her true self.

Raul stood there for a moment before laughter took over. He could not help it. This was the most entertainment he had since he set the fire, to begin with, next to almost having the Princess, now that had been a great time indeed. The tiny vial that was about to hit Raul's face cut his laughter short. He caught it in midair and held it up before him.

"What is this? And do not lie!" he warned, as he clenched his fist together.

The old woman immediately grabbed her scarf, trying to pull it from her neck. She could barely breathe, as it enclosed tighter around her throat.

"It is a power-stripping potion," Liza gasped.

"Where did you get this?" Raul questioned, looking at the vial, then he smiled at her. When she hesitated, the scarf tightened. "Let us try again, you miserable wretch. Where did you get this?"

"I got it from the alchemist," Liza choked out.

"Good. Did he say how you were supposed to use it?" questioned Raul.

"Please, I can… not… breathe," the crone pleaded. The scarf then gave way to easier breaths. "The alchemist said that if I threw it at you, it would strip you of your powers, leaving you defenseless."

Laughter broke the awkward silence and Raul could not have had better luck. He had been trying to come up with the final ingredient for the potion, since his raven never returned. It had been driving him mad, but now he had exactly what he wanted. Now all he needed was to know where he could find the Princess.

"Did he mention to you where the Princess was hiding?" Raul inquired.

As much as Liza had wanted to see Princess Ellyria suffer, she wanted the wizard dead more; if she divulged the Princess's whereabouts, then there would be no one left who was powerful enough to kill him. Unfortunately, she would have to rely on the Chosen One to exact her revenge for her on the monster in front of her that had taken her life away.

"You can tell me, I promise to kill you mercilessly this time. You look as though you have suffered enough," the wizard coaxed.

Liza stood her ground. She may have failed in her pursuit to use the potion against him, but she was not going to make things easy.

"I do not know where the Princess is," Liza lied, then felt herself being pulled until she was standing in front of the wizard.

"Are you sure about your answer?" Raul challenged the old woman, scarcely able to look at her revolting face, but he would not have to endure it much longer.

"Please sire. I told you. I do not know," Liza gasped, barely making out the words. Her eyes were blinking rapidly, with tears streaming down her hollowed face, as the scarf began to tighten again.

"I am growing quite weary of your lies. Tell me the truth, before I cut out your tongue," Raul threatened, stepping back away from her grisly hands as she tried to grab him. He kept his distance, then held up his hand and the athame came to him. "Yes. Were you trying to say something?" he mused, loosening his grasp on her.

"The Princess is not where you have been told. I am not going to be the one to tell you where she is either, you evil bastard!" Liza swore, then spat in Raul's face.

Out of complete reflex, he quickly brought the athame to her neck and sliced through the charred flesh. Blood spilled as her body crumpled to the floor.

"How many times do I have to kill you?" he pondered, kicking the lifeless figure out of his way, then vanished from the cottage…

Toby ran towards the cottage after he heard the screams. He waited for his mentor to join him in his escape, but after he could only assume that the wizard had killed her, Toby hurried from the safety of the woods.

Raul appeared before him so abruptly that the boy ran straight into him. Standing there out of breath, Toby looked up at the wizard, who still had the athame in his hand.

"Going somewhere?"

"I heard the screams. I got scared, so I ran," Toby stammered, then began to cry.

"Whom were you running from? There was no one here to harm you. I took care of that," the wizard proclaimed.

"My tutor, what did you do to her?" Toby asked.

"The woman you are referring to never really existed. She was an imposter, playing as your tutor when her true identity was that of an evil woman who just now tried to kill me. I was only acting in self-defense," Raul confessed.

The boy knew it was no use. He would never be able to escape.

"Did she mention where the Princess was by chance? I know that you must have been incredibly busy with all of your scheming, but perhaps some bit of information may have been dropped by her?" inquired the wizard.

"She mentioned that she was with the gypsies, sire. I do not know what that meant," answered Toby, unable to understand the relevance, but he would be punished if he did not reveal what he knew.

"Oh yes, you have done well my boy. Go on inside and clean up the mess. Oh, and get rid of that body too. I suggest that you take it out back and burn it," he ordered, then vanished again…

Chapter 15

Captain Jake and the remaining crewmembers had finished repairing the tear in the mainsail and hoisted it back up into place on the mast. Captain Jake's brother, Lord Brom, Rob the Red, and the rest of the crew should have been back by now; it was not like them to be late. Captain Jake decided to go out looking for them, leaving one man to guard the ship and taking the others with him. They lowered the last lifeboat into the water, and lit the lanterns, to guide their way through the darkness until they reached the small beach. Captain Jake searched for a way up the face of the cliff, when one of his men started shouting.

"Captain! I found some hidden steps," a surly man announced, as Captain Jake walked over to him.

"Good, let us see where they lead, come on."

They scaled the side of the cliff; the lanterns lighting the way on the stone path. When they finally reached the top of the cliff, they saw a lit-up tavern in the distance.

"They are bound to be in there. I do not see anything else around," Captain Jake observed. They approached the building and saw the sign on the door that read "The Nixen." That was when they heard the screams…

Captain Jake tried turning the knob on the door, but it was locked. The blood-curdling cries became louder and not a minute was wasted. Captain Jake and his men broke down the door. They were inside but saw no one in the room. From the double doors across the hall, they heard the screams again, and what sounded like vicious animals.

"Come on, follow me," Captain Jake ordered.

The twin doors were locked and they could not get in.

"We need something to knock it down with," the captain instructed.

Another man found a heavy chair, that they used to break down the door; they never expected to see what was before them. Blood covered the doors, as men had tried to escape, even more blood was splattered on the walls and the ceiling. Some of the crew were still alive they were fighting off women that had mouths of razor-sharp teeth and serpent tongues.

Rob the Red was grabbing heads and twisting them until he heard their necks break; a few others had been able to grab their knives from their boots and were in the process of slashing the monsters' throats.

Captain Jake and his men drew their swords and began running through the room, leaving heads to roll in their wake. They were nearly no match for the incredible strength and prowess of these vicious beasts. One of them jumped on Captain Jake's back and he reached behind him, grabbing a handful of her long hair and flinging her off before she could clamp those mighty jaws into him. She hit the floor and hissed, then quickly stood up, only to meet steel as it slashed through her neck, leaving her head to lie beside her body in a puddle of blood. It took everything Captain Jake had to help fight them off, but victory was finally theirs. Out of all the ten crewmembers that came in with Rob the Red and Lord Brom, only three survived. Rob made the fourth, but Lord Brom was still missing. The few men Captain Jake had brought with him survived, since they had swords to protect themselves with. Now he had to find his brother. Before they could get out the door, the few women that only had their necks broken or throats slit, stood up. They had healed and were coming straight for them again. Captain Jake and the others that had swords in hand advanced on them; one by one the monstrous heads fell, rolling at their feet.

"That should do it this time," Captain Jake said, out of breath. To be on the safe side all the remaining heads were severed, to ensure they would not come back from the dead again.

"What were those things, Captain?" one of the younger men questioned, clearly still in shock.

"Sirens, lad, Sirens. They seek seed from men and then they eat them," Rob the Red informed, throwing his arm around him, as they walked along. "So they bed you, then they devour you. Cheer up lad, they are all dead now. You will not have to feel bad, for having a bastard man-eater running around killing people in the future," Rob the Red consoled the young man.

"That is the way to cheer a guy up, that was nearly eaten himself. Let us go find my brother," Captain Jake laughed, shaking his head.

They made it out of the room and split up, to search through the brothel…

Lord Brom was still pinned down underneath Lorelei on the bed. She was playing with him like a cat does with its prey; his struggles were futile against her immense strength.

"Why do you not just kill me and get it over with, you vile creature!" Lord Brom shouted, at the woman who was taunting him and licking her lips with her snake-like tongue before licking him.

"You taste so sweet. I want to take my time, and enjoy my meal," she purred. "Perhaps play with you a little while longer. I have never enjoyed my food, as much as I have with you."

Lord Brom yelled out as she bit into his shoulder, not tearing his flesh, only enough to draw blood. He tried to fight her off again, but she held him tight with her thighs and held him down with strong arms.

She licked the blood that was flowing freely from his wound, then rose up smacking her lips together.

"Mmm, so sweet. I can not wait to taste the rest of you," she laughed with anticipation. She leaned down to kiss him full on the mouth again; when she stopped, he spat at her. She wiped herself off and then struck him hard across his face. "You did not complain earlier when I kissed you."

"I did not know that you and your whores were going to try to eat me and my men," he declared, trying to fight her again, but it was no use.

"Why are you still hard inside of me, if you did not like it?" she enlightened him, moving her hips a little more over his, then hovered over him and licked the side of his face again.

"It is not so bad if you do not fight me," she purred, then started riding him vigorously.

Lord Brom could not fight his body, as he neared release again.

"No!" he screamed.

"I am only insuring the continuation of my kind. We breed every year at Midsummer, taking in those lost souls from the sea that were brought here by their misguided fortunes. Once we lure them in by thinking we are all a bunch of lusty whores, we bed them and then feed upon them. We raise our babies, then send them out into the world, so they can continue the cycle," she informed him, then threw back her head, as she felt herself ride her own waves of pleasure and his release as well.

"You are sick! "Why are you even telling me all this?" Lord Brom yelled angrily, exhausted from trying to fight her off, and her raping him.

"I am a Siren, not sick at all, but I am offering you a deal," she said, trying to bait him.

"What deal?" Lord Brom asked, wondering what should he do now, pondering whether or not to play along.

"I shall spare your life, and you can become our stud," she smiled sweetly. "How can you resist having your choice of beautiful women every night, catering to your every whim? You could even help to lure others here, so we can feed upon them," she added, while she flicked her tongue at him.

"I have your word you will not kill me?" he inquired.

"Yes," promised Lorelei.

"All I have to do is make love all day long?" he inquired again, needing to come up with a plan fast and saw exactly where this was leading.

"Yes," she whispered in his ear, then stuck the tip of her tongue inside it. "Alright. On one condition."

"Name it," Lorelei offered.

"Let me take you from behind this time," urged Lord Brom.

She grinned wildly and sprung up from him, flipping herself over on her stomach. He grabbed her hips, pulled her to her knees, then drove himself hard and deep within her. While she was in complete ecstasy, he grabbed a hold of her long, blood-red hair in his hand and heard her moan, as he pulled her head back towards him. She had never been consumed by such pleasure before, as he pushed himself deeper inside her. Without letting go of her hair he yanked it back even further, to grab both sides of her face. Lord Brom quickly twisted her head with his hands, until he heard her neck snap. He pushed her body onto the floor and hastily put on his clothes.

As he was about to fling open the door, his brother Captain Jake and a few of the crewmen came to his rescue.

"I am so glad that you are alive," Captain Jake said, embracing his brother. He looked over at the naked woman on the floor. "You know that is a Siren, do you not?"

"Yeah, I found out the hard way," Lord Brom responded, revealing the bite mark on his left shoulder.

"We will have to get you cleaned up. How did you kill her?" Captain Jake asked.

"I broke her neck, why?" Lord Brom stated.

Before Captain Jake could reply, she had jumped up and leapt onto Lord Brom's back, taking another bite into his right shoulder blade. Captain Jake raised his sword and detached her head from her neck. Her lifeless body fell to the floor beside her head.

"You have to remove the head, dear brother," Captain Jake enlightened him.

"Good to know for the next time we run into a nest of blood-thirsty Sirens," Lord Brom mused, then let out a sigh and winced in pain, from the fresh bite on his shoulder.

"Seeing that they are all dead now, I suggest that we get out of here," Rob the Red suggested.

Everyone agreed, so they all immediately ran down the stairs. When they arrived, Lord Brom took a detour and ran behind the bar, to collect a few bottles of alcohol.

"This is not the proper place to have a drink now, brother," Captain Jake chided.

"I am not. We are burning this place down. Help me with the rest of these bottles," Lord Brom instructed.

The men grabbed all the bottles they could find and began to pour them throughout the entire brothel. After they made sure everything was completely saturated, they grabbed the lantern and threw it onto the floor. Flames engulfed everything within its reach, as the men ran out of the burning building. They watched from the top of the cliff, as the fire reached the sky; it gave them more than enough light to descend the rocky steps to the beach below…

Once they had returned to the ship, they immediately set sail for home. Captain Jake helped his brother to his cabin and began to clean Lord Brom's wounds. Captain Jake had to stitch them and Lord Brom drew up his shoulder when the needle went in.

"Well, I do not ever want to do that again," Lord Brom stated, as his brother finished sewing up the left shoulder, then moved on to the right one.

"So, did you make love to the Siren again, even after you found out that she was a monster?" Captain Jake queried, as his brother remained silent with only a dumbfounded look on his face. "Oh brother, you did? That is disgusting," he gasped.

"I had to. It was the only way I could get her off of me long enough to get the upper hand," Lord Brom confessed.

"Rob the Red said that they turned on him as soon as he spilled his load. How is it that you prevented her from killing you?" Captain Jake interrogated his brother further.

"I am just that good. Apparently, she wanted to use me as

their stud. If I serviced all of them and lured more innocent men to them, she would let me live," Lord Brom stated proudly.

"So you agreed?" enquired Captain Jake.

"Yes, but only to get away."

"Well, you definitely think on your feet, or should I say off of them," Captain Jake teased his younger brother.

"I think you are a sick man, brother," Lord Brom chuckled. "Thank you for stitching me up. How soon before we are back to Regnuom?"

"Well, we were way off course, so it will be a few days."

"Good, I shall catch up on my sleep. I will see you in the morning then. Oh, and Jake, would you mind keeping this to yourself? I would hate for this to get out to the wrong people," Lord Brom asked.

"Do you mean the Princess?" teased Jake.

"No. Just keep it to yourself please," Lord Brom pleaded.

Captain Jake smiled and left his younger brother alone.

Lord Brom eased himself down onto the bed, then looked up at the ceiling. He could not believe that he was still worried over her. He did miss her and he had never really stopped thinking about her. He wondered if she ever thought about him or where she was right now. After he had left her the last time, he promised himself that he would not let her rule his mind again.

No matter what he did, or how hard he tried, he could not erase her from his memories…

Chapter 16

Alfar entered the cottage, setting the firewood beside the hearth. He looked over to Princess Ellyria, who seemed as though she was in a daze, and his mother was acting strangely.

"What is going on?" he inquired of his mother. She walked over to him and grabbed his arm.

"Nothing that concerns you," she answered, as she squeezed the fleshy underside of his arm. "Go back to your chores!"

The young man did as he was told and left the room.

Princess Ellyria's head began to throb as her senses returned to her. She remembered why she was here, but could not remember anything that had happened in between. Then as if she were inside of the Seither's head, she could almost hear her thoughts. Closing her eyes she tried to focus harder, because it was not coming in very clear. She knew that Vala wanted to use her to get back at the wizard, but why was still unknown to her. The desire for revenge was strong inside her, but she did not know to whom she was seeking retribution.

Vala had moved to sit at the table, waiting for the full effect of her persuasion spell to end on the Princess. She could not try again now, because it was past the point of her still being under; she would have to start all over again.

"What is it that you need of me? Why do you not simply ask for help to kill the wizard?" asked the Princess.

"Are you willing to help me kill the wizard then?" Vala enquired, in a bit of a shock.

"I do plan on killing the wizard, but it will be for the betterment of the entire realm, and not simply for you," Princess Ellyria said sharply, sensing the witch's anger.

Vala stood up abruptly, walking over to the trussed-up girl. She stood there for a moment, before striking her across her face.

Tears stung in Princess Ellyria's eyes, as she slowly turned her head and sent Vala flying back. Anger took over her, since she had picked up on her emotions, as Vala hastily rose back onto her feet.

The Seither grabbed the young girl's face and tried to kiss her. This was the only way she would be able to keep her under control. Alfar walked in on his mother kissing the Princess and nearly vomited.

"Mother! What is it that you are doing?" exclaimed Alfar.

"It is not what it looks like son," Vala lied, turning to face her son, shock washed over her face.

Princess Ellyria did not succumb to the evil woman's majick. This time she was able to keep her focus.

"Alfar, you must listen to me. This woman is not your mother. I have seen your real mother, and she is trapped in the Elder Tree," Princess Ellyria tried to explain.

Tears appeared in the young man's eyes, and he did not know what to believe.

"What are you talking about? Mother, is this true?"

"Of, course it is not. She has the wizard inside her talking. I know that you care for her, but do not let your feelings cloud your judgment," Vala warned.

"She is lying to you! Do you not see it in her eyes? She is a Seither! She is the one seeking revenge on the wizard! Who is in fact evil to the core, but she only wants to avenge her sister's death!" the Princess shouted, as the emotions building in the room were becoming too much for her to handle.

"Do not listen to her, son. I promise you that I am not the monster she says I am," she pleaded with him.

Alfar did not know whom to believe at this point. He covered his face with his hands and began to cry.

Princess Ellyria began to cry as well; Alfar was experiencing so much pain and confusion right now, that it was beginning to break her heart. She pondered how to get free of her bonds, but was not certain whether or not she could untie the ropes with her telekinesis.

"Tell me the truth, are you my real mother?" Alfar questioned, looking up from bloodshot eyes to the woman he had only known as his mother, then to the one that he was sure he was in love with.

"Yes, of course, I am. How could you even think that I am not?"

"Princess Ellyria, please tell me what you saw in your vision. I need to know the truth," he stated.

"No, you do not need to hear it from her! You need to hear it from me. I am your real mother, I raised you!" shouted Vala, moving towards her son.

Alfar pushed her out of his way to go to Princess Ellyria. He lifted up her chin and wiped the tears from her sun-kissed cheeks.

"Please. Tell me what you saw," he questioned, looking into her emerald eyes.

"I saw a woman with golden hair, being cursed into the tree by Vala. She was crying and calling for her son. The woman that raised you, stole you from the hollow of the enchanted tree. Your real mother has been trapped inside that tree, all of these years, as well as the rest of the creatures in this forest," she said now, feeling the old woman panic.

"Is this true? Did you take me from my real mother and curse her into that tree? How could you lie to me all these years? I endured your beating me, starving me, and making me do everything for you. You blamed the wizard for all of your problems. When it was you all along that was the evil one!" he screamed, tears blinded him. He went after the one that betrayed him with the poker from the hearth.

"No! Wait, stop!" Vala cried out. "Gagarr!" The Seither's pet came in from her room. "Grab him!" ordered Vala.

Gagarr took hold of Alfar, then held him tight in his arms.

"No! What are you going to do to him? Please, I will help you kill the wizard if you do not hurt him," Princess Ellyria pleaded in tears. She watched as Vala walked over to the Halfling, caressing his face with the back of her hand.

The Princess turned away in disgust, knowing what the witch was about to do. He could not move to resist, she had a handful of his hair and pulled him down to take her spellbinding kiss. Princess Ellyria felt him succumbing to the spell.

"No, Alfar! Fight it!" she shouted, but it was too late. She had control over him now.

"Gagarr, leave him and go gather more faeries. I shall need them for my strength when we summon the wizard," Vala ordered her pet.

"What do you mean by 'summon' the wizard?" Princess Ellyria inquired, but the older just woman laughed at her.

"You still do not get it, do you? My sister was Volva, a much more powerful Seither than I could ever be. Raul was her apprentice, and once she taught him everything she could, he killed her. He not only took her power by eating her heart, but he also took my sister whom I was very close to. She raised me when our mother died, and I was very young when he killed her. I had to practically raise myself. Then I realized I had a natural talent all my own, to control others' free will just by kissing them. So I preyed upon men, which was not difficult since they are so easily swayed. I used my wiles to attract them and they desired me to kiss them, so when I did they were under my spell. When I became much older, I discovered by accident that I could control the dead. I was hiding in a wagon, where a corpse was waiting to be hauled away and when I touched it, it moved. I know this is mad, but when I knew my kiss controlled the living, I tried it out on the dead man, and he awakened. My sister had schooled me well on spell work, but I wanted to know more. So I went deep into the forbidden mountains, where it was said the oldest living dragon held the secrets to all majick. He protected it for his former master that had been killed. The old man was said to be the father of all majick, a powerful wizard that was not good, nor was he evil. He was The All, the one who could bend time and space, one who was chosen by the Gods themselves. He gave his dragon the ability to speak to anyone of any race or any creature and speak his or her language, so he had someone to talk to, that did not fear his power. He found out how intelligent and wise the dragons were, so he taught his dragon the secrets only he knew," Vala explained.

"How did you know that he existed, and how did you get him to give you these secrets?" the Princess questioned in confusion.

"Dragons are ancient creatures, outdating the existence of mankind. When mankind was born, the dragons took pity on us and tried to protect us. It should have been the other way around. Mankind could not understand the dragon tongue or the dragon ways. One by one they were hunted and killed out of fear. They were made to go into hiding, only trusting those with the true gifts of majick, not ones that sought after it. My people had been at peace with dragons, so I was able to seek the wisdom from the Ancient One himself. He gave me enough knowledge, to figure out the rest on my own. I was only a young girl then, still a virgin, it made me look pure in the eyes of a dragon," Vala recalled, smirking at the girl, who was poorly schooled in history.

Princess Ellyria was confused, she knew the woman was telling the truth, but she did not understand how everything came together.

"So why curse the forest? Why can you not fight the wizard on your own?"

"I am centuries old, and an immortal being. Unfortunately, I can still be killed by another immortal, or by a Chosen One such as you. I would look much older, but I chose to know the secrets of youth and beauty from the dragon. I came to live in this forest because I have caused the faery population in every forest I have lived in to be nearly extinct, but this forest had an abundance of faeries to choose from. Unfortunately, it also had a Queen to protect them. I could not very well fight the majick of the Queen every time I needed to harvest these woods, so I cursed her into the Elder Tree and trapped all of the faery folk within these woods too. It has been the perfect place ever since," she beamed.

"Why did you keep her son? Why did you raise him?" questioned Princess Ellyria.

"I was lonely. Not too many humans ever came into the forest, for me to capture and use to my advantage, like Gagarr here," she said, motioning to him as he walked in the door, with several sprites trying to escape from the bag.

"You have a lively bunch, my mistress," Gagarr stated.

The Princess was mortified, as she watched Vala pull out the tiny creatures, rip off their wings, then eat them whole.

"You are a monster!"

"Yes, perhaps. Although, you have not even seen the half of it," she laughed, as she went to her cabinet and pulled out several ingredients, then set them on the table. A large bowl was used to collect the many things she threw in. Then she called to Alfar, who like a good dog, came when she called.

"Give me your hand," she ordered the Halfling. Alfar extended his hand to be cut with her athame and let her squeeze his blood into the bowl. Vala then cut her own hand and clenched her fist tight, to squeeze out the blood.

"No! What are you doing to him? You said you would not harm him!" the Princess shouted to the white-haired Seither.

"I only need a little of his blood to make this work."

"What work?" asked Princess Ellyria.

"The spell to summon the wizard to me," Vala answered. "Once I get him here, you can kill him, then I shall take his powers."

Princess Ellyria should have known better, but she could only sense the anger and vengeance from her, not her desire for the wizard's powers. She tried to concentrate on the ropes again, but she was too easily distracted by all the chaos.

Alfar was beginning to come out of the spell and it did not last as long as Vala had expected. He looked about the room in a daze, his head ached, and he could not remember anything after he found out that Vala was not his real mother. He saw that Princess Ellyria was still tied to the chair, since Vala was not paying attention to him, he snuck over to help his love escape. He kissed her quickly, to let her know without speaking, he was back to himself again before he tried to loosen the bonds. Time was of the essence and Vala had begun the chant, to bring the wizard Raul right where she wanted him. She had not paid any attention to the Princess, or the Halfling, she was in total concentration. Smoke filled the room, as a strange energy took over…

Without any will of his own, Raul was transported into a strange little cottage. Once he gathered his senses, he searched his surroundings…

"Where in the realm am I? Who dared to summon me here?" the wizard questioned.

"I did," Vala confessed, moving to face him head-on.

"You obviously do not know who I am, otherwise, you would not have called me here, unless you have a death wish. What is it that you want?" Raul questioned, looking up and down at the attractive white-haired witch.

"You do not recognize me, do you?" Vala replied.

"I would have remembered a beautiful woman such as yourself, if we had met before," Raul said, approaching her. He reached out and touched her long, soft hair, then peered over her shoulder. He could not believe his eyes. "What have we here?" he inquired, moving Vala out of his way, to see a vision so lovely before him. "Do my eyes deceive me? Or is it the Princess I see before me?" Raul asked, exaggerating his excitement. "Is she a present for me? Is that why you have summoned me here? You will be greatly rewarded for your gift, madam."

"Not so fast. She is not the reason that I had called you here," Vala informed him, stepping in between him and his quarry.

Raul became agitated; the Princess was right here all trussed up for him and it was all too easy in fact. This was a trap! Raul grabbed Vala by the hair and bent her petite body backwards.

"So, witch! What did you think to accomplish by bringing me

here? If it was not to gift me with the girl, then what are you after?"

"She is yours if you want her, but I want to strike a deal with you," Vala said breathlessly. She had to think fast.

Raul set her upright again and waited impatiently, for what she was going to say.

"I want to strike a bargain. I give you the Princess and we take over the realm together. What an unstoppable force we could be. With both our powers combined working as one, we would be the Lord and Lady of the entire realm," she tried to persuade the wizard.

"No! You said that..." The gag that was shoved back in her mouth by Alfar, abruptly cut off Princess Ellyria. He looked at her and put his finger over his mouth, then stood at attention beside her as if he were being obedient to his mistress. Vala motioned for her pet to come to her.

"We could create an army of undead to storm all the kingdoms, they would have no choice but to give up their realms to us," she added.

The wizard looked over at her undead minion, who did not have the appearance of a corpse. He was impressed by this majick she had.

"How did you come to make him?" Raul inquired, watching her flash a large grin as she trailed her fingers down the front of his black robes.

"I used sex majick to trap him, then I killed him. While he was still inside me, I cut out his heart, drank his blood, then feasted on his heart, before I put it back inside his body. I used the sex majick again to bring him, not only back to life, but also as my servant. I can use the will of my mind, to make him do as I please," she explained. To prove her point she had her pet come to her and kneel at her feet.

"That is remarkable, but you are a sick witch. I do not bed the dead," Raul stated, but was still impressed by her majick. "May I give him an instruction?"

"No, only I alone can command him due to the bond we share," she confessed, then commanded Gagarr to rise and walk to the prisoner to guard her.

Alfar hurried and leaned down into Princess Ellyria's ear and whispered for her to play along when the wizard was not watching.

"How do you kill him?" Raul queried.

"He can only be killed if the heart is severed, or his head for that matter. Also, if I die, then the spell is broken," Vala offered her secrets.

"If I agree, what exactly do you want from me?" Raul pondered, looking to the Princess, then back to the Seither.

"Only to rule at your side," Vala offered, as she seductively ran her soft hand down the side of his face. "Let us be as one force and take over this realm as one," she purred, pulling his face toward hers. Her piercing ice blue eyes held the evil wizard's gaze, as she tried to manipulate his desires. He was still a man and all men can be controlled by their own lust.

"On one condition, then I shall agree with your terms," he counter-offered.

"Name it," Vala eagerly stated.

"I want you to give yourself fully to me," Raul declared.

Vala smiled knowing that was coming closer to her revenge. Their mouths came together in an instant, tongues entwined in the heat of passion.

Princess Ellyria and Alfar both felt themselves becoming sick, by what they were subjected to watch, it was too gruesome to look at, but too horrifying to turn away.

"You kiss just like your sister did," Raul confessed, then pulled Vala from his mouth by her hair and looked deep into her eyes. He wasn't surprised by her lack of words, or the shocked look upon her face, as he forced his mouth over hers once more before she pushed him off.

"You bastard! You killed my sister!" Vala screamed, trying to fight him, but he kept his grip tightly on the back of her head and kissed her again even more violently than before.

"We can truly be one," Raul hissed, after yanking her head back. Before she could scream, he reached into her chest and slowly pulled out her still-beating heart. He held the witch tightly in his grasp, as he peered into her eyes once more, biting into her quivering heart, then leaned into her ear. "Now I can be a necromancer and create life from death," he whispered, then laughed maniacally.

Princess Ellyria gasped, as she watched Raul devour Vala's heart, after he had let her lifeless body hit the floor. Gagarr also fell to the floor, since his creator was dead.

"Ahh the Princess is all wrapped up to go, how nice," Raul snarled sarcastically, then kicked the Seither's corpse out of his way, feasting his eyes on his perfectly wrapped package. He went to approach her, and she pushed him back only a few feet, but he was too strong and fought against her power. When he started towards her again, Alfar stepped in front of her. "Out of my way, you filthy Elf," he said, then waved his hand and sent the Halfling flying into the front of the hearth.

Princess Ellyria knew by seeing the fresh bloodstain on his tunic, that he had been injured. She began yelling from underneath her gag, then Raul pulled it down for her.

"If you have hurt him, I swear that I will tear out your heart and feed it to you!" she threatened. Her temper was now flared and she finally broke free from her bonds, sending the chair to the floor as she leapt up from it. She combined all the energy she had absorbed from the emotions in the room, concentrated them into a ball, and hurled it at the wizard.

The blow did not affect him and Raul laughed at her weak powers. To the wizard, it almost did not seem worth the effort to take them from her, but power is power. The more he had, the closer he was to becoming the most powerful being in all of the realms. He reached inside the folds of his robe and held the potion vial in his hand; now he would have her powers. Raul threw the potion vial at the Princess and she stopped it in mid-air.

"Impressive, girl, but that will not last long," he sneered, before he tried to send it back to her.

The Princess caught the vial in her right hand and quickly

threw it back at him. He was expecting her to use majick to send it and he was not prepared for the turnabout. He was able to send it away from him, then it smashed up against the wall.

"You little bitch! I will get you for that, I promise!" he screamed, then vanished out of sight.

Princess Ellyria ran to Alfar, who was alive and bleeding badly. She took him in her arms and cradled his head in her lap.

"Oh, Alfar. I am so sorry that you had to get dragged into this. Please hang on, tell me what to do and I shall do it," she offered while sobbing.

He felt her warm tears drop onto his face and opened his eyes.

"Ellyria, it happened."

"What happened?" she questioned.

"The curse, it is broken. I feel her calling to me, my mother," he breathed, looking up at his love.

"Well let us go then. She can heal you and everything will be alright," she offered while smiling and helping him to his feet.

Alfar pulled Princess Ellyria to him and kissed her softly, before he let her help him up. They kissed passionately for a few moments, then she pulled away.

"There will be plenty of time for that later. Right now I have to get you out of here," she chided.

Alfar cried out in pain when she tried to help him walk forward. It was at that moment she noticed how deep his wound was and what it was that had inflicted it. When Raul hurled him into the hearth, Alfar had landed on the poker, which had pierced his flesh and broken off upon impact.

Princess Ellyria had to pull the end of the poker out. She grabbed the leather strap that had always been used by the Seither to beat him and ordered him to hold it between his teeth. He took a deep breath to prepare himself for the pain. When she pulled out the wooden rod, blood followed uncontrollably. She felt his pain, and although she tried hard to block it, she could not. Her breath was cut short, as she felt a sinking in her chest. He fell limp in her arms and she ripped part of her dress to wrap around him, to try and stifle the bleeding. Then she lifted him up, concentrating hard to not let him fall. She had to use her power, for he was too heavy for her to carry and he was too weak to walk. As she walked out of the cottage, he followed her in midair.

Once they had arrived outside, a glorious sight welcomed her. A beautiful, white horse, with a single ivory horn spiraled into the air reaching to the sky. It pawed the ground and tossed its magnificent head up and down snorting.

"I can help you bring him to his mother, lay him over my back and I will carry him to her for you," the unicorn offered.

Princess Ellyria could not believe that she could hear the unicorn's thoughts. She had received her final power. She raised her hands hoisting Alfar onto the mare's back, gently laying him across.

"Thank you for helping him," she said, stroking the unicorn's soft muzzle.

"We must go quickly. I can feel his life force leaving him, hop on behind him and hang on. I will run fast as lightning to the Elder Tree."

Princess Ellyria climbed on the unicorn's back and they rode faster than she had ever ridden on a horse. The mare was even faster than her brother's horse Odin.

Princess Ellyria cradled Alfar in her lap to keep him from falling off, then looked down at him and realized that she could indeed love another. Although now, she was tangled within her own guilt…

Chapter 17

Prince Ian was pacing back and forth so vigorously, if the floor were made of anything less than the stone, he would have fallen through already. His man should have sent word by now that he had reached Inamor, and to tell him of what has happened with his sister. Was she safe? This waiting, worrying, and being held up in the castle was not helping him. He needed to be the one protecting his sister, not some strange man that he had sent in his stead. The guard came running in, after Prince Ian had beckoned him.

"Yes, Sire. You called?"

"Yes, I need you to send word to my father, that I have not yet heard from my man in Inamor and that I am worried for my sister's safety. Tell him that I am leaving to take care of this matter personally. Regnuom was perfectly fine without me before I sat on the throne and will continue to be fine without me for a few more days. Send that message by your fastest bird. Tell them to ready my horse. I am headed for Inamor," the acting King ordered.

"Yes, Sire. Right away, Sire," the man said, before he hurried out of the room.

Prince Ian left for his bedchambers to change his attire for the journey; the ride would take the better part of a day, even if he never stopped. He hurried to don lighter clothes, simple trousers, and a tunic, the lighter the better. He would carry only his sword and water pouch in the saddle; it was all that he needed.

Once he arrived in the courtyard, his horse had been made ready for him and he placed his broadsword into the leather holster, that he had custom-made into the saddle. He mounted his steed and looked to his man, to see if he was ready to accompany him. He nodded he was indeed ready, but before Prince Ian set out, he motioned for the squire not to leave just yet.

"If you do not hear from me by nightfall tomorrow, send word to my father to call upon my brothers for help. If anything happens here, send word to Lord Thomas and he will know what to do," the acting King ordered, before he kicked his horse and rode off into the night. Prince Ian's decision to bring his personal guard with him was last minute, he felt he might need his services if he ran into danger. He could fight well on his own, but not if he had to go up against the wizard. His father would be furious with him; it was a chance he had to take. Ellyria needed him…

The King and Queen awakened to the sound of knocking on their bedchamber door. King Jason grumbled, as he settled Queen Anna back down and told her that he would tend to the matter. She had been ill from grief over the news of the wizard looking for her only daughter and stayed in bed most of her days. He did the best he could to see that she was not disturbed, so whoever this was in the middle of the night pounding on their door, better have a good excuse for the disturbance. He opened the door to see his courier holding a message in his trembling hand. King Jason stepped out into the hall and pulled the door closed behind him. He stood there in his dressing gown waiting for the nervous boy to hand him the message.

"Oh, just hand it over boy. I am starting to catch a draft," he said, snatching the parchment from the boy's hand.

The young man stood there and waited, to see if a reply message would be sent in response. When King Jason finished reading the long message from his son Ian, he was furious. Why does his son never listen?

"What are you still standing here for?" the King questioned.

"I was only waiting for your response, Sire. Should I take

down a message for you?" the boy asked.

"No, that will not be necessary, but if anything else comes bring it to me at once," he ordered.

"Yes, Sire," the young man bowed and left, to wait for any new messages there might be for the King.

King Jason returned to bed, where he thought his wife would be sleeping, but she was sitting up in the bed waiting for him.

"What has happened? Is Ellyria alright?"

"Everything is fine. Ian sent word that he will see to his sister's safety himself and to not worry," he lied. He did not want his wife to worry that the man Ian had sent to look after their daughter never reported in, so that made Ian concerned for her safety. He curled up beside his wife until she fell asleep. Although he could not sleep himself for his own worries, he had to stay strong for his wife…

CHAPTER 18

The Black Forest was once again a place of beauty where all faery folk and enchanted creatures alike, could finally come out of hiding and return to their lives and playful antics. No longer did they have to live in fear of being hunted and killed, for the Seither was dead. They were finally free to roam as they pleased; now they could leave the forest to take care of all the plants and flowers, that only the sprites could properly care for...

The tiny, winged beings flew around their savior, as Princess Ellyria arrived at the Elder Tree, to see the Faery Queen herself. The unicorn kneeled for those to help transport the wounded forest Prince from her back, setting him gently upon the ground at the base of the grand tree. Even though the curse had been broken, the Queen had not yet emerged from the tree, for fear her son would not be returned to her. Then she sensed her son was near and left the protection of her home. Sparkles and shimmering beams of light encircled her, as she floated down from the highest branches. She was so lovely, hair of spun gold, sun-kissed freckles upon her nose, rosy cherub cheeks, and her bow-shaped pink lips shone brightly as she smiled. Her dress was sheer, sky blue, that was held together with gold ribbons, and white flowers, which dangled from her petite shoulders. Princess Ellyria noticed the Queen was as tall as her, as she floated down in front of the Princess.

"I am Redomredlyh, and I thank you, Princess, for breaking the curse put upon this forest by that evil woman. How could we ever repay you?"

"You could start by healing your son," Princess Ellyria stated, as she pointed to Alfar.

"How could he be my baby? He is almost grown," the Queen cried out, looking down at the nearly grown young man, that lay on the ground beside the Princess.

Time had not passed for his mother while in the tree. She was frozen in time and had no idea that nearly eighteen years had passed, since she was cursed by the white-haired witch, that had stolen her only son. Redomredlyh knelt beside the boy, whom she never believed would come back to her. She healed his wound, but it was too late.

Alfar's breathing was sparse, as he looked up at the woman. He remembered her, she used to swaddle him in large leaves from the tree and sing to him, until he fell asleep. This was the happiest day of his life.

"Mother," he cried, barely breathing.

The Faerie Queen held him in her arms and cradled her only son whom she never knew, but always yearned for. He had been returned to her and she never wanted to let him go.

"Yes, my son. Oh, how I have waited for this day. I will never let you go and I will always love you," she said, as tears cascaded down her cheeks.

Princess Ellyria could not help but cry too, she knew that Alfar was not going to make it and the emptiness that was filling her made her feel helpless.

Alfar looked up at his mother and began to feel at peace. He heard the song that his mother used to sing to him at bedtime; a lovely song about how the forest came to be and the love that brought him to her. Her voice carried through the trees and up through the branches into the sky.

"Love planted this seed in Mother Earth, she carried it inside her until its birth, a song brought the rain to help it grow, into the Elder we all know. Then our hearts grew with wonder, for a love so fair, we traveled far and we traveled fast, for a love so pure to share. Out of love you grew in me, so fair, so pure, you be, my love I share with you, my blessing you shall be. My innocent baby boy, my little bundle of joy, my innocent baby boy, my little bundle of joy," she sang.

Alfar closed his eyes and fell asleep, as he used to as an infant, when his mother cradled him in her arms as she did right now. His mother wept, as his life force could be felt no longer.

Princess Ellyria held great pain inside her, from the heart of the mother that had been left with emptiness and sorrow. She wished that she could help her, but she could only kneel beside her and embrace her, as she wept for the only son she ever had, but never knew…

The entire forest wept for their Queen and mourned the young Prince Alfar, who had been taken from them a second time. Flowers were gathered and adored on his mound, which was constructed for him as his final resting place and to then become one with Mother Earth. She would cradle him within her bosom, until he became one with Her once again.

The forest creatures and all faery folk alike, gathered around to each place their offerings, so their Mother could care for him in the afterlife. They laid garlands of flowers over tiny seeds that had been sewn into fresh earth, with hopes of renewal and growth, so Alfar could become one with them. Water from the stream was poured over the seeds with love, so one day, they would become a tree that Alfar could be swaddled in once more. When everyone had left, only a childless mother remained to say not her farewells and to offer Alfar good tidings, for his new journey into his next life.

Princess Ellyria watched as the Queen floated back into the Elder Tree, which she guarded both day and night. The sun was rising into a colorful sky and Princess Ellyria welcomed the dawn, but the inhabitants of the forest settled in for a long peaceful slumber. She turned away from such a glorious sight, for she needed to head back to the gypsy camp where Mala was most assuredly waiting for her return…

The Princess left The Black Forest with a heavy heart. She wiped the tears from her emerald eyes, as they silently fell. The river continued to flow with tears of a lost love, from the empty heart of a weeping mother. Princess Ellyria could not understand the love between a mother and child, but she could feel it. She hoped to never know such a barren feeling. Her own heart ached for a young man that she had grown to love, who had been taken away from her before it could blossom into something that she knew could have been magical.

"Goodbye Alfar. I shall never stop thinking of you and I promised that I would never let you go. I will always keep that promise that I made, blessed be my love," Princess Ellyria whispered, looking back to the forest, where she had left the love she would never forget.

Princess Ellyria knew that her message would be heard by the wind, which blew through the trees, carrying it to the one she would never forget…

Chapter 19

Raul returned to the cottage, only to find his apprentice missing. He was not pleased at the moment and his patience was wearing thin. A new power-stripping potion would be made and there was still one peach left, one last chance to get the Princess's powers. Toby would have to wait; he would deal with him later. Right now, it was all about the potion…

Toby carried a small sack with him filled with bread, fruit, and a change of clothes. He decided his only chance to get away was while the wizard was off chasing the Princess. After Raul left, so did he. The boy had not made it too far out of town; he did not even know where he was going. If his father had still been alive he would have gone home, but he was all that was left of his family, no mother, no father, no grandparents, just him. He had been walking for several hours during the night and it was now morning; he was hungry, so he stopped to rest for a while. An old oak tree, with great branches full of greenery, made for the perfect place to prop himself up under a natural canopy and provided enough shade to keep him cool. He did not want to eat too much, just a few bites of the bread and an apple would satisfy him for several more hours of travel ahead. He tried to come up with an idea of where he should go, yet nothing came to mind. How would he even survive? He had always been taken care of by someone that provided him with food, shelter, and the clothes on his back. What could he do to provide for himself? His skills were few, but he was a good apprentice; the wizard must have believed it too, or he would have been killed like everyone else who displeased him. Even though he hated Raul for killing his father, he did learn a lot from him; the wizard also made sure that he had learned to read. Of course, he killed his tutor before he had a chance to complete his final lessons, but he knew enough and had become an excellent reader to continue his education on his own. He hated himself for becoming slightly fond of Raul, but Toby considered the fact that when someone brings you into their home and takes care of you like family, then you do tend to care in return for that individual…

After Raul finished making the potion, he had the time to go search for his apprentice. He could not decide how he would punish him. Should he make him do extra chores, torture him, or kill him and find a new apprentice? The possibilities were endless, but right now he needed him, and finding a new apprentice to train this late in the game he did not have time for. It was up to Raul to find Toby. It would not be difficult, with the binding spell he used to link them together by majick, so he would always be able to locate him…

Toby had finished his breakfast and finished packing his little brown sack, when the wizard appeared from out of nowhere and scared him out of his wits.

"Where did you think you were going, boy?" Raul snarled, at the frightened lad.

"Nowhere, just out gathering fruit, sire," he lied.

The wizard knew he was lying and why, but he would deal with that later. First, they had work to do. If his next plot against the Princess was ever going to work, he had to do it now…

They returned to the cottage, so the wizard could prepare for the next phase of his plan. Raul knew the Princess would want to go back home, after the little incident at the Seither's cottage and he would be waiting for her.

"Will there be anything else you need for the potion, before I continue with my chores, sire," Toby questioned humbly, as he approached the wizard with heavy feet, clanking loudly as he walked.

"No, that will be all for now," Raul stated, then looked up at the boy nodding his head in compliance, who then turned away clanking again as he walked. "You know I hate having you in shackles, you move way too slow, but until I can trust you again they shall remain on. Understand?"

"Yes, sire," Toby responded, only after he had come to a stop, then continued with his chores, while his ankles created a melody of shame.

Raul pulled a souvenir he had stashed away, that he had taken from the gypsy camp when he was searching for the Princess, right before the white-haired witch summoned him. He had barely made it back to the cottage to hide it when he felt tingly from the spell, then he found himself within reach of the very person he had been searching for all along. The crystal ball was the gypsy's most powerful scrying tool; now he had one of his very own. He peered into the translucent crystal and concentrated on finding his minion, whom he had sent for information regarding the new King on the throne of Regnuom. Smoke filled the globe, and when it cleared the image of his minion appeared. Raul clapped his hands together and laughed. This was going to be marvelous fun. His minion appeared to be nearing the cottage. He could get his information and then try out his new power. Where was the Princess? The crystal ball clouded again, making the previous image disappear, then new images appeared. It was the Princess walking back to the camp. Ah, she looked so sad. What a pity. It would be the perfect time to ambush her, but with his minion fast approaching the cottage, he could not leave. He would have to see where she was later…

Raul's minion arrived just as he expected. He was inclined to find out his name, he had never bothered to ask, simply because he did not care. Although, he did grow tired of referring him to as 'guard' or 'minion' all of the time.

"So, what did you find out about this new king?"

"Good news, sire. He is Prince Ian of Toledya," he answered proudly. This was the first thing he had ever succeeded in doing right by his master. "His father, King Jason, put him on the throne for protection."

"Good news indeed. Could be useful information. Good work. What is your name anyway?" Raul inquired, tapping his fingers on the table.

The man stood in shock; his master had never asked him his name before. He must have finally pleased the wizard, to his own surprise.

"I am called Draug Noinim, from the northern parts of Regnuom. My family was killed in the war. Liza's father, King Harold, took me in when I was just a boy, among several others they had taken, to become a soldier for their army. I was one of the best, so they made me one of Liza's personal guardsmen. I am here now as your loyal servant," he said admiringly.

"I do not care about your life story, and your name is too long. I shall simply call you Draug," the wizard grumbled, shaking his head and rubbing his temples.

"Yes, sire. I would be honored."

"That is splendid Draug, you said you gave your loyalty. Am I correct?"

"Yes, sire. I will die in honor of you if I have to."

Raul showed his ugly blackened teeth, as he thought about an idea, which had been marinating in his mind for some time. He walked around from the table and slipped off his athame, hiding it within the folds of his robes.

"Is that so? It makes me so proud to know that I have the most experienced, noble, and magnanimous man at my side," the wizard said, placing his hand on the surly man's shoulder.

Draug smiled wide before blood escaped his lips. Raul had stabbed him with the knife, into his chest and cut out his heart. While it still beat, he drank the blood from the main artery and bit a chunk out of it. He rolled the beating heart in a bowl of ingredients the spell called for, before placing it into the dead man's chest.

"We are one, rise and awaken," the wizard chanted. Nothing happened. "I order you to rise and awaken. I am your master and I call forth the power within to control you," he chanted once again.

The man stood up, he had no idea where he was, or who he was.

"Yes! It worked without having to bed him!" Raul shouted, letting out a sigh of relief. He tried to telepathically control him, but that did not work. It must have been the reason the Seither slept with her dead, to have that connection. Well not he, there was not a great amount of desire to control this corpse with his mind. He would do it the old-fashioned way and speak his orders. "You are Draug, I am your master, and you will obey no one else, but me. Do you understand?"

"Yes, master," Draug answered, nodding his head.

Raul was pleased. This would help with most of the hard labor around here, so the boy could focus on his lessons.

"Toby," the wizard called to his apprentice, hearing the sound of chains rattling along the floor, as the boy approached. "I altered this man for us. He will be completely submissive to our needs. I should have him be under your command as well, so if you need something you can send him to get it for you," Raul informed him, then turned to his walking corpse. "Draug, this is Toby, and you will do as he commands you. Is that understood?"

"Yes, master," obeyed Draug.

"Good. Go outside and bring in more firewood. The boy and I have work to do," Raul ordered his dead minion, then returned his gaze to the crystal ball, to see where the Princess was. "It looks as though our little Princess has returned to the gypsy camp. Hmm, and who is that young man with her? Toby go and put on your attire, that you wear for cleaning," the wizard declared.

"Sire, I have a problem with that," he said, pointing down at his chains.

"Oh alright. Now you better not try to run away again, or I shall put on a large stone for you to drag around. Or maybe I could alter you, like I did with our friend, Draug. Understand?" Raul threatened, watching the boy nod his head in agreement, then unlocked the chains with a snap of his fingers.

The boy left to change his clothes, upon his return he was shocked by what he saw...

Chapter 20

Prince Ian had been in Inamor for only a few hours and his sister was already dragging him around. She was showing him the entire gypsy camp, including her very own private tent, that had been first on their tour. It allowed for the privacy needed away from Mala, who she had not informed regarding everything that had happened in The Black Forest. She feared it would upset her, that she deliberately disobeyed her warning about the forest. Prince Ian listened closely to her tale of what had happened within the short period of time she had spent with Alfar, and how she came to fall in love with him, only for him to be ripped apart from her. She told him how she was able to reunite him with his mother for one last moment before he died in her arms. Prince Ian could not imagine what it must have been like for him to have never known his real mother, and only know the monster that raised him. He would have done the same thing, to help his people be freed of the Seither's tyranny. His heart was so full of pride for his sister. She amazed him more and more, with not only her kindness to others, but the sacrifices she made for the sake of others.

"Ian, I really miss him. I think we would have been great together. We are both majickal and possess powers, that only we could sympathize with one another. It is hard sometimes to feel normal again, after everything that has happened to me, it is like I am an outsider," she informed her older brother.

Prince Ian hung his head, he felt horrible. His sister had never confided in him like this before; he never knew she felt this way.

Could it be his fault for leaving her here?

"Ian, please do not blame yourself for leaving, you did not know what was going to happen. I did not even truly see how all this would affect me either. I do not even have the power to foresee my own future, just those around me," Princess Ellyria explained wisely. She reached out and grasped her brother's hand and looked at him.

He knew her empathy power worked now and her power to communicate with animals. Although he never would believe that a unicorn would be the first one she would carry a conversation with. What would be next a griffon?

"Probably not, dear brother, griffons only exist to serve themselves, they would never answer to my call," she teased.

"Will you stop doing that!"

"I am sorry. I have not gotten control of this empathy power yet. I have finally managed not to get headaches before I feel someone else's emotions, but I still can not block them."

"Do not worry. I am sure you will get the handle on this before too long, just like you mastered your telekinesis power," he said reassuringly.

"That is the thing. I have not mastered empathy, but I was still able to converse with the unicorn. I do not understand."

"Maybe you should ask Mala. You have to tell her everything that happened out there. She probably will not be as disappointed as you think."

"Ask me what?" Mala questioned the Princess, as she entered her tent. "I am sorry that I could not help but overhear something about you entering the Black Forest."

"How did you know?"

"I do have a crystal ball you know," she teased. "I was worried after you never returned to the Summer Solstice celebration. So I took a peek as to where you were. That is when the wizard appeared. He spared my life, only because I ran as soon as he entered your tent and took your orb."

"So that is where it went. I was wondering where it was when I came back earlier."

"So you know everything," Prince Ian questioned Mala.

"I know only what happened to Ellyria before the wizard showed up. I only saw her with the boy in the forest, nothing after that. I did not worry so much since I knew it was a handsome young man that had struck her fancy. Are you going to tell me what happened now?"

"Yes, I will tell you," she said as she began to tell her what she had already told her brother. In the end, came the question about her telepathy powers with animals.

Mala giggled at the girl.

"What is so funny?" Prince Ian asked Mala.

"Unicorns are majickal creatures themselves, so they can communicate with anyone if they so desire. You will not get the ability to communicate with animals until you master your empathy power. It is going to be hard, and you are going to have to focus more than you ever did with telekinesis. Empathy for others can cause you to go mad. If you do not learn to control the power soon, you will have to shut yourself from humans until you can shut out all the voices in your head. Do you understand?"

Princess Ellyria was not sure, but she knew Mala meant it, and that she was fearful of her.

"Why are you afraid of me?"

"I am afraid for you. Afraid that you might not be able to control this in time, before the wizard uses his new power in combination with the Amulet of Elements. I will help you channel your energy to control it as best as I know how. I promise," Mala reassured her before she gestured for them to follow her from the tent.

"Thank you, Mala. I am so grateful for all your teachings. I also promise to listen to you, and respect your advice this time," she said, embracing the older gypsy woman.

"Of course, for you, anything my dear," Mala replied. "I must be going now. Prince Ian, enjoy your tour, and do not forget to visit the marketplace, you never know what you might find," Mala said, then left the siblings alone, and continued her business for the day.

Princess Ellyria smiled at Mala, watching her leave, then

looked up at her brother and grabbed his arm.

"Come now, let us head to the marketplace. We shall see most of the camp on our way," she laughed excitedly.

"Will I see any pretty women there?" Prince Ian inquired.

"You might, you never know," she teased.

They toured the camp as they headed to the marketplace. Princess Ellyria had not been there, since she and Lord Brom had been when they were looking for the amulet…

Prince Ian was enjoying his tour with his sister, and as predicted, he saw many pretty women. Even though his sister would not allow him to stop long enough to get to know any of them, he still had such a good time looking, that now he found himself growing hungry.

"I am famished after all this walking, dear sister. How about you? Are you not hungry?"

It had been a while since she had eaten. Mala made sure that she ate as soon as she returned to the camp, but she had barely touched it.

"Yes, I could eat something. What would you like, dear brother? The merchantmen that have the food are over there, so let us go see what they have, shall we," she said, leading the way. They linked arms and headed in the direction led by their empty stomachs.

The first vendor had many different loaves of bread, but they did not really want bread. The second vendor had various dried meats, but they did not want any meat. The third vendor had various delicious, exotic fruits, and fruit would be a good idea on such a hot day.

"How about some fruit?" she suggested to her brother.

"That sounds good. It is so hot out, that it will prove to be refreshing indeed," he answered.

When they approached the table, a small boy appeared.

"How may I help you?"

An older man hobbled over to the young pair speaking to his boy.

"I hope that my son is taking good care of you," he said.

"He is, thank you. Have we perhaps met before?" Princess Ellyria inquired, looking at the strange older man. Something was familiar about him, but she could not place where she might have seen him before. He was standing with a cane, he hobbled when he walked, and his grey streaks of hair complimented the grey flecks of color in his piercing eyes. He looked as though he was a handsome man in his early years, but time had not been kind to him.

"I do not believe so child. What is your name?" he asked, clutching his cane.

"Oh, my name is Ellyria, and this is my brother Ian," she answered the curious man, watching as Prince Ian was busy pointing out to the boy what fruit he desired for himself, and his sister.

"Are you visiting here? You do not look like one of the natives," the old man questioned, leaning closer to the Princess.

"I am visiting, yes, from Toledya. Have you ever been there?"

"I can not say that I ever have, my dear."

"Where do you hail from?"

"I come from a region that is far away, my dear."

Princess Ellyria began to get one of those headaches again. Perhaps it was from the heat and the fact that she had not eaten much. She hardly noticed when Prince Ian was handed the basket of fruit, after he gave the boy a few gold coins.

"Are you ready to go eat?" he asked his sister.

"Yes, I am," she replied, then turned to tell the man thank you before she left, because he had been so kind to her. Thank you for your kindness, sir."

"Wait! I see that you have no peaches in your basket?" he shouted, shaking the fruit at her.

"Oh, no. I do not suppose we do," Prince Ian answered the older man.

"Here, dear. A gift to you," the merchant offered, then handed Princess Ellyria the most perfectly ripe and fuzzy peach that she had ever seen.

"Thank you kindly, sir," she said, reaching for the peach from his outstretched hand. When she took it, she held it up to her nose to take in its wondrous aroma.

"You are very welcome, my dear. Why do you not take a bite to make sure you enjoy it? If it is not the best fruit that you have ever tasted, I shall give you another to replace it," he promised, giving her a wicked smile.

The young boy backed away from the table. Princess Ellyria felt tremendous amounts of fear from the boy. Why would he be afraid of them? When she started to take a bite, she felt the excitement from the old man building, and the fear from the boy turned into worry for her safety. Suddenly, she pushed Prince Ian out of the way. A few of the innocent bystanders began to scream and run away. Princess Ellyria threw down the peach, that turned black as soon as it touched the earth.

"I knew it was you, wizard! Show your true self, you coward!"

Toby ran to the other side and hid under the tables. Raul snapped his fingers, and in the blink of an eye, he turned back into his true image.

"How could you possibly know that it was me, you wretched girl? I am going to rip out your heart and eat it!" Raul shouted, then sent her flying into another table.

The people that were close by screamed, then ran away from the majickal battle that had just begun.

Princess Ellyria could not get to her feet before she saw her brother bravely draw his sword, then she sent him flying out of the way with a gentle wave of her hand, before the wizard had time to harm him. She quickly got to her feet when Raul made a move for her, but she avoided his attempt and sent him into one of the tables behind him.

Toby was hiding under the table when it collapsed on him by the wizard's weight, and he lay unconscious beside Raul. The wizard knew that he would not win this fight so easily, when an angry mob of gypsies came running toward him. He grabbed the boy and vanished before the Princess, and her allies had the chance to attack.

Once the wizard had gone, Princess Ellyria ran over to help her brother.

"Are you alright?"

"Yes, I am fine."

"I am so sorry, Ian, I had to. I was afraid the wizard was going to kill you. I would not be able to live with myself if he had," she confessed.

"I do not want to hear it. You are obviously not ready to go up against him. I am taking you home right now," he declared.

"What? I am not ready to go now. Mala was going to help me control my new power," she pleaded, trying to reason with her brother.

"You are going home. Dakota can help you with your empathy problem. End of discussion," the Prince commanded.

Princess Ellyria reluctantly gathered her things and bid Mala farewell. Mala told her everything that she could during the time she was packing.

"I will watch over you, no matter where you are. I will help when I can, perhaps even stop by for a visit when we move south for the winter," Mala offered, embracing her young student.

"I do hope so. I will be back as soon as I can. I promise," she cried, wiping the tears from her face.

Prince Ian had the horses ready and was growing impatient waiting for his sister.

"We must go, Ellyria. Now," he commanded.

She mounted her horse, leaving her trunks behind, and had only packed what she could fit into the saddlebags. She did not say another word to him, as they headed home for Toledya, Prince Ian had not said a word to her either.

Princess Ellyria did not have to ask, she already knew. Her stepping in and becoming the hero had hurt his manhood. She could not help that it had been a reflex. Her brother could be angry with her from now to the end of his days, but at least he was alive…

Chapter 21

The return to Toledya was a welcome one. After more than a few days of traveling in near silence, Princess Ellyria was grateful to be home. Her parents, her brothers, and Isis all customarily greeted her in the courtyard, as they had always done before when she arrived home. It felt as though she was in a daze, like she was there, but she was not. The warm greetings from her family were pleasant as always, but as she was being passed around sharing one embrace after another, she could not bear it any longer. She was overwhelmed by the outpour of all the emotions around her.

"I am so grateful that you are alright my darling. I have been worried sick ever since I heard you were being hunted down by the wizard. I do not know what I would have done if he had found you," Queen Anna said, embracing her daughter.

"He did find her, but she is still not strong enough to go up against him yet. We barely got away," Prince Ian announced.

"What? Is this true?"

"Yes, mother. We did get away, and that is all that matters," Princess Ellyria added, flashing her green eyes at her brother.

"The fact of the matter is that she is home safe. How about we have a grand ball in your honor sweetheart?" their father inquired.

"No, thank you. I do not want a ball thrown for me. I do not deserve it. I only want to go to my room so I can shut all of you out of my head for a while, please."

"Ellyria, wait!" her mother exclaimed, running after her.

Princess Ellyria stopped at the grand staircase and turned around to face her mother. She was not ready to explain what had happened in the Black Forest, not yet anyway.

"Please do not cry, mother. I need some space; a lot had happened while I was gone, and I just need to be alone right now. I shall be alright, do not worry about me, and I do not want to talk about it either. Please leave me be," she asked of her mother, then quickly ran up the steps with Isis trailing behind…

Later that evening, the family gathered for supper in the elaborate dining hall. Both parents looked proudly at all of their children; Prince Anthony, Prince Dakota, Prince Ian, and Prince Rowan, were all together once again. Well, almost all of them. Princess Ellyria refused to come down to join them. Queen Anna did not want to pry Prince Ian for information without hearing it from her daughter first, but she could not wait any longer.

"Ian, please tell me what happened with your sister. I know that you were not with her the entire time, but did she tell you anything?"

"She told me everything, mother. What would you like to know first?"

"Why is she pulling away from me, and why are you two fighting?" Queen Anna waited eagerly for some explanation, and by the look on her son's face, it was not a pleasant visit to Inamor.

"What would you like to know first? What happened before, or after the wizard tried to kill us?"

"Son, I do not know what has gotten into you, but you need to show your mother the respect that she deserves," his father chided.

"I apologize, mother. It was a very difficult time for both of us. Ellyria has received her power of empathy full force. She is not able to control it. Mala said that she must do the controlled breathing exercises she did with her telekinesis, because this will be the most difficult of all her powers combined. If she does not learn to control them, it will drive her mad. I can not tell you anything else. I promised her," Prince Ian told his mother.

"What happened? Did she get hurt again?" Queen Anna sighed, fighting back her tears.

"No, mother. She met someone, a Halfling Prince of the Black Forest. She fell in love with him, but the wizard killed him. She blames herself I think, even if she will not admit to it."

"What was he like?"

"I never met him. She said that he was a magical being, half dark elf, half-human, who had been kidnapped by a Seither and raised by her. He had never met his real mother until after this curse was broken, and he died in his mother's arms. According to Ellyria, she felt he was her equal," Prince Ian explained further.

"She must be heartbroken," King Jason chimed in.

"Ellyria has been through so much. Is there anything I could do to help?" Prince Anthony asked.

"She probably would not want to know that we all know her business now," said Prince Rowan.

"Rowan is right. We should not let on that we know, but with her empathy power, she is going to find out," Prince Dakota mentioned.

Before anyone had noticed, Princess Ellyria had changed her mind about coming down for supper; she now, however, felt that it was a huge mistake, since everyone at the table was using what had happened to her for their evening entertainment.

"Find out what exactly? Oh, do not bother because Dakota is correct on one thing, I do know that Ian told you what had happened. Thanks, Ian for telling everyone my business! Although if you all must know, yes, I did fall for a Halfling. I cared for him very much. I am so sick of this wizard hurting everyone that I love! I need to get a handle on these powers, I know this, but I have to do it alone. Please, understand that I love you all, but I do not want anyone else that I love to be killed by Raul. I am going to try and stay in my chambers, alone. If I need anything I shall come and get you," the Princess said, before returning to her chambers.

The entire room was silent for the remainder of the meal, and when they had finished eating everyone went in separate directions for the duration of the evening. Prince Anthony went to secure the grounds as he did every night, making sure the watchman had nothing to report on before he retired for the night. Prince Dakota went back to his tower to research empathy powers, and what their effects were on the person with the power. Prince Ian left to check on Migata, whom he had not seen since he left for Regnuom, then retired with her for the night. Prince Rowan decided to call for his giant dragon, Gaia, for a night ride, so he could relax before he retired for the night with her in her favorite cave nearby. King Jason had retreated to his study, as he spent every night since he had been King, and Queen Anna followed him in there, sitting across from her husband at his desk.

"What is the matter, my love?" King Jason asked, with concern for his wife.

"Why do you think Ellyria would not open up to me?" the Queen whispered, keeping her gaze in her lap.

"I can not answer that. I never know what to think about that girl. She has her own mind now, her own destiny. You are going to have to accept the fact that she is not a little girl anymore. She has grown into a bright, and powerful young woman. It might not be you that she is shutting out, it might be that she is shutting herself in. Give the girl time," her husband said, as he got up from his chair, taking his wife's hand. "Come on, let us go upstairs to bed."

"Perhaps you are right. I shall leave her be," she said reluctantly, then followed him out of the study.

"I know that I am right. Do not worry. She will come around eventually, you shall see."

King Jason and Queen Anna retired to their chambers for the night, and slept peacefully knowing that all of their children were safe at last, under the same roof...

The next morning came heralding a new day, and a new outlook for the Princess. Isis was asleep beside her bed as usual, while she took in all the wondrous surroundings of her home. She felt refreshed, after a full night's sleep, and perhaps it was all that was needed. If she got up and went downstairs, perhaps she could beat everyone to breakfast and hurry to eat alone, without the constant flow of emotions to absorb. Being an empath was not as easy or as forgiving as she had believed it to be, and it was not at all as she had desired it to be either. She donned a cotton day gown and ran quickly downstairs, to not run into anyone. As luck would have it, her brother Prince Dakota was up waiting for her.

"I have prepared a breakfast picnic for us. Do you care to join me?" he asked.

Princess Ellyria sighed. He had gone through all of the trouble and was concerned for her wellbeing.

"Yes. I will come with you," she agreed reluctantly.

The two walked out into the beautiful field, beside the broken wall by the courtyard. It was so pretty this early in the morning, as the sky was still painted by the sunrise. The flowers were waking up themselves allowing for their sweet smells to linger on the gentle breezes that carried them. Prince Dakota spread out a large blanket on the dewy mix of sweet grasses and clover, motioning for his sister to take her seat. Then he spread out an abundant feast of sweetbreads and fruits, that were of a colorful variety.

Princess Ellyria watched as her brother prepared her a plate, then one for himself, before he turned to her waiting for her response.

"Is this a test to see if I can read your mind? It does not work that way you know," she giggled.

"Tell me how it does for you?"

"Well, at first I had headaches, then I would become incredibly dizzy, before I felt the emotions from the person I was the closest to. Then I felt them without the headaches or dizziness, and I was able to pick up on more feelings from more than one person at a time. Now, I can not seem to stop the flow. It is like feeling and hearing everyone at the same time. Not so much hearing what the other person is thinking, but hearing their feelings, as though it is being said by the other person."

"So, you can hear what I am feeling, just not my thoughts?"

"No, I can not read your mind, nor can I distinguish between what is real or not."

"How so? Are you not able to tell if it is real feelings that someone has, or their thoughts? I am confused," Prince Dakota questioned further.

Princess Ellyria was becoming frustrated already and knew that her brother meant well. She understood that he was only trying to figure out how her gift worked for her, since it worked so differently for others.

"If someone is thinking about what they are feeling, then I can pick it up and hear it since it is an emotion. If they are only feeling pain, but have their mind clear, then I only feel it, and do not hear it. Make sense?" she tried to explain to her brother.

"I see. If I am sad over something, but not thinking about it, then you only feel it. However, if I am thinking of the sad feeling that I have, then you can hear it and feel it. Right?" he nodded, finally catching on.

"Yes, exactly. You finally understand what I was trying to explain. I can not shut it off. It is deafening me."

Prince Dakota leaned back on his elbows, then looked up at the bright blue sky, before breaking the few moments of silence between them.

"I did a lot of research before bed last night. Even though there was not too much on the subject, there was enough information that I think could help you. A lot of breathing exercises, and something called blocking that I think you could benefit from. When you close your eyes, you have to first focus on yourself only, your breathing, your heartbeat, and your thoughts. I want you to try."

Princess Ellyria closed her eyes. Her legs folded together, she sat upright with her palms turned towards the sky, the backs of her hands resting on her knees. She focused on breathing deep and slow, in through her nose, then out her mouth. She listened to the beat of her heart that was in unison with her breathing. Her mind was racing, as she tried to capture the emotions that would not hold still long enough to even sort out. Once she had control, she immediately heard her brother saying that she could do it, and to shut him out too. She smiled and could feel him smiling, even with her eyes still closed. It was not working, she seemed to be going deeper inside his mind instead. He was worried that if she could not control her power, she would go mad.

"Do you think I am crazy now? I thought you were on my side. I believed that you were trying to help me, but I was wrong!" she shouted, tears falling from her emerald eyes. She got up to leave, but her brother grabbed her hand, then stood up beside her.

"No of course not. I do not think that you have gone mad! Where and how did you get that idea?"

"I ended up going deeper into your head, that is where. I do not know how that could have even happened. You said to focus and shut you out, but I could not. I only found myself going in deeper into your mind."

"I do not think your empathy works on just emotions alone. I think your telekinesis allows for your empathy to cross into telepathy. Maybe Vadoma was not aware that this would happen. What did Mala say about it?" Prince Dakota consoled her, wiping the tears from her face.

"There was not much time for her to tell me anything. Ian was determined for us to leave right after the wizard left. I do not know what to do. I am scared, Dakota," she said crying, as her brother embraced her.

Even in his effort to comfort her, Princess Ellyria was feeling as though she was being ripped in two. Not only did she have her own emotions to deal with, but she was also dealing with Dakota's, who was also feeling completely helpless. What was she going to do? What was he going to do? How could he help her? This was becoming too much to handle, and all she could think about was Alfar.

"Ellyria, wait!" Prince Dakota shouted, as his sister pulled away from him, then ran back to the castle. "What happened?" he said out loud. Prince Dakota gathered all of the picnic supplies and headed back to the castle, to speak with his father. He would know what to do…

King Jason was already in the study speaking with Prince Ian. It was a heated conversation that took Queen Anna to intervene, to stop the two men arguing long enough to chime in.

"Both of you are acting like children!" she chided. "You need to talk to each other like rational adults, not a couple of toddlers fighting over a toy."

King Jason stopped pacing long enough to look out of the large window, that overlooked the courtyard. He was not paying attention to his daughter running back into the castle crying. He was too busy trying to talk to his thick-headed son, Prince Ian.

"I am only trying to talk some sense into the boy!"

"You do not need to browbeat him to death over what he has done. It is over now, give him a break. He was only doing what he believed to be the right thing," his wife added.

"Do I get a say in the matter at all?" Prince Ian asked. "I am the one that decided to leave my post in Regnuom, but I was the only one that knew of the wizard's search for Ellyria. I only reacted on instinct, since I never heard from the person that I had sent in my stead, and by your own advice, father."

"I am not saying that what you did was wrong, son. I am only saying that when you are at your duty station, you can not just leave based on a gut feeling," his father added. "You have to stay and protect your kingdom, unless you are going to war. A king must remain calm during any situation, no matter what it is. Do you understand?"

Prince Ian knew his father was right. He had an endless amount of men he could have sent to Inamor to see to his sister, he was not the one that had to go. He should not have gone.

"I am sorry, father. You are correct. I should have stayed in Regnuom. I understand your disappointment in me," he said humbly.

King Jason sat back down and looked at his son. He was so proud of him and believed he will make a fine ruler one day.

"I am glad you know now, that what you did was wrong. I hope that this was a good lesson, and I do hope that you have learned from it."

"I do, and I have. I also understand why you may feel I am no longer able to be the acting King of Regnuom."

"No, after I had received the report from my secret advisor, that was in charge of monitoring you, I know for certain that you are indeed ready to return to your station," King Jason said proudly.

"Really, father? You want me to return to Regnuom as the acting

King?"

"No, son. I want you to return to Regnuom as King Ian, their newly appointed true ruler. We shall hold the coronation here, followed by a celebratory ball. If that pleases you?" he announced. Prince Ian could not believe what he was hearing.

"I do not know what to say, father. Thank you, it is an honor that you think of me as being worthy of such," he beamed.

"Why have the coronation here, Jason? Would it not be better for the people in Regnuom to see him as their new ruler?" Queen Anna questioned.

"Yes, it would be. I am only concerned for Ellyria. I do not think it wise for her to travel right now."

"Why do we not plan it for a later time. It does not have to be right away, does it?" Prince Ian inquired. "Or could you escort me yourself, and have a small coronation there, without an elaborate ball? They are Vikings after all, father. I am sure that if we have the ball there, they will not stop celebrating for days," he teased.

King Jason chuckled, Queen Anna just shook her head and smiled.

"I do not think that having a ball with so many people here would be good for Ellyria, not with that empathy power of hers.

Too many emotions all at once without her ability to control them would possibly be devastating, father," Prince Dakota chimed in, upon hearing the end of the conversation as he entered the room. "I spent the better part of the morning with her, and she is not only dealing with the power of empathy I believe. I think she has the ability of telepathy as well. She was trying to block me through an exercise that I was trying to teach her, to help her block out my emotions. When she did, she tapped further into my mind, and knew what I was thinking and feeling before I had even thought it, or felt it myself. This was not supposed to happen, I do not think. So I do advise against having a ball or anything else, where that many people could overwhelm her," Prince Dakota stated to his parents.

"He has a point, dear," Queen Anna added.

"I agree, father. Besides, I do not need such a big celebration. I am proud to simply serve as the people's new leader," Prince Ian confessed.

"Well, I supposed that it is settled then. I shall make arrangements for us to return to Regnuom, and declare you as the King of their realm," his father declared, then turned to his wife. "Will you be alright with me gone?"

"For how long?"

"A week possibly, but you shall have Dakota and Rowan here. Unfortunately, I will need Anthony to come with us as a proper escort, since he is head knight," he added.

"Very well. I think that I can manage then," Queen Anna said, then stood up to kiss her husband before taking leave. "I am going to go upstairs and check in on our daughter."

King Jason smiled at her, watching her leave. He then turned to Prince Ian, who was getting up to leave himself.

"Well now, see to it that your lion is prepared for the journey. She is going with you, just make sure she understands that she is not to harm the farmer's livestock when you get there," he teased, before Prince Ian left the room.

Now that Prince Dakota was alone with his father he had more time to press him about his sister.

"What do you think we should do with Ellyria? She needs a proper tutor to get a handle on all this power she is developing too soon, too fast," he questioned, seeking his father's advice.

"I have only heard of one person that could have helped her, and that was a great wizard that lived amongst the dragons in ancient times," the King mentioned.

"I have read about him, he was the wizard who practiced The All, was he not? I know that I could do more research on him, in the library perhaps. Thank you, father, you have helped me tremendously. I know exactly what to do!" he said, running out of the study.

King Jason watched him leave. How did he help Dakota anyway? He pondered for a time, before he left to seek out Prince Anthony and prepare their departure for Regnuom. They would leave at first light…

Queen Anna knocked on Princess Ellyria's chamber door before she entered, and found her daughter lying on the bed. She entered quietly since she did not want to wake her.

"I am not asleep, mother, so you can stop tiptoeing around the bed to see if I am."

"I did not want to disturb you, darling," her mother confessed, before she joined her daughter on the bed. She lay down beside her daughter and stared up at the lovely lace material, that hung above them.

"I know, mother. It is not you, please do not blame yourself. I know that you are trying your best to understand what it is that I must be going through, but I am still trying to figure all of this out for myself. The best thing for me right now is solitude and rest. I am very tired," Princess Ellyria stated.

"Alright, darling. I shall leave you be. If you need anything, please do not hesitate to call me, or Nan. I love you, and I will always be here when you need me." Queen Anna embraced her daughter, brushing her hair from her face before she rose from the bed, then began to leave the room.

"Mother."

Yes, Ellyria."

"Thank you. I love you too."

"Get some sleep. I shall see you when you are ready to come downstairs," she told her daughter, before she closed the door behind her.

This was not easy for her, and this continuous situation had to be difficult for her entire family. Of course, she knew it was the hardest on her mother, it always had been. Princess Ellyria lay back down on her bed. She was not sleepy, as much as she was overwhelmingly tired. It seemed difficult to come up with the energy to do anything. Even as hot as it was outside, she had no desire to play in the fountain with Isis. She only wanted to remain in this bed and do absolutely nothing. She could only think of Alfar, she missed him, but he remained alive in her memory. If he had only lived long enough for her to say goodbye and to tell him how much she cared for him, then maybe she would not feel so empty right now.

Princess Ellyria turned to her side, curled up around her pillows, and stared out her window. The sounds of the birds chattering outside her window were quiet and peaceful, almost comforting in a way. The trees reminded her of the joyful time spent in the forest when she was with Alfar.

Now, they were just a constant reminder of what she had lost…

Chapter 22

Raul was pacing back and forth in his cottage angrily creating a path of fire as he walked. Toby tried desperately to put out the flames, with several buckets of water he had run and drawn quickly from the nearby stream. The wizard's feet began to slosh when he walked, as he stood still for a moment, long enough to catch the boy before another bucket of water was hurled at his feet.

"Toby! Will you cease throwing that blasted water on me!"

"I am sorry, sire. I was only trying to keep the cottage from catching fire," the boy stated, setting the water bucket down.

"No matter boy, continue with the chores," he grumbled.

"What about the fire?" questioned the young apprentice.

Raul waved his hand and put out the fire, then dried his wet feet with a snap of his fingers.

"See, all gone. No worries. Off with you."

Toby hung his head low, then took his fresh bucket of water he already had so he could use it for cleaning.

The wizard sat down at the table and looked at the amulet around his neck. It was such a beautiful stone, so many colors shown at once with the slightest tilt, and yet it was still so powerful. He needed to come up with a new plan to obtain the Princess's powers, getting her to eat, or drink the power-stripping potion did not work, and neither did throwing the vial at her. The potion was not the solution. She was too powerful now for him to simply kidnap her, but he still had the crystal cage. If only he could get her in the cage, that was the main problem he faced. How could he get close enough to kidnap her and put her inside? Toby! That is it! He would use him as bait! If he put the boy in the cage with the key hanging beside it, then lead the girl to his rescue, he could be watching and waiting to slam the door on her! He was so brilliant that he amazed himself. He must get to work on how he would do it, and where to have the boy in the cage. Raul looked into the crystal ball on the table. He peered deep inside and images of the sleeping Princess emerged.

"So pretty you are, my dear. I will have you, and I shall take what is rightfully mine. You shall see," he said at the image in the clear globe. When her image vanished, Raul pushed the sphere aside to continue laying out his new plan…

Toby entered the room and saw the wizard had left. He always enjoyed the time when the wizard was gone. He noticed a strange clear globe on the table. He looked at it, as he wiped off the smudge marks left behind, it began to fill with smoke. The boy was amazed by such an interesting object and knew at once it was majickal. He saw images emerge of the Princess, she was sitting in front of a mirror, and it was reflecting her image straight into the globe.

Princess Ellyria could not believe her eyes, it was the little boy from the gypsy market that had been with the wizard. She put her hand up to the mirror and Toby jumped back.

Could she see him too? The boy touched the crystal ball, and suddenly he could hear her.

"Can you hear me? You have to help me Princess Ellyria! The wizard is planning to kill me, and you must save me before it is too late," he spoke into the globe.

She could hear the boy, but how? What if this was a trick? He seemed sincere, and she could not take the chance to risk his life if it were not.

"Where are you?" she questioned through her mirror. There must be a connection between the crystal within her mirror, and the crystal ball Raul had stolen from her tent.

"I am in the forest outside of Narruc. Please help, the

wizard plans to kill me and use me in a potion," the boy pleaded desperately. The connection between them began to fade, then the crystal filled with smoke again. "Wait, no! Princess!"

Where did he go? The image of the boy was lost, but she had to go to him. She had to save him…

Raul laughed maniacally, as he covered the globe with a black cloth. He went to the mirror and the reflection was that of the boy's, then he waved his hand over his face and the reflection was now his own. Now it was time to set the trap.

"Oh. Toby. Come here boy, I have a job for you," he said wickedly.

The boy obediently obeyed, and in a blink of an eye, they were in the woods just outside of Narruc, well away from his hideout in the forest. The boy found himself inside of a cage, he grasped the bars and looked in confusion at his master.

"Why, sire have you put me in here? Was I bad?"

"Oh, no, boy. You are going to do something wondrous for me," he announced.

"How, sire, if I am to be locked in this cage?" Toby questioned, scratching the side of his head.

"The less you know, the more you shall seem innocent," he answered. "I will be back to check on you later. Enjoy your confinement."

Raul vanished leaving the boy alone in the middle of the woods and locked in a cage. This was not how he had believed that his day would start. He looked all around at his surroundings and saw the key hanging on the branch of a tree, that was about five feet away. Toby sighed, he would not be able to reach for the key, for his arms were too short, and the tree was too far away. What was he going to do? He sat down and propped himself up against the bars, while he waited for the wizard to return…

Princess Ellyria was careful to not alert anyone of her sneaking out of the castle, it was easy as many times as she had done it before, she was almost an expert at it. She found her way to the stables, readied her horse for the quest, then rode out quietly. When she was far enough away, she kicked her steed into a hard gallop, and on to Narruc they rode...

She arrived at the border, then took a shortcut through the forest to not draw attention to herself, and followed her instincts, letting them be her guide to the boy. The further she rode into the woods, the louder she heard him cry, pushing her horse on harder now, that she knew where he was. When she approached a clearing, she saw the top of the cage through the canopy of the trees. Slowly she dismounted and left the horse, so she was able to make a quick getaway if she had to. The wizard could be anywhere. She walked around the side of the cage and saw the boy inside. The cage appeared to be of a simple metal structure, she was sure it had a lock that could be picked easily.

Toby saw the Princess and rose to his feet immediately.

"You came!"

"Shush," she whispered, placing a finger over her mouth.

"The wizard left, but he said he would return shortly. Please you have to get me out of here," the boy begged.

She walked over to the front of the cage and saw an old rusty lock on it. After removing two hairpins from her hair, she started to pick the lock.

"Princess, the key is hanging on the branch over there," he motioned.

"Oh, thank you, that will help," she muttered, going to the tree where the key hung. She hurried back to the cage, inserted the key, and turned it until it clicked. Toby smiled as the door opened and he stepped outside. That was when she saw him.

"Princess Ellyria it is a trap, run!"

"Alfar? Wait!" she shouted. It was too late, she felt herself being shoved into the cage and the door slammed shut behind her. She watched as the ghost disappeared into the forest, and she was once again behind bars. Toby had run away before she could see where he had gone, and he was too far away for her to pick up on his emotions or thoughts. She tried to use her power to open the door, but it would not budge, then she remembered she had dropped the key. There it was lying on the ground! She went to the door of the cage, outstretching her hand with her palm turned towards the sky. The key floated up and was almost to her hand, when it went flying in the opposite direction. Princess Ellyria looked up and saw the wizard standing on the outside of the bars.

"Hello my dear, so glad that you could join us," he laughed wickedly.

She thrust her hands forward to try and break down the bars again, but they would not give.

"Do not bother wasting all of your precious majick," he advised, waving his hand in a circular motion before her. The metal cage was just an illusion, and the true appearance was shown with only a wave of the wizard's hand.

"No!" Princess Ellyria shouted, grasping the bars in shock. It could not be.

"Oh, yes. You are locked in the crystal cage that I had majickally constructed to keep you, and your majick in. Clever am I not?" he smirked.

"I will get out of here, and when I do, I will kill you this time," she threatened.

"You are no match for me little girl, and you never will be. I have more than enough power to destroy you right now, but I need you alive in order to take back what is mine."

"You shall never take my powers, Raul, so go ahead and try!"

Raul reached up to the sky and screamed. The ground shook, the sky grew dark, then lightning streaked through the sky.

"Now, you are just showing off. It does not frighten me," she said bravely.

"No? Maybe this will," he proclaimed, then vanished.

Princess Ellyria turned and looked all around her. She was no longer in the woods. Where was she? She was still in the cage, but not in the forest. She could not sense the wizard, she was now in total darkness…

Princess Ellyria awoke to the sound of a familiar voice. She got her bearings and saw Raul staring at her through the bars. The area was lit with torches, it was cold, and the air was musty. Rats scurried over cracks in the walls, and stones lay scattered about in a pile on the ground.

"Where am I?"

"We are underneath the castle's dungeon. These are the old catacombs, that were used in times of war to escape if the castle was ever taken over by the enemy. It also makes for a great place to conceal an army."

"What are you talking about? What army? Most of Liza's men were killed in battle, or ran away when my father and brothers came for me two years ago, when she had held me captive."

"You ignorant little girl. How you were selected by the Gods to be the Chosen One, I shall never understand," the wizard laughed at the innocent girl before him, how naive she was, it was quite comical.

"What are you ranting about?"

"How about I show you?" he offered, motioning to the shadows for his new pet to emerge. "Draug, come forward."

The undead soldier emerged from the shadows in full battle armor.

"Yes, master."

Raul snapped his fingers, and the man collapsed. The perks of not being majickally bound to the undead, the wizard mused to himself.

"Why did you kill him?" she questioned, recognizing him as one of her brother's personal guards.

Raul could not help but laugh at the shocked expression on her face.

"I did not kill him, he was already dead," he informed her, snapping his fingers once again, and the man returned to his feet.

"How did you?" the Princess whispered, she was in too much shock for words to express her confusion.

"Oh, it is a part of the new power that Seither witch in the cottage so graciously gave to me. The necromancy power is truly an art form in itself. Do you not agree?"

"You are a sick monster of a man!"

"Oh, I am just getting started, my dear!" the wizard declared, walking over to his drone, then touching him with the Amulet of Elements.

Princess Ellyria could not believe her eyes. She crawled away from the door of the cage and watched in horror, as the undead man began to multiply. Not one, not two, but hundreds of them were emerging from his body! She was powerless to stop the wizard's madness, as he placed his new army in single file lines that filled the entire underground tunnel.

"What are you going to do with that kind of an army?"

"I am truly surprised that you even have to ask, my dear. You can stop me you know. Oh wait, no I am afraid that you will not, since you are all locked up!" His evil laugh echoed in the tunnel, as he watched his one undead minion become thousands.

"You will not get away with this! I will find a way to stop you, I promise!"

Raul pulled a small vial from the folds of his robes.

"What is that?"

"The end of you, my dear," he mused, throwing the vile through the bars at her.

The Princess could not use her powers to stop it, but she reflexively tried to catch it and prevent it from breaking, but she was too late and the vial crashed at her feet. Smoke filled the cage, and Princess Ellyria fell to the floor.

Raul opened the cage to let out the rays of sparkling light. He closed his eyes and held his hands open to either side of him, allowing the majick to enter him.

"No!" she screamed. Princess Ellyria pushed herself up to sit on her hip, her knees still tucked underneath her. It was too late, he had all the power now. She hung her head, knowing she had failed.

He stood in front of the opened cage for a moment, before he walked inside and knelt down beside her. He lifted up her chin, which was now soaked in salty tears.

"Do not be sad, little one. I have set you free from your burden. Now, you no longer have the great obligation to kill me. We can still be together, even as powerless as you are, I will let you rule the four realms at my side," he offered, before kissing her gently.

Suddenly, she had a vision. She saw him storming the castle in Toledya, then Regnuom, and Inamor with his undead army. The wizard devastated everything and everyone in his wake, leaving no one alive that fought against him, and burning out those who feared him, leaving a warning of what would happen if they did fight. She tried to push away from his brutal attack on her lips, but he held her tight in his arms, pushing her to the back of the prison bars. Flashes of destruction invaded her mind; women were being raped, children were being eaten, grown men were ripped into pieces by the undead, and no one could hide or escape. She grabbed her head that felt as though it was going to explode, taking her heart with it. How could she still feel them? All of those innocent people calling out to her for help, when all she could do was stand there and watch them suffer. She could not snap out of her vision, even when she felt the wizard's hands upon her, groping her breasts, and tugging at her clothes. Why could she not stop the premonition? When she looked out before her, all she saw was her father and brothers leading their own army into the battlefield. Swords clashed, and many men were pulled down from their horses by the incredible strength of the wizard's men. If she could not break free soon, Raul would have her there in the crystal cage! She was helpless to fight him, as the images continued to hold her prisoner. The battle on the field grew dim, her father's men were no match for the wizard's army. They fought hard against them, but there was no hope left. Princess Ellyria fell to her knees in the middle of it all, calling out for anyone to help her. The sky seemed to become engulfed with flames, then a loud, thunderous roar was heard overhead. She looked up and was taken aback by the sights before her. Dragons circled the sky, before one by one, they had landed in the middle of the great battle. The undead were quickly bit in two, or scorched in a breath of dragon's fire.

Princess Ellyria snapped back to reality just in time to try and fight off the wizard's advances. Her dress was ripped away from her body, and she could barely breathe from the weight of him, but she brought up her knee right into his hard member that he had released from under his robes. He rolled over in pain, and she scrambled out from under him.

"Get back here, you tricky bitch!" he screamed, grabbing her ankle before she could get away. He dragged her back, pushing her onto the flat of her back. He used magic to keep her from moving, then wrestled himself between her legs. She felt him trying to enter her, and she spat in his face. "You ungrateful bitch!" he screamed, slapping her hard across her face with the back of his hand…

Princess Ellyria sat up straight in her bed and caressed the side of her face. She slowed her breathing and tried to relax, to slow her heartbeat. Everything was so real, almost as if she was really there. It was the most intense premonition that she had ever had. She got up from her bed and walked over to her washbasin, to splash the cool, inviting water over her face. Then she walked over to her vanity and sat down in front of her mirror. She looked at herself and saw a bright red mark on the side of her face. How could this be? Her mirror began to cloud her image, and new images appeared in its place. It was Alfar. He was in the forest watching over his mother and his loved ones, when suddenly the forest was ablaze. She watched as the tiny sprite's wings began to curl from the intense heat, causing them to be helpless as the flames consumed them. Tiny screams were heard followed by the cries of all that dwell in the enchanted forest. Alfar tried to help them, but he only passed through them, like the smoke that filled the sky. His mother held firm, protecting the sacred tree from the flames. Alfar could not get his mother to leave with him, she stayed, and he watched helplessly as the Elder Tree was surrounded by the flames, then they were consumed by them. Princess Ellyria covered her ears from the shrill cries of the Faery Queen. She looked away from the mortifying scene, but still felt Alfar's pain.

"Why will these images not go away!" she screamed, pushing out the energy from her hands into her mirror. The crystal broke into thousands of tiny shards all around her, she quickly raised her hands in front of her face to protect her eyes, and the broken glass froze instantly. Slowly she lowered her hands, looking at all of the tiny pieces of crystal that were suspended in mid-air. She took a deep breath, and slowly guided her hands to the mirror. The crystal shards of the broken glass returned to the empty wooden frame in a fluid motion, becoming flawless once again. She reached out to touch the mirror, then she was pulled through...

Princess Ellyria looked all around her. A bright light encircled her, and incredible comforting warmth. She saw Alfar coming from the light, reaching out his hand to her.

"Alfar, where are we? Am I dead?"

"No, my love, you are not," he said smiling, taking her hand, and helping her to her feet.

"What happened then? How did I get here?"

Alfar led her out of the light and brought her into his arms. His arms felt like the light that had surrounded her only moments before.

"You are between worlds. When you broke the enchanted mirror you created a portal, a portal that opened because of its sister crystal ball that Vadoma had left you, the one the wizard has. As long as he has the orb in his possession, you have a connection between you. You must get it back, as well as the Amulet of Elements."

"How? I did not even know that I was able to shatter the mirror," the Princess asked.

"Your powers are growing way more than anyone expected, and in more ways than you can handle right now. Vadoma sent me to get you and help you back to your world, because you can not get back on your own," he told her.

Princess Ellyria held Alfar tight in her arms. She did not want to let him go.

"I do not want to leave you. Can I not stay here with you?"

"No, I am sorry, but it is not your time. You are the only one that can stop the wizard. I have to get you back home. There is another mirror that is parallel to yours in this world, you only have to touch it, and you will be transported back. Come, I know where it is," he informed her.

"How can I stop the wizard when I can not even control my new powers?" she questioned, pulling him to a stop.

Alfar looked into those beautiful sapphire eyes, that he was drawn to the moment he first saw her.

"I am not supposed to help you, Vadoma's orders. However, I can tell you who can. You must go to the Ancient One, in the mountains of Ormr."

"The dragon mountain?" asked the Princess.

"Yes, find him, and then he can answer all of your questions. I must get you out of here before it is too late. Raul is planning his next move, and you have to stop him before he has his revenge," Alfar warned, leading her to the mirror that connected the two worlds.

"Alfar, wait. I never had the chance to say goodbye to you," she said, standing in front of the portal.

"Ellyria, I know how you feel about me. I knew before I died, but you have to let me go. I am not who you are supposed to be with. I have said too much already." Then he began to fade away.

"No! Alfar, please! I love you. Do not leave me!" she cried, reaching out to touch him one last time.

Alfar touched the side of her face, but his hand moved through her, yet he still felt the wetness of her tears.

"I love you, Ellyria, now touch the mirror and return home. The fate of the realm is in your hands," he said, and then he was gone.

The Princess stood there for a moment in total darkness, all but the light from the mirror shown before her. Tears fell from her eyes as she reached out to touch the mirror…

Princess Ellyria Rose opened her eyes and saw the dawn reaching into her window to wake her. Her pillow was wet from her tears, and she could smell him on her cotton nightgown. Was it all just a dream? It could not be. She felt him and talked to him like she was with him, only a moment ago. He sent her back, to defeat the wizard once and for all. How could she defeat him? Then she remembered what he had told her about the Ancient One, that he could help her. How was she to get all the way to the Ormr Mountains?

Princess Ellyria could only think of one person that knew of those mountains, also the only one who could take her there as well. Her brother, Prince Rowan…

Chapter 23

Queen Anna wiped the tears from her cheeks, as she bid farewell to her husband and two of her sons. King Jason was going with Prince Ian to Regnuom to officially declare him king, followed by a short coronation ceremony. Prince Anthony and a group of ten knights were escorting them properly to the kingdom. Royal banners were carried, and the elaborate coach was teamed with four horses to carry the men not only in style, but also for added protection.

"Please do not cry, my love. I shall be home in a week, and you still have Dakota, Rowan, and Ellyria to keep you company," the King said to his wife.

He wiped the never-ending trail of tears, that refused to stifle the flow from her cheeks, and kissed her gently on her quivering lips. She returned his kiss as though she would never see him again, then they embraced one another before King Jason had to pull away so they could leave.

"Ian, I am so sorry that I can not accompany you to Regnuom. I am very proud of you. I might be losing a son, but Regnuom is gaining a great leader. I love you," she said to her son, embracing him.

"It is alright, mother. Please do not cry. I shall visit soon, and when you can, come to visit me. Promise?" Prince Ian questioned his mother, then kissed her on the forehead.

"Yes, I promise," she said, before turning to Prince Anthony.

"I want you to watch after your father, and see to it that you keep a close eye on your brother," she whispered in his ear.

"Yes, mother, I promise," Prince Anthony said, he too kissed her on the forehead and smiled confidently, as he mounted his horse.

King Jason and Prince Ian were fixing to climb into the carriage when Princess Ellyria came running through the courtyard after them.

"Wait! I want to say goodbye too!"

King Jason smiled at his daughter, embracing her and swinging her around in the air like he used to do when she was a little girl.

"Please, be careful, father. I am sorry that I have not spent much time with you lately, but it has been hard trying to deal with things as of late," she apologized.

"I understand that you need to take care of yourself. Watch over your mother too, please," King Jason said, as he kissed her on the top of her head.

Princess Ellyria looked at her brother Prince Ian, who had not been on speaking terms with her since they left Inamor days ago.

"I wanted to congratulate you on your coronation. Regnuom is getting a fair, bright, and gracious ruler. Blessed be to you, brother," she said cordially.

"I thought I was going to be King?" Prince Ian teased in her ear, wrapping his arms around his sister.

"Always the jester. I hope the Vikings are ready for you," she teased in return.

"Let us hope he is ready for the Vikings," his father joined in. "Come along now, Ian, it is time to go."

The men climbed into the waiting carriage and Prince Anthony gave the signal for them all to move out. Queen Anna, Princess Ellyria, Prince Dakota, and Prince Rowan all waved as the carriage and its entourage rode out of the courtyard.

"I am going in to see about breakfast, if anyone wants to join me," Queen Anna announced.

"We shall be there in a while, mother," Prince Dakota

informed her. He turned to his sister, who had grabbed both her brothers by their shirttails and pulled them to stay with her.

"What is it, sister?" Prince Dakota questioned.

"Yes, tell us what is more important than breakfast is right now?" Prince Rowan added.

Princess Ellyria linked her arms in theirs and led them to the summerhouse to speak privately.

"I need to know what you have heard about the Ancient One," she questioned her brothers.

Prince Dakota and Prince Rowan looked at each other before they turned to her.

"Why do you need to know about the Ancient One, Ellyria?" Prince Dakota inquired.

"When I was trapped by the Seither in The Black Forest, she told me of him, and how she sought him for answers about majick. Then last night, I had a premonition. Alfar came to me and told me about the Ancient One. He said that was the only one who could help me to control my powers and tell me how I can defeat the wizard. I need your help to get me there," she told them.

"I thought Alfar was dead?" Prince Rowan questioned, before Prince Dakota slapped him on the back of his head.

"He is you, idiot. Can you not practice some sensitivity?" his brother questioned.

"Please, I would not have come to you with this if I thought that you could not help me," Princess Ellyria pleaded, her eyes welling up with tears.

"I will help you, especially if it means that this Ancient One can help you," he offered. "I shall go to the library and look up what I can about him as well. You do not want to go unknowingly into foreign territory," Prince Dakota consoled, taking his sister's hand and patting it reassuringly.

"I will transport you there. Gaia is forbidden to go any further than the edge of the border, but at least we can get you that far," Prince Rowan added.

Princess Ellyria wiped her eyes and grabbed them both by their necks squeezing them tight. She could not imagine doing this without her brothers.

"Oh, thank you both. I would not have been able to have come this far without you, and I will do my best to not let either of you down," she beamed.

The trio left the summerhouse and split off to do what they could to assist each other with the upcoming quest, to seek out the Ancient One. Prince Dakota retreated to the library seeking out anything he could find on the subject. Prince Rowan left to quiet his rumbling stomach and find his mother who mentioned something about breakfast earlier. Princess Ellyria headed to her room to begin packing and prepare for her quest, to seek out the only possible being that could help her…

"Is it true? Are you going to the Ormr Mountains alone?" Queen Anna asked of her only daughter, after storming inside her room. "Were you even going to tell me, before you went gallivanting off on another one of your adventures?"

Princess Ellyria could only sit there quietly, while she let her mother rant.

"I was planning on telling you after I knew more about it. Rowan has a big mouth. Nothing has ever changed with him, always running to tell you everything that I ever did as a child. I should not expect any less of him now," she complained.

"This has nothing to do with Rowan, young lady, and you know it. It is about you constantly running away to go and fight the good fight, without telling me anything!"

Princess Ellyria sighed, as tears formed in her eyes. She never knew that her mother had so much resentment concerning her destiny.

Mother, why have you not told me that you hate my being the Chosen One?"

"I do not hate it. Hate is a strong word, darling. I simply have deep, strong emotions against your destiny," her mother replied.

"Are you no longer proud of me?" questioned her daughter,

"Oh, no! Of course, I am very proud of you, dear. It is just that I am scared of losing you," the Queen finally admitted.

Princess Ellyria got up, rushed over to her mother, and wrapped her arms around her. She looked at her and wiped the tears from her mother's eyes, as she had always done for her.

"I promise you that I will not let that wizard hurt me, or anyone else for that matter. That is exactly why it is of grave importance that I find out how I am supposed to stop him before it is too late," she swore to her mother, as she held her hands.

Queen Anna no longer saw the little girl standing before her, she only saw the woman that she had grown to become.

"I am so proud of you, Ellyria. I love you very much. I am going to try to not be so overprotective of you and support the decisions you know that are right, for not only yourself, but for the entire realm," she declared proudly.

"Thank you, mother. You have no idea how much that means to me. I shall do my best to not let you down," she promised. "Not to change the subject, but I heard you have a lovely breakfast prepared downstairs, and I am starving," the Princess giggled.

"There is indeed. If your brother has not already eaten it all," Queen Anna teased, laughing at her daughter.

The two went downstairs followed by Isis, who had awakened at the mention of breakfast, and eagerly joined the pair for her share as well…

Meanwhile, Prince Dakota skipped breakfast to do his research on the Ancient One. He was amazed by how he came to be. The first wizard to have and use majick as a way of life, and the first human to have won the dragons' trust after mankind betrayed them. The wizard practiced The All, a form of majick that was neither good nor evil, but all of it combined with control of absolute power. He was a gentle man, so the lore stated, but the human race feared him and his power. The wizard went to live in hiding with the dragons in the Ormr Mountains, well away from those who would covet his powers. Other beings and wizards that sought only dark majick would go after him for his powers. He was said to be an immortal, but he was also a man. A man that had fallen in love with a woman who did not fear him, but held a great love for him. She gave him a son, but died immediately after he was born. The wizard knew not how to raise a child on his own, so he carried him to the nearby village, leaving him with a family who could not have children of their own. The wizard only requested that the child knew he was born from love and born in the time of dragons. The wizard went back to the seclusion of the mountains, mourned the loss of his wife, and grew bitter for abandoning his only son. The wizard watched his son from the majick crystal that he had discovered encased deep in the mountain. It allowed him to see his son and his future. He saw the coming war between man and beast, then saw that his son was leading the angry mob, that was coming to invade the solitude of his mountainous home. Over the years, the wizard had taught his dragon friend everything that he knew about majick, and how to speak in his native language. With the knowledge that his own death would be nearing soon, he sent his dragon and all the others back into the deepest depths of the caves. Pleading with them to remain in hiding, so the ancient wisdom that he had passed down to his best friend would be protected for all eternity. He conjured his final spell to give his dragon immortality and made him give his word that he would remain hidden, no matter what happened to him. Some of the dragons stood beside the wizard by choice, and to honor the only human to ever earn their respect. War came to the mountain, as the wizard predicted, returning his only son to his side, not as an ally, but as an enemy. The young man came with vengeance in his heart for his family that had been killed, by one of the dragons that had ransacked the village. It was not a dragon from their mountain, but they were blamed nonetheless, and slaughtered, as if they were the ones that had destroyed the village. The wizard fought the other villagers off with majick, but he could not bring himself to harm his only son. The young man was unaware that he was the only one who could kill the powerful wizard, when the battle was over it was only he and the wizard that were left standing.

"What are you reading?" Princess Ellyria questioned, causing

Prince Dakota to jump. "I did not mean to frighten you," she teased.

"I was reading about the Ancient One, and about the wizard that practiced The All," he informed her. "I am at the end. It has been the only thing I could find on the dragon, or the wizard," he added. He continued reading aloud so that she could hear as well.

"'The wizard told the young man before him that he was his father, telling him how after his mother had died, he could not care for him, and that is how he came to be with the family that raised him. The wizard asked his son if he would like to stay with him and learn from him everything that he knew. His son agreed, becoming a great wizard, but he wanted more power. The wizard refused to teach his son any more majick, for fear that his lust for power would turn him into a monster. The wizard's dragon was angry, and despite the promise he made, he came out of hiding to protect him upon hearing him pleading with his son to not go into the darkness. The dragon was too late. His master had been slain by the young man standing before him, holding the master's still beating heart in his hand. The dragon knew it was the only way to obtain the ultimate power that was inside the wizard, and the only way that he could have been killed."

"Is that it?" the Princess asked.

Prince Dakota turned the page in the ancient text. The words had faded, but he tried to read the last paragraph that was still intact.

"'The dragon tried to go after the boy, but it was too late, he had already eaten half his master's heart before he could attack. The boy dropped his heart and ran away from the flames that followed. It is said that the dragon still protects the other half of the wizard's heart and swore to avenge him. No man has ever entered the dragon mountain, those that have never returned."

"I am so glad there is more to go on than just folklore found in a dusty old book," she said to her brother.

Prince Dakota closed the 'dusty old book,' as she called it, turning to her.

"'This is going to be a dangerous quest. The dragons do not just dislike humans, they hate humans. Do not pout either. Gaia is an extraordinary exemption, only because Rowan raised her from an egg that our parents gave to him. They are bonded because of that trust, which he earned. You will have no trust going in there, and you do not have years to earn it. Time is of the essence for you to destroy the wizard," Prince Dakota informed her.

"I have to take that chance," she declared, leaving the room to search for Prince Rowan. He was the only one who could take her there, to the Ormr Mountains…

Prince Rowan was waiting by the fountain in the courtyard for his sister, while Gaia was in the nearby field, watching butterflies. He saw his sister coming his way and stood up to greet her.

Did you find out anything helpful from Dakota?"

"Yes, and no. There was very little mentioned in the book about the Ancient One, it was more about some wizard, but even that seemed more like old folklore," she mentioned. She was not sure what to think about it. None of it made enough sense to her, to heed something that was over a thousand years old.

"So what do you want to do?" he asked. He was concerned for his sister to just leave on a moment's notice, on a whim to ask some old dragon a few questions.

"Yes, brother. I did plan on going on a whim without considering anyone's feelings. Oh, and thanks for ratting me out to mother about my quest, to begin with. I was planning to tell her in my own way," she chided.

"By not telling her at all and leaving anyway, or were you actually going to tell her this time?"

"I did tell her, she knows my plan, and she knows that I am leaving. I will even say goodbye to her this time," she informed her brother.

"I hope so, she will be heartbroken if you do not, especially with father gone," he advised. Prince Rowan looked out in the field at his dragon. Gaia was lying on her back rolling back and forth in the thicket. He chuckled out loud at her silly antics and tapped his sister motioning to her.

"Dakota told me that if you had not raised her from an egg, she would have been a man killer. Is that true?" she asked, laughing at the frolicking contradiction out in the field.

"Yes, he is correct about that. Dragons and people were friends long ago, but some dragons hated humans, killing their livestock, making mankind an enemy," he informed her. He was lucky that his parents found the egg and brought it home for him to hatch. Gaia was his best friend.

"Is there a chance that I might not make it out of there, out of the dragon mountain?" the Princess asked. Even if there were a chance she would not get out alive, no matter how scared she was, she had to try.

"There is always a risk no matter what you do in life, but if you are not brave enough to take it, you run an even bigger chance of missing out on all of the great things that could happen. I know that you are scared, Ellyria. I do not have to be gifted to know that. I know you, and I also know how brave you are," he advised, putting his arm around her. "It is a natural human reaction to be afraid, but bravery comes from within," he added, looking at his sister in amazement. She was so strong willed that he had no doubt in his mind that she could do anything, that she put her mind to. Even if that meant walking right into the Ormr Mountains and finding the Ancient One, she would make it back out alive…

"Mother, I promise that I will be careful. Rowan will be with me all the way, until we get there anyway," Princess Ellyria explained to her mother. She was trying to bid her farewell, but it was not going as swiftly as she had planned.

"That is exactly what I am worried about, is after he leaves. You will be all alone in a foreign territory, where no humans dare go, especially alone," she said, concerned for her daughter. Queen Anna knew this was all part of her destiny, but she still could not help but worry, she was her mother after all.

"I shall be fine," her daughter replied.

"How long will you be gone?" her mother questioned.

"I do not know. As long as it takes to get my powers under control," she vowed, then leaned down to pet Isis before she left. "Goodbye, girl. I will be back soon, keep mother company. Alright, girl?" Isis gave her mistress sloppy wet kisses, as Princess Ellyria was making kissing noises at her. She stood up, embracing her brother Prince Dakota.

"Remember what I said about the wizard, information sometimes holds the keys to locked doors. Use your head when it comes to this dragon. They are highly intelligent creatures," Prince Dakota advised, before letting his sister go.

Princess Ellyria embraced her mother one last time, before Prince Rowan assisted her onto Gaia's monstrous back.

"I shall return as soon as I can!" Princess Ellyria shouted, back down to her mother and brother.

"I will take good care of her, I promise!" he said to his mother and brother, before he gave word for Gaia to fly. He looked over his shoulder at his sister. "Are you ready?" Prince Rowan asked his sister, as he climbed onto his dragon's back and waved in farewell.

"Yes, I am ready."

"Well, hold on."

Gaia let out a loud roar, and now that they were well away from the castle, Gaia took full flight, letting her wings take over. The dragon was so huge, that if she flapped her wings any harder they would have blown down her mother and brother, from the gusts of wind they created. They were now soaring into the clouds, flying back to Gaia's homeland…

Princess Ellyria had ridden on Gaia's back many times before, but at this very moment, she could feel what it was like to really fly. The feeling from the giant wings' movements was incredible, and she could feel underneath her the powerful muscles hard at work to keep them in the air. The sky was so peaceful, and she reached out to touch one of the puffy clouds that they flew by. It was wet to the touch, she pulled back her hand to see if she was able to take a piece, but it evaporated immediately. They were heading east to the mountains that could be seen from Toledya. It was a long journey, even on the back of a dragon. She looked down at the kingdom, everything was so tiny from her eye in the sky, which made the city look all the more fragile.

The Princess had finally let go of Prince Rowan's waist, feeling more relaxed, as she sat on Gaia's vast back. They had passed her home kingdom and now glided over the thick forest, that was a barrier between the realms and the mountains. They were getting closer to the dragon border, as it was nicknamed. The border was in between the forest and the mountains. It was almost like a desert, from where many dragon wars had been fought, and nothing could grow from the damage by the many fires that had left the ground to waste.

"I see the dragon sands, it is time to land. Hold on!" Prince Rowan shouted into the wind.

Princess Ellyria wrapped her arms around her brother's waist, as he commanded Gaia to land. He made sure to land in an open clearing, so he could be sure that there were not any dragons patrolling.

Prince Rowan slid down from Gaia's back and helped his sister down.

"You will have to be cautious where you walk. Try not to lose a shoe in the sands, the ground can get quite warm on a hot day like today," he warned her.

"I noticed," she giggled, picking up her shoe that she had already lost, pouring the sand out of it before putting it back on.

"I can not stay, Gaia is forbidden to come here. She associates with humans, therefore she is an outcast. Be safe sister, and I hope that you find all of the answers you are searching for," he said, before taking her in his arms.

Princess Ellyria looked up at him and smiled. She knew he was frightened for her.

"I shall be fine, do not worry about me. Go home and take

care of mother. I am sure that she is a wreck right about now," she told him, then kissed him on the cheek, before pulling away.

Prince Rowan did not want to leave her, but he knew that she had to do this on her own. He smiled one last time at her, before he climbed on his dragon's back.

"I shall give you a few days before I return. Meet me in this same spot, and I will bring you home," he called down to her.

"I will," she promised, waving him on. She closed her eyes and covered her face from all of the sand flying around her as Gaia took off. When the dust settled she opened her eyes, as they were already almost out of sight. Now she was alone.

Princess Ellyria walked out from the edge of the canopy, and out from the shadows. Her eyes widened to take in all of the beauty before her. The mountains were breathtaking. She had never imagined that if she had ever gotten this close they would look like this. They were not only vast in size, they touched the clouds in the sky, gracing them with their snow-capped peaks. She was half a day's walk away from them, and yet they still seemed so close. Tall grasses and enormous ancient trees, that even dwarfed the Elder Tree from the Black Forest, surrounded the bottoms of the mountains.

Princess Ellyria walked toward her destination, leaving her fears behind her to melt away in the sands, as she began her quest to seek out the Ancient One…

Deep in the mountain, Princess Ellyria stumbled upon a cave to the right, several feet from the entrance. It was cool and dark inside, which was a relief from the intense heat outside. Large red eyes opened from a deep slumber to the sounds of footsteps. A loud growl escaped powerful jaws, as the scent of flesh filled his nostrils.

"Who goes there? State your business here human."

Princess Ellyria stopped dead in her tracks, to the grumbling deep voice behind her. Cautiously, she turned around to see who was speaking to her in such a menacing tone. Her eyes widened not only in surprise, but also to take in the extreme size of the beast in front of her. She could only make out the silhouette of his gigantic head, which was held slightly above his sharp talon feet, which he was now tapping on the stone floor.

"I beg your pardon, my Lord, for my intrusion into your lovely cave. I did not mean to disturb you. I am Princess Ellyria Rose of Toledya, and I am the Chosen One. I have come to seek your guidance," she announced, standing far enough away from the monster's head full of sharp teeth, while being wary of him that he may consider her to be his next meal.

"I am well aware of who you are. You are the prophesied girl child foretold centuries ago. Come closer so I can get a better look at you."

Princess Ellyria timidly stepped closer.

"Closer child. Come into the light."

She stepped into a small sunspot on the floor and looked up to see a crack overhead in the cave, allowing for a small beam of light to permeate the darkness.

The hot breaths coming from his mouth made a bead of sweat trickle down her back. He looked at her for a moment before he snorted. Slowly she reached up to wipe her face.

"It seems quite unfair that you can see me, but I have yet to be able to see you, my Lord."

The beast let out a ground-shaking roar. Princess Ellyria covered her ears and braced her stance. He raised his head up, followed by his enormous body, stepping out of the cave. After nearly falling backward, she managed to run away from him, before she was accidentally crushed. Now that he was outside the cave, Princess Ellyria was in awe over his tremendous size. He dwarfed

Gaia by a few feet, and she had thought she was the largest dragon that ever lived. She was proven wrong. The solid black monster before her stretched out his mighty wings, almost touching either side of the interior room of the cave. His four legs stood under him like that of trees, supporting the thick girth, long neck, and extra-long, whip-like tail. His head was covered in a ring of horns, that gave the appearance of a crown. Which made perfect sense, since he was the King of all the dragons.

"You are the Ancient One, are you not?"

"I have not been referred to as that in over five hundred years," he mused. "My name is Nidhoggr," he added, stepping closer to the Princess, then lowered his head to face her.

"I need your help. I can not control my powers, and if I can not control them, I will not be able to defeat the wizard, Raul," she pleaded.

Red eyes looked her deep into her own sapphire blue eyes, and it was as if they could see right through her.

"I know why you are here, but I will not help you," he grumbled, as his tail wrapped quickly around Princess Ellyria's body.

"What are you doing? I was told you would help me to control my powers," she pleaded, trying to wriggle free from his tail, but he tightened it around her petite body.

"Yes, I can teach you to control your powers, but I will not help you destroy the wizard. That is part of your own destiny."

"So you will help me then? To control my powers?" she asked breathlessly.

Nidhoggr crouched his body closer to the Princess, curling himself around her. He gave a dragon's grin exposing sharp teeth and flicked his forked tongue. She smelled so sweet to him, he could almost taste her, but he knew if he ate her that the Gods would surely strike him down.

"Majick takes a long time to master. Each power requires a select amount of time for practice, and you seem as though you are in a hurry," he scoffed.

Princess Ellyria leaned closer to him, placing her tiny hand upon his large nose, looking him straight in the eyes.

"I will do what it takes to ensure my people are safe. I do not care if I am here until the following year. I will do whatever it is that you ask of me."

The stone floor of the room trembled beneath her feet, as he began to laugh.

"Alright, so be it. You will be here until the next Summer Solstice."

"My brother is coming back for me in a few days. I am to meet him at the sands by the forest."

"You will meet him then, and inform him you shall be my apprentice for the next several seasons. Do you have a problem with that?"

"No, my Lord."

Two days hence, Princess Ellyria met with Prince Rowan and told him what the dragon said. Reluctantly, he left after scolding her for such a foolish idea. She insisted she would be fine, and to come back for her before the full moon next Midsummer. They embraced, then she watched her brother and Gaia, fly away…

Princess Ellyria could not believe how fast the past year had gone by, as she recalled when she had first arrived at the Ormr Mountains. She had been walking most of the morning, now arriving at the sands, she saw her brother waiting...

"There you are. I have only been waiting for you most of the morning. How long does it take to walk from the mountain?" Prince Rowan questioned his sister, as he embraced her.

"Nearly a half a day's walk. I left at dawn, but I may have

lingered a little," Princess Ellyria admitted, then looked up at him and smiled.

"Well, are you ready to come back home?"

"Yes, I am definitely ready to go home. I have missed you all so much. How is everyone?" she asked.

"Let us hurry and get you home then. You shall see for yourself, once you get there," he said smiling at her.

Prince Rowan helped his sister onto Gaia's broad back, before climbing on in front of her. Before she knew it, they had taken off into the sky...

Princess Ellyria turned to look behind her, at the mountains that appeared miniature now that they were several miles away. She smiled inwardly, as she tapped into her brother's thoughts. He really did miss me, she mused. At least she had control of her empathy powers, and she could finally go home to be with her family…

Part Two: The Wizard's Revenge

A deep ominous voice echoed thunderously in the great hall, beckoning her to kneel before Alfodr...

"I am sending you to the realm of Ragnarok on an important mission. A great deal of events has come to my attention within the kingdoms of Toledya, Regnuom, Inamor, Narruc, and the two great forests. The Black Forest was cursed by the evil Seither, Vala, who was harvesting faeries and had made a slave out of the Elvin Halfling child, Alfar. She used him to lure the Princess to her, so she could manipulate her into killing the wizard Raul for her own revenge. Vala failed miserably and was killed by Raul, lifting the curse and freeing the Faery Queen. Alfar died at the wizard's hand in his mother's arms. Raul, with his new powers of necromancy, had returned to The Dark Forest of Woe, to prepare his revenge on Princess Ellyria Rose, who was still in Inamor with her brother Prince Ian. He had left his duty station in Regnuom as the acting King, disobeying his father. King Jason of Toledya, who was unable to help any of his children, was waiting patiently on word from them. Prince Ian arrived in Inamor, where his grieving sister was mourning the loss of her new love, Alfar. Raul then disguised himself as an old peddler selling fruit to trick Princess Ellyria into eating a peach, that was laced with a power-stripping potion the wizard made in the attempt to obtain the Princess's powers. Her power of empathy alerted her to the evil wizard's scheme, and she managed to fight him off. Prince Ian worried for his sister's safety and brought her back home to Toledya, where the reunion was not a pleasant one. Princess Ellyria became quite overwhelmed by her new power and shut herself off from her family. She then had a premonition of Raul, trying to take her powers, and creating an undead army. Alfar came to her in a vision and told her to go seek out The Ancient One, a dragon in the Ormr Mountains, saying that he could help her get control of her empathy power before it drove her mad. She enlisted the help of her brothers, Prince Dakota, and Prince Rowan. Her actions have affected not only her destiny, but also those who are unaware of its strong impact on them as well. Off the coast of Regnuom, in the Rhine River, Lord Brom has proven himself to be worthy after defeating the Jormungandr and annihilating a nest of Sirens. He will be one to watch over in the near future, but he is not the one that I am sending you to watch over. I am sending you to watch over Princess Ellyria Rose. She will need our help, but it will be up to her to find the correct path on the road of destiny, as the Chosen One."

"Yes, Alfodr. If that is what you wish of me."

"Understand that you are not to meddle in the personal affairs of these mortals, let the Princess seek you out, do not try to find her. Now go Hrafn. To Ragnarok!"

The sound of thunder bellowed and a crack of lightning streaked across the room, then Hrafn was gone...

Chapter 24

Toby packed up the tiny camp that he had made in the woods, just outside of Toledya. He had left the Dark Forest of Woe yesterday on a quest that Raul had sent him on, but he had no intentions of returning. The wizard had been obsessed with the Princess, after his old apprentice showed up at the cottage door a year ago, telling him she was at the Dragon Mountain. Raul surprisingly, went into a sort of a humorous fit, before sending his informant back to gain more information on why she was there. Toby was exhausted from all of the errands his master had sent him on, gathering a stockpile of certain herbs and other ingredients, for the creation of his latest spell to get the powers from the Princess. Raul had not left the cottage at all this past year, as he was too busy formulating potions, and planning his next move. Toby came to the assumption that Raul would not even notice he was missing yet, which would give him plenty of time to warn the Princess, and get back to the cottage. His revenge would finally be fulfilled, as the memory of the wizard killing his father was still fresh in his mind.

Princess Ellyria Rose was his only hope…

The castle was bigger than Toby had ever imagined, as he approached the outer gates. Guards immediately grabbed the boy and alerted Prince Anthony of the trespasser.

The boy's hands were restrained behind his back, as he was escorted to the courtyard where Prince Anthony awaited with his men.

"Who are you boy, and why are you here?"

"My name is Toby, and I am the apprentice of the wizard, Raul. I am here to warn Princess Ellyria of the wizard's plan."

"Take him to the dungeon, while I inform my father, the King," he said to his men.

Toby was taken away, as Prince Anthony hurried to alert his father…

King Jason had returned to his study after his son Prince Rowan had returned with his daughter Princess Ellyria earlier. She retired to her chambers to rest, his wife had said. Unfortunately, he had not had the chance to speak with her much about her studies with the Ancient One. The King looked up to the sound of the door opening, bringing him back from his thoughts, to seeing his son, Prince Anthony entering the room.

"Father, I have the wizard's apprentice locked in the dungeon."

"What? How? Who is it?"

"The boy just showed up, said his name was Toby, and that he was the wizard's apprentice."

"What does he want?" King Jason was confused. Why would the boy come here?

"He said that he had to warn Ellyria about the wizard, and his plans," Prince Anthony informed him, then waited for orders on what he should do.

His father sat quietly for a few moments before he spoke.

"Go interrogate him, find out everything you can, especially his master's whereabouts," King Jason ordered, running his fingers through his thinning, brown hair, and sat back down. "I want to know where that evil wizard is. Do not allow the boy to know your sister is here. He may be trying to get information for the wizard."

"Yes, father," Prince Anthony agreed, then left the room, passing his mother on the way out.

"Where is he going in such a hurry?" Queen Anna questioned. Her husband's silence worried her.

"Anthony apprehended the wizard's apprentice. The boy came right up to the gates and admitted to having important information regarding his master's plans. He said he wanted to warn Ellyria," King Jason informed her, then watched his wife sit down slowly in the chair across from him at the table.

"What did he say?" Queen Anna asked, then searched her husband's face waiting for the bad news.

"We do not know. Anthony was on his way out to question him," he answered.

"How bad do you think it could be, to make his apprentice come to warn us?"

"I do not know, dear, but we shall find out. How is our daughter doing anyway?"

"She was asleep, when I peeked in on her earlier, before I came downstairs."

"That is good. I am sure that she needs her rest after traveling. I do not want her to know about the apprentice until I have all the information from the boy. The less she knows, the better for now," King Jason stated, as he stood up, walked around the large oak table, and kissed his wife on the forehead.

"Where are you going?" she asked, looking up at him.

"I am going to the dungeon to greet our new guest, and find out what it is that he knows," King Jason replied, leaving the room.

Queen Anna sat for a moment alone, before deciding to return upstairs to check on her daughter one more time…

King Jason arrived just in time for the important news that Toby was giving to Prince Anthony.

"So you are telling me that Raul is working on another potion, in order to strip the Princess's powers, am I correct?"

"Yes, your Highness," Toby confessed, before he saw the King approach, then bowed before him rattling his chains.

"Is it necessary to chain the boy?" King Jason questioned his firstborn.

"I did not want him to escape, father."

"If he came willingly to give us this information I do not believe that he will try and escape," King Jason stated, then turned to the boy and motioned for his chains to be removed.

Toby wrung his wrists after the cuffs were taken off.

"Where is your master located?" King Jason questioned the boy.

"He is in the Dark Forest of Woe, Sire."

"I went to the forest, the cottage was burned to the ground. I will ask only once more. Where is he?" Prince Anthony inquired.

"He made a new cottage, just behind the castle in the forest of Narruc," Toby revealed.

King Jason walked away while grabbing Anthony's arm and leading him to a far corner, so that the boy could not hear.

"Have your messenger send word to Lord Brom. I have a feeling that your sister is going to want to go after the wizard once she finds out where he is," he whispered to his son.

"How do you think Ellyria will find out? I did not plan on telling her. Did you?"

"She is an empath now, son. What do you think?" King Jason added, turning around to watch the apprentice patiently waiting for them to continue. "Where is your master now, Toby?"

"Raul is at the cottage. He has not left, and he has been sending me to do everything for him this past year. He will be waiting for my return, and he can sense where I am if he starts looking for me," Toby confessed, but not yet worried that he had been gone long enough for the wizard to wonder where he was. "How long were you going to keep me here?"

"I suppose that you can let him go now. We have what we need from him," King Jason told his son.

Toby was escorted back out of the gate, so there was no chance of the boy trying to contact the Princess. He would be back in Narruc in time for supper…

Princess Ellyria was standing at her window looking out to the courtyard, watching the boy being escorted out of the gate. She could not sense his feelings from such a great distance, but she knew something was up. There would be no other reason for the wizard's apprentice to be here. Just then her mother came into the room. She knew her mother did not know why the boy was here, only that he was being questioned.

"I see that you are awake now."

"Yes, I woke up a few minutes ago, mother."

"Did you get enough rest?" Queen Anna questioned, then saw that look in her daughter's eyes that told her Ellyria was up to something.

"I did. What is it that you know about the boy that just left? I know he is the wizard's apprentice. Why was he here?"

"He came to warn you about the wizard's plans for you. Anthony was questioning him," she replied honestly. The Queen knew there was no way that she could keep the information from her daughter.

"Where is Anthony now? I am guessing that father would know what is going on?"

"Yes, your father knows. I think that he was going to find out exactly what the boy knew."

"Good, that is who I will go talk to then."

"Ellyria, wait. Your father did not want you to know that he was here, not yet anyway."

"Why? Why would he keep anything pertaining to the wizard from me?" she questioned her mother irritably. She hastily headed for the door and walked right past her worried mother. Not caring to wait a moment longer for her father to come to her himself.

Princess Ellyria would find out what the boy confessed…

Chapter 25

Lounging on a warm rock in the midday sun was a luxury for any dragon to enjoy. Favnir stretched out his mighty wings, flapping them for but a moment to cool down. It was a very hot afternoon, too hot for him. He slid off his perch and headed to the waterfall on the backside of the mountain to cool off. Taking his time walking to the other side of the mountain, he found himself to be distracted on his mission by the dragon's call that announced a meeting. Now what? He rolled his eyes, shook his head, then turned around to the meeting place where all the dragons gathered before their King…

"Dragons… It has come to my attention that the war of Ragnarok is nearing. I am giving a warning now that we will not be partaking in this war. It is not our fight, but the fight amongst the humans," Nidhoggr declared, looking out to the hundreds of dragons that came from all around, and out of hiding to answer his call. He found it quite endearing. "I am ordering that no one is to meddle in this coming war. Do I make myself clear?"

The Earth shook from the vibrations made by the deep bellows of agreement from the dragons below the rocky perch, where the King stood proudly. Favnir was standing beside him, as he was the Hand of the King. He was also the next in line to the dragon throne if Nidhoggr was to pass, since he had no heir to take over.

"Did I leave anything out?" Nidhoggr leaned over to ask of his predecessor.

"No, you did not, your Highness."

"Meeting is adjourned."

One by one the many different species of dragon that did not live amongst the protection of the mountains, headed back to their homelands. The King turned towards his Hand and held out his claws, preventing Favnir from his retreat into the cavern.

"Yes, my Lord? Is there a reason I am being detained?"

"I have been curious about your whereabouts lately. I have been hearing reports of your flying off alone in the daylight hours. You are aware of how dangerous that is, with so many dragon hunters out there itching for a prize to brag about. Correct me if I am wrong, of course."

"Yes, Sire. I do venture off sometimes, but I am careful to remain hidden."

"So where is it that you 'venture off to so carefully' then?"

"I just need a change of scenery every now, and again. Do you not? You have been here for centuries held up in this mountain, a lot longer than I have."

"This is not about me. However, I should warn you that it is not the best time to embark on such adventures. Stay close. I need you now more than ever, to keep a lookout for anything suspicious. War is coming, and I do not want it to follow us here. Do I make myself clear?"

"Yes, your Highness," Favnir agreed reluctantly, then moved along back into the cavern angrily. He must get to his master somehow and give him the great news, that he would not have to worry about the dragon's involvement in the coming war. If only he could sneak away…

Nidhoggr watched his successor until he was out of sight…

"Ari, come down. I know that you are up there," Nidhoggr called out, then looked up to the branches to search for the one he called to.

A beautiful eagle flew down before him. She looked at him and cocked her head to one side awaiting his request.

"I want you to follow, Favnir. Tell me everything that you see. I need to find out what he is up to."

Ari flew down the tunnel, then up into the sky, effortlessly soaring over the mountain, as the wind carried her magnificent, outstretched wings. She landed on the tree that stood above the opening of Favnir's private cave, to wait and see what he did, and where he went.

Favnir left that evening unaware that he was being followed…

Chapter 26

Nicole pulled the tiny parchment from the messenger bird's leg. She felt the tug of her dress by her son, Gabe, as he was trying to get her attention. Since he started walking, he had been getting into everything, causing a very pregnant mother to be beyond exhausted. Her husband, Captain Jake, had promised that he would remain inland until the birth of their new baby. Captain Jake and his brother, Lord Brom, were out in the field with their father planting the spring crops. Nicole picked up Gabe, then placed him on her hip, as she waddled out into the field to give Lord Brom the message that was addressed to him.

"Brother, this came for you!"

"Do not move! I shall come for it!" Lord Brom shouted back to her.

She was standing at the far end of the field and he could barely hear her, as he was all the way in the middle. It was only a few moments for him to walk to her, his long strides enabled him at a much faster pace than hers would have been. With her time only a few months out, there was no reason for her to be out in the field, especially carrying his nephew on her hip.

"Who is it from, dear sister?" as he reached for the rolled up piece of paper.

"It is from Toledya," Nicole said, then turned away to head back to the keep with a fussy toddler.

Captain Jake walked over to Lord Brom, to see what news he had.

"What is it, brother?"

"It is word from the King. He wishes me to go to Narruc to wait on the Princess. He says she is going to go after the wizard on her own, and fears for her safety. It also says that the wizard's cottage is in the forest behind the castle, that is all it says, nothing more."

"Are you going to go?"

"I have to, it is the King's orders."

"Are you sure that it is not just about the Princess?" Captain Jake questioned, as he raised a brow at his brother.

"Well, maybe. I have not seen her in over two years, brother."

"What difference does that make?"

"I am sure that she has moved on with someone else by now," Lord Brom sighed, running his fingers through his shoulder-length, golden-colored hair, fidgeting with his golden beard that he had grown out over the past few months. The beard was not long enough to braid yet, unlike his hair, which he usually kept braided while working in the field. He no longer favored his brother, who was clean-shaven and kept his dark hair cropped short.

"You can not possibly believe that? Can you? You left her so she could focus on her life as The Chosen One. I am almost certain that she has been busy trying to kill the wizard. I do not believe that it would give her adequate time to see other men," Captain Jake chided.

"I suppose you are right. Although, I am sure that she will be different, and have most of her powers by now."

"Does that even matter, Brom? You do still love her, do you not?"

"I never stopped loving her," Lord Brom confessed, then turned and walked away from his brother, leaving him to stand in the field alone to pack for his journey to Narruc…

Later that evening before the sun began to set, Nicole packed

Lord Brom some food for his saddlebag. She handed it up to him, as Lord Thomas said goodbye to his son, and she bid him a safe trip.

"Be careful, my son. If the wizard is as evil as you say that he is, then I will pray to the Gods to keep you safe from harm."

"Thank you, father. I will be there to watch over the Princess, and I plan to avoid the wizard the best that I can."

"Brother, be safe. If you need anything, send for me and I will come to your aid," Captain Jake added.

"I will, thank you. I hope that it will not come to that. You have a baby on the way after all. Your family needs you here right now. I shall be fine," he promised.

Lord Brom hoisted himself up onto his horse, then waved goodbye as he began his next adventure. Which once again, involved the Princess…

Chapter 27

Princess Ellyria stormed angrily out of her father's study, after having spent the past several hours arguing with him over her leaving to go after the wizard. He had questioned her about what the Ancient One had advised her to do. She could not count how many times she had told him that she had to get the Amulet of Elements back, and the crystal orb that he had stolen from her tent last summer in Inamor. She could not understand why it seemed as though her father did not believe her. He acted as if she was going on another one of her 'flighty adventures' as he put it. The conversation they had earlier still echoed in her mind...

"Ellyria, I am just worried for your safety is all. Think of your poor mother. She has been a complete wreck ever since you left for the Ormr Mountains. When I came back from Regnuom, I was shocked to hear the news that you had left. I was even more so when Rowan had returned from the dragon mountain, to inform us that you were going to be staying there an entire year. That is when your mother lost it. I had never seen her so upset, not since Liza kidnapped you two years ago. Why are you going to put her through this again?"

She watched as her father paced the floor in his study while yelling at her. All she could do was sit there and listen, until he had gotten over his tirade. When he stopped for a moment, she thought it was to catch his breath, because there was no other explanation to how he could have continued talking without him passing out from lack of oxygen. It was the only opportunity she had to confront him with her point of view.

"Father, I am not trying to be the obstinate daughter. I am trying to explain how important it is for me to get the amulet and the orb, back from the wizard. I can not defeat him without the Amulet of Elements, and I can not let him keep the orb in his possession either. Please understand, that it is my destiny to protect the realm from that monster. If I fail, who knows what will become of us all." It was at that moment, that she left the room. She passed her mother at the door, but she said not a word to her as she brushed by her…

When she arrived back in her chambers to pack, she had a peculiar feeling of déjà vu. She heard a knock at the door, and with a flick of the wrist, she opened it to find her mother standing in the doorway.

"What is it that you want, mother?"

"I have come to speak with you, if that is alright."

"What do you wish to talk about? I am sure father filled you in on my next dangerous venture."

"Yes, he did. However, I did talk him down from off his angry pedestal. I reminded him of the importance of your destiny, and how even I have come to terms with it," Queen Anna admitted, as she walked over to sit on the bed next to the satchel her daughter was cramming provisions into. She grabbed her daughter's hands into hers, preventing her from continuing her present task. "Ellyria, please hear me out. I love you so much, and I do not want anything to happen to you. You are too precious to me to lose now, or ever. Listen to reason, but listen to your heart first. The heart never leads us too far astray from where we need to go in this world. Trust in your heart, and you shall never be wrong. I did, and now I have you."

Tears welled up in Princess Ellyria's emerald eyes, changing them to sapphires. She bent down and embraced her mother.

"I am so sorry that I have hurt you so many times within

these last few years. Can you forgive me?"

"Of course I can. You are my child forever and always, no matter how old you are, or how long we may be apart. I will always be here for you," Queen Anna conveyed, but could not help to shed a tear of her own, while her daughter was still held tight within her arms. She did not want to let go, but she knew she had to.

"I love you, mother. I promise that I will make you proud."

"You already have," Queen Anna said with a loving smile, then got up from the bed, and looked her daughter in the eye. She could not bring herself to say goodbye, but she knew her daughter could sense it. Before Queen Anna left her room, she looked at her daughter one last time, praying to the Gods that she would see her again…

It was dark when Princess Ellyria finally headed out for Narruc. She said goodbye to no one, and left without a sound into the night…

CHAPTER 28

Raul was obsessively working on his potion when a knock at the cottage door broke his concentration.

"Toby! See who is at that door, before I blow someone up!"

"Yes, sire," Toby replied obediently, then went to see who was at the door, when he opened it he was not at all pleased with whom he saw. The young apprentice stepped aside and motioned for the houseguest to enter. "It is Favnir, sire."

"Well show him in!" Raul shouted, from the other side of the room.

"Thank you," Favnir said to the boy, as he walked to where Raul was sitting at his table working on the potion.

"What news do you have for me this time?"

"Nidhoggr has declared that no dragon is to participate in the upcoming war, sire," he stated, waiting for the wizard's response, who still had not raised his head up for even a moment to look at him.

The wizard gave pause, then stood up from the table.

"That is good news, but I do not trust him to not get involved, especially if that meddling princess persuades him to change his mind."

"How do you think we can stop her?"

"There is no stopping that little wretch. However, there may be a way to prevent Nidhoggr from changing his mind."

"How?"

"You will have to kill him of course. Once he is dead, you shall become King, then I shall have a guarantee that the dragons will not get involved in this war, and take the Chosen One's side," Raul stated, then went to the cabinet and pulled a potion from inside. "Here, this should do the trick. You must use all of it, pouring it into his water, or on a fresh kill. Then you will be the King of the dragons."

"What is it?"

"It is poison you idiot."

"What happens if he catches me?"

"You are a dragon, are you not? A fight to the death seems to be the next logical explanation that I can give to you. Now, go. I have more work to do here," Raul advised, sitting back down at his table and motioning for Toby to see him out.

Favnir took the poison vile, then left the cottage. Once he was outside he vanished.

Raul waited until Favnir left, to pull out the orb he had hidden in the cabinet. The power-stripping potion was almost ready, only one ingredient to add, then it would be complete. He wanted to see where his little nemesis was, so he could formulate his next move.

"Show me where the Princess is," he said to the globe. The crystal filled with smoke, showing images he was shocked to see. The Princess was at the edge of the forest and heading this way. Why? He was not ready for her yet! This was not in his plans!

"Toby!"

"Yes, sire?"

"Fetch me the seeds from the cabinet, and meet me outside," Raul instructed, then grabbed his grimoire, and went out to the far end of the cottage into the woods.

"What are you going to do with the seeds, sire?" Toby questioned, as he ran up behind him with the seeds.

"What does it look like to you? I am going to do some fanatical planting. Pass me the seeds."

Toby handed the tiny seeds to his master. The wizard began to chant a spell from his grimoire throwing the seeds far away from the cottage.

"Now what?" the young apprentice inquired, excited to see

what was going to happen next.

"Be patient boy, all things take time to grow," Raul told him, then held up the Amulet of Elements from his neck, and summoned water. A small cloud began to form over the spot where the seeds had fallen, then the rain began to come down on them. A few moments went by, and nothing happened.

"Is something supposed to happen, sire?"

"Shh, patience, boy," the wizard hissed, raising his hands in the air after the clouds had done his bidding. "Grow!" he shouted.

The ground trembled beneath Toby's feet, as he watched vines springing forth from the ground, where the seeds had just been planted. The vines began to wrap around each other and grew nearly ten feet into the air, then consuming the rest of the forest, concealing the cottage. Walls of the vines formed, and the thick greenery continued overlapping, making paths in between the walls.

"What is it, sire?"

"It is a labyrinth, Toby. One that has only one way in, but no way out."

The wizard turned around to go back into the cottage. Toby followed and was still in awe over his master's creation.

Raul never looked back, he planted his seeds, watched them grow, and now it was time to reap what he had sown…

Chapter 29

Deep in the forest, darkness had taken over the land, turning day into night. Wolves howled their loneliness in song, serenading the moon, while owls cried out to warn their prey. The dense fog crept over the ground, while enveloping a thick veil around old and withered trees...

Princess Ellyria could barely see in front of her when she came to a wall of greenery. Vines entwined the perfectly trimmed hedge that scaled up over her head nearly ten feet, she followed the length of it, and it seemed to go on and on in either direction. Then she saw an opening and walked through in between the hedge line, only to see more of the wall of shrubbery. The path she was taking led her to more green walls that seemed never ending, getting her absolutely nowhere. Every turn she made led to yet another turn, that ended with more of the giant brush. New openings only led to dead ends. She seemed to have found herself in a labyrinth of sorts. Just when she thought she had gotten one step closer to finding her way out, she found herself getting lost all over again. She had had enough of the maze and was going to see her way out.

Princess Ellyria stood in the middle of one of the green walls, after placing the backs of her hands together, she made a parting motion, then separated the hedge wall. She continued to go straight through her self-made paths, for what seemed like hours. Feeling herself beginning to tire, she became angered by the endless amount of vines and brush, that she just used her right hand to move the greenery out of her way.

The Princess thought that she would never get out, and just when she felt she could not go on anymore, she stumbled out of the labyrinth and into a clearing in the woods. After she had gotten her bearings, she looked all around her. The lush green was now brown decay, as she walked, she could only hear the sound of her feet crunching dried leaves, twigs, and the sound of her own heartbeat. The tiny hairs on her arms stood up, as she rubbed her forearms with her hands to ward off the sudden chill. She no longer heard the sounds of the forest animals, nor the sound of the wind howling in the distance. Another clearing in the woods allowed her to see a small cottage just up ahead. The closer she came to the cottage, the more ill she became. There was a definite evil presence, it had to be the wizard's hideout. She continued to walk to the cottage, trying to fight off the urge to be sick, but it was too late, she bent over and expelled the contents of her stomach.

Princess Ellyria stood back up and wiped her mouth with the back of her hand, she was not about to turn back now. The cottage appeared to be empty, as she crept up beside an open window. She peered inside but no one was there. She walked over to the porch, turned the doorknob, then slowly opened it. Her heart began to race, as she cautiously stepped inside. The feeling of déjà vu had returned. Looking all around her she found the place to be empty, but she was still going to be careful in case the wizard was hiding out in another room. Princess Ellyria moved slowly through the cottage and began to search for what she came here to find. She saw the black cloth on the table, covering what had to be her stolen crystal ball. It was revealed to be the orb when she pulled off the cloth, now that she found its location, she left it to look for the amulet. She walked past the hearth to the tall cabinet that stood in the next room. Many jars of different herbs, body parts, and vials of potions graced the shelves that she had never even heard of, as she skimmed the labels. All of a sudden, she heard a noise coming from the backside of the cottage. She went to inspect who it was and looked out the small window on the back door. Nothing. She continued to complete her search of the cabinet, finding no luck with the amulet being there. When she turned back around, Raul stood by the hearth.

"If I had known that I was going to have company, I would have tidied the place up a bit."

"Drop the sarcasm wizard, I think you know why I am here," Princess Ellyria stated, then spied the amulet around his neck.

"Looking for this?" he inquired, catching her staring at it, then held up the amulet in his hand, "Lovely is it not, yet so powerful. Here, let me give you a demonstration."

Before Princess Ellyria had a chance to see what he had done, a deep growl vibrated the floorboards. She looked down and standing beside the wizard, was a giant two-headed dog that stood at his waistline, slobber dripping from its large jaws filled with sharp teeth.

"I only have to give but one command, he will be after you and rip out your throat," he laughed maniacally. "There is nowhere for you to hide, Princess. I have got you where I want you now, bitch!"

Princess Ellyria made a run for the door behind her, but it was locked. She pushed out her hands in front of her and blew open the door, running out of the cottage as fast as she could. Suddenly, she heard a familiar voice call out to her.

"Ellyria!"

She turned to the sound of the voice and could not believe her eyes. It was Lord Brom! She ran to him, as he was running to her.

"What are you doing here?"

"There is no time to explain. I need you to run as fast and as far as you can until you see the little cabin in the woods. Go, hurry!"

Raul appeared in the doorway with the two-headed dog and pointed at them.

"Kill them both!" he ordered, knowing someone had to have

disclosed where his lair was. He did not think about it earlier with the Princess being here, she had the power of premonition to find him, but not Lord Brom, someone tipped him off. Who then? He had a pretty good idea who it was. Before Raul had a chance to blink, his dog was running the intruders into the forest. He had hoped that he would at least catch Lord Brom, and rip out his throat. The Princess he wanted alive. He could not steal her powers if she died by anything else besides his own hands.

Lord Brom and Princess Ellyria ran into the forest, out of the wizard's sight.

"Run, Ellyria, we have to split up. I will distract the beast! Get out of here now!" he shouted.

The dog became confused as the couple ran in two different directions. The Princess tripped over a fallen tree branch and lost one of her shoes, so she just kicked off the other, then got up to run again. The dog saw her fall and stopped chasing Lord Brom, to go after her. When Lord Brom saw the two-headed dog go after her, he grabbed a rock and threw it at the beast to get his attention diverted back to him. The dog yelped and turned in the direction where it came from, no longer paying attention to the Princess, as it was now angered and ran after Lord Brom. He stood his ground, but only for a moment as the giant dog lunged after him. Snapping its jaws, it salivated over his next meal that was standing there for the taking and leapt into the air to attack his quarry, but then was met with a large tree branch that Lord Brom pulled up in front of him. The two-headed dog impaled himself on the branch, as it went straight into his chest, Lord Brom pushed it into him further before he let go of the branch. The beast hit the ground, moments later, vanishing into thin air before his very eyes.

Lord Brom took some time to catch his breath, before following Princess Ellyria in the direction he had sent her...

Running barefoot through the woods, she ignored the sticks breaking under her feet, and sharp stones cutting into them. While branches snagged her clothes and slashed her tender flesh, she was out of breath, but could not stop now. Without looking back, she had to find a shelter of some kind, if only to hide and rest for just a little while. The full moon in the night sky gave enough light to see directly in front of her, but the dense fog made it difficult to see out ahead. She wished that she could remember where Lord Brom had said to go, 'the little cottage in the woods'. Where was it? Exhausted, and terribly sore from running for so long, she began to recognize her surroundings.

After looking behind her, realizing she was not being followed, she was able to slow down and catch her breath. It was the same cottage Lord Brom had brought her to, when he brought her to Liza, so long ago. It seemed as though no one had been here in a very long time, not even to maintain its upkeep. Peering inside a window, she could see that no one was there, so she went on inside. The mice were now the only inhabitants, cobwebs covered the corners, and thick dust had lain undisturbed on the furnishings. The mice scurried away, squeaking their fear of her, as she entered the very room in which she had freed herself from Liza's grasp.

Princess Ellyria then walked to the other end of the house, and before she could turn the knob of the backdoor, she heard a loud crash in the parlor. Deciding to go and investigate, she thought it would be wise to arm her person with something just in case. She found a piece of a broken chair leg and thought it would suffice. She slowly walked back to the parlor, retracing her steps from whence she came in, and saw nothing in front of her, or up ahead. She peered into the room, but there was nothing there. All of a sudden, a mouse ran across her foot. She screamed, then on pure instinct, threw the broken chair leg at the mouse as it ran off.

"Stupid mouse!" she squealed at the nasty vermin. Her heart felt as if it would beat right out of her chest, but before she could slow down her breathing, someone grabbed her from behind. Quickly, and on pure impulse, she reached for the broken chair leg, which she then used to hit her attacker. Eyes clenched shut, she hit her assailant hard with the chair leg, and he yelled out in pain, releasing his grasp on her.

"Wait, Ellyria! It is just I, Brom! Take it easy! What did I say about fighting with your eyes closed anyway!"

She looked at the man, who she was on a first-name basis with now, which made her wonder if it really was him or not.

"I am so glad that you had escaped. I was so worried when you were not right behind me that he had trapped you," she said relieved. Searching his eyes for any trickery, she decided to test him.

Princess Ellyria pulled him into her arms and kissed him passionately, Lord Brom smiled and returned her kisses with fervor. She pushed him away and saw the bewildered look on his face, she knew he was no imposter.

"Why did you stop, Princess?" a very aroused Lord Brom questioned. He stepped back, then looked at her and laughed, as she stood there tapping her bare foot and arms crossed, giving him her classic glare. "Did you really think that it was not me?"

"I am sorry, but I had to be sure. So I tested you," Princess Ellyria confessed, as she walked over to embrace him again, looking up into his bright blue eyes.

"Kissing me was your test? Well if that was your way of testing me, I think you had better do it again, just to be sure," he teased her.

The Princess pushed him away and slapped his arm. She could not believe after all their time apart that he was still the charmer.

"I can not believe that after all of these years, you still have not changed a bit."

"Well, dear Princess, neither have you," he jested.

She was surprised to see him in the Dark Forest of Woe and searching for the same majickal object, it could not have been just a coincidence. Then after the giant, horrible, two-headed dog came running after them, there was no time to reminisce about old times together. Princess Ellyria caressed the side of Lord Brom's face, wondering what his part was in all of this, and why he was there in the first place.

"Why, may I ask, did you happen to be at the wizard's house at the very same moment I was?"

He avoided her gaze, knowing she could look him in the eye and know whether he was lying to her or not.

"What are you not telling me?" she questioned, taking his hand and placing it to her heart. She closed her eyes, she could feel what he felt in his heart and hear the thoughts in his head. She could not believe what she saw. "My very own father hired you to watch out for me. When did this happen?" she asked angrily. She stared at him, waiting to hear what he had to say.

"When your brother Prince Anthony heard the apprentice's confession, your father sent word to me before you headed out on this quest, asking me to protect you," he informed her.

Princess Ellyria raised her arms and slowly the objects about the room began to float up beside her. Then in a single fluid motion, she sent them flying across the room, barely missing Lord Brom in the process. She could see the look of fear in his eyes.

"Does it look as though I need protection?"

He looked at her in awe. Her father never mentioned that she had harnessed all the power within her already.

"I see that you have learned to develop your powers," he observed.

"Yes, well, it took time over the past few years, but I am finally able to utilize and control them better. I do hope that I did not scare you too bad?"

"I was not scared," he replied hastily. She gave him that glance again. How she knew was incomprehensible to him.

"I know," she smiled. Many nights had passed when the full moon was high in the sky and the stars shone brightly, that she thought of him.

Lord Brom looked out the window to see if the coast was clear, then she came up behind him, wrapping her arms around his waist.

"We should be heading out, but I am afraid that it would

be better if we stayed here, and then leave at dawn," Lord Brom advised, turning around to face her. She was no longer the girl child of his past, she had grown into the woman standing before him. He cupped her beautiful face into his gentle hands, leaning down to kiss her passionately.

Princess Ellyria returned his kisses with equal ardency, as familiar feelings stirred within her. Their kissing ignited the fires of long ago, the love that had to be buried in the ashes between them like the Phoenix rising from the flames. He paused for a moment to look at her, to see if she was feeling this between them as well. She pulled him to her, as her hands searched his sculpted body.

Lord Brom picked her up and carried her to the bedroom, setting her on the bed gently. He tossed off the tattered blanket, then laid her on the flat of her back. They searched each other's mouths with eager tongues entwined. Lord Brom caressed her face with featherlike strokes of his fingertips. He saw her smile, as he placed tiny kisses from her mouth, down her cheek, to the inside of her neck, as his lips softly caressed her skin. His hands began to explore the hard hidden peaks of her nipples beneath her dress, acknowledging the fact that her cumbersome corset was not containing them.

Princess Ellyria arched her body to meet his touch, with a newfound feeling in her loins that she could not ignore. She urged him on to touch her, pressing her body into his, and kissed him more passionately than before. Then he paused only for a moment to pull his shirt over his head. It was then she noticed the scar on his abdomen and remembered when he had been stabbed by one of Liza's guards. With his shirt removed, she caressed his naked chest and explored his body as he had done to hers, placing kisses on his chiseled form; he looked like a perfectly sculpted statue.

Lord Brom returned to her mouth with his, reaching down to fumble with the ties of her dress to release her beautiful, full breasts. He fondled them gently, as they molded perfectly within his hands, kissing each breast, taking care that each nipple had equal time for him to suckle.

Princess Ellyria arched her back up into his lean body, over the sensations that he caused to inflame within her. Lord Brom picked her up to sit on his lap, the heat of his desire underneath her equally matched her own. She rocked her body into him, swaying back and forth in a rhythmic motion. They continued their exploration of each other's bodies and he could wait no longer.

Lord Brom flipped her off his lap onto her back and removed his trousers. He carefully removed the rest of her dress, displaying all of her beauty for him to see. He returned to her side for more of her sweet kisses, and she arched her body into his waiting for him to take her. He wanted to be gentle with her for the first time, so he placed his fingers inside her to help her relax and be able to invite him in without hurting her. She was beside herself with a fever so strong, that she felt as if she would burst at his touch. When he rested himself in between her soft thighs, she felt his fever for her as well. When he thought she was ready, and he was about to enter her, she trembled.

"Are you alright?"

"Oh, yes, Brom. I want to be with you," she replied breathlessly. She pulled him to kiss her again, as he entered her gently and felt the dam breaking within her. She took a deep breath and flinched, only for a moment, when he completely filled her.

Lord Brom began to move inside her slowly at first, then he pushed himself into her harder, and deeper. She wrapped her legs around him, arching her body to receive him even more. Princess Ellyria had no idea how wondrous this could be, as she lost total control over the pleasure that was consuming her body. He could not contain himself any longer when she soaked his loins, as he released at the same time, spilling his life into her. Lord Brom fell over, resting his body on hers. They were both drenched in sweat, exhausted by their lovemaking. Lord Brom withdrew from her and rolled over beside her. She looked at him with those big, sapphire-blue eyes and smiled.

"How are you?"

"I am well. You?"

"I am very well indeed," he said, a wide grin shown on his clean-shaven face. Lord Brom gently brushed the hair away from her face, tucking it behind one ear.

"So, what do we do now?"

"Well, we could do it again if you would like," he teased her.

"That is not what I meant," she giggled.

"What is it that you would like to know then?"

"How am I going to get the amulet back now?"

"That is what you are worried about? I thought you were more concerned about us."

"I can not think about that right now. This was lovely and all, but I have a wizard to kill. Remember?"

He sat up in the bed, brushed his shoulder-length, golden hair from his face, and looked at her with those sky blue eyes of his.

"I will help you with anything that you need. Just promise me that when this is all over, you will marry me."

"I promise," she said smiling, rolling over on top of him and kissing him tenderly.

Lord Brom and Princess Ellyria made love once more that night, before falling asleep in each other's arms…

Chapter 30

King Jason and Queen Anna were in the parlor when the messenger announced his presence.

"A message from Regnuom, your Grace."

"Thank you, that will be all," King Jason dismissed him, then unrolled the parchment and read it out loud. "It is from Ian. He says that he is doing well, the people respect him, and asks how we are doing here, especially his sister," he finished, then looked over at his wife who seemed like she was in a daze.

"What is the matter, my love?"

The Queen did not answer him, she kept gazing out the window.

"Anna, are you alright?"

"What? Oh, yes dear, I am well. I suppose I am a little preoccupied with my thoughts," she replied, without bothering to look at him.

King Jason knew something was bothering her. He did not want to push her about it, so he left her alone. They sat quietly almost waiting for the other to speak, when the tower guard came in disrupting the silence.

"Your Majesties, Lord Brom has returned with Princess Ellyria, they approach the gates now."

"Thank you for alerting me, you may go now," the King dismissed him. He looked over to his wife, who seemed very much excited with the news of their daughter's return…

Once they had arrived in the courtyard, Princess Ellyria was shocked that her entire family was not there outside to greet them. Lord Brom left the horses in the stable boy's care and escorted the Princess inside. Still, no one was at the door. This baffled her. When they walked into the parlor, her parents stood up to greet her.

"I am surprised that you were not in the courtyard to greet us, mother. Did anyone come to announce our arrival?"

"Yes, my dear. I did not want to bombard you as soon as you had arrived," her mother confessed.

"I am glad that you have returned, darling. Good to see you again, Lord Brom. Thank you for your help again, in bringing my little girl home safely," King Jason stated proudly.

"Yes, father thank you for sending, Lord Brom. I would have never made it without him. I am capable of taking care of myself you know. I am not that damsel in distress anymore in need of someone to rescue," she announced brazenly.

"Now, you listen here, young lady. I was only doing it for your protection, because that is what I do, by sending in the reinforcements. I am sorry if that upsets you, but it upsets me and your mother more, not knowing what might happen to you if I did not send in someone to help you. I know this is your destiny, but where in that prophecy does it state you can not get a little help along the way?"

"I am sorry, father. I did not think about it in that way. You are right as always. I am going to go upstairs now to my chambers if anyone needs me."

Lord Brom stood there silently not really knowing what to do. The only thing that was best to do, was stay out of that conversation completely. Queen Anna was feeling out of place to say anything either, but followed her daughter upstairs to prepare her a bath.

"Lord Brom, I do not want you to feel the blame for my daughter's feelings. I am sure that you know by now, how stubborn and thick-headed Ellyria can be," King Jason admitted.

"Yes Sire, I do."

"Come join me in the study, so you can tell me everything

that happened," King Jason insisted, then escorted Lord Brom to the study unaware of what really happened between them…

Princess Ellyria had already disrobed when her mother had arrived with the handmaidens behind her, carrying in the buckets of hot water for her bath. Queen Anna added some scented rose oil to the bath as the hot water was being poured in. Once the maids had finished, they left the room leaving mother and daughter alone.

"Are you not going to tell me what happened?"

"I did not get the amulet or the orb back, if that is what you are referring to," Princess Ellyria replied, avoiding her mother's gaze, and slowly easing into the bath. She also did not bother to acknowledge her mother, when she had pulled a bench up alongside her.

"Well, what happened then?"

"There is not anything to tell, mother. I failed in my mission, I barely escaped the wizard and the two-headed dog," she stated hastily.

"You have not really talked to me about anything since you left the Ormr Mountains. Has that experience with the dragons left you to be so different now?" Queen Anna stared at her daughter, who was not acting like the daughter she knew before. What has made her so hard that she could not confide in her?

"I apologize, mother. I do not want to cause you any more worries than you already have, that is all," she sighed.

"You could not worry me any more than I have been before. I have accepted your destiny, I told you that. Can you not trust to tell me what is going on?" Queen Anna asked, wringing her hands together, constantly smoothing out the wrinkles in her dress.

"When I trained with the Ancient One, he told me that I had to get the amulet back, or I would have no chance of defeating the wizard. I failed miserably in my quest to do so. Unfortunately, he took me by surprise, and as much as I had tried to be brave, I was actually terrified," Princess Ellyria confessed, then slid down into the tub further, keeping her gaze on the steam rising up from the water. The scent of roses was comforting, and she began to feel relaxed.

"It is a natural reaction to be scared, dear. Do not feel like you are weak, because you are not. Bravery comes from within, as do those powers. I could never have been as brave as you have, after everything you have been through. It is not over yet. What else did you learn from the wise old dragon?"

"I learned to control my powers, learned about The All, and the wizard that harnessed its power. He was from the Niflheim, the Underworld. His mother was said to be the Queen. When the wizard Yggdrasill was slain by his apprentice, his dragon took the remaining half of his heart and buried it in the center of the mountain. The heart grew into a beautiful Ash Tree that could reach its mighty branches to Valhalla, its roots grew deep into the Underworld, stretching out into the Black Forest and the Dark Forest of Woe. Both forests pull from the majick within the root, which all majickal beings are drawn to its power. The main root that grew into the Underworld, is said to have done so he could be closer to his mother. The tree is said to have great power, making it the most sacred tree in all of Ragnarok. I learned all that I could from him, then he sent me on my way. Now I must go back and tell him that I have failed."

"There must be something he can advise you on, and how to get the amulet back. Do you think that he will help you if you return?"

"I am not sure. I must go there as soon as possible. He is my only hope right now if I am ever to get the amulet back from the wizard," she said, as the droplets splashed back into the tub, and out onto the floor when she stood up.

Queen Anna was ready with the drying cloth to help wrap it around her. As Princess Ellyria was tucking in the corner under her arm and then turning around, the soft light from the window cascading over her face made her look different somehow. Her mother noticed it.

"How did things go with Lord Brom?" she questioned curiously, looking at her daughter.

Princess Ellyria had finished drying off and had just slipped on her blue cotton day gown over her head.

"What do you mean, mother?"

"Well, you had not seen him in two years. I was just curious if it was awkward for you to see each other, after such a long time apart?" Queen Anna questioned, then watched as the expression on her daughter's face changed, her cheeks suddenly had a rosy glow about them.

"No, mother, everything went well," Princess Ellyria responded hastily, her cheeks were quite warm, but she tried to keep a straight face.

Queen Anna decided to not press the issue further, but she knew that look. It was the same look she had after she had been with Ellyria's father for the first time. She and Lord Brom had been gone for a few days, and had to have spent at least one night together alone.

"Are you joining us for supper?"

"Yes, mother. I shall be down after I brush out my hair."

"Very well, I suppose that I shall leave you to it then. I will go downstairs and make sure Lord Brom is well."

"Why do you think he would not be?" she asked her mother in a worrisome tone.

"Because we left him alone with your father and brothers, that is why," her mother mused, leaving the room.

Princess Ellyria brushed out her long black hair, coiling it up into a bun to the mid-crown on the back of her head, securing it with a lovely silver comb, before she headed downstairs…

Everyone gathered at the grand table in the dining room. The King and Queen were seated at the ends of the table, Prince Anthony was to the right of his father, across from him sat Prince Dakota, beside him sat Lord Brom and Prince Rowan, and Princess

Ellyria sat beside their mother across from Lord Brom, and Prince Dakota. Lord Brom could not take his eyes off the Princess, she looked so beautiful in her blue dress with her hair neatly swept up off her shoulders. He had not paid much attention to her father, as he was in deep conversation with Prince Anthony over military strategy in preparation for the coming war. When the King addressed him, he barely caught what was asked of him.

"So, Lord Brom. What are your thoughts on how we should defend the castle walls? By using boiling oil, as we have done in the past, or use what the young folk are using these days?" he questioned.

"I am not sure tossing boiling oil over the side will keep out the wizard, Sire. No disrespect, but you should let your daughter handle the wizard," Lord Brom informed him."

"I agree, father. Ellyria needs to handle the wizard. We just need to be prepared for whatever accompanies him," Prince Anthony added.

"I will have plenty of various kinds of potions made, father, as well as barrels filled with black powder to set around the perimeter to set it off, if need be," Prince Dakota offered.

"I shall have Gaia waiting to surprise whatever enemy the wizard decides to throw at us," Prince Rowan added.

"It sounds to me, Sire that you have your strategy planned out," Lord Brom stated.

"Yes, apparently I do," King Jason chuckled. "I am proud of all of you, for pitching in your ideas, and skills."

"You are being awfully quiet this evening, sister," Prince Anthony noticed.

Princess Ellyria looked up from her plate of food that she had been toying with for the last hour, while they were in midst of their conversations. She had not wanted to chime in, she was too afraid of losing her temper.

"I am fine," she announced quietly.

"Are you sure?"

"Yes."

"Very well then. What is your battle plan, darling?" her father inquired. Everyone was watching her, waiting for her to reply.

"I do not have one yet, father," she answered sharply.

"What do you have?" King Jason asked, in a more regal tone.

"I am going back to the dragon mountain, to get more answers. If that is not a problem. Rowan, do you think you can take me there tonight?" the Princess inquired, turning to her brother.

"What? Tonight would be dangerous, going there unexpectedly," Prince Rowan advised.

"No, it would not actually. The dragons are more active at night, silly brother, you should know that," she teased.

"Could you talk some sense into your daughter?" King Jason asked of his wife.

"No more than I can talk sense into you, my dear," Queen Anna laughed, then smiled lovingly at her husband.

King Jason threw up his hands, then left the table. His sons followed suit, as did Princess Ellyria chasing after her brother, Prince Rowan. Queen Anna was left at the table with Lord Brom, when she looked over at him staring at the doorway.

"Well, what are you waiting for? Go after her," she advised.

Lord Brom nodded his head and went after the Princess…

What are you thinking?" Lord Brom questioned Princess Ellyria outside in the courtyard, as Prince Rowan was placing her small travel bag onto Gaia's saddle.

"I am going to the mountain, as I have stated within the past thirty minutes that you have been asking me. How is asking me again going to help your cause to keep me from going?"

"Take me with you. I can protect you."

"I do not need protection. Besides, I have to go alone. Dragons hate humans, and the King trusts me, end of discussion. I shall be back as soon as I can. I will send a dove when I am ready for you to come get me, brother."

"That is good. I hope it will not be another year that you will be gone this time," her brother teased.

"You were gone a year with the dragons?" Lord Brom asked. He could not be without her another moment as it was, but another year, he could not.

"I will not be gone another year, I promise. Do not worry. I will come back to you," the Princess said with a wink.

"Just promise that you will come back to me as soon as possible," he said, kissing her gently, before helping her up onto Gaia's back.

"Oh, stop it. You two are making me ill," Prince Rowan teased them.

"Please be careful," Lord Brom shouted up at her.

"I will," she replied, smiling down at him. This was strange for her. Usually, it is him that rides off and leaves her behind. It was time that he knew how she felt, even though she was only going on a mission, and not actually leaving him.

Lord Brom watched as Princess Ellyria took off through the sky. He would try not to worry about her, or how much he was going to miss her…

Chapter 31

Ari had been cautiously following Favnir, since he had left the mountain to the wizard's cottage and back to the mountain. She sat on a branch watching, as he poured something over a fresh leg of lamb he was preparing to bring out for Nidhoggr. Before he could start walking to the throne room, Ari had taken flight to warn the King…

Nidhoggr was patiently waiting for the promised tasty treat that Favnir was bringing out to him when Ari began screeching overhead. He was well versed in the eagle language and knew what she was warning him about. He sent her on her way just before Favnir came out with a mouthwatering leg from his favorite livestock, that smelled as though it had just been killed.

"Ahh, I see you have brought me my favorite snack. Well, done Favnir."

"I always make sure to have only the very best for you, Sire," he stated humbly, waiting for the King to consume it, but he was nervous.

"You are such a good servant. You deserve a reward for your loyalty to me. You may have the leg. I am still quite full from the ox I ate earlier," he offered, watching his expression change dramatically as he pushed the leg aside.

"I do thank you, but mutton is quite gamey for my taste. I prefer cattle," Favnir lied.

Nidhoggr could not wait any longer to call him out on his treachery. He flung the leg away and pushed himself into Favnir, hard pinning him up against the wall.

"Do you take me as such a fool that I would not find out that you were trying to poison me?"

"I do not know what you are talking about, my Lord," Favnir pleaded, sliding down to try and escape his King's grasp.

Nidhoggr grabbed him by the throat so that he could not get away, then dug his claws deep into his neck.

"Where do you think you are going, traitor?" he shouted, as he flung him to the ground.

Favnir tried to scramble to his feet, but Nidhoggr's foot came down on his neck before he could get away. Favnir bit into his leg, causing the older dragon to pull it back off him. The younger more agile dragon quickly lunged for his elder, then chomped down on his throat. Both dragons began to roll around on the stone floor, neither giving up the fight. Nidhoggr slashed sharp claws across Favnir's face, leaving the blood to drip down to the floor. Favnir then leapt for Nidhoggr again, but he was ready for the attack. He crouched down in time to allow Favnir to jump him, but then he flung him over his back into the wall. The young dragon had not the chance to get up, and the more experienced dragon was on top of him fast. He pushed himself onto his traitor, bringing him to the floor, the full weight of him crushing the smaller dragon.

"Why? Why would you betray me?"

"I had no choice," he confessed. Now weakened from his Lordship's weight, he struggled to fight until the end.

Nidhoggr smashed the back of his head into the stone floor, even with the claws that were piercing his flesh, he did not let up. He continued his attack, opening up his chest with his sharp talons, then crushing him, with the sheer size of his body. Favnir could no longer protect himself, he was too weak to fight anymore.

Suddenly, to Nidhoggr's surprise, Favnir transformed back into his true form, as that of a man. He shrunk between his massive legs, as he looked down on his former predecessor.

"How can this be?" he questioned him in disbelief.

The man lying before him was barely breathing and looked up at him from the stone floor.

"I was an apprentice for the wizard, Raul. I became too greedy wanting more power, so I could become more powerful than he was. So, he cursed me into the dragon you had always known me to be, and the curse allowed for me to change into a human when I was around the wizard. I was made to be his informant, reporting back anything that he deemed useful to him. I am sorry for my betrayal, but as I said, I had no choice," he gasped, then took his last breath.

Nidhoggr mourned the loss of the friend he still held in his memory, as he carefully laid his head down on the ground. When he looked up, Princess Ellyria was standing at the entrance…

"What happened? Who is he?"

"That is no concern of yours, Princess. Why are you here?"

"I came for your help. I went to try and get the amulet from the wizard, but he took me by surprise, and I failed," she confessed to him, walking over, and kneeling beside the naked man before her. "Who was he? Did you kill him?"

"You ask too many questions. As far as the wizard goes, I can not offer you any more advice," he stated irritatedly. The dragon was covered in blood, and his wounds were deep.

"Let me help you," she said, pulling a dry cloth from her travel bag. She began blotting off the blood.

"Stop it. That is enough. Leave me be," he grumbled.

Princess Ellyria was not going to give up.

"Please, at least tell me how he can be killed, you must know that at least," she begged.

"In order for the wizard to be killed, you must remove his heart and destroy it. If the heart is not destroyed, the majick will resurrect him in time."

"Well, can I do this without the Amulet of Elements?"

"No, I am afraid that you can not. He is protected by the amulets' power. You must take it away from him, for you to have enough power to take his heart."

"Do I need the amulet to kill him?"

"No, but it must be out of his possession. The amulet was made for you Princess, it is rightfully yours, it will enhance your powers."

"How do I get the amulet back then?" she questioned irritably and was about to lose her temper.

"I can not answer that either. However, I do know who may have an answer."

"Tell me who then!"

The dragon looked at the desperate girl, feeling almost sorry for her.

"You must seek out Hella, in Niflheim, it is the Underworld. She may have the answers you seek."

"How can I get to the Underworld? I am not that powerful."

"Follow the root of the Ash Tree, and it will lead you there."

"Where is this tree?" she asked, seemingly getting nowhere fast with this dragon.

Nidhoggr walked away, into the depths of the mountain.

"Where are you going?"

"If you want to find the Ash Tree, then I suggest that you follow me, Princess," he advised, leading her to the centre of the majestic mountain.

Even during her stay here, Princess Ellyria had never been this far into the mountain. He usually kept her confined to the areas he was, never letting her out of his sights. Once they arrived at the base of the tree, she looked up at it in amazement. Never in her life had she seen such a tree, besides the Elder Tree from the Black Forest which paled in comparison just from the sheer size alone. The Ash Tree was wider than she could have ever imagined, the branches reaching into the sky and heading for Valhalla, and the great roots branching off into three directions.

"Follow this root, it will lead you to the Underworld."

"Are you not coming with me?"

"No. I am not permitted to go with you. You are on your own, Princess. Good luck."

"Thank you, for all of your help. I appreciate all that you have done for me," she said, before kissing him on his giant nose.

Nidhoggr let out a grumble, then gave her a dragon's smile.

"Just go, before you change your mind about me," he growled almost playfully.

Princess Ellyria smiled, then followed the root into the Underworld, unaware of what a long journey she was in for…

The Underworld was not as she had expected. In all the lore she had read about this place, this proved to be quite a surprise. It was not cold, nor damp, nor did it feel empty, or melancholy. The hidden world beneath Ragnarok was filled with mist dancing around ancient trees, that were filled with apples, the fruit of the Gods. A large pool was at the center, with huge lilies floating on top of the crystal clear water, allowing for tiny sprites to rest on them.

Princess Ellyria kept walking, observing all of the beauty that was covered by sparkly dust from the pollen of exotic flowers, and the faeries that fluttered about. Up ahead she saw a magnificent throne that was covered in gold, and decorated with precious stones of rubies, diamonds, emeralds, and sapphires. She was completely awestruck the closer she came to the throne, then a woman appeared before her very eyes. Assuming her to be the Queen, she never would have believed it by how she was depicted in the ancient texts. She was unusually exotic, and her skin was a dark ashy tone that anyone would mistake for a shade of blue. Her face was almost that of a young girl, with the eternal youth she had been blessed. She had enchanting ice blue eyes, that were decorated by the thick eyelashes that lowered slightly, more than likely from the weight of them, very large, and round in shape, like that of a doe. Her nose was petite, her cheekbones were round, sitting high up on her face, and her lips were full and almost curled up at the corners when she smiled, like that of a cat. Her hair was the most interesting, as it was the color of the sapphires from her throne, it was all one length reaching to the back of her thighs, and straight as an arrow. She was very tall, most likely a trait she inherited from her mischievous father, Loki who was said to be a giant. She did not know much about her mother, and was not about to ask. Standing before the throne, Princess Ellyria decided to take a knee, to show respect to the Queen of the Underworld.

Hella stood up, picking up the ends of her long gown that was transparent and had a long v in the front, exposing her large ample breasts.

"You may stand, Princess."

"You know who I am?" she asked returning to her feet.

"Yes," she replied with a voice that was almost hypnotic, even soothing.

"Then you must know why I am here?"

"Yes. You are here for answers," she answered almost cryptically.

Do you know how I can take the Amulet of Elements from the wizard?"

"No."

"What do you know?" she asked, before minding her tongue. This was her realm, and she was a Goddess, who could strike her down at any moment.

"You think you know me, foolish girl?"

"I apologize. I meant no disrespect to you, your Grace," she quickly responded, feeling her heart skip a beat.

"I am the daughter of Loki, who is hated by Alfodr. I did not choose my father. I was born of his loins only, not out of love. I tried to declare my loyalties to Alfodr, but this is where he sent me. A lonely place where I am visited only by the dead, I hate it here. She began to sob, as her tears flowed down to the floor, and into the crystal pool in the center of the room.

"This place is so beautiful. How could you hate it?"

"No matter its beauty, in which it appears to you, in my sights, it is a dark, cold, and damp place. Where those that die a worthless death come to torture me, leaving me to feel their agony and despair. I am tormented by my own empty heart and imperfections. Do you not understand?"

"You are so beautiful. How could you possibly feel that you are imperfect?" she questioned, then watched as Hella walked to the pool, motioning for her to follow.

"Look here, child. See the reflection in the water?"

Princess Ellyria looked down into the pool and saw herself, and that of Hella.

"I still see your beauty."

"I only see a monster, half rotten, half whole, light, and dark. There is no beauty in my eyes. I am the ugliest of all the gods, and not permitted to grace my presence to those in the heavens," she confessed, taking Princess Ellyria's hand into hers. It was cold to the touch, but she felt that her heart still had a little warmth left inside. "This pool can reveal to you all of the answers that you seek, you only have to peer deep inside for you to see," she advised, waving her hand over the pool. It darkened at first, but then it gave way to light, showing the images of the realm above.

Princess Ellyria could not believe her eyes. She saw that the wizard had trapped the boy in a cage in the woods. She could hear his cries for help and feel his pain. The images vanished, before she could say a word, Hella placed her hand on her shoulder and looked deep into her eyes.

"You must seek out the one they call the Raven. She can help you. I am sorry I can not give you the comfort that you seek. I hope the pool has answered your question as to what you must do, but I must tell you that the one you seek lives amongst mortals," she told her, before turning away from Princess Ellyria, towards her throne, where she spent most of her days filled with despair.

"How do I get out of here?" she questioned, then watched as Hella looked back at her, while she continued to slowly walk away.

"Jump into the pool, and it will return you to your realm. Oh, and Princess, when the time comes, you will need to pray to Freyja, and warn her."

"Warn her about what?"

"When the wizard takes his revenge," the Queen declared before she vanished.

Princess Ellyria was left to stand beside the pool alone. She could not just jump in. She looked out in the direction of where she came in, but the root had disappeared. Oh, what was she to do now? Hella said to just jump in, but could she trust her? She saw the image of the young apprentice locked in the cage before her again.

After taking in a deep breath, Princess Ellyria jumped into the icy cold water that lit up as brightly as the sun…

CHAPTER 32

Raul added the final ingredient to the power-stripping potion. He made it extra special for that bitch of a princess, and since he had finished, he was ready for his plan to be set in motion. The masterful vision that he had sent to her through the crystal ball of Toby being locked in a cage and stranded in the woods was such evil genius, that he amazed even himself. Now, he would look into his majick orb to see where the Princess was. The crystal filled with smoke, as the smoke cleared it revealed to its seeker the one he was searching for. Much to his excitement, she was already in the forest searching for the boy. It is time to give her what she was searching for, then Raul vanished from the cottage…

Toby sat in the cage alone in the woods, waiting for his master's return. He was not certain what the wizard had in mind while keeping him in this cage, but he could not get out. The key was hanging on a tree branch nearby, that was just too far away for him to reach. All of a sudden, the wizard appeared before him.

"Is my punishment over, sire? Are you going to release me?"

"Yes, I am, but do not think your punishment is over, if I find out that it was you who tipped off to Lord Brom as to my whereabouts," he snapped. "I am sending you back to the cottage, now go."

Raul sent Toby back to the cottage with a snap of his fingers, then with a wave of his hand over his face, he changed into his apprentice, and placed himself inside the cage…

Princess Ellyria slid down from the tired horse that she obtained in town, where she appeared completely dry upon her return from the Underworld. She tied the horse to a tree, behind several overgrown bushes to keep it concealed, until it was time to make her getaway. Again, this strange feeling of déjà vu vexed her. She made her way through the woods in search of the wizard's apprentice, whom she had seen locked away in a cage, in these woods. As she walked around the corner of the forest, she spied the top of the cage. She crouched down from view behind a bush and waited a few minutes to see if the wizard was going to show up in his unexpected ways, which always took her by surprise. After a few moments, she ran to the cage.

Toby recognized her right away and was relieved she had come to his rescue.

"Princess Ellyria! I thought that you would never hear my call," the boy said excitedly. She pulled some pins from her hair, then began to pick the lock.

"The keys are over there on that tree branch," he said, pointing in the direction they were in.

Princess Ellyria quickly ran over and got the key, inserting it into the lock, which clicked and fell from the door.

"Toby, run quickly. There is no telling when the wizard will come back. I have a horse hidden behind that large bush," she pointed out. "Wait for me there."

When she looked up beyond the cage, at the edge of the woods, she saw an unbelievable vision. It was Alfar. She slowly walked around the cage, afraid if she moved too fast he would vanish from sight. He was trying to tell her something, but he was too far away to understand. Princess Ellyria was suddenly grabbed from behind, and a cloth was placed over her mouth. She faded into unconsciousness…

Princess Ellyria awoke to her body trembling. Why was it so cold? It was the beginning of summer, but it felt like a winter storm had blown in. She finally opened her eyes to see where she was. The light was dim, her eyes followed the source of light that was created by only a few torches mounted in the corners of the walls. Once she got her bearings, she was horrified to find herself back in the very crystal cage that Liza had locked her in a few years ago. She stood up, then grasped the bars on the door to see if perhaps it was never locked, since she had been unconscious. Unfortunately, the door was locked, so she focused all her energy, pushing her hands out and hurling the energy ball she had created into the door. It still would not open.

Suddenly, Raul appeared from out of thin air before her.

"Enjoying your stay? I believe that you recognize the cage, do you not? It is the same one that I had constructed for that wretch, Liza. She was such an idiot for letting you get away. Not once, but twice. I do not know how she was ever able to function on a daily basis. I will not be so easily fooled by you, Princess. Not this time. I have got you where I want you," he sneered.

"I keep hearing you say that, but I never stick around long enough to see if that is true or not," she antagonized him. "Where are we anyway?"

"We are in the catacombs underneath the dungeon. It has not been in use for centuries I am sure, but I do plan to hide my army within these hidden passageways, that are miles and miles of empty tunnels leading out into different parts of the city and the forest."

"What army? My father destroyed most of Liza's army two years ago in the battle, and those who were not killed ran away like cowards. What army are you trying to rally? No one is going to fight for you!" she declared. She was now quite angered by him, she looked around for anything that she could use if she managed to get out of the cage. How would she get the wizard to release her? It was beyond any current ideas that she had at the present time.

"You can drop the innocent act, you stupid little girl. I do not understand how you were selected by the Gods to be the Chosen One, they must have been having a bad day," Raul scoffed, then laughed maniacally at her.

"What are you ranting about?"

How about I show you?" he offered, then motioned to the shadows for his new pet to emerge. "Draug, come forward." The undead soldier emerged in full battle armor.

"Yes, master."

Raul snapped his fingers, and the man collapsed.

"Why did you kill him?" she asked, recognizing him to be one of her brother's personal guards.

"I did not kill him, he was already dead," he explained, snapping his fingers as the man returned to his feet.

"How did you?" she whispered, too shocked for words.

"It is one of the new powers I took from that Seither bitch, from the Black Forest, which she so graciously gave to me. After I ripped out her heart of course."

"You are a sick monster of a man, wizard!"

"I am just getting started, my dear!" the wizard declared, then walked over to his drone and touched him with the Amulet of Elements.

Princess Ellyria could not believe her eyes. Stepping back from the cage she watched in horror as the undead man began to multiply. Not one, not two, but hundreds of them were emerging from his body! She was powerless to stop the wizard's madness, as he placed his army in single file lines filling the entire underground tunnel. She had no idea what she was going to do now, or how she could even stop him.

"What do you think you are going to do with that kind of an army?"

"I am surprised that you even have to ask, my dear. You can stop me, you know. Oh, wait, you are all locked up!" he bellowed. His laugh echoed through the tunnel, as one undead minion became thousands.

"You will not get away with this, I promise!" she screamed, then watched Raul pull a small vial from within the folds of his robes.

"Wait. What is that?"

It is the end of you, my dear," he smirked, then threw the potion vile through the bars at her.

The bottle shattered before her, as smoke filled the cage, causing the Princess to fall to the floor. Raul opened the cage door to let out the sparkly rays of light. He closed his eyes, then held out his hands open to either side of him allowing the powers to enter his body.

Princess Ellyria pushed herself up to sit on her hip. Her knees were still tucked underneath her, as she saw the majick being absorbed by the wizard.

"No!" she screamed, but it was too late, he had all her powers now.

The Princess hung her head low, knowing that she had failed. It was all over now, the wizard had won, then she passed out once more…

Princess Ellyria sat up screaming, sweat drenched her body, wondering where she was. She looked all around her from the bed that was not her own, both her hands and feet were restrained. She began to panic and started screaming.

Just then Lord Brom came in.

"Oh, Ellyria. I have been so worried that you would never awaken," he said, embracing her, before untying her bonds.

"What do you mean you thought that I would never wake up? Where are we?"

Lord Brom looked at her, placing his hand on hers.

"You had another one of your episodes. You started acting like you had these powers that you do not have again, and I had to restrain you. It was for your protection. I see that you are well now, so I can take them off."

"Where are we?" she asked again. Confused that she could not feel anything from him, or read his thoughts.

He looked at her and was puzzled that she did not know where she was.

"Do you not recognize our home? You always talked about that little cottage in the woods, so that is where we are," he said reassuring her.

Princess Ellyria stood up from the bed and began to walk around the cottage. It looked familiar, but she could not remember anything prior to her waking up. As she walked into the main living area, she saw a small boy.

"Brom, who is that boy?"

"Do you not remember him?"

She shook her head no.

"That is our son."

What happened to her? Why could she not remember anything? She swayed as if she were about to faint.

"Here why do you not come back here and lay down in the bed?" he urged, then picked her up gently and carried her to the bed. As he set her down, she looked up at him.

"Why do I not remember anything? I do not recall any of it. We have a house, a child, and I am guessing that we are married then?"

Lord Brom leaned in to kiss her, deeply, passionately. He closed the door, after making sure the boy was occupied. He returned to the bed, removed her clothes, then ravaged her body with kisses.

Princess Ellyria succumbed to his attack on her body, helpless to resist him. She felt his mouth cover every square inch of her body, and she returned his kisses with equal passion. He quickly removed his clothes, his magnificent body stood at the foot of the bed in front of her, then he crawled up between her legs spreading them wide. He rested his body between warm thighs, then returned to her mouth to kiss her with ardent fervor. She arched her body into his ready for him to enter her, but he stopped and delayed taking her right away. He grabbed her breasts, then squeezed them in his hands roughly taking a nipple into his mouth, biting it.

She pushed him away and sat up in bed, the feeling of déjà vu came back to haunt her.

"Why are you being so rough with me?"

"I am sorry, my love. I will try to be more gentle."

She started to speak again, but he silenced her with kisses before she ever had the chance to breathe a word. He laid her back down on the bed and nestled himself back in between her legs. She could feel his excitement for her, his hand was rubbing as he was probing her using his fingers. She arched her body into him, to let him know she was ready for him to take her. He plunged himself deep inside of her, the full length of him penetrating her very core. She received him fully and wrapped her legs around his back. The pleasure of him inside her was intoxicating, she closed her eyes, enveloping her arms tightly around his neck. He began to thrust harder and was at the point of release. She was near her release as well, they both were consumed with the throws of passion as they experienced releasing at the same time, completely spent. He withdrew himself from her and left her alone in the bed. Curious, she got up and followed him out of the room, to see what made him get up so suddenly. When she opened the door, she was back inside the cage…

Was this all a dream? She could not remember anything besides the very vivid dream she just had of Lord Brom. What was happening to her?

All of a sudden, Raul appeared again before her.

"I see that my dream spell has worn off. I knew that I should have given you a heavier dosage," he mused.

"When are you going to let me go? You have what you wanted from me, and I am no longer a threat to you. Please let me go."

"You are correct on one thing, my dear. You no longer have the burden of killing me. As to what I want from you, I think you already know the answer to that one, my pretty."

Princess Ellyria stepped back away from the cage as he opened it and went inside to claim his prize. He pinned her back up against the cage by her wrists, which he held tight in his hands. She cringed as she felt him lick the side of her face, dragging it to her mouth to thrust his tongue inside. He stopped instantly as he leaned over, the rolling pain in his loins were short lived as he caught the Princess trying to run out of her cell. He grabbed her, slinging her to the back of the cage, striking her hard across the face with the back of his hand. She fell to the floor helpless to fight him. He pinned her down with his power of telekinesis so that he could have full use of his hands, as he ripped open the front of her dress.

"You can be my Queen and rule at my side, when I take over the entire realm," he said breathlessly, as he forced himself between her legs."

"Never!" she screamed trying to fight him, but she could not move.

He leaned in to kiss her, she settled down for a moment, and as soon as he stuck his tongue in her mouth again, she bit it as hard as she could.

"You ungrateful bitch!" he screamed, splattering blood across her face as he spoke. Raul backhanded her again harder than the last time, leaving her there in the cage, locking the door behind him. "I shall return, and this time you had better be grateful that I chose you as my Queen. I can always fill you with a potion to make you more compliant," he said before he vanished.

Princess Ellyria tried to cover herself with the remnants of her dress, to fight off the cold that was consuming her. She had no way out of the cage, no powers, and no one knew where she was...

Chapter 33

Two days had passed, and still no word from the Princess. Lord Brom had begun to worry. Without wanting to alarm her parents, he took the gut feeling he had first to Princess Ellyria's oldest brother, Prince Anthony.

"Do not be so hard on yourself, you did not know, Brom. However, we are going to have to take this to my father. You need not worry, he is not as easily panicked about what my sister does, as much as my mother."

"Very well then, let us go see your, father. The sooner we tell him, the sooner we can leave."

"Then I take it that you have a plan in mind?"

"Yes, I do."

Prince Anthony and Lord Brom left the courtyard, where they were talking in private, to go see the King before they embark on their very important mission to find the Princess…

King Jason looked up to find his eldest son and Lord Brom standing before him in his study.

"Is there something that I can help you both with?"

"Yes, father. Lord Brom has it upon good reason that something bad has happened to Princess Ellyria."

"Is this true Lord Brom? What is it that has you concerned for her safety?"

"I have a feeling in my gut, Sire. No one has heard from her in two days, and I can not help but worry that something is wrong," Lord Brom explained.

"I know my daughter, and if I thought for one minute she was in danger, I would send out a search party for her. However, she is with the dragons, so I am not overly concerned at this time. I know that you have not been around her for quite some time, so you can not possibly understand that this is normal for her. Besides, two days is nothing, she has been away for longer periods of time than this. So I would not fret too much about her now. Give her a week, and I am sure that she will send word by then. She always does," he informed him.

"Sire, I do not think that I can, or should wait a week. Please, I mean no disrespect, but there is no way that I am going to wait around long enough to see if we do hear from her."

"Father, perhaps Lord Brom is correct. Can we afford to take the chance? She might have decided to go it alone on some hair-brained adventure, and has gotten herself into trouble. Perhaps just Brom, Dakota, Rowan, and myself can go looking for her? I know that you do not want to exhaust your men on a goose chase. What is the harm in sending us?"

"Perhaps you may have a point there, son. I shall allow it. As soon as you have any information, send word to me right away. That way if you need help, I can send it," he assured.

"Thank you, Sire." Lord Brom said.

They both had turned to leave the room when the King called to his son.

"Do you really think his gut feeling is on to something?"

"Yes, I do. He has always been right before when it came to Ellyria. Must be the connection between them. Thank you again, father," Prince Anthony said, before he left the room, passing his mother on the way out.

"Where is he going in such a hurry?" Queen Anna questioned. She pulled up a chair and sat down, while waiting for an answer from her husband, who looked perplexed about something. "Are you alright, dear?"

"Oh, yes. I am fine. Do you think there is a connection between Brom and Ellyria?" he asked. Her long pause let him know the answer already.

"Honestly, I believe there is. I think they are destined to be together somehow. What made you ask that?"

"Oh, nothing really. Something Anthony had said before he headed out."

"Where was he going? You never did tell me," she questioned again, worried by his silence.

"Brom had a feeling since he had not heard from Ellyria in two days, that something must be wrong. I told him it would be fine if he, Anthony, Dakota, and Rowan could go looking for her, just in case."

"What do you think? Should we be concerned?"

"I do not want you to worry, my love. I think that she is fine, because you and I both know that she goes for days on end with no contact. She may not have a messenger bird available to her, besides, she can take care of herself. Our daughter is very powerful," he said confidently.

Queen Anna stared at the floor, then looked back at her husband. She let out a quiet sigh to not let on to her husband that she was just as worried as Lord Brom was…

Prince Anthony had gathered his brothers. They each knew where they were to go in search of their sister. Prince Anthony would be going to Regnuom, to see if his brother King Ian had seen her. Prince Dakota was to go to Inamor, to speak with Mala and see if she had seen his sister. Prince Rowan was going to go to the Ormr Mountains, to speak to the Ancient One, even with the knowledge that it could be incredibly dangerous for him, as well as for Gaia. If Princess Ellyria were still with him, she would be able to vouch for him, since she was not, then he was on his own. Lord Brom was going to go looking in Narruc, to inquire the locals about the Princess's whereabouts. If no one had seen her there, then he had planned to travel into the Dark Forest of Woe, to the wizard's cottage and see if he was holding her hostage. He would find her, no matter the cost. Even if the price was his life. Lord Brom was given a horse to ride, Prince Anthony would ride Odin, Prince Dakota on Luna, and Prince Rowan on Gaia. They left on this quest with hopes of finding the Princess unharmed, but their worry for her well-being kept them focused and ready for whatever challenges that may arise. Prince Anthony carried his sword, Lord Brom carried a knife hidden in his boot, as well as a potion that could turn the wizard into stone if needed. Prince Rowan had Gaia for protection, and Prince Dakota carried a small armory of potions in his pouch, that he wore on his hip.

"Everyone knows what to do if they find Ellyria. The best thing is to get her back here as quickly as possible, then send word to the King that she has been found. I will do the same," Lord Brom instructed.

Lord Brom led them on the mission, with each brother going in their own direction on the same quest, to find Princess Ellyria and hopefully bring her home…

Lord Brom arrived in Narruc late that evening, when the sun was setting in the sky. His horse was exhausted, and so was he. He had decided to go look around in the marketplace and ask some of the merchantmen if they had seen, or heard of where the Princess might be. A young boy of the age of thirteen approached him, pulling him aside.

"I hear that you are looking for a princess. Would it be Princess Ellyria Rose that you are searching for?"

"Yes, how did you know?"

"I heard you asking around. I know where she is. At least I have a pretty good idea where she could be."

"How? Who are you?" he asked, grabbing the young boy's shirt, almost pulling him up off the ground. "If you know where she is, then I suggest that you had better take me to her at once!"

"I do, and you can put me down now, sir. I am not the one who has taken her, the wizard has. Harming me will not get you any closer to getting her back."

"How do you know this? Who are you?" Lord Brom asked again.

"My name is Toby, and I am the wizard's apprentice. I was the one that told the King where the wizard was hiding in the forest."

"Why betray your master then?"

"The wizard killed my father. He was the only family I had left in this world, and he killed him mercilessly. I know that I can not kill him myself, but the Princess can. Only then will I have my revenge, so I want to help her the best way that I can, without the wizard finding out."

"Do you know where he is keeping her, and can take me there?"

"Yes, I believe that he has her locked away somewhere beneath the castle's dungeon. I am not sure where exactly. I have only been down there once, from Raul dragging me along with him. I should be able to lead you there without him finding out. If he does, I know that he will kill me for sure for my betrayal, and then he will bring me back to life."

"What do you mean by bring you back to life?" Lord Brom questioned, confused by what he said.

"Raul can bring the dead back to life and make them do anything he commands of them. I saw him do it," Toby explained.

"Great. Now the wizard is a necromancer too? How did that happen?"

"He said that he got it from a Seither, in the Black Forest."

Toby tugged at Lord Brom's shirt. "Come, let us go now. We do not have much time."

Lord Brom followed Toby to the cellar, that he had used to get into the castle two years ago in search of his father and the Princess. He pulled open the doors, and the memories came flooding back to him...

Toby led Lord Brom through a maze of corridors, that seemed to go on forever in the near darkness. Many rats were accidentally stepped on, as they went deeper into the depths of the castle. When they had finally arrived, Toby stopped dead in his tracks, as Raul was there spooning something into the unconscious Princess's mouth.

"Stay hidden. I will go and distract him. As soon as we are gone, you go in and get her out of there. It will not take long for the wizard to figure out that I have lied to him," Toby advised him, as he went on to risk his life…

"Toby, what are you doing down here?" Raul asked, as he saw the boy running from the shadows.

"My Lord, come quick!" he said out of breath. "They have attacked the cottage!"

"Who did?"

"The King, and his men! They are searching for the Princess as we speak!" Toby shouted, in hopes that his ruse would work.

The wizard finished pouring the liquid into her mouth, to make sure she would not wake up while he was gone.

"Quick then, take my hand boy. Let me show you how we defend our home."

They vanished in a matter of seconds, giving Lord Brom maybe only a few minutes to get Princess Ellyria and himself out of the depths of the castle. Toby had told him that if he followed the tunnel strait it would take them to the other side of Narruc, well away from the forest and the castle walls. He found a key hanging on the wall and tried it, even with the possibility that it was not the right fit. However, the wizard did not have enough hindsight to have locked the cage door. He figured as much, as he was in a hurry to get back to the cottage, whatever he was feeding to Princess Ellyria, made him not be too worried about her getting up and walking out.

"Ellyria, wake up. It is I, Brom. Please wake up," he pleaded, then kissed her, but she would not awaken. The potion must be too strong. It had always worked in the storybooks, that his father had read to him as a child, so it was worth a try. He gently hoisted her up onto his back and began to make his way out of the cage, when Raul returned without the boy.

"Just where do you think you are going, Lord Brom? That is my future Queen you are carrying!"

Lord Brom did not hesitate to throw the potion at the wizard. Raul was not expecting it and began to turn to stone as soon as the vial crashed at his feet.

"That will hold you for quite a while. It was made especially for you, wizard!" he shouted, then smiled as the stone continued to consume him.

"No!" Raul shouted, before his head became entombed in the stone.

Lord Brom did not look back, as he headed into the tunnel and far away from the wizard. What he did not know, was that the wizard had taken Princess Ellyria's powers, making him all the more powerful, allowing him to break out of his

stone prison sooner than was expected. However, it was long enough for Lord Brom to get away with the Princess…

"Where is everyone at? You said that the King's guards, who were looking for the Princess, had attacked the cottage? Where are they? I see no one here, or any indication of them being here! What say you, boy!"

The wizard's words echoed in Toby's aching head. He pressed the sides of his temples, barely recalling what had just happened, when he saw the blood on his hand. The wizard had struck him with the back of his athame, promising that he would return to punish him soon enough. Well, soon enough would have to wait, as he struggled to get to his feet, after a loud jingle, he was back on the floor.

The wizard had chained him to the hearth, there was no running away now…

Lord Brom had finally made it out of the tunnel and carried the still unconscious Princess into the small nearby village. A slender, black-haired woman watched the man carry a woman, with the same color of hair, into the village. She knew this had to be the Princess...

"Pardon me, sir, but I think you had better follow me. It is for your own protection."

"Who are you, and why should I follow you?" he questioned the strange woman.

"I know that you do not know me, but I know that she is Princess Ellyria Rose of Toledya, and she needs my help."

"How do you know this, and who are you anyway?"

"My name is Raven, but we have no time for pleasantries. There is a wizard after you, right?"

"Well, yes. How did you know that?"

"Like I said there is no time, you must follow me if you want her to live," she pressed on. She led him to a small one-room cottage on the furthest side of the village.

Lord Brom laid Princess Ellyria on the cot, she was still sleeping from the potion.

"Here take my hand, we must pray."

"What? We have no time for pleasantries, but we have time to pray?"

"That is the only way that we can save her. It is not in my power to heal her, we must call to Freyja."

"Wait! What? Call to Freyja? Who are you really? I am not helping you call to anyone until you answer me!" Lord Brom demanded.

"I am a Valkyrie, and Freyja is my boss so to speak. Now, take a knee, mortal, and pray!" she ordered.

Lord Brom took a knee. Then he and Raven both prayed for Freyja to come to their aid.

Lightning cracked and thunder rolled as the Goddess appeared before them. Lord Brom stayed on the floor in sheer awe, that standing before him in all her beautiful glory was Freyja. He was speechless.

"Hrafn, I see that you have come to the Princess's aid, as our Father had requested of you."

"Yes, your Grace, I have. She is under a deep spell, that I can not awaken her from."

"Lord Brom, you may stand. Do you know what the wizard gave to her?"

"Only that it made her sleep," he said, and could not believe that Freyja had just spoken to him. His ears would never hear things the same as they did, upon hearing a voice so lovely as hers.

"I can undo what he did," Freyja announced. She simply touched Princess Ellyria's forehead, she opened her eyes, taking in a deep breath.

"Where am I?" Princess Ellyria questioned, trying to sit up. Her head ached, she could not remember what had happened.

"You are safe now. Are you alright?" Lord Brom questioned.

"I am not sure. Everything is still blurry," she said.

"Princess Ellyria, I am Raven, and she is the Goddess Freyja. We are here to help you, and to take you to Valhalla."

"Valhalla! What do you mean you are taking her to Valhalla? Does that mean she is dead?"

"No, Lord Brom. We are taking her to Valhalla to see Alfodr. He is the only one who can return her powers to her," Freyja explained.

"She is not dying then?"

"No, she is not. You are so gallant for your concern," Raven said smiling, trying to reassure him that the Princess would be alright. "You need to say your goodbyes now, Lord Brom," Raven added.

"What? You are taking her now?"

"Yes, we must. She is too weak and vulnerable to remain here. Trust in the Alfodr, he will heal her, then she will be returned to you, under your protection," Freyja informed him.

Lord Brom leaned over to kiss her and she smiled, too weak to even return his kiss.

"Step back, Lord Brom so you do not get caught in the Bilrost," Raven warned.

Lord Brom stood back, well away from the light that began to glow around them.

Thunder bellowed deep within the walls of the cottage, and lightning lit up all around them. When Lord Brom opened his eyes, they were gone…

Chapter 34

"Riders approach the gate, Sire," the tower guard said, upon his entry into the parlor where the King was spending an afternoon with his Queen.

"Thank you. Do you know who they are yet?"

"Not yet, Sire."

"Let me know as soon as you do."

"Right away, Sire."

The guard left the room, leaving the royal couple alone.

"Do you suppose it is our sons?" Queen Anna inquired, while looking out the parlor window.

"Perhaps, my love. It would be nice to have good news for a change," King Jason suggested. He tried to be optimistic with his wife, even though deep down he expected the worst of news. It is better to plan for the worst than to expect something better, he had always believed. He looked at his wife, still beautiful as always, but no matter how hard she tried to mask it, she was very vulnerable.

"Yes, it would indeed," she mused, then saw her sons approaching the courtyard.

The guard came in to announce their arrival before the Queen had the chance to relay it to her husband.

"Your sons have returned, your Grace."

"Did you see the Princess?"

"No, your Grace."

"Very well then, carry on," King Jason said, as he walked out with his wife to greet Prince Anthony, Prince Rowan, and Prince

Dakota…

"I am surprised to see that you all made it back here all at once. I take it you were not able to find your sister?"

"No, father. I am afraid we did not," Prince Anthony answered for the group.

"Did anyone hear as to whether she had been to any of the locations that you had searched for her in?" Queen Anna questioned.

"No, I am afraid not, mother," Prince Dakota said.

"Why do we not all go into the parlor, so you three can tell us what you did find, shall we?" their father suggested.

The group retired to the parlor, each son with his own story to tell…

"Anthony, why do you not start? How was Ian? Did he look as though he was keeping Regnuom under control?"

"Yes, father. He is doing quite well. He did say that it was so peaceful there most of the time, and he becomes bored without something to do. He wanted me to ask you what you did to keep your sanity during your downtime. Besides that, he had not seen, or heard from our sister since he had left," Prince Anthony explained. King Jason laughed over learning about his son's boring reign.

"You will have to send word to your brother that I have no complaints. I have all of my children to worry over, and a beautiful wife that keeps me plenty occupied during my 'downtime' as he called it."

"I shall be sure to tell him that, father," Prince Anthony replied.

"Dakota, what did you find out in Inamor," Queen Anna asked.

"Well, mother, I spoke with Mala, but she had not heard from Ellyria since she had left for Inamor last summer. She was surprised to hear that she went to study with the dragons. I was surprised she had not spoken to Mala since then. I had believed them to be close, after everything that she had gone through with Alfar and the entire Black Forest adventure from last summer. Alas, she had not heard anything from anyone else that might have seen her," Prince Dakota informed his family.

"That is strange, that even Mala has not heard from Ellyria. I also thought they kept in close contact," Queen Anna stated.

"What did you find in the dragon mountain, Rowan? Where you able to find out where Ellyria had gone to?" King Jason questioned.

"I was able to speak to the Ancient One, and he told me that he had sent her on a quest to Niflheim, the Underworld, to seek out the Goddess, Hella. I was not permitted to go after her. Nidhoggr did say that it would be a long journey for Ellyria, and that she may have received information on how to acquire the Amulet of Elements from the wizard. So my guess is that is exactly where she went too," Prince Rowan suggested.

"You are half-correct," Lord Brom interrupted, upon entering the parlor. Everyone turned to the entryway and saw him standing there, looking very travel-worn.

"Did you see Ellyria? Do you know where she is?" Queen Anna questioned, fighting back her tears.

Lord Brom walked into the parlor and sat down beside Prince Rowan.

"Yes. The wizard lured her into his trap, by allowing her to think she was rescuing his apprentice, Toby. When in actuality, it was Raul disguised as the boy. He trapped her in a crystal cage and stole her powers somehow. Toby led me to her and caused a distraction, but when the wizard realized Toby's deception, he came back for Ellyria. I used the potion Dakota gave me, which encased the wizard in stone, allowing me enough time to grab Ellyria and escape. I took her to a small village outside of Narruc, where a Valkyrie approached us. She called to the Goddess Freyja to heal

Ellyria, since she was weakened by Raul's sleeping potion. Then they both took her to Valhalla," Lord Brom relayed his story.

Everyone else finally closed their gaping mouths, as King Jason was trying to calm his fretting wife, who was now crying into her hands.

"You do not mean to say that she has died, do you?" King Jason questioned.

"Oh no, Sire. She is to go before the Alfodr, so that he can restore her powers in order for her to defeat the wizard once and for all."

"She is going to be alright then?" Queen Anna asked, in between sobs.

"Yes, your Grace. Princess Ellyria will be returned under my protection. I am to help her with whatever she may need, to complete her destiny," Lord Brom stated.

"Well, that is what we all should do," Prince Anthony chimed in.

"Yes, I agree." Prince Rowan said.

"As do I," said Prince Dakota.

"Good. Ellyria will need us all behind her, every step of the way," King Jason announced.

"So, what do we do now?" Prince Anthony asked.

"Nothing for now. We can only wait for her to return from the heavens," Lord Brom said, before he got up to leave the room…

Lord Brom left for the courtyard to where the big fountain was, where he had seen Princess Ellyria play in the water with Isis. He had watched her for several minutes that day, before he had gotten ready to leave. The same day she had followed him into the stables, wearing only the cotton dress that clung to her besotted, curvy body, making it transparent to see the succulent peaks of her rosy nipples. He sat down on the edge of the fountain and raked his hand through the cool water, imagining her dancing around him, wet, and carefree…

Chapter 35

Raul appeared in the small village that was between Narruc and Toledya. He looked around at all the people too busy with their work, to even take notice that he was there. Farmers were busy working in their gardens, or herding livestock into small fenced-in areas. Women were by the well, hoisting up water to put in their pots to cook in, or to wash their clothes. Children were at play, running amuck, laughing, oblivious to adult responsibility, and completely innocent. Raul was only passively amused by all of the business steadily going on around him. Without warning, he began sending objects into the air with just a flick of the wrist. People screamed, then ran in fear for their lives as axes, spades, and carts fell down all around them. Using the power of the Amulet of Elements, he was able to shoot fireballs from his hands onto straw houses, which immediately burst into flames. His favorite part was watching those who lived there run out screaming, or become trapped inside. Panic swept over the village. Fathers ran to protect their homes and families, and mothers ran to find their children. No one was safe from the wizard's wrath of destruction. Out of the corner of his eye, Raul noticed a small child had run into the safety of his cottage.

"Just where do you think you are going, you little bastard!" Raul shouted, as he walked over to the cottage. "Do not make me blow your house in, boy!" he threatened. Crying was heard from inside the small one-room cottage. Raul took in a deep breath before he expelled the air from his lungs, his breath came out with fury, as he watched the house collapse in on itself. Raul laughed wickedly as the villagers ran screaming into their homes, from the dust storm he created by simply waving his hands in the air. He was too powerful for anyone to dare stand against him, and those who remained in their homes out of fear, did not realize that it would also become their tomb.

Raul closed his eyes, outstretched his arms to either side of him, and slowly came off the ground, hovering in the air. He made a fist with each hand before punching a crater into the village, causing all the homes to fall with a loud boom. The screams were heard from his pedestal above, as they drowned out his maniacal laughter. What could he possibly do to top what he had done so far? He burned their homes, blew them down, created a giant crater, and now there was nothing left. What should he do now? The wizard must have had a muse on his shoulder when the next idea came to him. He would create his very own lake. With the power from the amulet, he created such a storm over the village. That in no time at all, those who could not swim, drowned, and those who could, were still pulled down from the vacuum created by the debris, while lifeless bodies surrounded them. The wizard reappeared on the nearby hill, watching the devastation that he created with his limitless powers. Now that he had his new powers under control in unison with the power from the amulet, it was time to show Narruc their new leader, and proclaim himself a god.

Raul appeared in the middle of the bustling city. He snapped his fingers, and about a dozen of his undead minions appeared on either side of him.

"Good citizens of Narruc. For those who do not know me, I am the wizard Raul, your new King, and your new God! Bow down before me now, profess your loyalty to me, and you shall live. Turn against me, or try to fight me, and I promise that you will die," he proclaimed.

The people of Narruc stood there dumbfounded, absorbing

what they had just heard. A few of them took a knee, but others grabbed axes, pitchforks, and spikes.

"Our loyalty lies with the King in Toledya!" one man shouted.

"Yeah, our loyalty is with our King, not with the likes of you!" another man yelled.

Those carrying pitchforks and axes made their way towards Raul. The wizard merely waved his hand, sending the weapons in the air before turning around to face the men. They began to run, but it was too late. Raul had already killed them with their own weapons. Panic took over, as the people ran, screaming with fear, and scrambling to get away from the tyranny of the wizard.

"See, that is only a small warning. How about I set a real example of my power," he laughed maniacally. "Go, my minions! Go, and teach them a lesson they will never forget."

The minions began to pillage the city, every man who had tried to fight against them was slain, every innocent child was slaughtered, and every woman was raped, and murdered. It was only a small demonstration of his power, but it was enough for them to get the message, as he watched his minions do his bidding.

"Hear me now!" he screamed to the heavens. "Hear me, people of Narruc! I am your new God! Pledge your loyalty to me, and I will stop the murder of your men, raping of your women, and the slaughter of your children. Proclaim me as your new King, and pray to me as your God!" Thunder sounded in the distance and the people did as they were told out of fear of their new ruler, and deity.

Raul now had one kingdom under his rule, but soon he would have the other three...

Chapter 36

Princess Ellyria arrived in Valhalla with Freyja and Raven. She was still weak from Raul's potions, but was able to take in all the beauty of the magnificent great hall. Golden shields adorned the ceilings, spears aligned the walls, chest plates and armor made up most of the benches, it was truly a sight to behold. The Princess could not help but stare when they finally arrived before the Alfodr. Freyja, Raven, and Princess Ellyria all took a knee before him.

"Rise my children. Hrafn, I see that you have completed the task I sent you to do. Well done, I am very pleased. Freyja, my child, I want to thank you for answering the call, when they were in need of you. Princess Ellyria Rose, my Chosen One, you have been through many challenging obstacles. I believe this one, may be your greatest challenge yet," Alfodr declared.

"I am sorry that I have failed you. I am no longer worthy of being your Chosen One," Princess Ellyria responded softly, unable to keep her butterflies in line.

"That, my child, will be up to me to decide. I have taken up with the council about what I should do with you. It was unanimous that I give you second chance. You have already proven yourself at times with your honesty, bravery, and wisdom. At times, I know that you have been lost, but I know it was from the lack of guidance that you truly needed. I am challenging you to a test. A test of three, to be exact. The first will be of wisdom, the second of courage, and the third of virtue. These tests are to see whether you really are the Chosen One. If you fail, you will be returned to your world without any previous memories, or any knowledge of who you once were. If you pass, you will be returned to your world with the knowledge of who you will become. Do you accept this challenge?"

"Yes, Alfodr. I will accept your challenge, and I will complete the tests to the best of my ability," Princess Ellyria stated confidently.

"Excellent. The first test is wisdom. I will ask a question, and you will answer as honestly as humanly possible. Whom would you protect first, your family, or the realm?" Alfodr questioned.

"The realm. As much as I love my family, the fate of the many takes precedence over the fate of the few," she said without hesitation.

Both Freyja and Hrafn looked at each other and smiled. Alfodr gave them a knowing glance before he proceeded with the next test.

"The second test is that of courage. For this test you will need a spear," he ordered, then motioned for a spear to be given to the Princess.

Hrafn handed the Princess a spear and took one for herself.

"I do not understand. What am I to do with this?" Princess Ellyria questioned.

Hrafn wasted no time in challenging her to a fight, as she lunged straight for her. Princess Ellyria avoided her attack, but paused in confusion.

"I can not fight her! I have no training in battle, or with a weapon for that matter," she exclaimed fretfully. Her words were nearly cut short as the Valkyrie led her attack again, this time swinging the blunt end into Princess Ellyria, knocking her to the ground.

Freyja looked at Alfodr, casting a worried glance his way. He only signaled that he was not stopping the test for the Princess's lacking skills in combat. Hrafn waited for Princess Ellyria to get back up before she resumed her attack. This time, she was surprised when the Princess swung the spear around to block her move. Squaring off again, the women walked slowly around in almost a full circle before Hrafn lunged again. Princess Ellyria waited patiently, before twisting herself around with the blunt of the spear to relay the attack on her aggressor. The Valkyrie smiled, impressed by the girl's quick thinking, and her desire to continue the fight. This time, it was Princess Ellyria who caught Hrafn off guard by leading the attack, swinging the spear back and forth into its rival.

Alfodr became amused by the display, Freyja never took her eyes off of Princess Ellyria, who was not backing down. Hrafn tried to disarm the girl, but was shocked when her feet were kicked out from under her. She landed on her back, dropping her weapon in the process. Princess Ellyria stood over her, with the spear aimed at her throat, and had a foot firmly pressed into her adversary's chest. Hrafn was not only surprised, but also slightly frightened by the wild emerald eyes staring down at her.

"I may have accepted the challenge to fight you, but I will not harm you," she said holding out her hand for Hrafn, to help her to her feet.

When the Valkyrie rose, the two women embraced each other and smiled.

"You showed tremendous bravery," Hrafn said to Princess Ellyria before walking away.

"That was a true test of courage indeed. There are two kinds of courage, physical, by acting in spite of possible harm to one's body, and moral, acting in a way that depicts one's belief that is good despite others' disapproval. Your actions have encouraged me to allow you a glimpse into what life may be like for you if you choose for yourself not to be the Chosen One. This will be your choice alone, and it will lead you to continue to the third and final test, or it can lead you back to a normal life. Close your eyes child and let me show you what life could be like for you, if you give up your destiny," he advised.

Princess Ellyria closed her eyes. At first, she saw nothing, only darkness that gave way to light. She was with Lord Brom. They seemed happy together, and she had no powers or visions, just a normal life that seemed to be full of love. They had a child between them, a son who looked like his father. She smiled at the vision in her mind, which swiftly led to tears staining her cheeks. Raul had taken over the land, the wizard's tyranny showed no mercy on all those who challenged him, and those that followed did so only to stay alive. Great sorrow was felt even without her powers, as she came out of the vision barely able to catch her breath in between sobs. She fell to her knees before Alfodr and looked up at him with a humble heart.

"Please, I must get back to those people. The men, women, and children, they need me to save them from the wizard. His undead army has helped give him power that he is abusing, without any remorse for the pain he is inflicting on these people. How can I save them? I no longer have my powers. Is there any other way he can be defeated? I know his heart must be cut out, and destroyed, but is there another way I can get close to him to do so? He still has the Amulet of Elements, and I still have no idea how to get it back. Tell me what I must do, and I will do it," she offered courageously. She watched as Raven, Freyja, and Alfodr exchanged glances.

"You have proven yourself to have great wisdom, it is always a difficult choice to choose between the lives of the ones that we love, and the lives of strangers. You fought bravely even though you lacked the skills needed in combat. You also proved the greatest amount of fortitude by not killing your opponent when you had the opportunity to do so. Your actions in valor proved that your heart wins in the battle over bloodlust, which can lead to self-destruction. The third test was proven by your tremendous amount of virtue. No matter how much you want to be with the one you love, you put the love for everyone else above your own personal desires. The fate of the realm lies in your hands and no one else. It is your destiny alone to save the innocent from the evil that wants to consume them. Princess Ellyria Rose of Toledya, the Chosen One, the only one who was prophesied long ago to destroy evil and bring peace throughout the lands again. I bestow upon you The Power of Litha!" Alfodr proclaimed, then struck the floor three times with his staff, before directing it towards Princess Ellyria.

A bolt of lightning shot out, and thunder echoed throughout the great hall. A colorful array of dancing lights surrounded her, as she held out her hands on either side of her, this time accepting the power to enter her once again. Freyja and Hrafn went to Princess Ellyria, then embraced her after she had been blessed with her powers once more.

"Now, I will return you to Toledya so you can prepare for your greatest challenge yet. You must get the Amulet of Elements from the wizard. He still has the powers he stole from you, making him nearly impossible to kill. The amulet will be your greatest tool to utilize against him. Without it, I am afraid that you will fail, and the entire realm will perish."

"How can I get the amulet away from him? He wears it around his neck, and I have already tried many times to get it back," Princess Ellyria explained.

"I can not tell you that. It will be up to you to figure out a way to get it back on your own. However, I can tell you that it is alright to call for help when needed," he advised.

"Thank you, Alfodr. I will not let you down," she swore.

"Do not let the people of the realm down, my child. I must send you back to your world alone, to complete your destiny. To Toledya!" Alfodr shouted.

The thunder bellowed in the distance, a crack of lightning streaked from the ceiling encircling Princess Ellyria, then she was gone…

Princess Ellyria appeared in her bedroom chamber. She walked over to her vanity and sat down before her mirror. After a quick glance at herself, she ran downstairs to the parlor where everyone was still gathered together. It was like time had paused until her return. Lord Brom was the first to run and embrace her, followed by her family.

"I am so happy to see you," Lord Brom whispered in her ear. He also took notice that her dress was no longer ripped, and her hair had appeared as if it had never been disheveled.

Queen Anna was next in line, and she looked at her daughter who had returned looking as though nothing had happened.

"I was so worried about you," her mother said.

Her father and brothers all greeted her next, taking turns to embrace her. Princess Ellyria turned to everyone and smiled, grateful to be home with everyone around her that she loved.

"I have missed you too," came a strange voice in her head. She looked around in confusion. It was not coming from Lord Brom, or her family.

"What is the matter, dear?" the Queen asked her daughter, who looked to be quite distracted.

"I am not sure," she said, walking over to Isis, who was sitting in the doorway waiting to greet her as well.

"I have missed you too," the voice said again.

"Who are you?" Princess Ellyria questioned.

"With whom are you speaking to, Ellyria?" Prince Dakota questioned, watching his sister start talking to herself.

"Tell him you are talking to me," the voice said again, only this time Isis placed a paw into Princess Ellyria's hand.

"Isis? Is that you?"

Prince Dakota knew exactly what was going on, but he thought he had better clear it up with everyone else, because to them it looked as though the Princess had gone mad.

"Ellyria, are you hearing what Isis is thinking?" Prince Dakota asked.

"Yes! I think I am! Isis? Are you really talking to me?"

"Yes! Finally, you can understand me! Tell them that you are not crazy."

"Dakota, are you thinking what I am?"

"Yes, sister. I believe that you have received your third power," he mused.

Lord Brom and everyone else in the room were speechless.

They knew she would be receiving the power to call upon the aid of animals and communicate with them, but they just were not sure when.

"I understand what the Alfodr meant, when he told me I could call for help if I needed it," she burst out.

"What does that mean?" Lord Brom inquired.

"It means that I have an idea of how to get the amulet back from the wizard."

"Wait, Ellyria! You just got home. Should you not rest for a few days and get your strength back?" her father asked.

"I plan to rest tonight, but tomorrow is a new day. I can not give the wizard any more time to have the upper hand. I must get the amulet back."

Lord Brom was amazed by the differences in her, how she appeared to be so confident, and more fearless than ever before.

"What do you need from us?" King Jason questioned.

"I need a plan to go with my idea," she stated.

"Strategy is my specialty," Prince Anthony offered.

"We will help too," Prince Rowan and Prince Dakota chimed in at once.

"Good, then it is settled. We shall work on the battle plan tonight, then tomorrow we go to Narruc to take back what is rightfully mine," Princess Ellyria announced. She led her brothers and Lord Brom out of the parlor to go over the plan.

This was to be Princess Ellyria's greatest challenge yet…

CHAPTER 37

Princess Ellyria, Lord Brom, and Prince Rowan left before dawn, riding Gaia to the Ormr Mountains to warn Nidhoggr of the wizard's undead army. When the trio arrived, it was Princess Ellyria and Prince Rowan who left to speak to the Dragon King. Lord Brom stayed behind with Gaia, who kept nudging him with her head playfully, knocking him over.

"Will you stop that? You overgrown lizard. Has your master not taught you any manners? Ouch! Cut that out!" Lord Brom chided. Gaia stopped and flopped over on her back, kicking her legs in the air. Lord Brom shook his head at her odd behavior, then sat down beside her. "You are a peculiar dragon, are you not?" he mused, then heard her let out a snort before she rolled back over, and curled up to take a nap. She had the right idea. It would help pass the time, while they waited for Princess Ellyria and Prince Rowan's return from the mountain…

Princess Ellyria and Prince Rowan were glad they had left so early, before it had gotten too hot for the half a day's walk to the mountain. When they had finally arrived, Nidhoggr stood at the entrance, as if he knew they were coming.

"Princess Ellyria, this is beginning to become a habit for you. Is it not? What will the other dragons think of your constant visits?"

"See, I knew he could be charming when he wanted to, brother," she teased.

"If you say so," Prince Rowan said unimpressed.

"What can I do for you this time?" the dragon growled.

"I have come to you with a warning. The wizard Raul has created an undead army of thousands. He must be stopped before he wages war on the four kingdoms. I am going to take the Amulet of Elements away from him, but I am going to warn everyone to prepare for war first. Do I have your aid in this? Can I count on you as an ally?"

"I am afraid not, Princess. I can not justify being a part of this human war. Dragons have already gone to war for humans and mankind turned their backs on us, saying we were the enemy. I will not subject my race to such needless deaths again. This is not our fight, it is yours. I am sorry that I can not help you. I do suggest that you go and warn the others. They are the ones that will need your help. The wizard would not dare bring an army here, because he will fail upon arrival," Nidhoggr advised, turning his back to his visitors, and waiting for them to see themselves out.

"He will bring this war to your doorsteps, just as he will bring it to every corner of the realm. You will have to decide what side to fight on, but I can guarantee you that I will not let the wizard win this war. Come on, Rowan. He is no help to us, let us go now," she warned. Princess Ellyria looked back to find Nidhoggr watching her as they were leaving. She had wanted not only to warn him, but to gain him and his kind as allies in the fight against the wizard, and his undead army…

As the midday sun was approaching in the summer sky, Lord Brom saw Princess Ellyria, and Prince Rowan coming back. When they approached, the look in his love's eyes told him that she did not achieve her goal.

"How did it go with the Dragon King?

"He is not going to help us."

"At least he is not going to be on their side either, sister. Be grateful, because that would have greatly put a damper on things."

"Well, where to now?" Lord Brom asked.

"We go to Regnuom and work our way over to the Black Forest, then to Inamor. We must warn everyone. I have a feeling we will not be needing to warn anyone in Narruc," Princess Ellyria suggested.

They all mounted Gaia and headed to Regnuom, to warn their brother, Ian, and to warn Lord Brom's family as well...

Upon their arrival in Regnuom, newly crowned King Ian gave them a warm welcome. Although, he suspected their visit was not just a social call.

"So what brings you here? How is everyone in Toledya? I hope all is well," he said, as he embraced his sister, his brother, and Lord Brom. King Ian sat down at his desk and ran his fingers through his thick dark brown hair.

"I am sorry to be the bearer of bad news, brother. We have come to warn you that the wizard Raul has created an undead army and plans to attack all of the kingdoms. We are on our way to warn everyone. You must gather your armies, and prepare for war."

"Of course, we will fight alongside our father, and together we will fight to the death if we have to," he said proudly, standing up from his desk, and leaving the room for a moment. When he returned, he brought his head knight with him. "I am having my man gather all of the able-bodied men, to fight for us in this war. We will protect Regnuom, and we will fight to protect the other kingdoms as well," he assured them.

"Good. Then it is settled. We must go and warn my father and brother, to take his family, and go back out to sea," Lord Brom told them.

"Send word to our father that we were here to warn you, so he knows that you are going to gather your men for the war, and that we are safe," Princess Ellyria added, then embraced King Ian before she prepared to leave.

The trio left for Lord Thomas's province, to warn him as well of the coming war...

A knock at the door alerted Lord Thomas to company, that he was not expecting. When he opened the door, his guests were pleasant ones indeed.

"Brom. What a nice surprise! I see that you have brought friends. How nice to see you again, Princess Ellyria, and Prince Rowan too. What brings you here, Brom?" he said, holding the door for everyone to come in.

"I am afraid that this is not a social call, father. Where is my brother? He needs to hear this too," Lord Brom announced.

"He is in the kitchen helping Nicole. Wait here, and I shall go get him."

Lord Thomas left, and a few moments later produced Brom's brother, Captain Jake.

"Brother!" Captain Jake shouted upon seeing him. As they embraced, the Princess caught his eye. "And hello again, your Highness," he said bowing before her, then watched her laugh at the gesture.

"It is good to see you too. This is my brother, Prince Rowan. Prince Rowan, this is Captain Jake, Lord Brom's brother," she introduced.

"Father says this was not a social gathering, that you had something important to tell us."

"Yes. Is there somewhere we can go to talk? I do not want to upset Nicole in her delicate condition."

"Yes, of course. We can go into the study," Captain Jake offered, then led everyone to the study, and shut the door.

"Now, what is going on, Brom?" Lord Thomas questioned his son.

"The wizard, Raul, has created an undead army. He plans to attack the four kingdoms and start a war. I thought it would be best that we come to warn you personally, so you can take the family to the Draki, and go out to sea where everyone will be safe," Lord Brom advised, allowing for his words to sink in for his father and brother, to absorb what they had just heard.

"Will King Ian need every able-bodied man to fight in the war?" Captain Jake asked.

"Yes, and he is gathering men right now to prepare for the wizard's attack," Prince Rowan chimed in.

"It will be better that you stay with your wife during her time of need, brother. She should not bring your child into this world without his father there, only to find out that he has gone to war," Lord Brom suggested.

"I can not just sit back and watch my crew be led into battle without me," Captain Jake said worriedly.

"Then appoint Rob the Red as acting Captain. He is a great leader, and I know that you will not be able to keep him away from a good fight."

"I suppose that I could, but I should still be there to fight for my family."

"You are. You are keeping them alive, and without a full crew for that ship, you will have to be the one to stay and run it," Lord Brom added. He knew that he had finally gotten through his brother's thick skull about the whole thing. Now it was up to Captain Jake to break the news to his wife.

"We really need to be going. I am so sorry that we brought such bad news. After we have finished alerting everyone else, I am going after the wizard to increase our odds of winning this war. Congratulations on the newest addition to your family, Jake," the Princess said, embracing him before they left the room.

Just as they began to file out of the room, Nicole had come out of the kitchen looking for everyone.

"Where is everyone going? I have not had the honor of meeting any of you yet."

"Dear, I would like you to meet Princess Ellyria Rose and her brother, Prince Rowan," Captain Jake said, making the introductions. "I am afraid that they can not stay, and they must be going now."

"It was lovely meeting you," Princess Ellyria said. "I am sorry that we can not visit longer, perhaps next time, when we are not just passing through."

"Yes, good to meet you both," Prince Rowan added.

Lord Thomas showed them out, as Captain Jake stayed behind to explain the purpose of their visit. Princess Ellyria could feel Nicole's fear and pain. She could not imagine what it must be like for her to be with child and hear such horrible news, without any sure way of knowing the outcome of it all.

"Thank you, father. I am sorry it is by such bad circumstances that brought us here."

"It is alright, my son. Just be careful, all of you. I hope to see each and every one of you when this is all over," Lord Thomas announced, embracing his son. "You take care of my son, young lady," he teased the Princess, before they walked out the door.

"I will, sir. I promise."

As the door was closed behind them, there were still many more to open, with the hope of getting the warning out to everyone, before it was too late.

"To Inamor, sister?" Prince Rowan shouted, as they rose up into the air.

"Yes, brother. To Inamor, then we shall go to the forest, and warn the Queen."

Princess Ellyria watched from above, as the kingdom grew smaller the higher they climbed

into the sky. They appeared as though they were tiny ants scurrying about the land, and that is exactly how the wizard would see them. She had to stop him before he crushed them all…

Mala was equally surprised, as she was grateful to see her friend. Princess Ellyria introduced her brother and Lord Brom to her, as they entered Mala's tent.

"What brings you on such a pleasant visit?"

"Not so pleasant, I am afraid," Princess Ellyria said.

"What do you mean?" Mala was concerned.

"Raul has created an undead army, which he plans to use to storm the kingdoms. Mala, I know your people are peaceful, and they only fight when it is brought to them, but I need you to rally them together and prepare for the war that is coming."

"How will we defend ourselves against an army like that? We are not capable of such a battle."

"Perhaps not in battle, but you are capable of majick. This army was created from majick, so you should be able to fight them back with majick of your own," Princess Ellyria suggested.

"I will alert the rest of the gypsies," Mala said.

"I am going to warn the Faery Queen in the forest as well after we leave here, then I am going after the wizard to take back the amulet."

"That is good of you to warn her. Even though faeries are mischievous, they do a lot of good to help nature flourish. How do you plan to get the amulet back?"

"I was going to ask if you could advise me on that very subject."

"I do not understand."

"I have received my gift to call upon the aid of the animals, but I need to know which animals to call, to help distract the wizard long enough to take the amulet off his neck," Princess Ellyria asked.

"The woodland creatures of the forest. They have had their homes destroyed by the wizard. They will make the strongest allies in this case. Use your own judgment, and trust your instincts. They will lead you in the right direction," Mala advised, as everyone prepared to leave.

"Thank you again, Mala. I will see you soon. I wish that I could stay longer, but we really must be going to the Black Forest, and warn them before it is too late," Princess Ellyria said.

"Take care and be careful, my friend," Mala said.

"I will, thank you, Mala," she replied, embracing her friend.

Princess Ellyria, Prince Rowan, and Lord Brom waved farewell to their friend, leaving for the Black Forest to warn the Queen of the coming war...

The Black Forest was just as she had left it, in all of its beautiful, natural glory. Tiny sprites came out from the protection of the trees, to greet the one that had saved their lives. Before she called to the Queen, she looked over to the tree that stood where Alfar had been buried. She walked over by herself, leaving Prince Rowan and Lord Brom waiting by the Elder Tree.

"What is she doing, Rowan?"

"Did she ever tell you about Alfar?"

"No. Who is Alfar? What does it have to do with that tree?"

"If she has not told you, then I had better not. I shall let her explain it," Prince Rowan told him.

Princess Ellyria touched the baby Elder Tree that was not yet fully grown, but was still taller than her, and equally as wide as her body. Placing a hand gently on the tree, she closed her eyes to see if she could sense him. Although she could not, she then returned to the Elder Tree to call upon the Faery Queen, Redomredlyh. She looked up into the branches of the ancient tree, stretching her arms high above her.

"Redomredlyh, great Queen of the Faeries, please grace me with your presence, as I call you near," Princess Ellyria chanted.

A bright light descended from the highest bough. The Queen landed softly before the Princess and smiled at her.

"Welcome, your Highness. I see that you have brought friends."

"Yes, my brother, Prince Rowan, and my friend, Lord Brom. We are here to bring you important news. The wizard Raul has created an undead army, and he is using them to conquer the kingdoms. I know your forest is well protected, but it will not be from him, or his army. You must prepare to protect yourselves against his assault. I am going to try and stop him, but if he strikes before I can get to him, lead your people out of the forest, and go as far away from here as you can. Do you understand?" Princess Ellyria advised, watching the peaceful being smile at her, although she did not appear frightened.

"I will place a protective shield over the forest once you leave. It should be strong enough against his majick," she said.

"He is a very powerful wizard, the force field may not prove to be enough protection. You may have to flee the forest," Princess Ellyria warned.

"I promise that we will be alright, thank you for the warning, Princess," the Queen said, then embraced Princess Ellyria, before she returned to the safety of the tree.

"Do you think she comprehends the gravity of the situation?" Prince Rowan inquired.

"I am not sure, brother. However, I will have to come to their aid, if they are attacked," she informed him.

"So, who is Alfar?"

"Thanks, Rowan."

"What did I do?"

"It is not his fault. I asked him what was up with that tree over there," Lord Brom interrupted.

"Come with me, and I will tell you," Princess Ellyria offered, then led Lord Brom to Alfar's tree.

"Last summer, I met a Halfling who was kidnapped by an evil Seither, the one who had cursed this very forest. I rescued him from her, only to lose him at the wizard's hand. The curse was lifted, but it was too late, and his mother, the Queen, could not heal him in time. I loved him, and I was surprised that I could. I never thought I could love another, as I had loved you, but I did," she confessed, then kept her head down to shield her eyes from falling tears.

Lord Brom lifted her chin gently to wipe the tears from her cheeks, before he kissed her soft lips. She kissed him back, but could not shake the image of Alfar's face. It was as though he was watching out for her, making sure that she was happy.

"We have to go to Narruc," she said, pushing him away.

"Are you sure that you want to go now?"

"The sooner we leave and get the amulet back, the sooner we can start preparations for the coming war."

"Will he not give up once you get the amulet?"

"No. In fact, it will make him come after me with a vengeance," Princess Ellyria said, as they turned to tell Prince Rowan they were ready to leave.

Princess Ellyria waited for a moment, as she allowed Lord Brom to walk out ahead of her, at least long enough to say goodbye one last time to her Elvin Prince…

As they flew over Narruc, Princess Ellyria was struck by all the pain, fear, and misery coming from the people down below. When they landed at the edge of the woods, she was surprised by the animals that had already gathered, as if awaiting her arrival.

"What are all these animals doing here?" Princess Rowan questioned.

"I do not know."

"Perhaps they sensed you're here, just as well as you can sense them." Lord Brom suggested.

"Could be," she said giggling.

"Well, how is this supposed to work?" Prince Rowan asked.

"I am not sure exactly. I am thinking it will be the same way it was when I spoke with Isis, telepathically," Princess Ellyria said. She closed her eyes, before she had the chance to focus her energies into one of the animals, she heard the voice of the wise owl sitting in the nearby tree.

"We need your help. An evil man has taken over the forest, and we need your help to get rid of him," the owl screeched.

"I will try, I promise, but first, I need your help, as well as all the forest creatures that you can gather. That evil man has something that belongs to me," she informed the owl.

"You tell me what you need us to do, and we will do it," the owl offered.

"I need the amulet he is wearing around his neck. Once I have it, it will make it easier for me to have the power to fight him."

"Very well, Princess. Consider the task done," the owl stated, flying from the tree screeching his message to the other animals.

Princess Ellyria, Prince Rowan, and Lord Brom watched in amazement, as many different species of animals gathered together and made their way toward the wizard's cottage.

"What do you think they will do?" Prince Rowan asked.

"How do you think they will manage to get the amulet off of the wizard's neck?" Lord Brom questioned.

"I am not sure how, but they are going to go get it. I feel guilty in sending those poor, innocent animals to their possible death," she sighed.

"I think they will be alright. They are wild creatures after all," Prince Rowan said trying to comfort her.

"Try not to think about it. It is for the good of the entire realm, remember that. If they do not help you, they will not have a home at all. I am certain that if the wizard succeeds, the first thing he will wipe out is the forest, since he will no longer have to hide in it," Lord Brom stated.

"You both have a point, and I hope that they can succeed."

Princess Ellyria stood at the edge of the clearing, watching as the forest animals disappeared into the Dark Forest of Woe…

Chapter 38

Raul was working diligently on his strategy for the upcoming war he was going to wage on the remaining three kingdoms. He had already taken Narruc as his home base, and he would launch his undead army from there. Right now, his main concern was taking Toledya, and how. Once he had the kingdom, the others would fall silently behind without its protection. Regnuom would put up a good fight, but the Vikings were superstitious, his majick, as well as his undead army, should frighten them enough to be careless in battle. Inamor would be the easiest for him to take, for his majick surpassed all of the gypsies' majick combined, even if they tried to put up a good fight, they would be no competition for him. Once he had the kingdoms under his control, he would massacre all of the leaders, destroy the forests, and conquer the Ormr Mountains, annihilating the entire dragon race.

While Raul was drawing his map for his tour of world domination, he began to hear strange noises at the front door. He tried to ignore the chattering, scratching, and clattering, but it was beginning to get on his last nerve.

"Toby! Go see who that is at the door making that racket! I can not fully concentrate on my plans to take over the realm with all that annoying noise!"

"I can not, sire."

Why not?"

"My chains, they will not allow me to reach the door."

"Of course! Why do I have to do everything around here?"

Raul grumbled, then stood up from the table, and walked to the front door. By the time he had arrived, the noise had stopped. Instead of opening the door, he turned around to return to the table. Perhaps it had been the wind blowing the tree branches up against the side of the cottage. When he sat down to finish working on the map, the noise started back up again. He looked toward the door, and it was quiet again, so he continued his work. The noises started again, this time even louder than before.

"Argh! I seriously do not have time for this shite! All these unnecessary interruptions are keeping me from finishing my plans!" he shouted, then stormed to the door, flinging it wide open.

It was at this point the most horrifying things ambushed him: cute, cuddly forest animals. Raul screamed as he was attacked by a flock of birds that swarmed the cottage. Then all of the sudden, he felt several squirrels crawl up his legs under his robes. While he was busy trying to stomp his legs, to knock the fuzzy-tailed rodents off, a mob of other creatures joined the attack. He was still waving the birds away from his face, but it was too late when bird droppings temporarily blinded him. Raul screamed trying to wipe his burning eyes of the feces, he staggered outside where a family of bunnies jumped him from behind. He let out a shriek, as the pain in his ankles surpassed that of his stinging bloodshot eyes by the ferocious cotton-tailed vermin. Still unable to get his bearings, or see for that matter, he was not at all prepared for the large ten-point buck that was carefully lining up his sights on the wizard. The large buck charged toward him at an alarming speed, ramming himself right into the wizard's arse. Raul cried out in pain from the antlers that went straight up his backside, as he was sent flying face-first into a skunk. Before Raul could scramble to his feet, the skunk sprayed him in the face with a vengeance. If his eyes were not burning, they were now. He was completely blinded by the foul spray and could not even stand to open his eyes. The birds saw their chance and swooped in close to his neck, snatching the Amulet of Elements. Raul felt tiny claws scratch his neck, as the necklace was snatched right off.

"No!" he screamed.

The wizard had now become so enraged, that he no longer felt the painful bites of the rabbits, or the swelling in his buttocks from the buck's antlers, or even the burning of his red, swollen eyes from the bird droppings and skunk spray. He tried to conjure a great wind to knock the birds from the air, but it was too late, they had already flown away. The remaining animals were not so lucky. The buck was quick to run, but not fast enough. Raul was quicker. He grabbed him with his powers and wrung his hands together, effectively breaking the buck's neck. The rabbits and squirrels found themselves on a spit rotating over the fire with just a snap of his fingers, and the skunk he left alone to run away into the forest. He smelled bad enough, and he did not want to continue to smell it after killing it. Raul turned to walk back inside the cottage, when he heard hysterical laughter.

Toby had seen the entire display from the cottage door being left wide open, and in all this time with the wizard, he had never seen such an amusing sight. He quickly stifled his laughter when the wizard walked in.

"What is so blasted funny?"

"Nothing, sire."

"Is it the fact that I reek of skunk, or that I am covered in bird shite? Which neither is very funny to me," he stated calmly.

The boy could not contain himself, he let out a snicker and was snatched up from the floor, before he could shut his mouth.

"I have had just about enough of you, boy!" Raul shouted, then threw him back down on the floor. He had disappeared before Toby could blink, to go bath in the river that was a few miles from the cottage…

When Raul had finally cleaned himself up, after having to enlist the help of majick to remove the foul odorous scent of the vile black and white creature that had laid its waste upon him. His eyes no longer burned, but his rear end was still sore, even after his wounds had healed. Anger was an emotion of the past, as he had long since surpassed it. He needed to take his frustrations out on more than just a few annoying animals or a small village, because he had already done that. He needed to destroy something bigger, take out the entire existence of someone or something. After pondering for only a moment, he had an epiphany, then he vanished again…

Chapter 39

The remainder of the animals returned to the edge of the forest, where Princess Ellyria, Lord Brom, and Prince Rowan were patiently awaiting their return.

"Look!" Prince Rowan announced. "They are coming back!"

"I am amazed that they had made it out alive. Did they retrieve the amulet?" Lord Brom questioned.

"I am not sure. I can not see that far up ahead, but they are flying in fast," Prince Rowan stated.

"They have the necklace," Princess Ellyria informed them.

"How do you now?" Lord Brom asked in surprise.

"I can feel their excitement."

Princess Ellyria held out her hands, as her feathered allies flew down low dropping the prize into her hands. They fluttered all around her, chirping excitedly about their accomplishments.

"Thank you all so much for your help," she stated, then looked to the birds and the other animals that had bravely risked their lives for her. She waved them on, as they returned to the safety of their homes.

"So now what do we do?" Prince Rowan questioned his sister.

"You go home and tell father that I have the amulet. Tell him it is time to prepare for war."

"What are you going to do?" he wondered, concerned for her, but he had a feeling she had a plan in mind.

"I am going to be right behind you, but Brom and I need to see an old friend first."

"We do?" Lord Brom inquired.

"Yes, we need to go to Raven and ask her how this amulet works," she informed him, holding up the amulet.

"You should put that thing on before Raul shows up, or sends something to snatch it out of your hands," Prince Rowan chided, before calling to Gaia.

"He is right, Ellyria. You should put it on. It will be safer that way," Lord Brom added.

"I think you are right, Brom. Would you help me?" she asked, then turned around holding up the sides of the necklace for Brom to reach each side of the chain.

"There is nothing to hook it together?" When he placed the two ends near one another they fused together magically. "Well, you do not see that every day," he said in amazement.

"What do you mean?" she questioned.

"Look down, sister," her brother chimed in, pointing at the amulet.

Princess Ellyria looked down at the amulet. It was glowing!

"Oh, my!" she exclaimed, seeing the beautiful light the amulet was emulating. After a few moments of it being on her neck, the light slowly faded.

"It was truly made for you," Prince Rowan observed in awe.

"Yes, most definitely," Lord Brom quickly agreed.

"It is rather beautiful is it not?" she observed, holding it up and admiring it, "It never appeared so striking, when it was on the wizard's neck."

"Perhaps its true beauty and power were not able to be at its peak, since it was not made for him. It was made for you, and you alone," he added.

Gaia heard Rowan's call as she arrived before him. He climbed on her back after she crouched down on her belly to allow him on.

"I shall see you both soon in Toledya. Sister, be safe and practice using the amulet while you can before the wizard tries to come after it. He has to know it was you who has stolen it, or he is a complete idiot," Prince Rowan advised.

"I will, you be careful yourself. The wizard could be anywhere hunting us down," she responded.

Princess Ellyria watched as Gaia flew off, leaving her and Lord Brom to go to the small village he took her to after he had rescued her from Raul. They must find Raven, and quickly...

Lord Brom and Princess Ellyria had found a couple of horses in town and they rode toward the village. When they arrived, they were at a loss for words. There was nothing left of the village, it was now only a giant lake, where the once small village of only a few hundred peasants had lived. Bodies were bloated and had floated to the top of the water, men, women, children, all dead.

"It is a horrifying sight if you ask me," Raven interrupted, appearing from out of nowhere.

"The wizard did this, did he not?" Princess Ellyria questioned the Valkyrie.

"Yes, I am afraid so. I see that you have finally acquired the Amulet of Elements. Do you know how to use it?" Raven asked, propping herself up against what was left of an old tree.

"I am not exactly sure. I have an idea, but that is not going to help me much," she mused.

"I can only tell you this, the amulet was made for you. Anything that you can imagine from your heart's desire, you can make appear. You can use your power of telekinesis in unison with the power of the amulet as well. It is at your command, and its power is amplified by yours, and vice-versa," she divulged.

"Is that why the wizard was so much more powerful?"

"Yes, and no. The power of the amulet worked for him, but not with him. The Amulet of Elements comes from good majick, it is only half as powerful in the wizard's hands. Even with the powers he stole from you, it still did not allow him to use the amulet's full power. In your hands alone, may its full powers be unleashed."

"Does this mean Ellyria is indestructible?" Lord Brom questioned.

"No, I am afraid not."

"What? What do you mean? I thought that since he no longer possessed the amulet, he would be weaker?" Lord Brom interrupted again.

"The wizard had an unlimited amount of power before he took yours, Princess. Powers that you do not even possess. He knows that if he taps into the power hidden deep within him, he could destroy everything, including himself. Raul is wise, I hate to admit it, but he is. He knows when to use his powers, and when not to, so he does not lose control."

"What do you mean by him losing control?" Princess Ellyria questioned nervously.

"I have already said too much. I can not tell you anything else, or I will be meddling too much in your destiny. I must go, I wish you the best. I must take these brave warriors to Valhalla. They will serve us well in the coming war." Raven touched the water, and the souls were carried to the great hall where the fallen warriors before them awaited. Lightning streaked across the sky, thunder bellowed in the distance, and then they were gone…

"Are you alright?" Lord Brom asked of Princess Ellyria, who was staring out in the distance.

"Yes, I am well. Are you ready to head out to Toledya?"

"I am ready when you are."

"Good, let us go then."

Princess Ellyria Rose hoisted herself onto the

horses' back, and Lord Brom followed suit. It was not a long ride home from here, but the journey had only just begun. She had to prepare herself for what was to come, and decide how she was going to do it…

The heat of the afternoon made the horses tire more easily, so Lord Brom and Princess Ellyria allowed time for them to rest.

"Does this place bring back any memories?" Lord Brom asked curiously. He watched as a smile emerged from her serious facade.

"Yes," she giggled. It was the same lake that they had stopped to rest at a few years ago, when they had escaped the wizard from the castle in Narruc. Her cheeks warmed at the memory of what had occurred then.

"Are you blushing, Princess?" he teased.

"No, I believe it to be the sun, my Lord," she laughed.

"Care to go for a swim?"

"I thought that you would never ask."

She kicked her horse into a fast gallop, over to the large tree on the hill overlooking the hidden lake. Lord Brom caught up to her, as they both dismounted and led the horses to drink from the crystal clear water. The lake was just as beautiful and peaceful as they had remembered.

"I shall race you," she teased.

Before Lord Brom had a chance to catch her in his arms, she ran taking off her clothes at the same time. She paused only to pull off her riding boots, then to pull down her trousers. Lord Brom caught her as she was bent over, grabbing her hips, and pulling her back into his aching desire, that was still held firm in his pants.

"Where do you think you are going?" he chuckled.

"Nowhere now," she whispered breathlessly.

Princess Ellyria turned to face Lord Brom, he pulled her to

him, and kissed her deeply, passionately. He paused only to finish helping her out of her trousers. Then she returned the favor by helping him out of his clothes, before returning her mouth to his. Standing in the clover on her tippy toes to reach him, she soon found herself in his arms, as he carried her to a thick bed of clover by the water. Just as she thought he was going to lay her down, he surprised her by throwing her into the water.

Princess Ellyria came up squealing and took in a deep breath.

"I can not believe that you just threw me in the water!" she yelled after him, as he dove in the water. He came up and took a breath before he began to laugh at her. "What is so funny?" she questioned, splashing him a few times before he swam over to her.

"I was only having a bit of fun," he confessed, grabbing her before she could swim away, then pulling her to his warm body beneath the water.

Princess Ellyria felt his excitement for her, as she reached down to trap it in her small hand. Lord Brom let out a deep breath, as she stroked the swell of his large endowment. She let go of his member when he reached under her buttocks and lifted her up, then wrapped her arms and legs about him. He kissed her again, his tongue exploring her mouth, as she did the same. Lord Brom then carried her to the edge of the lake and pressed her up against the embankment. Staying in the water he entered her, he could not wait a moment longer, and she welcomed him just as eagerly.

The water splashed up over the bank, as he thrust deep within her. She arched into him and braced herself up against the wall of the lake. While remaining inside her, he hoisted her up onto the edge keeping her legs wrapped around his waist. He pushed himself even deeper, then heard a soft moan escape her full lips. Before she knew it, Lord Brom flipped her over on top of him. She sat upon his hips, rocking back and forth over him. He leaned up, pulling her to him, stealing more kisses, then grabbing her large breasts, which were bouncing in front of his hungry mouth. He managed to trap one of her nipples in his mouth that he suckled on, while he fondled the other. She let out an even louder moan, unable to control it. He thrust himself into her deeper, pulling her hips down harder into his, as she bounced up and down on him. She began to lose herself to the pleasure that was erupting inside her, and when she was riding it out, Lord Brom joined her. He let out a groan as he spent himself alongside her. She fell over on top of him, then kissed him softly…

Lord Brom finished packing up and collected extra water for the horses, as well as for themselves. He looked over at the young girl he knew before, and she had grown into the stunning woman standing before him now. She was so beautiful, and so brave. He would die for her before he would let any harm come to her.

"Are you ready? I am sure that your brother has arrived in Toledya by now, and has told your father everything already."

"I am quite sure that you are right about that. I am ready now," Princess Ellyria said, as she pulled on the last boot.

"Well, let us get back before nightfall. We have spent enough time playing this afternoon."

"I did not hear you complaining about it earlier," she teased.

"I was not complaining at all. It was a wonderful afternoon," he said smiling, then kissed her once more.

Princess Ellyria ran her fingers through his thick hair, and down over the side of his rough face.

"Good," she said, smiling at the man, who she would do whatever it took to protect. She could not imagine losing him to the wizard like she had lost Alfar. No matter what happened to her, she would make sure that he was safe.

Princess Ellyria and Lord Brom rode down the hill by the lake in the direction of home, unaware of what was happening on the other side of the realm…

Chapter 40

Meanwhile, on the other side of the realm, in the Black Forest, tiny sprites were busy tending to all the summer flowers that were in full bloom...

From one blossom to another, the Faeries assisted the bees in gathering nectar for the young ones and collecting pollen for their majick dust. The forest had returned to its peaceful state since the evil Seither had been defeated, and the curse that she had placed on the forest was lifted. The Fae were finally able to live life without fear, without worry, and have their freedom. They had no natural enemies. The animals were their friends, so they no longer had to fret over being hunted, or made into someone else's meal. At night, they danced to lively music and drank thimbles full of sweet nectar made into wine. During a beautiful day like today, they basked in the sunlight and happily focused on their daily routines. Without having a care in the world or troubles to worry over, the faery folk took comfort in the protection from their mother, the Queen of all Faeries. Redlomrdyh had no worries herself, and took into consideration the Princess's warning about the wizard. She made a protective shield around the entire forest, confident that would be enough majick to protect them from the wizard, but all of that changed in the blink of an eye…

The Faery Queen heard the tiny cries of her children, and she saw the bright flashes of light from the far end of the forest. She began to panic. The shield should have held up against the wizard's own majick, but it was not strong enough after all. Faery majick alone would not be capable of protecting them from the evil that was about to spread across their homes like a plague. The Elder Tree stood in the center of the woods, and the Queen could see for miles around her from the highest bough. Her tiny children fled with all of their might to the protection of the great tree, but some of the tiny sprites were too far from home to make it...

At the edge of the woods, a loud explosion of majick soared into the sky like fireworks, as Raul broke down the faerie's protection spell and entered the forest. Screams were heard, as they flew as hard and fast as their tiny wings could bear. Some were snatched out of the air, as their intruder steadily made his way through the endless array of greenery. One by one the sprites' wings were pulled off, as Raul did it slowly, without mercy. Blood trickled from newly emptied sockets, and their tiny lights faded. Once their wings were pulled, they were thrown carelessly aside, left to die a painful death, as they bled out into the earth below.

Raul trampled through the brush and tall grasses, grabbing faeries from mid-air, as they tried desperately to get away. He alternated between pulling wings from their bodies and squishing them in his hand, until they were nothing but a bloody ball of goo. Some he enjoyed stomping under his boot after he had pulled the wings from them, so they could not get up and attempt to fly away. Their tiny cries went unheard, they remained helpless in their efforts to get away from the darkness that was consuming them. The wizard became hungry during his long walk to the center of the forest, where he knew the Queen would be. He began to pop off wings more rapidly, in order to shove the squirming sprites into his mouth, as if they were nuts being shelled. Having not a bad flavor, he was pleasantly surprised by their sweet taste, as he had never partaken in such a delicacy before. He continued to trudge through the forest, taking his time with his lunch, savoring all the different samples that flew into his hand's reach. The tiny sprites' attempts to escape were futile, as one by one they were whisked from flight, then crammed into a hungry mouth. Raul had satisfied his appetite for the moment, but still enjoyed his leisure stroll through the woods, snatching the tiny Urmen from the air, ripping off their wings, then tossing them aside, as if he were pulling petals from a flower. He relished in their screams and cries, it was like music to his ears, as he continued on his bloody tirade…

When he came to the clearing, he saw before him the magnificent Elder Tree that stood proudly in the center of the forest. Raul needed to lure the Queen out somehow. He had already tortured and killed many of her children. Why did she not come out to protect them? Surely she would have enough majick to be a worthy adversary.

"Come down from your tree, you faery bitch! I have tortured, killed, and eaten several of your children. Are you going to stay hidden, while I kill more of them?" Raul shouted. He gave a demonstration next to the tree, slowly pulling the wings from one of the younger sprites to make it scream louder and longer. If that did not make her come out of hiding, then what would? A bright light flashed behind him, and when he turned around she was there.

"That is enough!" she screamed, sending a ball of bright light from her hands into the wizard, knocking him to the ground. "Leave now! We only want peace. You do not belong here! Now, go!" the Queen demanded.

Before Redlomrdyh could blink, the wizard had her by the throat, only a moment before she transformed into a tiny ball of light. She flew from his grasp, and flew into the Elder Tree for its protection, along with the rest of her children.

"Do you think that you have outwitted me, you wretched sprite! Well, think again, because I am just getting started!" Raul exclaimed. Without the power of the amulet to create fire for him, he had to do it himself the old-fashioned way, with a spell. He raised his hands in the air and began to chant. "Fire, fire that burns so bright, I cast you out into flames, ignite!"

The Elder Tree was consumed with the ravenous flames, that hungrily began to eat through the strong bark of the tree. Raul watched while laughing loudly, as the fire began to make its way up into the branches, turning green leaves black. He heard the screams from the Queen, as she told her children to fly away fast from their burning home. However, the heat from the flames grew too intense for them. Their tiny wings curled on ends, then they fell from the sky into the flames that spread over the sweet green grasses, which were now charred and brown.

Raul stepped back a few feet from the fire, that had taken over the entire base of the former great tree. He saw the sprites fall from the sky, some in flames, some still alive, but when they landed in the fire, he heard their little bodies pop.

The faeries swelled from the heat, until they burst into tiny bloody puddles, boiling and oozing into nothing from the intense heat of the flames. As much as this was amusing the wizard, he had more stops to make on his tour of world destruction…

The marketplace in Inamor was business as usual with all of the people bustling about...

The gypsies ran the marketplace only in the spring and summer months and left in mid-fall, after the last harvest before winter, going south of the realm. They were peaceful, living off the land, roaming according to the seasons, to the winds of change. Over the last several years, word of their wares had spread, they were now sought after by the other kingdoms coming to buy, sell, or trade with them, during the warm seasons. Fortune telling and spellwork were among the most famous of their trades. They were not just talented, or strong believers in majick, they also had strong family values and were very protective of their families. Family was sacred to them, and no one could break their beliefs. Never looking for trouble, the gypsies kept to themselves, but if intruders came to cause pain and grief, then they would need to watch their backs. An eye for an eye, a life for a life…

Raul cloaked himself with his robes, keeping his new youthful appearance covered. The faeries he had ingested earlier had a surprising effect on him that he had not expected. His skin became tighter, his graying hair grew darker again, and he no longer looked centuries old, he was not certain how long it would last. Once upon a time, very long ago, he was an attractive young man, after years of dark majick, he began to show his true age, turning so hideous that he had a face his own mother could not even love. He walked around the market for some time, blending in with the crowd, slowly making his way into the gypsy camp. With his youthful appearance, no one was the wiser, making it all too easy to creep along in search of the Bandolier…

Mala had been carefully planning for the wizard's attack. She wore her family's talisman, the Evil Eye, for protection, and a special potion to use against the wizard if he should appear. The other members of the clan were busy in their preparations as well. The men made ready their weapons, and the women were creating more potions to pass out amongst them, to deter the wizard long enough for them to escape. Without knowing exactly when the wizard might appear, they hurried with their tasks. The tribes' Bandolier wasted no time gathering what she needed, then taking it back to her private tent, which was furthest from the entrance of the encampment. When she arrived, she felt as if she were being followed, but she did not see anyone behind her. Shrugging off the strange feeling, she went on into her tent. After setting down her provisions, she was grabbed from behind.

"Hello, pretty. Stay calm, and do not bother to scream."

"I know who you are," she stated calmly. She felt herself being whirled around to face her assailant.

"Do you not recognize me?" he mused, seeing the surprised look on her face.

"Who are you?" Mala queried, honestly not knowing who he was. Then he began to laugh at her. "You are the wizard?"

"Are you not as smart as you are attractive? I was beginning to think that my appearance had you fooled," Raul added.

"What do you want from me?" she asked fearlessly.

"I need you to send a message to your Chosen One."

"Why should I tell her anything? Except that I hope she kills you slowly, and without mercy!"

"Ah, but you will not. I need a different message relayed to her, a private one only you can get across."

"What message would that be, wizard?" Mala gasped, choking out her last words, as blood poured out of her mouth. The sound of her still beating heart was held up before her open eyes.

"Tell her that you are dead, witch!" he exclaimed, laughing before taking a bite out of her pulsing heart, then let the gypsy's lifeless body fall to the floor. As he finished licking the blood off of his fingers, one of the other women of the tribe walked in on him. She screamed upon seeing her mistress in a heap on the floor of the tent, and a strange man covered in blood. He held the Evil Eye in his hand and the remains of a heart in the other. Before she could run away, he used the talisman to slit her throat and silence her, but it was too late. He had been discovered.

Raul waved his hand opening the tent wide, throwing out the dead bandolier, to serve as his message to the Princess. When the men saw what had happened, they made their attack with weapons ready, but the wizard was waiting for it. He stood patiently, not moving a muscle as the village men came at him with knives, swords, and pitchforks. Raul waved the men away as if they were flies, shooing them like the pests that they were. Then the women flanked him from the left, throwing their vials of potions at him. Smoke filled the air, causing Raul to be temporarily blinded, long enough for the women to grab their men, and get out of there. When the smoke cleared, everyone had taken refuge in the woods. He had no time to play cat and mouse games, for he had another kingdom to pillage…

In Regnuom, King Ian called for the presence of his Hand...

"Have the precautionary measures been implemented with the anticipation of the wizard's assault on the city?"

"Yes, Sire. All duty stations have a man on watch in the towers, and by the gates. I had the men put posts in the ground around the outside of the gates as well. Everyone is well-armed, with axes, spears, and swords. The women are prepared to hide the children in the keep, also armed with many weapons for protection."

"Very good. Alert me if you see anything out of the ordinary, or if the wizard and his army are spotted."

"I will, Sire. I shall have a man by your door at all times as well. No one will be able to get past him alive, I can assure you. He is our best guard."

"Very well. Where are you off to?"

"I am going to see to it that the men have come back with those able to fight from the surrounding villages. I will return as soon as I have word."

"Thank you. Report to me immediately upon your return."

"Yes, your Grace."

The Hand of the King left the room, leaving the head guard to watch over King Ian in the throne room. Migata was in his bedchambers, so if someone were thinking of assassinating him in his sleep, they would be in for a surprise…

One by one, the tower guards were taken out. Throats were slit to prevent them from alerting the others standing guard below by the gates. The men were suspended upright by their own spears, giving the illusion that all was well. The same was done to the men below watching the gates. With their backs turned away, and over a hundred yards from the castle, none would be the wiser. Like a serpent, Raul stealthily slithered his way past all the lookouts, inflicting them with his poison as he went. He entered the castle and began his search for the King's personal guard. He knew that he would be the one standing in front of his door for protection, but no one would be there to protect the guard. Raul stalked the man he found standing alone in front of the large double doors in the hall. He watched and waited, athame in hand, ready to strike…

A short time later, the Hand of the King returned to give a report as instructed earlier. When he arrived at the door, the guard was missing. He looked around the corner, to see if he had left the door to check something out, but there was no sign of the man on duty. When he turned around to walk back to the door, the guard was standing there, as if he had never left.

"How did you get back so fast? I just walked by here moments ago."

"I do not know what you are implying, but I have been here the entire time," the guard stated, then looked at him and smiled.

"I do not know what has gotten into you, but I am the Hand of the King, and you should address me as such."

"Does that mean you wash his arse for him too?"

"I will have you flogged for your insubordination!"

"Not if you are dead!" the guard snapped, bringing the knife to his throat before the King's Hand could call out for help, his words were garbled as he choked on his own blood. The guard stepped back from the body, letting it fall to the floor with a thud. With a wave of his hand, his true identity was revealed just in time for the King to open the door, who was alerted by all the noise.

Before King Ian could yell, Raul had him by the throat.

"Do not utter a word. Send a message to that cunt sister of yours. Tell her that I am coming for her, and her little boyfriend too!" Raul threatened, vanishing before the rest of the guards had been alerted.

"Are you alright, Sire?"

"Yes, although I can not say the same for my man though," King Ian reported, then knelt and closed his eyes. "Send word to my father, tell him that the wizard is coming. Prepare for war."

"What about you, Sire? Are you not worried for your safety?"

"No. If the wizard wanted me dead, he would have killed me just now when he had the chance. He was only here to send a message. Well, it was heard loud and clear."

"Sire! All the tower guards, and the guards at the gate, have been slain!"

"Why does that not surprise me? Take them to their families, and send more men to stand watch. It is going to be a long night," King Ian ordered, then left to alert the rest of his men to double up at the duty stations. War was coming…

Meanwhile, in the Dark Forest of Woe...

Toby wiped the tears from his eyes, as he saw the devastation the wizard had caused through the crystal ball. He was still bound by his chains, he had not eaten in days, and he was too weak to try and use the axe to break the chains. There was no escaping, there was no way to kill the wizard, and it was all he could do to maintain his composure. Toby looked into the magic orb one last time to see where the wizard was now, but he could not find him.

"I am not sure that it works with me standing behind you. Do you not think?"

"Sire, when did you return?" Toby inquired hesitantly.

"Now. What were you looking at in the orb?" the wizard asked, towering over the young apprentice.

"I was watching you, sire."

"Oh, really? Did you like what you saw?" Raul taunted, watching the boy fidget with the metal cuff on his ankle. "Well? Answer me, boy!"

"No, I did not!" Toby shouted, unsure where the tiny ounce of courage he finally found had come from, but it had not only surprised himself, but the wizard as well.

"No, you did not. What?" Raul scolded, standing over him like a menacing shadow.

"I did not like what you did to all those innocent faeries, or all those people you killed! Like you killed my father!" he screamed, then began to sob, but he did not care. He hated Raul, and he could not wait for the Princess any longer to kill him. He grabbed a knife he had hidden underneath him and made a lunge for the wizard's heart.

Raul just stepped aside and watched the boy trip over his chains.

"I think you had better try a lot harder than that, boy, if you wish to kill me!" he laughed. He made twirling motions with his hands, which caused the chains to float up and wrap around Toby's neck. "I know that it is not very sportsmanlike of me to not allow you a fighting chance, but I am not in the mood to die. I do not have the time to bother with you any longer, boy!"

Toby hovered just above the floor, kicking his feet and trying to pull the chains from around his neck, gasping for air.

"Are you trying to say something? I am so sorry, but I can not understand what you are trying to say to me," he smirked, letting out some slack in the links, to allow the boy to speak.

"I may not be able to kill you, but I know who can, and I hope that she makes you suffer before she finishes you off," Toby barely made out, in between breaths. His ears were pierced by the wizard's maniacal laughter.

"I wish that I could keep you alive, just to watch her fail. She will not kill me, because she can not. You have to be a killer in order to kill, and she does not have it in her. Does that not just crush your little hopes and dreams?"

"She will, I know she will!"

"You just keep that thought. I promise you this. I will kill her before she kills me." He saw the tears stream down his face. "Oh, you do not like that idea, do you? It is too bad, I can not help it. How about I end your suffering?" Raul threatened, making the chains tighten about the boy's neck again, and watched as he gasped for air.

"You are wrong. I saw your death in the orb," Toby whispered with his last breath.

"What?" Raul observed, letting go of the chains to get the boy to tell him what he saw in the orb. "Tell me what you saw, boy!" he urged, but it was too late, the apprentice had spent his last breath with a warning of the wizard's future. That could not be true. The little wretch had to be lying. He could not even bring him back, because he would not be able to regain his memories. Raul searched in the crystal ball for a glimpse into what his apprentice perhaps saw in the globe.

"Show me what my apprentice saw. Show me what you showed him," he said over the crystal. Smoke filled the globe, but revealed nothing to him. It remained dark, without image, and void of the future. "Damn it!" Raul sent the crystal flying, causing it to shatter as it hit the wall. "No! What have I done?" he shouted, falling to his knees, lowering his head to the floor. How was he to see his enemies? Sometimes his temper really got the best of him. He stood up and looked around him, as if he were in a daze.

Raul had let his anger take over once again, but he could not let it control him. He had to get his head together, and his temper under control. Toby was dead, and the crystal ball was destroyed. All that remained was his cottage, which he no longer needed to hide out in. He would leave for the castle in Narruc to gather his army and prepare them for war. Time was on his side, and it was his only ally in his pursuit of revenge…

The guards he had placed in the castle made way for him to enter the dungeon. He entered the secret passageway to the catacombs below. Raul woke up his sleeping undead army and lifted the invisibility spell he had cast on them, in case they were discovered.

"It is time my pets. Let us go to war!"

The undead army followed the tunnel out into the woods on the other side of Narruc, some were sent to Regnuom, some to Inamor, and the rest headed for Toledya…

Chapter 41

Prince Rowan dismounted from Gaia in the courtyard and ran into the castle to find his father. He first went to his study, flinging open the door.

"Father! I have great news!"

"Yes, what is it?" King Jason asked, looking up at his son, who seemed out of breath, and eagerly awaited the news.

"Ellyria has the Amulet of Elements!"

"That is wonderful news, but calm down. Have a seat, and tell me everything," he said, watching his son take a seat across from him at the table, and trying to slow down his breathing.

"Ellyria, Lord Brom, and I went to warn all of the kingdoms. When we went to Inamor, Mala told Ellyria to use her power to call the forest animals for help. So when we arrived at the edge of the Dark Forest of Woe, there were already animals that had gathered to greet her. She asked this owl if he could help enlist some of the other woodland creatures to assist her in getting the amulet back. The owl agreed, gathering together a small army of cute, cuddly animals to attack the wizard. It must have worked because a few hours later, they brought the necklace back to Ellyria. Once she put it on, it began to glow. It was the most beautiful thing that I have seen in a long time. After that, I started back home," Prince Rowan relayed the events.

"Where did Ellyria and Lord Brom go then?"

"She said they had to see a friend in that really small village between here and Narruc, but that is all I know about it. Knowing my sister, I am sure that she stopped somewhere to rest the horses, on the way home," Prince Rowan explained, then turned to see his mother enter the room.

"I see you have returned without your sister. Where is she now?"

"Rowan may have returned without his sister, but he did bring good news to share," King Jason told his wife.

"Oh, and what would that be?" the Queen asked.

"Ellyria has the Amulet of Elements, mother," Prince Rowan added. He saw his mother's face light up, and saw her smile for the first time in quite a while.

"Oh, that is wonderful news! I am so happy for her."

"It is a good day indeed," King Jason added.

"Ellyria wanted me to tell you to prepare for war, and the wizard will try to steal the amulet back. She said to gather your men and make ready the battle plan." Prince Rowan informed, then watched the happiness fall from their faces.

"I shall need you to go and find Anthony for me then. I will need him to prepare the men for the battle."

Yes, father," Prince Rowan said, before leaving the room in search of his eldest brother.

"Do you think it will come down to a war breaking out?" Queen Anna questioned her husband. She almost did not want to hear the answer, but she already knew what he was going to say.

"Yes. I am afraid so, my love. Although, you should have no worries that the battle will come here. Perhaps Ellyria will be able to distract the wizard, and keep the battle in Narruc."

"What if it does come here? Are we prepared to ward off an entire army of undead soldiers?" Queen Anna asked, searching his face for answers, that she was not so certain he had for her.

"Honestly, I believe we do. Besides, with Anthony in charge to lead our men fearlessly into battle, we should win this war. Not to mention we have Ian and his men, who will come to our aid if needed. The castles' defenses have never been breached in the history of our family. So, yes, I do believe we can defend ourselves from an undead army," her husband reassured her. "Does that make you feel any better?"

"A little. I just hope that Ellyria can destroy the wizard before it comes down to an all-out war," Queen Anna added, watching as her husband's attention turned elsewhere. Perhaps he was just as worried as she was.

Just then, Prince Rowan returned with Prince Anthony, who had already been caught up on the situation by Prince Rowan, as they walked to their fathers' study.

"Father, I have been carefully going over a strategy in my head for the upcoming battle. I believe that if we use a regular battle plan, the wizard could outsmart us, and flank us when we least expect it. I think we should do the unexpected, and have Dakota help us. I know he is not trained in the art of battle strategy, but he is a genius when it comes to alchemy. We must fight fire with fire, and Dakota has a lot of firepower," Prince Anthony suggested.

"He is correct, father. Dakota has several potions that could help us against the undead army, which is our biggest concern since we technically can not fight the wizard. It is up to Ellyria to do that," his brother added.

"I agree, dear. Your sons are very intelligent, you know," the Queen stated.

"Yes, they are, my love. Anthony, you go gather all the men, instruct them of our plans, prepare them for battle, and commence with as much training as you can before the wizards' undead army knocks on our gates. Rowan, you go find Dakota for me. Explain to him our plan on the way here, so his clever mind has a chance to start working on a plan of action we can use in the event of this coming war," King Jason instructed.

"Yes, father." Prince Rowan and Prince Anthony left the study to do as they were asked.

Queen Anna looked at her husband, who now looked completely confident. She beamed with pride for her husband and sons. She had complete faith in them and knew, that they would see to it that everything would eventually be normal again. They would be safe, not only under the castles' protection, but with the protection of her family, and their impenetrable plan as well…

Prince Rowan found his brother Prince Dakota in the tower with Isis, diligently working on a new formula for a potion he had been working on for some time.

"Hello, brother. What brings you on such an unsuspected visit?" Prince Dakota questioned, looking up from his alchemist work.

"Father sent me actually, but it was Anthony's idea."

"Pertaining to your visit?"

"Yes, I am afraid so," Prince Rowan chuckled. "What are you working on anyway?"

"I have been working on a new potion, that will hopefully take out an army of undead soldiers. Been working on it since Ellyria told us about them."

"So that is why we have not seen much of you lately. Been held up in the tower like Rapunzel, eh? That is funny because that is exactly why I was sent up here, to see what you could cook up to give us the upper hand in the coming war. They also want you to come up with a battle strategy," Prince Rowan informed his surprised brother.

"Really? Anthony and father want me to come up with a strategy? Well, I am quite flattered," he mused.

"Do you think that you can come up with something in time?"

"That I am not sure. I shall try. What do they want besides a plan and potions?" Prince Dakota queried.

"Anything that you can come up with that will keep us alive, and prevent the castle from being destroyed. We must be able to fight the army on our own, while Ellyria takes on the wizard. Either way, we need some pretty powerful potions, black powder, anything that will rain on their parade," Prince Rowan said smiling, as he could almost see the gears already turning in his brother's mind.

"Give me a little time. I will get back to you before nightfall."

"That is only a few short hours away, brother. Can you come up with something that fast?"

"I do not have as much of a choice, do I?"

"You have a point. I will leave you to it then. Come see father when you are ready. I know that he will be very interested in whatever you come up with," Prince Rowan disclosed, before he left the room.

Prince Dakota pondered for a few minutes, then recalled something that Rowan had said to him. 'Anything that will rain on their parade'. Which of course gave him an idea, and he quickly went to his Book of Shadows to see if what he had in mind was would work. He flipped through the pages, but what he needed was not there. He looked in another book he had taken from his shelf. Nothing. Prince Dakota pulled every book from the shelf and sat down to read through them all if he had to. With any luck, something would turn up. Once he came upon the oldest of his books, the one alchemy book he had not yet read through. He carefully turned the careworn pages, and finally found what he was looking for. Now, it would rain on the wizard's parade...

Prince Rowan found Prince Anthony out in the field, with a few of his second in command. They were going over military strategies in preparation for the inevitable attack on the castle.

"Did you find Dakota, and ask him for his assistance?" Prince Anthony inquired.

"Yes, I did. I just left the tower. He was already ahead of us, and had been working on a new potion soon after our sister told us of the wizard's undead army," Prince Rowan informed him.

"That does not surprise me in the least," Prince Anthony chuckled.

"How are you doing with devising some different strategies?"

"It is coming along well. These are my best men when it comes to strategic warfare planning. I have encountered only a few possible problems which may occur at any given time, so we are working on a backup plan to those methods."

"I am sure that father will be very pleased," Prince Rowan stated. He was confident in both of his brothers' plans and believed they would be able to merge strategies, to work in unison with one another. "Well, alert father of what your plan is, as soon as possible. I am going to let him know that I have spoken with both of you, and that you are hard at work on the battle plans," Prince Rowan added, then left his brother to continue his work, as he went to relay the information he had gathered to his father…

King Jason was alone once more in his study. He had already sent his troubled wife to her bedchambers for much needed rest. As worried as he was about her, he had to keep his mind focused, as he too was working on a battle strategy of his own. His son Rowan, who appeared to have some good news, momentarily interrupted him.

"What did you find out from your brothers?" his father asked.

"I spoke to Dakota, who was already hard at work on a new potion he had been formulating for some time. He said he would also come up with a strategy to use in unison with the new formula he is making. Dakota said that he would try to have it to you before nightfall," his son explained.

"Well, that is impressive, because it is nearing sunset now," the King observed, looking out the window. "What did you find out from Anthony?"

"He had his best military advisors still working with him, when I left him just a moment ago. Maybe between the two of them, they shall have something that will coincide well with each other's plans," Prince Rowan added.

"Let us hope so. There is no time to delay. We need to be ready. Especially since we do not know exactly when they will make their attack on the castle."

Suddenly, Prince Anthony ran into the room out of breath.

"Father, I just received a message from Ian. He said Raul attacked the castle in Regnuom, killing his second in command, and his best guards. He also said that the wizard left a message for Ellyria, saying that he was coming for her."

"This is not good. Go and prepare the castle for the assault. Gather the women and children, and move them to the keep. Arm the women for they will need to protect the children. Double the guards at the gates and send all men that you can, to reinforce the walls. Especially the side of the garden, where the wall is broken. It will be dusk soon, let us hope that Lord Brom returns with your sister before dark. Rowan, you go and tell Dakota we may be getting attacked tonight so be prepared. Tell him to hurry up with whatever it is that he is working on. I shall go tell your mother and keep her upstairs, with extra men to guard her door," King Jason ordered.

King Jason, Prince Anthony, and Prince Rowan all proceeded to leave the study together, when the messenger cut them off at the entrance.

"Sire, this just flew in for you," he said, watching his King read over the message, and seeing the alarm go off in his eyes.

"Inamor has been attacked by the wizard. Mala and another one of the women were both killed earlier today. Ellyria will be devastated," the King relayed the news.

"Maybe that is exactly what the wizard wants."

"What do you mean, Anthony?" Prince Rowan questioned his eldest brother.

"It is a mind game he is playing to daunt Ellyria. If she is distracted by heartache or anger, it will sabotage her concentration in her fight with the wizard," Prince Anthony explained.

"I understand. He is tormenting her mind," their father stated.

"Yes, unfortunately," he added.

"Do you think we should even tell her?" Prince Rowan questioned.

"If we do not tell her now, my sons, then we run the risk of her finding out at the wrong time. I suggest that we tell her after she arrives. At least she can make up her mind on what she wants to do after she finds out. She will be hurt, but it could also give her some ammunition against the wizard," King Jason advised.

"What do we do in the meantime?" Prince Anthony questioned his father.

"We continue to the tasks at hand, we do not have time to wait for Ellyria to walk through those doors. We must act now."

"I agree, father. We can tell her, whenever we see her," Prince Rowan suggested.

"Good, let us go then," Prince Anthony, added.

The men headed in their separate directions. Prince Anthony went to gather his men, then send them out to watch over the castle grounds. Prince Rowan went to check on Prince Dakota's progress and to get him to make haste with the potion-making. King Jason went to place more guards at his bedchamber to watch over his sleeping wife, whom he had to awaken and inform her as to what was going on. Dusk was nearly upon them, Princess Ellyria and Lord Brom had yet to return. His greatest concern now was for his daughter, he hoped that she would arrive safely before nightfall. He did not want her caught off guard by the wizard before she saw him coming for her…

Prince Anthony made his rounds, making sure the gates were guarded. The wall by the courtyard had been repaired, and the towers were brightly lit with torches to see the enemy coming. Prince Rowan alerted Prince Dakota, who was not quite ready with the potion, but he was nearing its completion. King Jason had gone to his chambers to inform Queen Anna of what was going on, and to ask her to remain in her chambers until he let her know when it was safe to come out. Many weapons were passed out among men, knights, warriors, and peasants alike, who set aside their class differences and banned together as men protecting their homes. Swords, spears, axes, and arrows were lined up ready to grab alongside the walls, as well as large vats of boiling oil, and barrels of black powder that had been strategically placed. Large piles of stones were staged on the upper level of the castle walls, and torches were lit all around as well. Even with all the preparations made, there was no way of predicting the outcome…

Chapter 42

Princess Ellyria and Lord Brom had stopped again to eat and rest since leaving the lake, where they had shared a lovely afternoon romp. Lord Brom had made a fire, then he went hunting for some food for them, and was lucky enough to catch a young boar. After gutting and cleaning it, he made a spit and placed it over the fire. It took some time to cook, but Princess Ellyria and Lord Brom found a way to pass the time. After they had finished eating, the sun began to set, so they had decided to head home before a search party was called out after them.

Princess Ellyria smiled at the fond memories of the day they had spent together when they arrived. The outer gates were heavily protected with armed men and long posts that were made into spears, which stood tall around the outside of the main entrance to the castle. Two guardsmen occupied the two towers above, they too were heavily armed with weapons. Everything was quiet. The torches were lit and were the only light that could be seen from the road leading to the castle gates.

Darkness had left her thick veil over the horizon, while her mistress lit up the night sky...

"Princess Ellyria, it is good to see that you have returned. Everyone has been waiting for you," the guard said.

"Thank you. If you will excuse us, we shall be going on into the castle now."

"Yes, your Highness," he nodded, motioning to the guards to open the gates, to allow Lord Brom and Princess Ellyria to pass.

When they rode the horses up through the courtyard, they were both amazed by the repair to the broken wall alongside the fountain, that she used to jump over when sneaking off of the castle grounds. The entire perimeter was heavily guarded, and the castle was heavily fortified. Once Princess Ellyria and Lord Brom reached the main doors, they had to be opened by four guardsmen to let them in. Security was exceptionally tight, and for good reason. Now that she had returned, there was no one else that needed to be let in the gates, no one could gain entry, or leave...

Princess Ellyria and Lord Brom entered the long hall, surprised that no one was out there to greet them. They walked into the parlor, which was empty, then walked over to her father's study. She found her father and three brothers all gathered around his table. When she came in, they all turned in her direction.

"Ellyria, you have returned!" King Jason exclaimed, being the first one to notice her. "When did you and Brom return?"

"We just walked in actually. What is going on? Has there been any word from Ian?" Princess Ellyria questioned, watching as the happy expressions disappeared from their faces.

"You had better come in and sit down, sister," Prince Anthony said, offering her a seat.

"What happened?"

"Ellyria, Ian was attacked at Regnuom by the wizard. He is fine, but several of his men were killed, including the head of the royal guard. Ian said the wizard sent you a message, that he was coming for you and the amulet," Prince Anthony revealed, then watched as his sister reached up to clutch the amulet around her neck.

"I know there is more. Pray tell me, what else have you learned?" she questioned.

"Raul also attacked Inamor. He killed a couple of the women from the village," Prince Rowan divulged.

"Mala."

"Yes, I am afraid so. I am so sorry, Ellyria. I know that you were close friends," Prince Rowan added, then saw the tears well up in his sister's emerald eyes.

"That is not all the wizard has done either. He obliterated an entire village," Lord Brom chimed in. He felt bad for his Princess, and felt helpless in bringing her comfort.

"Are you alright, dear sister?" Prince Dakota asked, worried by her silence.

Princess Ellyria stood up and then walked over to the window. The men were bustling about in the light of the lit torches and the full moon, while still making preparations for the assault. She watched for a few minutes, before turning back to the others in the room waiting for her to say something, anything.

"This is not going to be enough. The undead army was created with this," she said, holding up the amulet, admiring its beauty and the way the moonlight danced upon it, amazed by the power it contained. "Dakota, I know that you have something up your sleeve. Is it ready yet?"

"Almost. I am waiting for it to cool completely before I put it into place."

"That is good, but you might want to go check on it. The sooner we are prepared the better. They will be here when the moon reaches her place high in the sky," she advised, motioning to the moon through the window.

"I shall go now. Father, that is all I had to offer on the battle plan anyway. I am going to check on my formula," he said, before leaving the room.

After Prince Dakota left, Prince Anthony stood up to leave the table.

"I am going to relay this plan to my commanders, I shall be

with them if you need me," he stated, then took the map with the strategy they had been working on.

"Rowan, go call to Gaia. We will need her here to help in the fight, once our enemies have arrived," King Jason ordered.

"Yes, father. Should I have her waiting in the field by the courtyard to keep her hidden, and then jump out when it is time for the counter-assault?"

"Yes, that is a very good idea. Check in with Anthony, on when would be a good time to give the signal for her to attack."

"I shall see to it right now," Prince Rowan agreed, before leaving the room.

"Brom, I need you to come with me. You can help me in the weapons room to gather more supplies, and there is some armor that might fit you," the King offered.

"I do not think that I should leave Ellyria alone, your Grace," Lord Brom stated.

"No, Brom. You go, I will be fine. I need to go up to my room and see if I can descry anything from the mirror," Princess Ellyria interrupted.

"Are you sure? Raven told me to watch over you."

"Yes, I will be fine. I am in the castle, and we have not even been attacked yet. However, I would like to find out if we are about to be. Go with my father, and get yourself ready," she instructed, then pulled Lord Brom to her, and kissed him gently on the mouth, unconcerned by her father's presence. "I shall return soon enough," she added after the kiss.

"Come now, Brom, we do not have much time. I am sure that Ellyria will be fine," King Jason chided.

"Yes, Sire," Lord Brom humbly agreed, watching Ellyria leave, then followed her father to the arms room…

The cool night air blew through the open window into Princess Ellyria's bedchamber. She rubbed her bare arms to ward off the chill, as she entered the room and sat down in front of her ivory-washed vanity. She peered into the mirror that was made from the majick crystal, by the gypsies for her grandmother, that her mother had passed down to her when she was a little girl. Princess Ellyria looked upon her reflection, thinking about how frightful she looked right now. She began to brush her waist-length black hair, after she had pulled it down from its already loosened bun, and took her time with the tangles, pondering on whether or not she really wanted to see the wizard's destruction. The image of herself and her lustrous locks began to fade, as smoke filled the mirror. It appeared as though the mirror was going to show her anyway. As the smoke began to clear, images formed of men, women, and children were covered in blood. They had been slain by the undead soldiers, who ransacked the innocent as they made their way through the realm. Every village they came to was destroyed. All of their crops were destroyed, the animals slaughtered, and the men were helpless in their attempts to protect their homes. The undead dragged the women into their own homes, where they were raped, beaten, and then killed. Some were left alive to watch, as their children were not only mutilated but eaten alive in front of them as well. When the villagers attempted to try and fight back, they were killed mercilessly for their efforts. Hope had run out for them, as their cries to the Gods were left unheard. However, the Gods did indeed hear their cries, but could not meddle in the travesty occurring. Only the Chosen One could save them. Only she and she alone could end their pain and suffering. Where was their savior? She was doing nothing but watching the bloodshed from a majick mirror, in the safety of the castle. What was she doing?

"Show me everything the wizard has done! Show me how to stop this! Show me what to do!" she yelled at the mirror. She saw the wizard's image emerge. He was laughing, watching with amusement at what his minions were doing at his command. His tyranny had spread over the innocent, like the village where he started his reign of terror and the complete takeover in Narruc. She wiped the tears from her eyes, as the images played back all of the scenes like a stage show, as everything was reenacted for her.

All of those people had suffered mercilessly by his hand, as if it would aid him in his revenge against her somehow.

Princess Ellyria watched helplessly at those horrifying events. What he had done in that peaceful village, in Narruc, in Regnuom, and then in Inamor, where he had killed her good friend Mala. No matter the pain or anger she was feeling, she had to keep a clear head, but when the mirror showed her the graphic images of what he had done in the Black Forest, she nearly lost herself with the desire for vengeance. It was a natural instinct to feel such things, but for her, it could not be allowed. Vadoma, Mala, and even Nidhoggr had warned her that with great power, came the temptation for more. The pursuit of more power could lead her into darkness, allowing evil to control her. If the wizard knew that she could be easily swayed into darkness, then he would try to woo her to his side. His wish for ultimate power would be easily obtained if they joined forces, they could take over the world. All of the Gods in Valhalla could not stop them. Princess Ellyria calmed herself, before looking back at the mirror. She saw the forest in flames, and the Faery Queen desperately trying to save her children. It was exactly what Alfar had been trying to show her! This was the image from the premonition that she had. All at once, those past feelings of déjà vu made sense to her now! They were premonitions of the future that she had simply shrugged off as being just nightmares. She had no time to lose and must get to the forest before it was too late. How was she going to get there? As she was trying to figure a way out of the castle, she heard a voice coming from the mirror.

"Use the amulet," it called to her.

Princess Ellyria could not believe her ears. It had to be Alfar.

"How? How do I use the amulet?" she spoke into the mirror.

The voice came closer, then Alfar appeared in the mirror.

"How can it be? How can I see you?"

"Ellyria you do not have much time. I do not have much time. You must save my mother please! The entire Fae race is dependent on her. Without her, they will all perish. Please, help them!" he shouted, before his image began to fade.

"No, wait! How can I get there? How can I use the amulet to get there?" she questioned desperately.

"I am not supposed to be here. Use the amulet, focus on where you want to go, then touch the mirror. It will create a portal, but you must hurry! Time is of the essence!" Alfar warned, then faded from sight, as if something was pulling him from the other side.

"Alfar?" she whispered.

The mirror returned itself to the present circumstances. Tiny sprites were caught in the flames, one by one their tiny bodies burst like bubbles, while others simply melted away. Princess Ellyria could not wait a moment longer. She closed her eyes and concentrated on the forest. When she began to feel the heat coming from the flames, she rose from her chair and touched the amulet with one hand, and the other to the crystal mirror.

A flash of bright light lit up the entire room. When it had faded from view, Princess Ellyria was gone…

Chapter 43

The portal opened and Princess Ellyria covered her face with her hands, trying to mask the thick black smoke, after entering the forest. When she looked back, the portal had closed. Her eyes burned, she could barely see in front of her. The fire was so intensely hot, that she felt as though her skin might melt right off of her body. As Princess Ellyria walked through the charred woods engulfed in the flames, she walked past several species of animals, as well as faery folk, some that she had never even seen before, lay wingless and bloody, on the ground. She had to ignore them, keep her focus, and find the Queen. When she arrived at what used to be the great Elder Tree, she gave pause, in shock from witnessing the flames consuming it. Unharmed by the flames and protected by the amulet, she called to the Faery Queen, Redlomrdyh.

"Great Queen, I call you near, hear my voice, hear my cry, I call you to thee," she chanted. There was no response. She tried once again, louder. Nothing. Without giving up, Princess Ellyria continued her chant, until a tiny light emerged from the top of the tree.

Standing before her, the tiny light transformed into the Queen.

"Oh, Princess. Can you save my children? They have all died! The wizard came, he killed, and ate my children, then set fire to the entire forest! I am not powerful enough to stop the fire. Please, can you help me?" the Queen cried.

"Yes, I have come to help you. I will help save your children and the forest. Keep your children from the flames, as I will try to put them out."

Without having used the amulet to create anything, she was not just sure how to trigger its magic. She had to focus her mind, she closed her eyes shutting out all the noises around her. The tiny cries and screams began to slowly fade from her ears. She visualized a great downpour of rainwater to snuff out the roaring flames, she kept that image in her mind and willed it to happen. Thunder sounded in the distance, as white puffy clouds became darker, banding together until the sky was completely shrouded. Princess Ellyria opened her eyes and felt the cool moisture in the air on her skin. The rain came and trickled down slowly at first, soon giving way to larger, heavier droplets that started coming down hard on the forest. The flames began to go out, as the waves of water came down like Thor's hammer.

The Queen came down from the trees to play in the rain with her children, as they danced together rejoicing. The fire was finally extinguished, and the Queen could now return the forest to its natural glory, as it was before the wizard had tried to destroy it…

Using the power of the Amulet, Princess Ellyria helped the Queen restore the forest to its former beauty. The charred black grass returned to the green succulent blades it was once before. The green then began to spread to bushes, then it climbed up into the trunks of the trees, returning them to their former healthier selves. The branches stretched out before her, as the green sparkly dust continued to sweep onto each branch, growing once again tiny shoots, that bloomed into new green leaves. The many sprites and animals that had died unfortunately could not be brought back to life, but they were returned to Mother Earth, to become new blossoming flowers and new growing saplings. Princess Ellyria was awestruck. Only moments before, the forest was engulfed in flames, but now it was once again the beautiful forest full of greenery, and full of life. The Queen returned to Princess Ellyria's side and smiled at her.

"I want to thank you, Princess, for all that you have done to help us. Please, let me offer you something in return for saving my children, and our forest. Tell me what it is you wish, so that I can grant it for you," she offered.

"You do not owe me anything," she smiled, "I wanted to help you. It was my duty to do so. Your survival is payment enough," she said humbly.

"There must be something that you wish for. Is there not?"

"All I wish for is the end of the wizards' tyranny. I want to prevent him from taking over the entire realm. I want to stop him from destroying any more kingdoms, and taking innocent lives. That is what I wish."

"I can not help you with that. That is part of your destiny. However, I can offer you a glimpse into the future, if you would like," the Queen hinted.

"How?"

Queen Redlomrdyh motioned for her to follow. Princess Ellyria followed her to the pool beside the Elder Tree.

"Look here, deep into the water. It will reveal to you your heart's greatest desires. Know this, any future that you might see within the pool can still be altered by other events. So take heed in knowing that it can be changed in an instant."

"Why would it be worth seeing if it could change?"

"We are not bound by our destiny. Sometimes it changes. It changes by the choices that we make as our lives go on. Therefore changing our destinies, may not occur if we do not take chances, and chances, Princess, are what we take every day. Now, go on, look into the water, and let it show you what some of those chances could bring."

"Does that mean that I still have a chance to change the future, that may be revealed to me?" she asked, the Queen, but she had vanished before she could get an answer. "I suppose that I am on my own now," she said, gazing into the crystal clear water, that was once tears of the Faery Queen when she was cursed into the tree, crying for her only son. The pool remained and still flowed through into the river, that ran into the meadow just outside the forest. The deeper she looked into the water, the more images began to appear before her sapphire eyes…

Princess Ellyria could not believe what she was seeing. This was not at all her heart's desire, and she felt deceived by the Queen's promise to her. Her vision blurred as tears filled her eyes, and as she wept into the pool, the images changed with the ripples made by her fallen teardrops. No longer were the kingdoms the glorious cities she had visited in the past, only crumbled ruins, a mere shell of its former self. No longer did farmers tend to their lands, or mothers let their children play. All were in fear for their lives, as the darkness consumed the realm. Raul was on her father's throne, and she was sitting by his side. No! This could not be. More tears fell, then the ripples changed the images again. The halls of Valhalla were empty. No longer did the warriors train with the Valkyries. Their spirits were slain, and they had been sent to Niflheim to be with the Goddess, Hella. It was a bargain struck by Raul to the Hella herself; if he brought those in Valhalla down, she would help him into power. She betrayed Alfodr, as well as her own father, Loki, by letting the wizard into the Underworld. From there, he enlisted the help of the enemies of Asgard, and personal enemies of Alfodr himself. Raul and his undead army, as well as the help of his new allies, went to Valhalla and made the Gods bow down to him.

Princess Ellyria splashed the water with her hand. No, this could not be. Why was she being shown this? None of it makes any sense. She splashed some water on her face, before she looked back into the clear water. Another image appeared in the water, but it was more like a reflection. It was of Alfar. Princess Ellyria looked behind her, but no one was there. When she turned back to the pool, his image was still there. Was she seeing things that did not exist?

"Alfar? Is that really you?" she whispered into the water.

"Yes, Ellyria it is."

His voice sounded as if it were right next to her. Then she felt a hand upon her shoulder and took in a deep breath, trying to still her heartbeat. She looked to the hand on her shoulder, then up to whom it belonged. It was Alfar! She stood up immediately and placed her hands on his face, to see if he was real.

"It is really me, I promise. I am here with you right now," he said taking her in his arms. It was so good to feel her again.

"How?"

"It was your heart's desire, was it not?" he questioned.

"All I saw in the water were horrible images of a possible near future. I do not understand. How could this be? I have never forgotten about you, and I have never stopped loving you," she confessed to him, but still feeling as if this were a dream. "Am I dreaming?" she whispered, then feeling his lips on hers, kissing her gently, feeling the love from him deep within his heart.

"Did that feel real to you? Because it did to me."

"Oh, yes. Alfar, it really is you," she said breathlessly, afraid to question it, afraid she would wake up.

"Yes, my love. I am here because you wished it to be so," he assured her, cupping her face in his hands, looking deep into her sapphire eyes, then he kissed her once more. She fell into him, drawn into his kiss, his energy, she could not stop for a moment to doubt whether he was real, or not.

"So my wish came true?" she said pushing him away from her.

"Yes. I am here because my mother granted your deepest wish. My spirit was held in the young Elder Tree, but she released me for you."

"Does that mean you can come with me? Back to Toledya?"

"No, I am afraid that I am bound to the forest. The majick is protecting my spirit, without it I would fade away, and no longer be able to return," Alfar confessed, wiping the tears from her sun-kissed cheeks. "Why are you crying?"

"Because as much as I would love to stay here with you, I can not. I am the Chosen One. I must prevent the wizard from destroying the entire realm, and taking over the place of the Gods. If the vision I saw was true, then I must return to prevent that from ever happening. I am so sorry. I do love you, but I have to go," she cried, touching the side of his face with the tips of her fingers, committing it to memory.

"I understand. You have proven yourself to us all, and I believe that you will beat him. Love conquers all, Princess, remember that," he advised, pointing to the pool, then a new image appeared. "This can be your destiny if you let it. Do not let your heart be your downfall. Remember the love for your family and others that you are close to, that love will be your greatest strength in defeating the wizard. I am afraid that I must go now and return to the tree. I will always be watching over you, no matter what you choose to do," Alfar promised, before stepping back and fading into the tree.

Princess Ellyria reached out for Alfar one last time, but it was too late. He was gone once again...

The Princess dried her eyes and then got up from Alfar's tree. Did she fall asleep? It felt real, and she did not remember going to sit at the base of the tree, or leaning up against it either. She walked over to the pool staring at her reflection. In it, she saw herself as the timid, unsure girl she used to be, then the image changed, just as she had done over these past few years, always growing braver, and more confident. She smiled at the thought of how she was at this moment, then watched as darkness filled the pool. Princess Ellyria shook her head in disbelief, that could not be her. Could it? Uncomfortable, she stood up from the pool. She needed to get back. How was she going to return? Perhaps she could use the amulet again, but there was no mirror. Then she had a brilliant idea come to her. As she did with the pool in the Underworld, she would use the pool's reflection like the mirror and create the portal with the amulet. It had to work, for she was running out of time. She closed her eyes, then imaged herself back home sitting at her vanity. Keeping the vision in her mind's eye, she held the amulet in one hand, touching the water with the other.

A bright flash of light, which paled in comparison to that of the moon, alerted all of the forest dwellers to its majick. When the sprites opened their eyes, the Princess was gone…

CHAPTER 44

A flash of light illuminated the empty room, and Princess Ellyria was sitting once again at her vanity. She opened her eyes to find herself back in familiar surroundings. The visions she had in the forest still haunted her mind, and she still could not get her head wrapped around what had just happened earlier either. Sometimes, the line between fantasy and reality became blurred when concerning her visions. She knew that Alfar was with her in those woods, that it could not have been all just a premonition. Or was it? Needless to say, it felt real to her, and she would heed his warnings. He had been correct thus far. Why doubt him now?

Princess Ellyria grabbed the length of her hair and began to twist it around, until forming a fairly neat bun on the back of her crown. She slipped off her dress and then walked over to her tub, which had been filled a little earlier, for the bath she never had the chance to take. It was a good time to get a quick bath, even though it was probably cold by now. Skimming the water with her toes, it did not feel too bad, but when she settled herself down into the water, her nipples became erect almost immediately. She took in a quick breath at the completely different temperature than the room, which was still very warm, so the water felt very cool in comparison. Laying back into the tub, she sunk herself lower into the water, but her feet came out of the water slightly on the other side. She used to imagine herself as a mermaid when she was a little girl. Her mother said she could never keep her out of the water. Some things never changed, even when she was all grown up. She smiled at the few pleasant memories of her childhood, closing her eyes to have a better vision of them…

Princess Ellyria must have fallen asleep because when she woke up, it was to her mother's screams. She hurried out of the tub, still dripping wet from her bath, and frantically looked for something, anything she could grab to put on quickly. After finding a plain pale pink cotton gown, she quickly pulled it over her head. She ran out of her room to find her mother in the hall.

"Oh, Ellyria! I have been looking everywhere for you. Please come quick, they are here!"

"Who is here?"

"The wizard's army!" Queen Anna shouted, then seeing that her daughter seemed unmoved by her news, and could not imagine how she could remain so calm.

"Mother, it will be alright. Where is father?" Princess Ellyria tried to ask while consoling her.

"He is at the wall with your brothers and Lord Brom."

Princess Ellyria gave her a quick embrace, then she let go to head downstairs.

"Where are you going?" her mother questioned.

"I am going to help them!" she declared, knowing that her mother was crying, but she could not help that now. She needed to find her father, brothers, and Lord Brom before it was too late. If the wizard was out there, she needed to help them, they can not fight off the wizard on their own. When she arrived, it was too late. The undead army had rammed the outer gate in, and no matter how hard the knights fought against them, they just could not be killed. The wizard resurrected them as soon as they were slain. This could not be happening! How were they going to defeat them? She ran as fast as she could to the far end of the wall, where she saw her brothers. They could not hear her call and were struggling against the much stronger minions. Princess Ellyria was unable to help. If she used magic from the amulet, she risked hitting the ones she loved. She had to think of something fast. The castles' defenses were falling, with the undead unable to be killed, which made them all the more dangerous than she had imagined. Just then, she saw Lord Brom running straight into the middle of them, sword swinging in hand, lopping off their heads. That seemed to work, for they were not getting back up. She heard Lord Brom yelling to the others to do the same, but it was too late. Her father began to sound the alarm to fall back. Most of their defenses had been slaughtered, leaving very few alive. It would be better to pull back now. The wizard's army pressed on, attacking full force, with even more men, which seemed to have appeared out of nowhere. Princess Ellyria saw her brothers and Lord Brom become surrounded by the undead, trapping them between the wall and the main gate. She had an idea, but when she ran over to them to distract the minions, it was too late. Her father, brothers, and Lord Brom were all slain, and fell to the ground in a pool of their own blood…

"No!" Princess Ellyria screamed, sitting up in the bath, sloshing water all over the floor. She took in a deep breath, relieved that it had only been a dream, but it felt more like a premonition. Both Alfar and the Faery Queen told her the future could be altered. Perhaps there was enough time to change the outcome. Before she could get up from the bath, Raul appeared out of nowhere, pushing her down into the bathwater. She kicked with all her might, while trying desperately to hold her breath. The wizard's laughter echoed in the water, his smile was wide with blackened teeth showing, his cold grey eyes were filled with vengeance, as he only seemed to want her dead. Using the power from the amulet in unison with her telekinesis, she blasted Raul with an energy ball, sending him flying into the wall. He got back up and as soon as she tried to escape from the tub he backhanded her hard, causing her to fall back into the water. She was pushed down again, but this time she was too weak, and in too much pain to focus her powers. He pushed her shoulders to the bottom of the porcelain tub, his strength was unaffected by her meek attempts to fight him, she felt herself letting go, as the water began to fill her lungs…

Water flowed out from the sides of the tub as Princess Ellyria came up out of the bathwater gasping for air. She could barely breathe, as she coughed up the water from her lungs. The wizard was gone, but had he really been there? Her head began to throb, and her shoulders were very sore. Placing a hand to her throat, it was too sore to yell for help, so she slowly got out of the tub and grabbed the drying cloth from where it hung. After she had dried off, she donned a pale pink cotton gown. She left her hair wrapped in its bun, pulled on her shoes, leaving her room to search for her father, so she could warn him of the vision that she had just had…

The study was empty, and there were no signs of anyone in the parlor. Maybe they were outside defending the wall? Princess Ellyria opened the side door and exited the main courtyard, where men were standing on guard everywhere. The entire perimeter of the castle had a man on watch. She walked over to the main gate and saw her father, brothers, and Lord Brom.

"Father!"

"Ellyria, why are you not upstairs with your mother? She woke up earlier and has since been looking for you," King Jason said, upon seeing her.

"I told her that you had gone up to your chambers, but she said you were not there. Where did you go?" Lord Brom enquired too.

"You have to listen to me. I had a vision of the attack. You must double your men at this gate, and leave here now."

"What are you talking about?" Prince Anthony chimed in.

"I am talking about the vision that I just had. If you stay here, you will all die. Please, you must leave. The undead army can not be killed by simply running them through with your swords. Their heads must be taken off."

"Well, now that we know how they can be killed, we do not have to leave our station," Prince Anthony argued.

"That was even after Lord Brom found out that cutting off their heads was the only way to kill them," she said, desperately trying to get them to listen.

"She has always been correct with her visions, father. I would heed her warning," Prince Rowan added, coming to her aid.

"Thank you, Rowan. Come on all of you, there will be too many trying to get into this gate all at once. The outer gates, they used a battering ram to break it down."

"Anthony, go and tell your men to double their posts, and secure the outer gate with more stones. Block this gate better as well. We do not want them having easy access into our keep," King Jason ordered.

Prince Anthony left with a few of his men to brace the outer gates more securely, Prince Rowan left to secure the main gate.

"Where is Dakota?" Princess Ellyria questioned.

"He was in the tower last I checked. Why?" King Jason asked.

"Do you know if his potion is ready?"

"No, he left to finish it, but he has not yet returned," he replied, seeing the worry written all over his daughter's face. "What is on your mind, Ellyria?"

"I need his help with an idea that I have. Brom, take my Father safely away from this gate. I do not want to take any chances of either of you getting killed," she advised before running back to the castle.

Princess Ellyria ran to the tower as fast as she could through a hidden tunnel, remembering that the shortcut made for a great game of hide and seek with her brothers when they were children. Life was so much simpler than she thought, as he ran the rest of the way up the stairs and threw open the door.

"Ellyria, what are you doing here?" Prince Dakota asked, surprised to see her.

"There is not any time. Have you gotten the formula ready?"

"Yes. I am adding the final mixture to the last of these vials.

Why?"

"I need to know what it is they are supposed to do," she inquired breathlessly, then noticed her brother looking at her as if she were crazy, but she did not care what he thought of her right now.

"It is a highly flammable liquid. If we throw these at the undead army, then shoot arrows lit with fire, they go boom," Prince Dakota explained, amused by the look on his sister's face.

"How many do you have?"

"I have only been able to bottle twenty or so, but I have another twenty bottles that can be filled within the hour."

"Good, because we are going to need them," she informed him, looking out the open window. In the distance she could see the hundreds of torches marching toward the castle. Not even the tower guards were high enough to see from such a far range. She must get down there to warn them, and fast. "Give me some of the vials, and I need you to call for Luna. I have an idea that just might work to stall the attack on the castle."

Prince Dakota called to his giant white owl, which was large enough to fly two people on her back. She landed on the tree standing outside his window.

"What is the plan, sister?"

"Have Luna carry these over the outer gates, about fifty yards out, and drop them. I shall have father alert the archers to shoot flames onto that very spot. If it is as flammable as you say it is, that will derail the undead armies' march, giving you enough time to finish filling the vials," the Princess instructed.

Prince Dakota passed a few of the vials to Luna and told her what to do. She flew off in the desired direction and dropped the vials on the ground. When Luna flew back, his sister climbed out of the window and onto the giant owl's back.

"What are you doing?" Prince Dakota called out to her.

"I am taking a shortcut, it will be much faster this way," she replied fearlessly. Luna carried her off to the courtyard below, so Princess Ellyria could find her father…

King Jason looked up to see Luna landing beside them, with his daughter on her back. Princess Ellyria slid off the owl and ran over to her father.

"Father, Dakota made an explosive potion. We sent Luna over to a space, about fifty feet past the outer gates. When your men see the army pass onto that mark, have them shoot lit arrows, and we shall watch them explode," she said proudly.

"That is brilliant! Leave it to my little brother to come up with something like that," Prince Anthony beamed.

"Was that all he had? Or is there more?" King Jason inquired.

"He has about ten left, and twenty more vials that he is filling now."

"That is not a whole lot, Princess," Lord Brom added.

"I know it is not, but it will buy us enough time to go in and start rolling some heads," she acknowledged.

"What do you mean by 'us'? You do not honestly think that we will let you in direct combat, do you?" Lord Brom questioned worriedly.

"I can fight."

"You could not even carry a sword, much less swing one," Prince Anthony scolded.

"Watch me," Princess Ellyria declared courageously, taking the sword from her brother. She tossed it up into the air, then drew on her powers to manipulate the sword. Using her hands, she made motions carefully wielding it back and forth, slicing through the air. Everyone stood there speechless, as she proved her point.

"That was impressive," Prince Rowan announced, breaking the awkward silence.

"See, just because I am a female does not mean that I am weak," she added.

"That is cheating, you have powers," Lord Brom teased.

"I do not think that in this case, it is cheating, my dear Lord Brom," she teased back, kissing him on the cheek.

"Sire! The army approaches!" the man in the tower called down.

"Give the signal!" King Jason ordered.

Several arrows were ignited, by the guards in the towers, then shot out from the outer gates. A loud explosion was heard, as the entire path where the undead soldiers stood went up in flames. The front lines were killed upon impact, while the others stomped right over the charred bodies, walking through the flames unscathed.

"They are still coming!" Prince Anthony cried out.

"Let us hope that Dakota brings the rest of the vials down soon, or we are going to be fighting sooner than expected," King Jason observed.

"I shall go check his progress," Princess Ellyria offered, climbing onto Luna's back. "I will be back momentarily."

"I hope that she returns with more of those vials, I would hate to have to get all bloody," Prince Rowan added sarcastically.

"Oh, brother, you will be getting bloody. I can guarantee it," Prince Anthony informed him.

"That is enough you two. We do not have time for any foolishness," their father chided.

"Do you think that the potions will be enough?" Lord Brom questioned.

"We can only hope," replied King Jason.

Princess Ellyria returned to the tower, to see if Prince Dakota had finished filling the vials. When she arrived, he had some strange contraption on his table.

"What is that, brother?"

"This is going to be one of my greatest inventions," he responded, displaying the strange bag-like object, with a long tube on one side, and a small sac on the other end, resembling closely to a sheep's bowels.

"What is it exactly?"

"This is the sheep's stomach here," pointing to the center piece, "then this is the lower intestines," pointing at the tube, "and this is the sheep's testicles," he informed her, pointing to the sac on the end.

"So you have utilized the stomach as a water bag, and the intestines for like a pour spout. What are the testicles for? Dare I ask?"

"I put the potion in the main sack, then I pump it out by squeezing the smaller sack here, then it sprays out since I have sewn it together allowing the liquid to pass through. Once it sprays out, fire can be shot out on them from the towers," he explained.

"So they will be saturated in this stuff, then go up in smoke once the flaming arrows are shot out. Am I following you correctly?"

"Yes, that is basically the point. Although the unfortunate thing is, I will have to wait until they are under the wall, so I can spray this stuff on them."

"Meaning?"

"Meaning, that we will have to wait until they breach the main gate."

"That will pose a risk," she stated, frowning at the idea.

"I have nothing else. I am sorry."

"Well, I do. Come on, and bring your flame-throwing sheep guts with you."

"What did you just say?" her brother asked.

"I said bring your sheep guts with you," she repeated.

"No, before that."

"I said something about flames, and throwing."

"That is it!" he shouted, then kissed her on the forehead. "Flame thrower. You are smarter than you look," Prince Dakota complimented her affectionately.

"Hey, you better watch it, or I will turn you into a toad."

"Like that could happen," he teased.

"Alright, there is no more time for jesting, we have to go now before the army breaks down the gate."

Yes, little sister, we shall go now," he said, before he gathered his flame-throwing sheep guts, then followed Princess Ellyria out of the tower.

Prince Anthony, Prince Rowan, Lord Brom, and her father were all standing on the upper wall, looking down at the undead army trying to break down the outer gates, when Princess Ellyria showed up with Prince Dakota.

"I see that you have finished what you were making?"

"Yes, father, but she has an idea that I am not even aware of yet," he explained.

"What do you mean by 'idea', daughter?"

"I am going to use the amulet to create a larger version of this," she stated, watching Prince Dakota's face drop.

"How are you going to do that? You would be better off leaving majick out of this fight," Prince Anthony interrupted.

"Does it not go into that whole personal gain category?" Prince Rowan questioned.

"I do not believe so. Not if I am using it to protect the castle, our lives, and fighting off evil forces," she smirked.

"She does have a point there," Lord Brom added.

"What do you think, Dakota?" she inquired.

"I do not think you should try to make this bigger. I think you should create the fire," her brother suggested.

"What? I have never created fire before, only water, and a portal," Princess Ellyria confessed. She was trying to run the idea of fire creation through her mind, as she held out her hand a tiny spark appeared, turning into a tiny flame. She manipulated the image into that of a fireball, when she opened her eyes, she was amazed.

"Wow! Look at that!" Prince Rowan proclaimed.

"Do you think you could throw that?" Prince Dakota asked.

"I am not sure. I could try," Princess Ellyria mused, tossing the fireball out of her hand, landing it on the ground below, barely missing one of the guards. "Oh, I am sorry!" she shouted, looking down to make sure that he was alright, before she turned back to Prince Dakota.

"That is great! Try it again, but throw it further this time," Prince Dakota suggested. He watched as his sister concentrated again making another fireball, as she threw it even further. "Wonderful! Let us see if you can throw one straight up in the air."

Princess Ellyria threw the next fireball up into the air, while Prince Dakota squeezed his invention, spraying it out into the fire.

It burst into a stream of flames that went out several feet in front of them.

"I think that will work!" Prince Dakota rejoiced enthusiastically.

"I agree, brother. I am so sorry that I had doubted you, dear sister," Prince Anthony apologized. "Now, let us go kill those undead bastards!"

With their newly devised weapon in hand, they left the safety of the wall, marching down to the main gates, to rain fire on their enemies' parade…

The undead army breached the outer gates with their battering ram. Arrows were shot, but the minions were unaffected by them as they pressed on, even with arrows deep in their bodies. Knights fought gallantly, running straight into the enemy slashing off their heads with their swords. As hundreds of the undead horde filled the courtyard, their next mission was to bring down the main gates and storm the castle. They were using the battering ram again, as several of the undead were heaving it into the doors, trying to bust them open. On top of the wall, the men grabbed the sides of a large vat of oil, pushing with all of their might to tip it over onto those with the battering ram. Screams were heard, as was the sizzle of burning flesh. The undead were covered in the boiling-hot oil, but still stood back up after their affliction. Steam came up from their bodies and the skin on their faces had melted, revealing their bones. They picked up the battering ram again and continued to thrust it into the castle gates. King Jason's men flanked the undead at the battering ram, sending heads rolling upon the ground. More of the undead minions followed to take their place, as the battle raged on…

"Dakota, we must get down there now, to help them, come on," Princess Ellyria said fearlessly.

They both went down the stairs from the outer wall, that led to the courtyard. Prince Dakota brought his new weapon and stood beside Princess Ellyria, who was waiting for the right moment to create a fireball. As the minions saw them, they immediately headed in their direction.

"Now!" she shouted, sending up the flame.

Prince Dakota sprayed the potion into the fire, sending the flames into the enemy. The undead screamed, backing away from the flames that engulfed them, unaffected by the fire they kept coming as if they were immune to the flames.

"Dakota, run!" Princess Ellyria cried out, standing her ground, then conjured an energy ball, sending them back into the far walls by the outer gates. That seemed to have had little effect on them either, as they still kept marching on.

"Ellyria, get out of here, now!" Prince Dakota shouted.

Lord Brom heard her brother's cries. Prince Anthony, Prince Rowan, and King Jason, all with swords in hand, charged their enemies in the courtyard. Lord Brom brought Princess Ellyria a sword, and together they made heads roll. Princess Ellyria stood back, allowing the sword to do all the work, as she wielded it with her mind. She floated it above the undead men, then swiftly to their surprise, the sword that was in midair came down on them, removing their heads from their shoulders. One by one, they were cut down. The King's men were still outnumbered, by at least a hundred of the undead.

Prince Dakota had moved a few of the barrels of the black powder away from the castle, so the archers could have better aim. When the barrels went up, it was like fireworks in the sky, several of the undead soldiers were taken out in the explosions. He quickly noticed that as the undead men were killed, they faded away like the raven had. The amulet created these men from majick, meaning they could be killed by the amulet too. He tried to call to his sister, but she was too far out in the courtyard to hear him, so he grabbed a sword and ran in her direction. He was not a great swordsman, but he was good enough to swing the pointy end into the enemy. Chopping his way through the crowd, he finally made his way to Princess Ellyria, who was presently distracted at the moment fighting off the minions.

"Ellyria, use the amulet to take their life away!" Prince Dakota called out to her.

"What do you mean?" she asked, still focusing on the sword and decapitating the enemy.

"The amulet created them, maybe the amulet can destroy them too," he revealed, fighting to stay alive.

"I can try. Watch my back, will you? I can not very well keep a sword in mid-air, and try to figure a way to use the amulet to destroy them," Princess Ellyria mused, then focused her energies, imagining the amulet taking them out, or removing the life it gave them in the first place. The stone lit up brightly, casting rays of light outward, as the undead fell to the ground and vanished into thin air.

"That is it! Keep doing that, it seems to be working!" Prince Dakota advised, while trying to fight off the never-ending hordes of undead soldiers that kept coming to attack them.

"I will try," she stated, keeping her focus. The amulet remained lit, casting out great beams of light into the minions, effectively eliminating them one by one. Princess Ellyria continued to slowly walk through the courtyard, as the undead soldiers were dropping to the ground in her wake.

King Jason and the others were unaware of her actions, as they courageously fought the enemy. Lord Brom ran in between them, aiding them with his sword, taking every last monster he could and leaving them headless. The undead were strong, and they had taken down several of the King's men already, running them through like butter with their blades. Prince Rowan signaled Gaia to charge, so she flew up from the field and unleashed her attack on the undead army. At least a hundred of them remained, but as dawn approached, the giant dragon took them down. Gaia shot a furious blaze of flames, as they stumbled around blinded by the fire that melted their eyes shut. The dragon bit their heads off and spat them back out. As the battle raged on, the King's men fought the undead army with a vengeance, while Princess Ellyria wiped out their very existence…

Dawn broke on the eastern horizon, marking the beginning of a new day. The enemy had been slain and faded away, with the ending of their lives. The only dead that remained were those who died in service to their King, ensuring their kingdom's survival. The warriors were carried from where they had fallen, to be sent to their families to mourn them. All that remained from the battle was the blood-stained fields, when the rains came, it would cleanse the Earth of the evil that had soiled the ground…

Princess Ellyria stood at the center of the outer wall looking down into the courtyard. Her favorite fountain managed to remain standing, unscathed by the battle, but she could not say the same for the gates that were struck down, or the courtyard itself, which had been devastated by last night's events. As she looked out from the castle into the morning sun, the wind blew through her long black hair, she knew that this was not the last of the wizard's revenge. In fact, this was just the beginning.

The war on the realm of Ragnarok was coming, and there was no way to stop it…

PART THREE: THE WAR OF RAGNAROK

Heimdallr turned away from the young girl sitting in his lap listening to tales of old. He paused, momentarily distracted as he listened carefully to what was going on below. The sounds of battle cries and devastation rang in his ears.

"Hnossa quickly, you must go back to the safety of your mother's arms. You will be told when it is safe to come back out."

"What is going on? Heimdallr, I am scared," she cried out.

"Fear not, little one. I shall keep you safe, but you must go now. The war of Ragnarok is about to begin, and you will not be safe here. Now go!" he warned her.

Heimdallr watched as little Hnossa ran as fast as her little cherub legs could carry her. His gaze returned to the world below, as he watched what was foretold to happen centuries from now, prematurely unfold before his very eyes.

Even though he was a powerful God, he could not control the fates of mankind, or the fates of the Gods themselves. It would be in the hands of the Chosen One, it was up to her and her alone, to decide the fate of the realm…

Chapter 45

Bodies lay scattered along the ground. Blood-covered tables were turned over, and those who had managed to escape would not remain hidden for long. Nuri and a few of the others hid behind one of the large tents that remained standing, waiting for a small group of the undead soldiers to catch up with the others, before they left the sanctuary of their hiding spot. The gypsies' new Bandolier was not prepared for the assault. After her cousin Mala died, it was all she could do to assume the responsibilities of the new leader of their tribe. It was almost unheard of for one so young as she to assume the role of Bandolier, but Nuri was next in line, being the only living relative of Mala. Her eldest cousin was twenty years her senior and never had children of her own. So by rights, Nuri became the new Bandolier. She awakened from her daydream, as the lookout returned to alert her whether or not the coast was clear to move on.

"The stragglers have passed on, it should be safe to move on to the village if we hurry," the man informed her.

"Thank you. Come, let us go before we are seen. We must gather everyone we can that is still alive. If possible, we need to collect all the remaining potions to defend ourselves. Grab all the weapons as well, even from the dead if you have to. We must put our superstitions aside, so we can stay alive long enough to move south," Nuri advised, as she led the small group with her to the village, but when they arrived, they had not expected the horror before them.

The undead soldiers were ransacking the village, and the gypsies were fighting back with all they had, but the undead came back, even after being struck down. No potions or pitchforks seemed to have any effect on them, they continued to leave only terror in their wake. Nuri needed to come up with a plan fast, before it was too late.

The screams from the men, women, and children were deafening to the small group slowly making their way along the backs of the tents. The undead soldiers sliced open the men with swords, and ripped limbs from their bodies, leaving them to die without mercy. The women were dragged into tents by their hair, as they were brutally beaten, and ravaged until they too died. Orphaned children became easy targets with no parents to protect them, and nowhere to hide. Many of the older children were tortured and killed for sport, while the younger, plumper children became the main course, as they were put on a spit over a roaring fire. Some of the undead soldiers went on to Narruc to await new orders from their master, only a few remained to finish their meal.

The village was completely destroyed. Many gypsies were slain, but those that were able to run sought shelter. Nuri and her group went through collecting the living, and what little provisions they could gather to travel south. They walked through the village back out toward what was left of the marketplace, stepping over the bodies that were scattered all over the ground. A few of the widows, that managed to survive, could not give comfort to their heartbroken and scared children. It is such a shame when youth is jaded by such tragedy. One of the newly orphaned children held Nuri's hand, as they walked free from Inamor, then looked up toward her for answers.

"What are we going to do, Nuri?" the small child innocently questioned.

"We are going to migrate to our homeland in the south, where we will be safe."

"Are the monsters going to be there?"

"No. The monsters are long gone, and from the looks of it, they are heading in the opposite direction. Do not worry, you shall be safe. I promise." Nuri hoped that she did not just lie to the child, and she made sure that they were not being followed. She began to think about what Mala had said about the Chosen One, desperately wanting to believe what she had told her. Nuri did not look back at their former home and kept moving forward. All of the horses were slain, so it was going to be a long journey ahead on foot.

Unless by some strange chance, someone helped them along the way…

Chapter 46

King Ian wasted no time lopping off the heads of his enemies. With every stroke of his blade, the undead soldiers fell to their knees. It was beneficial that his father sent word on how to kill these bastards, just in the nick of time. Rob the Red and his crew fought bravely alongside him, taking them out one by one. Sweat dripped from his brow soaking his long red beard, but it did not slow him down, as he severed heads leaving a trail of undead soldiers in his wake. The undead army was not prepared for the fight the Vikings were dishing out…

Regnuom's city was prepared for the assault of the wizard's armies, but many of the villages were not. Captain Jake barricaded the door, but it was not going to hold for long...

"Father! Get Nicole and Gabe out of here now!" Captain Jake shouted. He was holding the door closed with only a few posts, but the undead soldiers had procured themselves a battering ram.

"Jake! What about you? I can not just leave you!" Nicole cried out, holding Gabe securely in her arms. The baby was scared and crying, from all of the horrible noises coming from the door.

"Nicole, do not argue with me, go with my father now. I will be alright, I can take care of myself."

"Should I not stay, and help you fight them off?" Lord Thomas questioned his son.

"No, father, I have this under control. Please, get my wife and child out. Take them out the back, and head for the ship. I shall fight them off. Now go!" Captain Jake heard Nicole weeping, but he could not look back at her or he would not attempt what he was about to do next.

With his sword in hand, he swung open the door and ran out wielding it with fury. The undead soldiers were taken aback by Captain Jake's courage and tried their best to kill him. Swords clashed with a piercing ring, back and forth they struck at him, but were no match for Captain Jake's cunning skills with a blade. Even though the odds were stacked against him, he fought them easily. After spending years at sea, he could hold his own, having fought way more men at once in the past than he was right then. Captain Jake kicked and pummeled his way between them, bringing up his sword for the finishing blow, leaving heads rolling around on the ground. It was fortunate the message from his brother came through and had given him plenty of time to prepare, before any of the undead soldiers came knocking at his door.

Nicole tried to keep Gabe quiet, as Lord Thomas escorted them out the back to the shortcut in the forest, leading to the docks, but his constant cries alerted one of the soldiers to their whereabouts. Jake heard his son's cries, and unfortunately so did the soldiers. They left in mid-fight, at the chance to eat the tender morsel that was crying.

"Oh no, you do not! Not my son!" he shouted, running up behind them. Before they could turn their heads, Captain Jake removed all interest that they had in his crying son by removing their heads.

Captain Jake heard Nicole scream and ran to the other side of the keep as fast as he could. He found his father on the ground, and one of the undead minions had Nicole by her hair, while trying to grab his son.

"Jake!" Nicole tried to fight the man off, but she could not with Gabe in her arms.

Captain Jake flanked the distracted man from around the corner and cut off his head. Nicole screamed as cold blood splattered across her face. Jake threw down his sword, then embraced his wife and child.

"Are you alright? Did he hurt either of you?"

"No, we are fine," she sobbed into his chest. "Was that all of them?"

"Yes, I believe so." At that moment, he remembered his father lying on the ground. He walked over and knelt beside him, luckily he was still breathing.

"Father? Father, wake up. It is I, Jake," he said, while tapping him gently on the face and trying to revive him. His breathing was shallow, and blood soaked the back of his head. After a few moments of persistence, Captain Jake managed to wake his father.

"Jake? Is that you? Where is Nicole? I am so sorry, I tried to fight him off, but he hit me with the blunt of his sword. He could have killed me, but he did not."

"Nicole and Gabe are fine. You did the best that you could under the circumstances," Captain Jake assured, as he embraced his father and helped him to his feet.

"Thank you, son. Now let us head to the ship before any more of those undead bastards show up," Lord Thomas advised.

"I couldn't agree with you more father. Nicole, shall we?" he said, extending his arm to his wife.

Nicole only smiled up at her husband, carrying their son tightly in her arms; they left for the ship, with her husband and Lord Thomas as her escort. They were together as a family, that is all that mattered to her, hoping that this was the last they would see of this war.

Although the Captain and his family felt they were safe for the moment, they were unaware of the dangers that were still to come… Meanwhile back in the city, King Ian and his army, with Rob the Red and his crew forced the remainder of the undead army out of Regnuom. Those that were killed vanished into thin air…

King Ian and Rob the Red were walking through the battlefield past all of their fallen brethren, neither of the men could find the right words to describe what they saw.

"I find it utterly horrifying and amazing at the same time that among the dead, the undead are not to be seen," he spoke up, breaking the silence between them.

"Well, at least you do not have to clean up after them," Rob mused.

"You do have a point there, but I do not think that it will be the last of them. Honestly, I do not think that will be the only battle we will see."

"What do you mean?"

"From what my sister warned me about, this wizard is going start a war. No one will be safe from his wrath. I just hope that we bought ourselves enough time to prepare for the worse that is yet to come," King Ian stated.

"You have my word, that my men and I will fight by your side, your Grace."

"Thank you, I appreciate that. Let us get these men home to their families, so they can lay them to rest."

King Ian and the others gathered the fallen warriors and prepared for the inevitable war, that they knew was coming for them…

The Draki were ready and waiting on the passengers to make their way aboard. The short trip to the dock had exhausted Nicole, who was very heavy with child. As soon as she arrived on the ship, Captain Jake escorted her to the captain's quarters.

"I shall take care of Gabe, you need to rest," Captain Jake chided.

"Are you sure? I could try and get him to take a nap with me."

"I can take care of our son, you need to take care of our other son," he said, patting her large belly.

"How do you know if it is another son?" Nicole asked, looking longingly into his eyes.

"The same way that I knew when you were carrying Gabe," he said with a wink and smile, kissing her gently on her forehead, before returning on deck.

"How is Nicole?" Lord Thomas inquired.

"She is tired, but I think once she has rested she will be fine," Captain Jake replied, taking his son from his father's arms and walking with him over to the wheel. "Let us see here, Gabe. Watch and learn my boy, I shall have you a captain of your own ship in no time," he told his son. Gabe giggled, as he tried to turn the heavy wheel of the ship, while in the safety of his father's loving arms.

"How long do you plan on having us out at sea, Jake?" his father questioned.

"As long as it takes. Lord Brom is supposed to alert me when it is safe to return home."

"You are aware that your wife could very well give birth while we are out at sea, right?" Lord Thomas stated, giving his son a worried glance.

"Yes, father. I am well aware that could happen, but between the two of us, I am sure that we could bring the child into the world in one piece," he laughed.

"Son, I just worry for you. With no midwife on board, if something goes wrong, we will not know what to do."

"You do have a point. We shall head to Inamor and pick up a midwife there, to bring along with us."

Captain Jake had no idea Inamor was left in ruins by the undead army, as he directed the ship southwest toward the home of the gypsies…

Chapter 47

"No!" Princess Ellyria screamed. In her rage, she sent several objects flying across the room, that went smashing against the walls. She would have fallen through the floor by now had it not been made of stone, as she walked back and forth in her bedchamber, like a caged animal. "Why does he keep going after everyone else, but me?"

Poor Isis, who was not at all comfortable with her rampage, had remained quiet until she was accidentally hit with one of the flying objects.

"Ouch, that hurt," the big wolf whimpered.

"I am sorry, girl. I am just really frustrated right now. I should not take it out on you. It is not your fault."

"I forgive you," Isis sighed, then laid back down in her favorite spot and went back to sleep.

An afternoon nap seemed like a good idea, but Princess Ellyria needed to inform her father of what she saw in the mirror…

King Jason was in his study preparing his next battle strategy, when his daughter came running in out of breath.

"What is it, Ellyria? Are you alright?"

"Father, I saw what the wizard has done. He completely destroyed Inamor and attacked Regnuom. They need your help. It appeared as though Ian and his men were able to fight the undead army off, but the undead army is just the beginning of Raul's assault on the realm."

"Are you sure Ian was alright?"

"Yes, I am sure that he was fine, but several men, women, and children died in Inamor. I do not want to see any more lives taken by that wizard!" she shouted, smashing her fist to the table.

King Jason looked at the wild look in his daughter's emerald eyes. He worried for her.

"I shall call for your brothers and gather my men. We will head out early tomorrow morning before daybreak," he assured her.

"Thank you, father," she said, embracing him before leaving the room.

King Jason then called to the guard just outside the door, to find his sons and ready the army…

"Father, you summoned me," Prince Anthony said, upon entering the room.

"Yes, I did. Where are your other brothers?"

"I am sure that they will be here shortly."

Moments later, Prince Dakota and Prince Rowan entered the room.

"What is going on, father?" Prince Dakota questioned.

"Your sister has informed me that Inamor and Regnuom have been attacked by the wizard's undead army. Many lives were lost in Inamor, and Regnuom suffered extensive damages as well."

"Is Ian alright?" Prince Anthony questioned.

"Yes, Ellyria saw that he was, but she feels that we need to go and assist them. I do believe that this was only the first in a series of assaults the wizard has planned. I do not want to take any more chances, and we must take action now. Perhaps if we cut them off before they regroup in Narruc, we can take the remaining undead soldiers down. I do not want to make anything easy for the wizard," the King instructed.

"Yes, father. I shall get the men ready. When should I tell them that we are leaving?" Prince Anthony inquired, before walking out the door.

"Before dawn, we will head out. Where is Lord Brom? We will need him to come with us as well."

"The last I saw of him he was speaking with Princess Ellyria out in the summerhouse, as I was heading this way," Prince Rowan answered.

"I need you to let him know of our plan as well," King Jason informed his sons. "Dakota, I shall need you to gather, as many potions that you think we will need, in case we run into the wizard. I need to go find your mother and let her know what is going on. I shall see you all in the morning," he added, before leaving the room.

"Well, you heard him. Let us get ready to go to war," Prince Rowan declared.

"I shall go pack the potions, you go find Lord Brom," Prince Dakota instructed his youngest brother.

"Very well, I shall see you in the morning then," Prince Rowan said, as they both walked out of the study together before parting ways.

"Yes, I shall see you tomorrow," Prince Dakota added, then headed back to his tower and watched his brother turn in the direction of the courtyard. He was not certain of which potions to pack, but he would collect the strongest ones.

Prince Rowan walked out to the courtyard, to see if Lord Brom was still in the summerhouse with his sister, but he could not see them from where he was currently standing… Meanwhile, Lord

Brom was in fact in the summerhouse trying to talk some sense into Princess Ellyria, but she was being too stubborn to listen to reason…

Princess Ellyria was pacing back and forth franticly, her thoughts interrupted by Lord Brom. She stopped pacing long enough to stand there and stare at him with her arms crossed, waiting for him to speak, but she already knew what he was going to say.

"Ellyria, you do not need more powers to defeat the wizard. You have more than enough, and you have the Amulet of Elements. What more do you think you need?" Lord Brom questioned, noticing she was furious, more so than he had ever seen her.

"I will do whatever is necessary to defeat him, Brom. I had hoped that you would have figured that out by now!" she shouted at him, stomping her feet as she walked off, passing her brother with haste, back to the castle.

"What is wrong with her?" Prince Rowan inquired.

"She feels that she needs more power to defeat the wizard. I told her my opinion, and now she is angry."

"I could tell. We are heading out to Regnuom before dawn. Raul sacked Inamor and left enough devastation in Regnuom, making my father want to go with his armies there. Ellyria was the one who told us," the Prince informed him.

"So, that is why she was so upset."

"She did not tell you what had happened?"

"No, just that she needed to find how to get more power, and asked if I would help her find someone who could," Lord Brom said, running his fingers through his golden hair. He looked out toward the castle and knew he had to go speak to her. "Tell your father I will be ready and meet you before dawn. Right now, I need to go and apologize to your sister," he added, before leaving the summerhouse.

Prince Rowan nodded, then stayed behind for a moment,

before leaving to inform his father that Lord Brom was going with them. He worried for his sister, but at the moment he worried for Lord Brom more.

While the army was preparing for their departure and the men were gathering supplies, another was preparing for tomorrow as well…

Chapter 48

Raul never considered vanity to be among his many traits, but as he looked upon himself in the mirror, he did now. The faeries he had eaten returned him to his youthful appearance, but it had since worn off and he was his former repulsive self…

The glass shattered as the wizard's anger took over once again. He needed to figure out a more permanent solution. Raul went to his grimoire and opened it, to search for a potion that he could use to regain his youth permanently. Faeries were the main ingredient in the eternal youth potion that he had found, as well as needing rose petals, rosemary, and sunflower oil. The faeries would be the most difficult to capture. He needed at least a dozen of them alive for the potion. The remaining ingredients he believed were in his cabinet. He did a quick inventory check before leaving for the Black Forest. He was sure the Faery Queen would try and attack him to protect her children, but he had a plan to stealthily gather the faeries he needed. After he had made sure that he had all of the additional ingredients for the potion, he vanished from the cottage…

Raul was not surprised to see the forest had regained its

former beauty, since he had set fire to it only a few weeks ago, he knew that it had to have been the Princess's doing. The forest was flourishing and was heavily abundant with faeries for the taking. He quickly disguised himself as an old woman, using Liza's likeness for inspiration. He knew faeries loved crème, so he brought some along with him, fresh from a cow in a nearby village that had been destroyed by his undead army. Raul was surprised the cow had gotten away and was left unharmed. He placed a large saucer down on the ground and then poured the rich crème inside. After patiently waiting a few moments, the Fae came out from hiding.

"Come out little ones," he said, disguised as the old crone, cooing to the faery folk. "Care for some fresh crème?"

Timidly, the tiny sprites came out of hiding and flocked to the fresh bowl of crème, and quickly began lapping it up.

"There now, did grandma not bring you some good crème? You drink it all up now," he urged, sitting back up against the tree, waiting for the sleeping potion to set in. At least fifteen faeries gathered around the bowl greedily drinking the intoxicating crème; there were more than enough for the potion. One by one, the fat-bellied sprites drifted off in a peaceful slumber, then he carefully placed them one by one into a brown sack. Once they were all nestled inside, Raul changed back into his natural glory, vanishing from the forest…

The cottage was so empty now that Toby was gone. The wizard missed him at times like these, when he would reappear from out of nowhere and startle the boy. It was so amusing the way he would almost jump right out of his skin. Raul refocused his mind on the task at hand. He needed to prepare the faeries for the potion. The grimoire called for the faeries to be ground into a fine paste, then mix in the rose petals and rosemary, then slowly add the sunflower oil until completely blended. The recipe only called for a minimum of a dozen of the sprites, but he would use all of them to ensure the spell's permanence. While they were still sleeping, he pulled each one out of the bag, laid them gently in his mortar, grabbed his pestle, and began triturating the tiny sprites. Cracking and popping echoed throughout the cottage, breaking the lonely silence, as the wizard ground the faeries together. One by one, he added in more of the sleepy sprites, that were dreaming of sweet crème and had no idea of their fates. Blood, bones, and faery dust soon turned into a thick paste. Raul then added the rose petals, rosemary, and sunflower oil, mixing it until well blended. He read what the next step was and laughed at what it said.

"I have to apply it to my what?" he read out loud. He saw a few faery guts had accidentally spattered on the page, wiped it off, then read it again, more carefully.

"Apply it to the face and drink the rest. Eternal youth will not be far away if you recite these words for old age to go away," he recited. That was the silliest spell he had ever seen. He went to another mirror that hung on the wall, then smeared the concoction all over his face, and slurped the rest straight from the mortar.

"Old age go away, may eternal youth forever stay," he chanted. Faery majick was powerful by itself, but combined with other ingredients, it really packed a punch. Sparkling lights surrounded his face for several minutes before Raul was completely astounded by what he saw in the mirror. He raised his hand to his face, it was smooth to the touch, free of wrinkles, blemishes, and free of warts that covered his former face. He had recaptured his youth once again, looking like he did when he was a young lad in his early twenties. He was as handsome then, as he was now, and forever.

"If this mirror could talk, I am sure that it would say I was the most handsome bloody wizard in all the land," he boasted. He raised an eyebrow at an idea that came to mind, a way to assist him in his efforts to bring about the final war to Ragnarok. Raul pondered for a moment, studying his new face when it finally came to him. He knew exactly who he would call upon to quench his bloodthirst for war.

After changing out of his robes, he returned to the mirror and admired his new hard body as well. He could not believe how godlike he now appeared. He was chiseled to perfection and was sure he could make even the finest sculptor envious. He quickly donned tighter fitting clothes and riding boots that he had stashed away from someone he had killed. Not that he even remembered who it was, nor did he care. Time was a precious commodity, and he had to put his plan in motion.

After checking his new image in the mirror one last time, completely satisfied with his appearance, he vanished along with his reflection…

Chapter 49

Princess Ellyria returned to her bedchamber and prepared herself for bed. She had already bathed and brushed out her waist-length black hair, when she heard a knock at the door. She already knew who it was before she had even opened it.

"I wanted to come and apologize for not listening to you earlier. I am sorry if I hurt your feelings," Lord Brom said sincerely.

"Would you like to come in?"

"Do you not consider it to be inappropriate?"

"Brom, I am a grown woman after all," Princess Ellyria stated, stepping aside so he could enter her bedchamber.

"I also wanted to inform you that I am going with your father and brothers to Regnuom. We are leaving right before dawn. I am not sure when I will be back," he began to inform her, then finally noticed what she was wearing, as she started fidgeting with her hair, pulling it over to one side and combing it with her fingers. It was her sleeping gown, too thin for the warm weather, and it left absolutely nothing to the imagination. He was so distracted by her large breasts, and rosy nipples, that he lost sight of what she was saying.

"I want you to be safe. I need you to come back to me," she whispered.

"Give me a reason to return," he added, then stepped a little closer to her, his desire for her was so overwhelming that it was hard to get out what he had to say to her.

Princess Ellyria threw caution to the wind and went to him,

covering his mouth with hers. Lord Brom was happily surprised by her brazen display of affection and kissed her passionately in return. He had not been with her in weeks, and her intoxicating kisses were sending shock waves throughout his entire body. Her hands searched his chest through his white, blousy shirt, her fingers nimbly finding the ties so she could remove them. While applying tiny kisses to his chiseled chest, his hands caressed her large breasts under her transparent gown. She found the ties to his trousers. After removing his belt, she pulled the ties and opened his package like a present. He let out a gasp as she fell to her knees before him. She took his throbbing member into her soft, petite hands. Curious if she could pleasure him in the same way that he had pleasured her, she slowly ran her hands up and down his hard shaft. When his breath became quickened, she knew that he was enjoying it, then she was curious. What if she kissed him there, as he had done before to her?

Lord Brom braced his hand up against the wall, as he felt her hot breath upon his manhood, and nearly fell over when she placed tiny kisses all over it. She knew this had a feverish effect on him, so she slowly put him in her mouth. He let out a moan, as she licked the head of his manhood, and then took him even further into her mouth. He then aided her in the art of fellatio, by gently pushing her head back and forth on him, while gently grabbing a handful of her long soft locks. She was a quick study and worked more skillfully on his member. He arched himself into her, close to release, which he did not want to do yet. She stood up as he assisted her to her feet, and was quickly swooped up into his arms.

Lord Brom carried her to the bed, his long strides allowing for a shorter distance, then threw her down swiftly. She giggled at the gesture, but was quickly silenced by lustful kisses, as he covered her mouth with his. He stopped only for a moment to disrobe her, to pull her closer to him, so he could continue to explore all her naked glory. She felt his hot breath on her neck, kisses trailing slowly down the side, down to her collarbone, and lingering still lower until he trapped one of her erect nipples. She arched her back, grabbing herself with her hand, feeling wet heat coming from between her own thighs, as he suckled from her breasts. When he left the comfort of her bosom, he returned his kisses to her flat stomach, and teased her belly button with his tongue. She flinched slightly, almost bucking herself into him. He smiled assuming she wanted his mouth where her hand was. Pushing her hand gently out of the way, he softly kissed her, then she arched herself into his face, grabbing his long, golden blonde hair. His expert tongue was parting her, as he plunged it deeper inside her. Her womanhood pulsated under his kiss, and her warm juices flowed over his lips. A small moan escaped her mouth, and she could not wait a moment longer to have him. She pulled his hair away to gaze longingly into his eyes, beckoning for him to take her right now. He stood up while removing his pants, climbing over her in the bed, and leaning down to share the sweetness of his kiss. Desire had taken completely over her, as she grabbed his manhood in her hand stroking him gently, slowly urging him to enter her. He teased her, allowing for her to only have the tip of it before pulling away, but when she held it firmly in her hand he had no choice but to surrender. Guiding him into her, she pushed him in and out of her, causing him to gasp at the sheer sensation of feeling her stroke him and go into her at the same time. He could not stand for her torturous pleasure anymore, so he quickly plunged himself deep into her. She sucked in her breath and followed his rhythmic strokes, by wrapping her petite legs around him and returning his thrusts. In a playful mood, he grabbed a hold of her waist, and then rocked himself back, until she was on top of him. She quickly found her own rhythm, and watched as he threw his head back into her bed. When she leaned over to kiss him, he took the opportunity to grab a hold of one of her bouncing breasts into his hands, gently massaging each one, then leaning up to latch onto one of her rosy nipples with his hungry mouth. She nearly fell on top of him from the sensations racing straight from her nipples to her loins, and grinding her hips into his. Her release dripped down over him, once he knew she had gone over the threshold, he picked her up off of him and bent her over the pillows. She was nervous about what he might do to her, when he gently pushed on the small of her back with his hand. He entered her womanhood from behind slowly, and she shuddered almost instantly. This sensation was completely new to her, as he plunged himself harder and deeper inside, pulling her hips into his. Her pillows muffled the screams of pleasure that consumed her, as she let go once again, then drenched his thighs from her intense pleasure. He was proud that he had created such an effect on her. He pulled himself out from her and then rolled her over onto her side to lay behind her. She was in amazement as he entered her once again, grabbing her hip to pull her towards him.

Princess Ellyria clutched the pillow that was under her head so she could moan into it. Never had she had dreamed of such pleasure, and Lord Brom brought it out of her all too easily. Quickly, he rolled over on top of her and erupted with his own pleasure. He filled her core with the very life from within him. He collapsed on top of her, as he tried to slow his heavy breathing. She wrapped her arms around him and held him until his heartbeat slowed. He leaned up to look into her beautiful, sapphire eyes, pushing a tendril of hair off to the side of her face. His swelled manhood remained within her, and he did not want to move from the comfort of her body.

"I do not have to be an empath to know that you do not want me to leave tomorrow, but I have to. I wish I could stay here in your arms and make love to you all day long. It would be way more enjoyable than going to war against an army of dead men," he teased her affectionately.

"I understand. I know that you are more worried for me since I will be going up against the wizard soon enough," she said, smiling as his face turned crimson confessing to the charges.

"Yes, I am very worried for you. I do not want to lose you."

"I promise that you will not lose me," she added, before leaning up to kiss him.

He returned her kiss gently, only for a moment, then backed away to look deep into her eyes.

"I need you to promise me that you will wait for me. I want to marry you when this is all over."

"Promise me that you will return, and you will have your bride."

"I shall hold you to your promise," he added, before he kissed her once again.

Lord Brom made love to Princess Ellyria, again and again, that night, until they were exhausted from their exertions. They remained wrapped in each other's arms, until they drifted off into a peaceful slumber. Tomorrow would bring a new day, but it also would bring about the beginning of the end...

A few hours had passed since their romp, Lord Brom looked over at a still sleeping Princess, cautiously slipping from the bed to not awaken her. It was still quite dark outside, but he needed to make his way to his room and prepare for the quest. He also needed to sneak out of her room without being caught by one of her brothers, or worse her father. Lord Brom hastily put on his clothes and stood a moment longer to watch his love sleeping peacefully, before leaving the room.

Lord Brom knew that if he did not say goodbye to the Princess one last time, it would upset her, but he could not have left if he had...

Unable to sleep, Prince Anthony decided he would patrol the halls making sure all was quiet in the castle. When he walked around the corner to check on his sister, he saw Lord Brom sneaking out of her room. He did not want to cause a scene in the middle of the hallway, so he followed Lord Brom instead, to see what else he had been up to. As soon as Lord Brom had entered the guest chamber, he was grabbed from behind and pushed up against the wall.

"What is going on? What is your problem?"

"I think that I should be asking the same of you, Brom?"

"I do not know what you are referring to," Lord Brom replied, thinking that the Prince had taken leave of his senses.

"Do not play innocent with me. I saw you leaving my sister's bedchamber at an inappropriate time of the night without an escort. That could only mean one thing. You have dishonored my sister and my family," Prince Anthony declared. He was so disgusted he could not even stand to look Lord Brom in the eye. "Do you have anything to say for yourself, before I wake up my brothers?"

"I have not dishonored your sister or your family. Ellyria is a grown woman and she can make her own decisions, about whom she allows in her bedchamber alone at night," Lord Brom added, then pushed the Prince off scowling at him.

"She is not one of your trollops, Brom. She is a Princess. You are supposed to be serving her father, the King, but you are dishonoring him by deflowering his daughter."

"I am not dishonoring anyone. She came to me of her own accord, she chose to be with me."

"So, this was not the first time, was it?" Prince Anthony enquired, before he took a swing at Lord Brom. He was able to dodge him and then grabbed his arm swinging it around behind him. Prince Anthony tried to break free of Lord Brom's grasp, but he could not.

"Are you going to stop trying to hit me long enough to explain, before I let you go?"

Prince Anthony nodded his head. Lord Brom let him go, and the Prince turned around to face him.

"What exactly, are your intentions with my sister?"

"I plan on making her my wife when all this is over. Listen, I love your sister more than life itself, I would never dishonor her," Lord Brom confessed, waiting for a reaction from Prince Anthony, but it was not the reaction he had expected.

"If you really loved my sister like you say you do, then you should not have slept with her first. I will not mention this to anyone, but I do expect you to do the right thing. You had better keep your word and marry my sister, or you shall have to answer to me," Prince Anthony threatened, lowering his head, for he was still too angry to look at the man standing in front of him, and left the room.

Lord Brom was not surprised by his reaction, but he could not worry about that now. He had to prepare for the coming war and keep his wits about him. Princess Ellyria was the reason for him to return home in one piece, and as promised, he would marry her upon his return...

The men gathered in the courtyard just before dawn, filling saddlebags with provisions and weapons for the long journey. They had carefully filed out of the castle careful, as to not awaken their women. King Jason left Queen Anna sleeping peacefully, even though he was fully aware of how angry she would be when she woke up. He told her that he was leaving last night, and they shared a wonderful night saying their farewells to each other. King Jason looked at his sons. Prince Dakota had gathered his potions and was placing them in the saddlebag on Luna's back. Prince Rowan had placed all his weapons in the bags on Gaia's back and sheathed his sword along the side. Prince Anthony had been the first one outside when he arrived in the courtyard earlier, and was already atop Odin waiting patiently to depart. His son's gaze was fixed on Lord Brom, almost as if he had angered him somehow. Lord Brom hoisted himself up onto his horse and was also patiently waiting to leave. He too was looking preoccupied with something. Nevertheless, it was time to lead the hundreds of knights to Regnuom, to assist his son King Ian in battle.

"Men, this will be one of our greatest challenges yet on the battlefield. You have always followed me into harm's way without any question before, and I am here asking for you to do the same once more. These enemies are not like anything you have not fought before. They are the same undead bastards we fought only weeks ago, to protect our home. Today we march for Regnuom, to help my son King Ian on the battlefield. I expect you to show him as much loyalty and respect as you give to me. Are you ready men? Are you ready to protect the realm and our homelands from the likes of those rotting corpses that are killing men, raping women, and eating children?"

The men shouted out their battle cries, raising their swords high in the air.

"Then let us move out and destroy our enemies, before they can take any more lives! To Regnuom!" the King shouted.

Lord Brom rode out of the courtyard amongst the hundreds of soldiers, but looked behind him one last time. He saw his princess standing in the window looking down at the plethora of horses and men leaving the castle grounds. Lord Brom was too far away to see her face, but he could almost feel her tears flowing down upon him.

King Jason led his army across the lands to Regnuom, unaware the undead army would not be their only adversaries on the battlefield…

Chapter 50

Swords clashed together echoing throughout the city. King Ian knew it would only be a matter of time before the next group of undead soldiers would come back for a second assault, after gathering more men. As predicted, hundreds more of the wizard's minions arrived to try and take down the city. The young King was not ready to give up the fight, no matter his need for a chance to catch his breath. Rob the Red was fighting alongside him, and back-to-back they fought against their enemies. Rob plunged his knife into the side of the walking corpse and lopped off its head with his sword. He felt the cold spray of blood splatter the side of his face before retrieving his knife, as the body fell to the ground at his feet. King Ian looked down at the body and watched it slowly fade away, before the ground was littered once again with another. Blood stained the ground, and many of King Ian's men were slain as they struggled to fight off the undead soldiers.

Hope was beginning to fade, and King Ian was not immune from thinking the same. He was exhausted, but still going through the motions. Rob the Red fought tirelessly, swinging his blade overhead, as he ran straight for his enemies. The battle continued for hours, but it felt like days had gone by, with no sign of it ever ending. The King's soldiers were being pushed back toward the castle, unable to hold their ground.

The men fought courageously, and they died just as fiercely…

King Ian looked up for but a moment and saw banners flying in the distance. It was his father! Suddenly, he felt courage emerging from deep within him to fight harder. He cut through the undead like butter, leaving a trail of heads, and their cold blood on the ground. The sound of thundering hooves came closer, as King Jason and his men arrived, attacking the undead army from behind. King Jason showed no mercy wielding his sword masterfully, and leaving heads rolling in the wake of his unrelenting fury against his son's assailants. King Ian's soldiers pushed hard against the enemy, right into King Jason's men, and together they fought against Raul's undead minions…

Hours later, the fallen soldiers both wounded and dead, were carried off the battlefield, then returned to their families. King Ian hung his head in despair, that so many lives had been taken. His father placed a hand on his shoulder, as they stood in silence watching the bodies being carried away. King Ian and his father were then joined by his brothers, as they came off the battlefield worn out and bloody. Lord Brom walked by as if to join them as well, but was warned off with a scowl from Prince Anthony. He walked past them and helped Rob the Red with the wounded.

"What was that look all about?" Rob questioned.

"A disgruntled, overprotective, older brother," Lord Brom replied.

"Ah, you have deflowered his sister I am guessing?"

"Not that that is any of your business, but yeah, that is exactly why he is angry."

"Not that it is any of my business, but do you plan on making her an honest woman? Because I would still marry the girl, deflowered or not."

Lord Brom flashed him a look that could kill if he had the power to do so.

"Yes, I plan on marrying her, as soon as I return from this bloody war."

"Well, that is good. I am proud of you, and I am sure your brother would be too."

"Have you seen my brother?" Lord Brom asked, quickly changing the subject.

"No, I am afraid not. I left to fight with your brother before they were to head out for the Draki. I have not heard anything yet. Not since we heard their village was attacked," he admitted.

Lord Brom stopped, then grabbed Rob the Red by the shoulders.

"What? Why did you not say something earlier?"

"I did not want to mention it when we were fighting off the undead."

"Come on now, let us go to the village. I want to make sure they are alright."

"What about the King?"

"I am sure that they will be fine without me for a little while," he acknowledged.

Lord Brom and Rob left for his father's village, while Prince Anthony was watching his every move…

Lord Brom was nearing his father's keep, when he grew tired of his shadow stealthily following him. Rob the Red mentioned they were being followed earlier, but they both did not let on that they knew.

Prince Anthony ducked behind a tree and waited a few moments for Lord Brom to move on. Instead, he was grabbed from behind, then shoved up against the tree.

"Why are you following me?" Lord Brom questioned.

"I wanted to see what you were up to. I can not trust you anymore. You betrayed my family!" Prince Anthony shouted.

"Are you that ill over Brom taking your sister's maidenhood?" Rob interrupted.

"Stay out of this, Rob. This is between us," Lord Brom retorted.

Rob moved out of the way, before someone accidentally hit him.

"There is nothing more to say to this traitor," Prince Anthony said, then spat at Lord Brom.

It was at that point Lord Brom had completely had enough, as he wiped the spittle from his face. He said not a word before he laid out Prince Anthony on the ground. The Prince tried to scramble to his feet to fight back, but Lord Brom was quickly on top of him throwing punches.

"Ouch, that looked like it hurt," Rob cringed watching Lord Brom and Prince Anthony roll around on the ground. He felt it was best that they work through their issues, before trying to break them up. After a while of watching them fight like a couple of children, he leaned in beside them, grabbed each one of their heads, and then smashed them together. Both men stopped fighting immediately to rub their aching heads.

"Have you two had enough?" Rob questioned.

Lord Brom and Prince Anthony looked up at Rob from the ground, all battered and bloody from fighting, before he helped each of them to their feet.

"I take it that you two have had enough, finally?" Rob repeated.

"Yes, we are done," Lord Brom admitted.

"I suppose," Prince Anthony added.

"Now, I am not the best at giving advice, but I will tell you this. Put aside your differences, for the time being, there is a war going on if you have not noticed, and we are on our way to see what has happened to your family, Brom. Prince Anthony, I do not know you, but I can tell you this, Lord Brom is stupid in love with your sister and he will make her an honest woman when he returns home. He can not if he is too busy having to kick your arse over something foolish. Do you understand my meaning?"

"Yes," Prince Anthony admitted, letting out a sigh.

"Brom, can you forgive the lad for trying to be a big brother, and looking out for his baby sister?"

"Yes."

"Good. You two had better kiss and make up, we have a village to attend to." Rob the Red walked out ahead of them, giving them a moment to start playing nice.

"I am sorry for not trusting you. You have been nothing but good to my sister," Prince Anthony apologized.

"It is to be expected, I suppose. I do not have a sister of my own, but I can understand that you have her best intentions at heart," Lord Brom admitted.

"So, you are really going to marry her then?"

"Yes, I am," he said proudly, putting his arm around Prince Anthony's shoulder to reassure him. "Let us go see if my family managed to escape, before the undead began their assault on the village."

Lord Brom and Prince Anthony caught up with Rob the Red and continued to the village. When they arrived they were mortified by what they saw...

The village was laid to rubble, and bodies were piled on the ground. The stench of burnt flesh invaded their nostrils, as they continued on. Once they had arrived at his father's keep, Lord Brom waved the men in opposite directions to circle the house. After making sure it was safe to go in, Lord Brom called out into the silence.

"Father, Jake, Nicole. Is anyone here?"

There was no answer.

Rob and Prince Anthony came in behind him.

"There is no one here," Rob announced.

"Do you think that they left in time?" Prince Anthony questioned, watching Lord Brom walking in and out of the different rooms.

"At least there is no sign of a struggle, or blood anywhere," Lord Brom said, as he walked back out the door, while the others followed.

"I bet they made it, Brom," Rob added, trying to be optimistic about the situation.

"It appears that way," Lord Brom whispered. He could not take the time to check the dock and see if the ship was in the harbor, even though he wanted to. The King would be wondering where his son had ventured off. He knew they had to be getting back, before there was another assault.

"I am sure that Captain Jake got everyone out in time. You can not allow yourself to worry about it now. Worrying will not keep you alive," Rob advised.

"He is right, Brom. We need to get back to the city, before my father starts to worry about me," Prince Anthony agreed.

Lord Brom nodded his head, looking at the empty keep one last time, before they returned to town…

Chapter 51

"Ellyria Rose! How can you just stand there like nothing has happened?" Queen Anna questioned.

"Because mother, I know where father went, and where my brothers and Lord Brom are. They are going to be fine. I promise they will come home," Princess Ellyria said.

"Well, I am glad that you know everything young lady," Queen Anna retorted, then continued her pacing in her nightgown. She had woken up to see her husband was gone and got up to find her sons had left as well. It was not that she did not know where they went. The point of the matter was that she did not get to say goodbye. What if something had happened to her loved ones? She would never forgive her husband for not waking her and allowing her to see him before he left.

"Mother, please. I think that you are overreacting to something that you have no control over," Princess Ellyria said, trying to comfort her mother the best she could, but she was being quite stubborn.

"And you do!"

"Yes, I do."

"If you have all this power, why then have you not killed the wizard? It makes perfect sense to me that if you kill the wizard all of this will go away. No war to send my husband or sons to, and I would not have to constantly fret over what happens to you!" Queen Anna shouted, then sat down on the chaise in the parlor. She sobbed into her hands, her long, black hair concealing her face from her daughter. Princess Ellyria walked over to her, sat down beside her, and placed a hand on her shoulder.

"I am sorry that I have failed you, father, and my brothers, but this is more complicated than you think. Do you not think that it has been difficult for me as well? I have given up my entire life to fulfill my destiny as the Chosen One, but I am still just a mortal. Yes, I have all this power, but sometimes I feel that it is not enough to defeat him," Princess Ellyria confessed.

Queen Anna turned around to face her daughter.

"I am sorry too. I thought that I had prepared you enough for your destiny, but I failed. I kept you locked away in this castle to keep you safe, but it was out of my own fears," Queen Anna admitted, looking into her daughter's emerald eyes. She watched as her daughter's face softened, and her eyes changed back to the color of sapphires.

"What do you mean?"

"I mean that I was selfish for keeping you confined to your own home. You should have had a normal childhood, one that you could have had fond memories of. I just could not fathom the thought of losing you," the Queen added.

Princess Ellyria wiped the tears from her mother's eyes.

"I did have a normal childhood. You gave me everything a princess could want. I had my brothers to play with, and Isis was my greatest gift of all. I also had the two most loving and wonderful parents a child could ever need, or want. I do not resent you, or my father for keeping me here, I know it was for my protection. I know that you did not want me to be harmed. I love you, mother."

"Oh, Ellyria, my beautiful baby girl, now a beautiful woman. I love you too."

Mother and daughter embraced one another for a few moments, both in tears. They paired off looking at each other and smiling.

"We can finally have some time with just the two of us, like we used to do when you were little," Queen Anna beamed at the idea, wiping her cheeks.

"No. I am afraid that I can not, mother," Princess Ellyria

stated, feeling guilty the moment the words escaped her rosy lips. She had an idea and wanted to see it through.

"What? Why? There is nothing more that you can do at the moment, but wait out the war with me. All of the knights have gone, all but fifty or so to watch over the castle. I need you here to protect me."

"I still have to go after the wizard."

"You said it yourself, that you do not have enough power to go up against him."

"That is exactly why I must leave. I need to find a way to get more power, so I can finally defeat him."

"How are you going to do that?"

"I am not sure, but I know who can steer me in the right direction," she informed her, before heading for the door.

"Ellyria, wait! Where are you going? When will you be back?"

"I am not sure, mother. Soon I hope!" she shouted back to her, as she ran up the stairs to pack for her journey.

Queen Anna watched her daughter leave from the window; she had not even said goodbye before she had left. It must be a family trait from her husband. She worried about her daughter going out on her own, but she had almost become accustomed to it by now...

Once Princess Ellyria had open ground, she kicked her horse at a faster pace. Why did she not use the mirror to create a portal? She would need to find a water source then. It would take too long on horseback to get to the Black Forest. The lake! That is where she would go, for it was not too far from where she was now. Princess Ellyria changed direction and headed to the very place that would always remain special to her and Lord Brom.

The lake remained untouched by the devastation surrounding it. It was still just as crystal clear and as beautiful as she had remembered it to be. She did not have much time for pleasant memories or daydreaming, she needed to continue her search.

Using the Amulet of Elements, she touched it to the clear water, after a flash of bright light, she was gone…

Princess Ellyria came up from out of the small pool of water, near the great Elder Tree in the Centre of the forest. The forest was quiet, almost too quiet, but she only had her task in mind. She walked over to Alfar's tree and knelt before it. Closing her eyes to call him, she went into a deep state of consciousness.

"Ellyria, what are you doing here?" Alfar asked.

"I need your help. I seek your advice. I am so lost, and I do not know what to do," Princess Ellyria confessed.

"What is it that you seek?"

"I need to know how I can get more power, so I can defeat the wizard. He has gained far more power than I have. I do not feel that I can beat him."

"Ellyria, my love. You have all the power in here," Alfar said, placing his hand to her heart, then he kissed her rosy lips.

"No, I do not. I need more," she pleaded, desperately in need of his help, but did not know how she could convince him otherwise.

"The power is in you, not in majick alone. Search your heart, it is in there, you just have to delve deeper."

"Alfar, my heart is full of love, but it is still not strong enough to conquer the wizard's hate," she confessed, looking into his eyes, but not seeing the answers she was searching for.

"Remember Ellyria, majick alone is powerful, but true power comes from within. Majick can consume you if you let it. Please heed my warning, I am sorry that I could not help you," Alfar advised, as he faded away with his final words echoing in the distance.

"Alfar, wait! No, please come back!" Princess Ellyria shouted, as she fell back on her knees and sobbed into her hands. There had to be a way…

Chapter 52

The wizard Raul was a foreboding foe to all. However, the memories of his past still haunted him, making it his only true weakness. As he stood at the entrance to the Ormr Mountain, the story of what once was returned to his mind with a vengeance…

"Please, do not do this, my son. Having absolute power is not worth the burden that you will have to carry."

"It seems to have worked for you all of these years. I am not going to ask you again. Teach me everything that you know, or I shall simply have to take what I want," the young man threatened, as he stepped closer to his father trying to intimidate him, but the old man stood his ground.

"Is this because I had abandoned you? I told you that I had never meant to hurt you. I was wrong to have given you up after your mother died. Please, can you find it in your heart to ever forgive me?" the old man asked, then walked to his son to embrace him, when his son welcomed him with open arms, he let out a gasp.

"No. I can not, father. I can, however, find what I desire from inside your heart."

"Why?" he questioned with his final breath, his eyes wide

with disbelief, as his heart was pulled from the cavity in his chest.

"So I can have absolute power, of course," he stated, before pushing him to the ground, while he held his beating heart in his hand.

The ground began to shake underneath him, he knew who was coming. Before his father's apprentice could arrive, he raised the beating heart to his lips and took a bite out of it. The taste was strange, but he quickly tried to consume it as fast as he could.

"What have you done to my master, boy?"

"I took what was rightfully mine!"

"His life was not yours to take!" he roared, charging at the young man. Before he could get to him, the young man had already thrown down the remainder of the heart and ran out of the mountain…

Raul wiped the past from his eyes, as he walked into the entrance of the Ormr Mountain. The old caves had not changed in centuries he thought, as he continued through the passageways to the center of the mountain. It was still daylight, so the inhabitants should still be sleeping if he remained quiet.

When he finally reached the entryway to the centermost part of the mountain, his path was blocked by a familiar foe.

"I was wondering when you would crawl back here, Ranulfr," Nidhoggr growled.

"After all this time, are you still holding a grudge? Is that not surprising," Raul was quick to reply, as he made a move toward the entrance.

The ancient dragon slammed his giant black tail across the threshold, curling it up to block him.

The wizard glared at his nemesis.

"I see that you are not going to make this easy for me?" the wizard mused, glaring at his nemesis.

"Now, why would I do that?" the dragon questioned, then stepped closer. "I shall not let you pass. So turn around and go out the same way you came in, wizard," he warned, as smoke filled his nostrils, patiently waiting to have his revenge.

"You are no match for me, dragon. Join me and then we can take over the entire realm. Try to fight me, then you shall perish along with the rest of them," Raul threatened.

Nidhoggr raised his mighty head opening his jaws wide, before he unleashed the fiery inferno onto the wizard. Raul stepped back, absorbing the flames into his hands, until the dragon stopped his assault. The Ancient One paused in disbelief and was surprised when the wizard hurled a giant fireball from his hands at him. Nidhoggr was taken aback by the blast and tried to shield his face with his wings. After the fire had dissipated, the dragon lunged at Raul, but he was sent into the side of the cave wall. Large rocks broke free and crumbled on top of Nidhoggr, as dust filled the cave all around him. He shook his crowned head free from the rubble, that had landed in between the spikes on his head. Once again, he lunged for the wizard, his sharp teeth snapping together. Raul waved his hands, sending the dragon back into the wall, but this time holding him there.

"You are no bloody match for me! Give it up, I grow tired of your pitiful attempts on my life. Stay out of my way, and you will not get hurt," Raul warned, laughing at the dragon's poor effort to break free from his spell, then stepped forward past him towards the center of the mountain.

The wizard followed the root leading to the Underworld. Instead of going further from his past, he was delving deeper into it. A chill crept up into his very core, as he descended to the world below...

"Who are you? Why have you come here?" A voice echoed through the silence.

"I am the wizard, Raul. I have come to make you a deal."

"I do not make deals," she hissed, as she appeared behind him. Her unique beauty took him aback. She was not at all the monster he had expected her to be.

"What if I told you that I could give you your heart's desire, and the revenge that you seek?" Raul offered.

The Goddess Hella looked at the strange young man before her. There was something so familiar about him, but she could not seem to remember.

"Who are you, really? Do I know you?" she questioned.

Raul pointed to the great root at the entrance and grabbed her hand. She pulled it away without hesitation.

"How dare you! Do you know who I am?" her voice bellowed.

Raul felt his knees buckle out from underneath him, as he was forced to kneel before the dark Goddess.

"I should destroy you for such disrespect."

"Would you kill your only son's child?" he asked, feeling her ice blue eyes looking right through him.

"Yggdrasill," she gasped, clutching her heart.

"Yes, he was your son. Remember?"

"You took his life?"

"I had to. He came at me. His only son, but that did not seem to mean anything to him. Not after he abandoned me. I never knew who he was until the war between mankind and dragons took place. He recognized me, as soon as he had laid eyes on me. To make himself feel better, he offered to teach me majick, to become a great wizard such as himself. He envied me and what a great wizard I became, then tried to take back his power. I had no choice, but to rip out his heart. It was the only way I could defeat him. I hope that you can forgive me," he explained, bowing his head before her.

Hella motioned for him to rise and embraced him.

"It must have been a heavy burden on you, after all of these years. I know how that feels. I have spent centuries alone, with only my regrets for company. While those who sent me here, relish in the joy of having their children all around them! He must pay for what he did to me. I will help you. What is it you require of me?" she declared proudly, and a smile widened over perfectly white teeth.

"I need you to open the gates of Utgardar."

"You know what you are asking of me, do you not?"

"Yes, I need you to release the Jotunn."

"Are you sure you want to release them? Once they are released, you may never get them to return," the Goddess advised.

"Yes, I am well aware of that fact. It is the only way."

"Are you ready to bring about the war of Ragnarok?"

"I am counting on it," the wizard said smiling.

"Before it is prophesied to occur?"

"Do you want your place in Valhalla or not? I thought you wanted revenge? This is the only way," Raul stated, waiting for a response.

"When do you need me to unlock the gate?"

"When I give you the signal. I have to tie up a few loose ends up there, then I will be ready for you to unleash them. Then you will be able to return to Valhalla, taking your rightful place in its golden halls. You have my word," he promised. Raul began to turn and walk away, but Hella called to him.

"When the time comes," she said, gazing into the pool. "You must lure the Princess into darkness. Make her your ally, and she will rule by your side. She will come to me first, and I will send her to you. In your new guise of youth, you are only your past self, she does not know that. Use it to your advantage, and I will do my part to see you as ruler of this realm. It will be my gift to you. Now go, I sense she is near. Ranulfr, make sure you are kind and gentle to her, it will complete your deception," she advised.

"So, you are telling me that if I woo her into the darkness, that she will forsake her duty as the Chosen One?"

"Yes, but she will still be bestowed with her powers. Use them through her, and you shall have what you desire. I have seen it in the pool, it is your destiny," Hella added, disappearing before the final words trailed from her icy blue lips.

Raul looked down at the pool, trying to see his future. The pool remained imageless, and he wanted to believe what the Goddess had said, but he still had his doubts. The Princess was very strong-willed, it would take a great amount of self-doubt to get her to crossover, but he did like a challenge…

Chapter 53

Princess Ellyria Rose left the Black Forest in search of answers, and she was determined now more than ever. There was only one that would have the information she sought. She returned to the pool touching the amulet to it, so she could travel to her next destination, then with a glimmer of light, she vanished…

The waterfall behind the Ormr Mountains was very peaceful, but Princess Ellyria could not linger any longer, she had to go see the Ancient One.

Nidhoggr had finally been released from the wizard's spell shortly after he left the cave. He returned to his place at the entrance to the World Tree and curled up to take a long nap. Unfortunately, he was interrupted by an annoyingly familiar voice.

"Nidhoggr, I do hope that I have not intruded, but I seek your wisdom."

"What is it that you want this time, Princess?"

"I need you to tell me how to obtain more powers."

Princess Ellyria had a look of determination on her face, but it did not change the answer he was about to give her.

"I will not be doing that," he declared, hoping to give her a hint to go away, as he laid his head back down, closing his eyes. It would have worked for most, but not for his present nuisance, as he felt her rubbing his giant nose. He should have eaten her a year ago.

"What is it you that expect me to say? I have already told you when you were training, that too much power leads down a dark path. Why the sudden desire for more power? Not that I care," he grumbled.

"I need more power to destroy the wizard, once and for all," she informed him and was not giving up now, no matter what he said. There had to be a way.

"You have all the power you need to destroy him. You must have faith in yourself. Now, go."

"I am not leaving until you tell me how. I know it can be done. How can I master, The All?"

"There was only one being on this planet that could wield the true power, and that was my master, Yggdrasill. Someone killed him mercilessly for his powers because they were so full of greed and hate, and they were blinded by it. My advice to you, is to give up the notion of obtaining such powers for personal gain," he advised, as he turned away from her, for now, he wanted a nap.

"Please Nidhoggr, you must tell me who I can speak with, to give me the answers that I seek. You must know someone!" she pleaded.

"Will you leave, if I tell you?"

"Yes, I promise."

"You must seek out the Norns. They can give you the answers you are searching for. Now go."

"Who is that, and where can I find them?"

"They are three, three sisters in fact. You can find them at the base of the World Tree. Now leave, no more questions. Do not bother me anymore," he growled, flashing a mouthful of razor-sharp teeth.

"Thank you," she said, bowing before she turned away. She did not hear anything more from him except for another deep growl, as she passed him to enter the way to the sacred tree…

Princess Ellyria saw no one, as she approached the base of the Ash Tree. She slowly walked around its massive perimeter finding nothing so far. How could this be? She had already walked around the entire tree, but saw no one. What now? She turned around to go back the other way, but then, as if it had appeared out of nowhere, a well was right in front of her. Curious, she peered inside. It looked very deep, but she could see the shimmer of water at the bottom.

"It is a long way down, if you are not careful, Princess Ellyria Rose," a strange voice called out.

She quickly turned toward the sound, which the voice was coming from. Three cloaked giants stood at the base of the tree spinning what appeared to be wool, on a giant spinning wheel.

"Who are you? How do you know my name?"

"Please forgive my sister, Urd, she can be rude sometimes. I am Verdande, and this is my sister, Skuld," she introduced herself while removing her hood. The other sisters followed suit, removing theirs as well.

"Are you the Norns?"

"Yes."

I have come for your wisdom. Can you help me?" the Princess asked.

"We know why you are here," answered Urd.

"We know you seek power," added Verdande.

"We can not help you," informed Skuld.

"Nidhoggr said that you could help me."

"We will not help you."

"Why not?" she asked.

"Do you know who we are, child?" Verdande questioned.

"No, not at all," she said, intimidated by their size, as they stood well over seven feet tall.

"We are the sisters of Fate. We create the Destinies of

mankind, and the Gods themselves. You are but a single thread in the web of mankind that we have created," Urd explained.

"Are you Goddesses?"

"No, child. We are above the Gods. We weave the destiny of all who live on this Wheel of Fate," Verdande added.

"I presume that you know of my destiny as well? Is that all you do each day, is spin the wheel to see where it stops for each living person?"

"You had better curb your tongue, young one," Skuld threatened.

Princess Ellyria grasped the concept that they were not to be tangled with.

"We also take care of Yggdrasill, supplying it with nourishment from the well. Feeding his roots, so that he can thrive," Verdande educated her.

"Do each of you do the same thing or have your own special talent?"

"If you must know, I am Fate, Verdande is Necessity, and Skuld is Being," Urd added irritably.

"You are all so young, to be the creators of Destiny," Princess Ellyria added, attempting to get them to warm up to her.

"We are maids, and must remain so, or we will not be able to spin the wheel," Skuld mentioned kindly.

"Why can you not tell me where I can get more powers?"

"As we have explained before, we will not tell you. We have already threaded what your destiny will bring long before you were born. It can not be changed. If we were to give you any advice concerning your destiny, it would change the course of the future. Your destiny can not be changed in any way, remember that others' lives are entwined with yours. Do not allow your personal gain to blind you from the fate of others," Urd disclosed.

"What can you tell me?"

"We suggest that you seek counsel from Hella. She can give you a glimpse of your future, and possibly give you the answers that you are seeking," Verdande advised.

"Be warned, child. Hella has two faces, which you may have

spoken with before, but may not be the same one that you might speak with now," Skuld forewarned.

"I do not understand. Wait!" she shouted.

Princess Ellyria watched as the three sisters faded from sight, stepping inside the tree. Now what, she thought to herself?

"Time is of the essence, child. The fate of the realm is in your hands. You are the Chosen One," the voices echoed through the caves.

Princess Ellyria had no choice but to seek out Hella, so she followed the root into Niflheim…

A familiar chill swept over her as she entered the Goddess's world. She knew where to find her, standing over her all-seeing pool. Princess Ellyria waited for Hella to emerge from the shadows.

"Princess Ellyria. What brings you here once again?"

"I have come to seek your counsel," she said, kneeling before her.

"Rise, young one. What questions do you seek to be answered?"

"I am on a quest for more power, to use to defeat the wizard, once and for all. Will you help me?"

The dark Queen sauntered over to the Princess, placing her hand on her shoulder. Hella's piercing, ice blue eyes felt as if they could see into her very core.

"I can not help you, but I know someone who can."

"Who then? How do I find them?"

"A Seidman named Ranulfr. He lives deep in Jarnvidr, the Troll Forest, between the forests of Toledya, and the Ormr Mountains. He is very powerful, and wise beyond his years. He can give you all the answers you are searching for, and perhaps more," Hella purred the information to her.

Princess Ellyria had a glimmer of hope, but still felt as if she was going to embark on a wild goose chase.

"Thank you, your Grace. I appreciate your help," she said, before bowing and turning towards the pool, but the Queen grabbed her hand before she could turn around.

"Heed this warning, Princess. The forest is full of grave dangers, so be careful. We do not need the Chosen One to be harmed now. Do we?" Hella stated, smiling wickedly, before letting go of her hand.

Princess Ellyria remained skeptical, taking her warning in stride. She could still feel the cold icy glare from the ruler of the Underworld, but ignored it as she vanished through the enchanted pool…

Chapter 54

Deep in The Troll Forest, between Toledya and the Ormr Mountains, where the Wood Troll Giants dwell, a new occupant took residence. The wizard erected a small cottage, gathered supplies, and prepared a new spell while he waited patiently for his guest to arrive. The locals kept at a distance and were not bothered by his presence, but he had not alarmed them to anything suspicious...

The grimoire was turned to the spell that would keep him alive for all eternity, if he did it correctly. If the Princess managed to kill him, his heart would be unable to be destroyed, then he could be resurrected once again. While mixing the ingredients for the potion, he happened to notice a clause at the bottom of the page.

"This can not be right," he read it again, "this adds a new detour in my plan." Raul finished the potion, then quickly drank it down. He clutched his chest, then leaned over the table, barely able to breathe. A few moments passed and the pain lessened. He stood up, took a deep breath, and closed the grimoire.

The wizard stopped by the mirror, to admire his reflection on the way to the cottage window. He flashed an evil grin while rubbing his porcelain white, perfectly straight teeth with his finger. After he was satisfied, he continued to his destination. The shudders were thrown open and Raul was greeted with a gust of fresh air, carrying the smell of newly blossomed flowers. He sneezed, waving his hands before him, as if it would prevent the sickly sweet floral scent from attacking his sense of smell. Raul could not stand the forest and all its beauty, but he had to keep up pretenses that he was not the wizard she knew before. While he was deep in thought, a small bunny hopped underneath the window, looking up at him with wide brown eyes.

"What are you looking at? Shoo, go away. Off with you now!" he shouted at the small rodent. He hated those small, furry, cute forest creatures. The bunny quickly hopped away, before the wizard had in mind to stew him for his supper. He was too small to bother with right now. Raul was too preoccupied with how he was going to ensure his resurrection upon his demise.

The only person that could resurrect the wizard beside the Princess, would be an heir…

Chapter 55

Princess Ellyria approached the lush green forest, where Hella had said she would find the Seidman deep within the home of the Wood Trolls. She walked along the worn, narrow trail, most likely made by its inhabitants, following the path that she had hoped would lead to the one she was searching for...

The animals timidly came out of hiding, curiously inspecting the new intruder. A wise, old buck led the others, as he slowly approached the Princess. She could sense his presence behind her, then turned around to speak to him.

"I know that you are all wondering who I am. My name is Princess Ellyria Rose. I will not harm you, I promise."

The eldest creature of the forest tilted his massive crown of antlers.

"You can speak to me?"

"Yes. I have the ability to communicate with all animals. I can hear your thoughts," she professed, then reached her hand out towards the stag.

"Why are you here?" he asked, sniffing her hand, then took

a step back.

"I am searching for the one they call the Seidman. I have been told he dwells within a cottage in this forest. Have you seen him?"

The wise old stag stepped closer to the Princess.

"I know not of this Seidman you speak of, but perhaps the wood giant Jarnvidr could help you."

"A giant? Is he friendly?"

"Yes, 'she' is quite friendly. I must be going now," he said, before turning away to lead the other creatures from the path.

"Wait! How do I find this giant?"

"By the waterfalls. Keep following the path to the right, and you shall find her," he advised, then quick as a flash he bounded back into the thicket, his white tail pitched high.

Princess Ellyria continued, keeping to the path, in the direction the stag had told her to go; what seemed to be hours later, she heard the sound of water. She ran toward the sound, knowing that it had to be the waterfall. Taking a shortcut through the trees, she came out into a clearing.

The breathtaking sight before her was unimaginable. Never before now had she seen such beauty. The waterfall was larger than expected, crashing down over a cliff, and covered with long flowery vines, that cascaded into a large lake. The banks were also covered with the same flowery vines, that seemed to take over as the predominant foliage. The clover grass was thick and lush, perfect to run through barefoot, or to lie upon for a short nap. Princess Ellyria had not noticed how sleepy she was until the lulling sound of the crashing water, and the inviting clover luring her to a peaceful slumber, that she could not succumb to. In an attempt to wake herself up, she took off her shoes and ran to the grass in the outer field, which appeared to be invitingly soft. Seeing was believing, and her feet would squeal with joy if they could, as she frolicked in the clover.

While the Princess was in the midst of her carefree abandonment, someone else was being entertained by the amusing show, sitting at the edge of the clearing. It was at that moment when Princess Ellyria opened her eyes after spinning about, that she noticed her audience. She had read many stories about giants, but none could have prepared her for the sight before her. Although she had not realized it yet, that staring rudely would get the attention of her onlooker.

"It is not polite to stare, or did no one teach you such manners human?" the giantess questioned.

"I do apologize for the rudeness. I am Princess Ellyria Rose. Are you Jarnvidr?" she asked, slowly approaching the giant.

"Yes. Why do you want to know?"

"I was sent by Hella. She said that you could help me."

The giantess stood up. She towered over Princess Ellyria, like a large oak tree.

"Help you? I do not understand what I could help you with."

"I was told that you could help me find the Seidman, who lives deep within this forest. Do you know where I can find him?" Princess Ellyria asked politely. She felt as if she was an ant in comparison to the giant, but was also surprised to see just how pretty she was. Giants were usually depicted as ugly fearsome creatures. This giant was none of those things. Jarnvidr's skin was a dark ashy color, and her hair was black as night. Princess Ellyria could not see the color of her eyes from so far away, she assumed they were just as pretty as her delicate feminine facial features.

Jarnvidr leaned down closer to the Princess, showing off a thick set of long lashes that accentuated her striking, green eyes.

"I do not know of this Seidman that you seek. But I do know of where his cottage is."

"Can you take me there?" the Princess asked, smiling up at the wood troll giant.

"No, I am afraid not. However, I can tell you which way to go." she said, flashing a cordial smile. "Follow the trail back to the far north side of the forest. There you will come across the cottage that you seek."

"Thank you. It was a pleasure meeting you, Jarnvidr. If you or your people ever need me, I will assist you," she promised, shaking the giantess's finger. As she turned to walk away, she heard the giant call out to her.

"Be careful Princess. These woods are not as peaceful as they seem," Jarnvidr said, as she disappeared into the forest.

Princess Ellyria was not sure what she had meant by her warning, but started her journey north, without knowing if she would arrive before nightfall or not. The path had remained unchanged, and nothing out of the ordinary appeared to her. She followed the path, as it slightly veered to the left, but was she still heading due north.

Up ahead was a dead end. A wall of vines blocked her path. A strange feeling overcame her and she rubbed her arms, to ward off a slight chill in the air, that had suddenly seemed to settle in. The Princess could sense that she was not alone and waved her hand moving the foliage away, to reveal the secrets it was camouflaging. A small cottage was revealed. She had finally made it.

Princess Ellyria slowly approached the door, keeping an eye out for anything that may perhaps jump out at her. Seeing nothing to cause her alarm, she knocked on the wooden door. She waited for a few moments, but no one answered. When she turned to look around, she was taken aback by the dashing young man, that seemed to have appeared out of nowhere.

"Is there something that I can help you with, miss?" he questioned, in a smooth, deep voice.

Princess Ellyria took a deep breath and tried to calm her fluttering heartbeat. "Yes," she barely whispered. It was all that she could manage for words.

The man affectionately touched her arm. The shock of electricity made the Princess pull away instinctively.

"I did not mean to offend you," he said sweetly. "Are you alright? May I offer you a drink?"

Princess Ellyria had forgotten her tongue once again. Why did she all of the sudden have no words? She reached up to touch her cheek and softly bit her lower lip. Why was he just standing there staring at her? Why did he have to be so handsome? She lowered her hand to her side and snapped herself out of his hypnotic gaze.

"Yes," she managed to say.

"Yes. Is that the only word you know?" he asked, then began

to ask the same question, in several different tongues.

Princess Ellyria laughed out loud taking him by surprise, by the look she saw on his face.

"I can say more than just yes."

"Oh, that is a relief. I only know five other languages," he chuckled. "Would you like to come in then, for some tea, or water?"

"Yes! I mean, yes I would like something. Thank you," she said, knowing that she was blushing by now. She followed him into a well-kept home, then seated herself by the hearth, and thought it to be peculiar that he had a fire going, when it was still warm outside. Princess Ellyria watched him diligently prepare something for each of them to drink.

He handed her a cup of tea, before joining her by the fire.

"I never caught your name by the way."

"Oh. It is Ellyria. Princess Ellyria Rose," she stated awkwardly, then sipped her tea, to avoid stumbling over her words any more than she had already. The tea was sweet and very pleasing to her pallet, but not too sweet, and slightly minty. Her mind had started to drift by the strange sensation of the tea, when she heard him speaking to her.

"Oh, I am sorry. What did you say?"

The young man, who appeared to be in his mid-twenties, flashed perfectly white teeth.

"I asked you if the tea was to your liking."

"Yes, it is. It is very sweet. What is it?"

"It is my very own personal blend of sweet flowers and various mints. Do you like it?" he asked.

"Yes, it is quite lovely."

"You never answered my question earlier."

Princess Ellyria felt his dark eyes upon her. They were almost piercing right through her. She crossed her legs, then tapped the side of her cup. The clinking was taking over the awkward silence, so she stopped.

"What question was that exactly?"

"What brings you here, my dear?"

His voice alone saying, 'my dear', made her uncomfortably

aroused. What was wrong with her?

"I am searching for the one they call, the Seidman," she asked, surprised by the laughter that came from him. What was so humorous?

"Is that what they call me?"

"You are the Seidman?"

"Yes, that is what I am, but that is not my name, dear girl," he informed her, stretching out his hand to take hers. "My name is Ranulfr. I am a Seidman, sorcerer, wizard, whatever you choose to call me."

"You are so young?" Princess Ellyria questioned. She could not have expressed the shock she felt, as much as it showed on her face.

"Yes, it is a family trait. I understand your surprise. I get that reaction all the time when I venture out of these woods," he paused for a moment to fill the girl's empty cup. "How can I help you?"

"How did you know that I came for help?"

"That is the only reason anyone comes into the Troll Forest this far to seek me out, for help with something that they need. What is 'your' need, Ellyria?"

Princess Ellyria ignored the fact that he did not address her properly. He said her name and that is all that mattered to her. She became fixated on his well-placed, full lips as he spoke. Then she looked at his strong jawline and perfectly sculpted cheekbones. His forehead equally balanced a prominent, regal nose. A thick tuff of soot-black hair was slightly covering it, matching thick, straight brows. She was able to regain her focus for a moment long enough to answer his question. What could he do for her? That was an almost tricky question. She could not let her imagination run wild. She needed to be serious. If that was possible.

"I was told by Hella that you could help me."

"Help you do what? May I ask?"

"Obtain more powers, to defeat an evil wizard where I am from."

"That is a lot to need help with. What makes you think that I would even help you?" Ranulfr questioned, crossing his arms, then slowly rubbed his chin.

Princess Ellyria's eyes narrowed, and she leaned in closer to him, accidentally spilling her tea in his lap.

"Oh, no! I am so sorry. Please forgive me. I did not mean to spill my tea all over you," she blurted out, while trying to keep from giggling. She had not even noticed, that during the spilling of her tea he had also spilled his own tea. "Your shirt, it is soaked," she added.

Ranulfr set his cup down, stood up, and removed his shirt. Princess Ellyria began to choke.

"Are you alright?" he questioned, patting her on the back.

She was so taken aback by his naked chest, that she had inhaled the wrong way.

"Yes. I am well now. Thank you," she said, in between gasps of air.

"Would you like me to open a window?" he said, hurrying to open the window anyway.

Princess Ellyria stood up, then tripped over her chair. He turned instinctually before he could open the window all the way, to catch her in time.

"Thank you, again. I am quite well, and I can assure you that I am competent," she said, while in his arms, then pushed off from his smooth muscular chest. "I am alright, really," she added, taking a deep breath.

Ranulfr helped her back to her seat, his hair glistening in the sunlight that penetrated through the crack of the half-opened window.

"Would you like some more tea? Since yours was lost to my pants," he teased.

"No. That will not be necessary," she said, practically writhing in her chair. "I need to be leaving anyway. Apparently, you can not help me anyway," she added shortly.

He grabbed her arm as soon as she stood up.

"Unhand me, sir."

"I am not going to let you leave without giving you what you came here for. I have never turned anyone away, and I am not going to start now."

"You said that you could not help me," she said, glaring at him with emerald green eyes.

"I never said that I could not help you. I said what makes you think that I would help you."

"I just assumed that..."

He placed a finger over her mouth and cut her off mid-sentence.

"I will help you, but you must follow my instructions carefully. Trying to obtain ultimate powers can be dangerous, for me and you."

"I never said anything about ultimate powers?"

"You did not have to. I already knew."

The Princess stepped back slightly, but noticed he still had her by the arm. "How did you know?"

"The same way that I knew who you were before you told me, and the same reason that I knew you were coming here. I am a Seidman after all," he said, peering down at her.

Princess Ellyria looked up at him. Gazing deep into his eyes, she wondered if she could trust him. Either he could block her power, or he was who he said he was. She had no other choice but to trust him.

"What do I need to do?"

"I have a potion that will make you more open to receiving ultimate power. If you let me, I can teach you how to obtain such power."

"Will it help me in defeating my enemy?"

"Yes. It will help you enhance the powers you already have, and develop the ones that you can have. If you follow my instructions. Is that agreed?" Ranulfr offered, flashing a perfect grin.

Princess Ellyria shook her head. She watched him retrieve a small vial, from a cabinet in the next room. He returned, presenting the potion to her.

"Drink it, and you shall be on your way to having ultimate power," he proclaimed, passing the vial to her. "Now drink, Princess."

Princess Ellyria looked at the vial in her hand. There was no turning back now. It was up to her to defeat the wizard. She touched the vial to her bee-stung lips, then turned it up and nearly choked, as the fiery liquid made its way down her throat.

"Here, this will help," he said, handing her a cup of water.

Princess Ellyria drank the water greedily, letting it cool her sore throat.

"Thank you," she said, returning the empty cup. "What do I do next?" she questioned, eagerly awaiting her new lessons.

"You become my new apprentice of course," he said, standing up straighter, then took her by the hand. "Follow me. As we begin your new lessons, you shall be staying here of course," he added, leading her to an empty room. "You may sleep here."

Princess Ellyria looked at the tiny room, that was smaller than her wardrobe at home, but she did not want to question him, nor be rude to him for his hospitality.

"Thank you," she said softly, before entering the room. "How long will I be staying?" she questioned, believing it was not too rude to ask.

"As long as it takes for you to grasp your new lessons, and to obtain the amount of power you shall need," he replied, leaving her to be alone.

Princess Ellyria closed the door behind him, then sat down on the tiny cot in the windowless room. She did not feel any different after drinking the potion. She did however feel tired after her long journey and decided to take a nap. Eyes wide open, she stared at the wooden beams in the low-hanging ceiling.

Instead of sleep coming to the Princess, she had an insatiable craving for power that had begun to consume her…

Chapter 56

Back in Regnuom, King Jason and his men were finally able to defeat the wizard's undead army. Those who were not killed were made to retreat. The city was devastated, many lives were lost, and the only building left standing was the Great Hall...

Lord Brom was in a daydream of sorts when Rob the Red tried to get his attention.

"Brom, the King is asking for you. He wishes for you to send a message to his wife and Princess Ellyria, to let them know that we are all safe and have defeated our enemies."

Lord Brom took his gaze from the distant horizon to acknowledge Rob.

"Yes. Tell him I will right away."

"Are you alright, sir?"

"Yes. I am well. Heavy in my thoughts is all. Carry on."

Rob the Red left Lord Brom alone. Lord Brom pulled some parchment and a quill from the tattered, bloodstained pouch on his hip. He began to write the words that flowed through him so freely. There was not a day that had gone by, that he had not thought about Princess Ellyria. He missed her. Once he finished signing his name, he tied it to a messenger bird and sent it home to Toledya.

Lord Brom walked back to the group of men he fought alongside, that were trying to restore some order to the chaos. Bodies were dragged away into a pile to be burned, while others that had been claimed by their families were laid to rest with a proper ceremony. Lord Brom covered his face as he passed by the fire pit. He saw the King up ahead in the distance, with Princess Ellyria's brothers.

The King was addressing the group of men, as Lord Brom approached.

"The enemy has been defeated. We have won this battle, but it is our duty to help the survivors and repair the damage that has been made. Although we can not bring back the loved ones that have been lost, we can give comfort to those that are in mourning. Let us rebuild Regnuom. Let us give back the city to the people," King Jason proclaimed, and then turned to his son. "King Ian, this is your kingdom, I will assist you in seeing to this city's reconstruction, and we will remain here until we are further needed elsewhere."

Lord Brom stepped up, unable to hold his tongue.

"What about Toledya? Should we not return soon, in case the city is attacked again?"

"Toledya has already been attacked once. I do not foresee it being assaulted again."

"Father. What if Lord Brom is right? What if the wizard is expecting you to think that he will not strike a second time? Right now, the castle is vulnerable. With very few men guarding it, and our mother has very little protection right now," Prince Anthony questioned.

"You may be right, son. Have you forgotten that your sister is also there protecting the Queen, and how powerful Ellyria is?"

"No, father. I was just stating a point, that Lord Brom is usually correct on these hunches of his."

"We will remain in Regnuom for the initial repairs and removal of the dead. After that, we shall return home based on Lord Brom's hunch that there will be an additional assault on Toledya. Is there anything else anyone would like to address?"

The men remained silent.

"Very well then. Let us finish our work here. We do not have much daylight left," the King added.

Lord Brom looked at the King, who did not appear to be too concerned with anything, other than assisting the others with the disposal of the bodies that were piled up everywhere. He hoped the message would get to the Queen soon. Even though he meant it for Princess Ellyria to read.

Toledya remained unharmed for the moment. Queen Anna Marie on the other hand, was very worried the wizard's armies would return while her husband was away. She was even more worried that her daughter had not returned, nor had she sent any word of her whereabouts...

"Oh, Isis," she cooed, while petting the large wolf's head. "Where is she? Oh. Why am I talking to you? It is not like you can understand what I am saying to you," Queen Anna said, then stood up and walked over to the window in the parlor. She watched as the sun set in the distance, and observed that the grass still had not begun to grow since the battle weeks ago. The ground was still stained with the blood of the fallen, and she knew that blood would be spilled once again.

The raven now perched on the windowsill, startled the Queen. A note was attached to its leg. She let out a sigh of relief, then removed the message from the bird. She did not recognize the handwriting, and it was addressed to her daughter.

"My Dearest Ellyria, your father's armies have defeated our enemies. He is well, and so are your brothers. I, however, am not.

Though I am physically well, my heart is full of sorrow. I long to be with you again and count the days until we are together once more, so that we can finally be married. The sun will rise and set many times until we meet again, but you will always shine brighter in my heart, I love you. Brom."

Queen Anna cried. She had no idea how he truly felt for her daughter. Although she knew her daughter loved him, she never knew how far their relationship had developed. She already had approved the couple's union and would see to it Ellyria's father did as well. She returned to the chaise to sit and finally relax now that she knew the war would be over soon.

"It is almost over, Isis, I do hope that they return home soon," she said with a sigh.

The Queen was pacified with the knowledge that the battle in Regnuom had been won. Her husband and sons were well, but she was still worried about the Princess...

Chapter 57

Deep within the Troll Forest, Ranulfr was preparing Princess Ellyria's breakfast, as well as her daily tonic…

The Seidman was busy with the morning's chores, having every intention to impress the Princess when she entered the dining area.

"Good morning, Princess. How did you sleep?"

"I slept well, then I woke up with this awful headache," Princess Ellyria complained, rubbing her aching head.

Ranulfr seated her at the table, then set breakfast before her.

"You shall feel better after you eat a hearty breakfast and drink your tonic."

"What is the tonic for?" she questioned, before smelling it, then smiled. It smelled the same as the tonic she had the night before. "Is this the same tonic you gave to me last night?"

"Go ahead. Be a good girl and drink it. Then eat your food before it becomes cold," he said, smiling down at her.

Princess Ellyria quickly swallowed the sweet smelling tonic. She was also very hungry and quickly began eating her plate of food. When she finished, she placed the empty dish in the basin and washed it. It was the least she could do, since her host graciously took her in as his apprentice.

"Are you not going to eat?"

Ranulfr peeked around the corner to answer her.

"I ate earlier. I am usually up before the sunrise," he informed her, then returned to his work and left her to the chores.

Princess Ellyria finished tidying up the cottage, while being considerate to not disturb her master. She was not certain what it was that he locked himself up within the other room, but it was none of her concern. She decided to go out and get some fresh air, but did not want to leave without letting him know where she was going.

Princess Ellyria gently knocked on the double doors. There was no answer at first, so she knocked a little louder.

"Yes," Ranulfr called out from inside.

"I am going out to get some fresh air."

"That sounds like a lovely idea. Enjoy the day."

Princess Ellyria closed the door behind her, stepping out of the cottage to enjoy the fresh air. The wind was brisk this early in the morning, as she stepped out onto the dewy grass, making her way into the woods. An outing was exactly what she needed.

As she made her way through the forest, a few of the animals came out to join her. A family of rabbits curiously hopped around the Princess, and a few chipmunks had just finished cramming nuts into their cheeks, before scurrying up onto a nearby tree stump. Princess Ellyria knelt down to pet one of the braver bunnies. She was curious to see the rabbit looking at her, as if it were trying to tell her something. The rabbit was ignored, as the Princess stood up and continued walking down the path. The animals looked at one another in confusion. The Princess should have heard their warning.

Princess Ellyria lost herself to the morning, while enjoying picking flowers and various herbs that she came across. The morning chill gave way to a warm afternoon, as she lost track of time. She stumbled upon the open meadow where the waterfall was. The soothing sound of the crashing water was inviting to her. Without wasting another moment, Princess Ellyria quickly slipped out of her white cotton day gown and eagerly ran toward the waterfall.

The water was chilly when she dove in. Her nipples hardened when she came up for air. She grasped her breasts in an attempt to warm them, but there was no relieving herself of the chill from the slight breeze that was blowing over the water. She held her breath, diving down once again before swimming over to the falls.

Princess Ellyria came out of the water, then flung her long black hair up and over through the air, letting it fall down along her back. She raked away the remaining tendrils that clung to the side of her face. A small alcove under the falls allowed her to sit on some rocks nearby. She pushed herself up out of the water and wrung out her hair, allowing it to cascade over one shoulder, then looked out from behind the falls. It was so peaceful within this little hideaway, giving her time alone with thoughts of Lord Brom. She felt herself growing with desire, as her mind drifted to the memory of when he had made love to her last. Simply on instinct, she reached down between her legs, to gently rub herself. How she wished that he were here in this beautiful place with her. Then she recalled the time in the lake when he first began to take her, but was interrupted by her father's guardsman. That was when he first kissed her down there. She lay down carefully on the rocks, then began pleasuring herself, while she envisioned Lord Brom kissing her deeply where her fingers were now embedded. She let out a soft moan, as she brought herself to climax. After catching her breath, she steadied her frantically beating heart and dove back into the cool water.

Princess Ellyria swam the distance to the edge of the bank. Her feet touched the bottom of the lake, so she stood up. Water dripped down her naked flesh, and the light reflecting the remaining beads made her appear as if she were sparkling. She wrung out her hair and let it fall down the length of her back, as it reached the curve right above her round bottom. She inhaled the fresh air deeply, then let it out slowly, closing her eyes as she exhaled. She outstretched her arms allowing the sun to dry her, without a care in the world. The swim had left her feeling completely rejuvenated. She was ready to face anything now.

Princess Ellyria opened her eyes, looking forward to whatever the rest of the day might bring her, unaware that she was being watched…

Chapter 58

The Queen of the Underworld peered longingly into her pool, awaiting word from Raul. He would let her know when it was time to unleash the giants from their icy prison. Until then, she must wait. Once she did as instructed, she would finally begin her revenge on all of Valhalla...

Raul arrived at the cottage before the Princess returned from the waterfall. He must contact Hella for her to open the portal from the Underworld, as he would open the portal from above ground. He would have to make excuses to Princess Ellyria, as to why he must take leave of the cottage. Until then, he would contact Hella through his scrying bowl. He poured the black liquid into the large bowl and peered into it until light shined through the darkness.

"It is time to unleash them," he said, then quickly covering the bowl with a satin cloth upon hearing the door open.

Princess Ellyria walked in, then headed straight to her room to change out of her damp clothes. After hearing her door close, Raul took the bowl and poured its contents out the open window, then placed the bowl in the cabinet.

The Princess emerged from her room wearing a pale blue

cotton dress. Her hair was coiled behind her head, and the smile she wore outshined the sun.

Ranulfr could not help but notice the glow about her. She was indeed beautiful. Although, he could not let his desire cloud his task at hand.

"Did you have a nice afternoon?"

Princess Ellyria followed the sound of his voice coming from the now opened doors.

"Yes. I had a lovely day," she replied, then noticed his attire. "Are you going out?"

"Yes. I have some errands to take care of in the nearby town. It is a few days away, but I shall be back before you know it."

"Shall I accompany you?"

"No. I need you to stay here and watch after the cottage. Keep it tidy, and make yourself at home. I must gather some much-needed provisions while I am there. I have provided an ample supply of your tonic. Make sure you drink it every day. To miss a dosage will set back your ability to harness the powers that you need, for you to defeat the wizard. Every day you will become stronger. Now, I must get going. I shall be back soon," he promised, then kissed her cheek and left the cottage.

Princess Ellyria touched her face, then in the blink of an eye, he was gone. She was not aware that he was so powerful, but somehow she still trusted him.

Without knowing when he would return, Princess Ellyria continued with her daily chores and studies. She had become a good apprentice, always busy reading the mountain of books Ranulfr left her with. Although, at what cost would she have to pay for such knowledge?

A few days later, Ranulfr returned to the cottage and found Princess Ellyria weeping. With haste, he went to her side to try and comfort her.

"Whatever is the matter, Princess? Why are you crying?"

She looked up at him from her window seat, in the corner of the room. Her emerald eyes were bloodshot. Rubbing her face with the back of her hand, Princess Ellyria sat up from her slumped-over position.

"Would you like to talk about it?"

"I do not want to burden you with my troubles. You have been so kind to me."

Ranulfr took her tiny hands in his and looked longingly into her eyes.

"There is nothing you could say that would cause me to feel such a burden. Please, go on, and tell me your troubles, my dear."

Princess Ellyria felt so comfortable around him. She could not understand what it was about him that seemed so familiar to her, but it was comforting, nonetheless.

"It is... It is the man that I love," she said, struggling with the words. Why did she feel guilty telling him such a personal thing?

"What about him? Did he hurt you in some way?"

"Oh, no. Of course not."

"What is it about him that has upset you so?"

"I am worried for him. He went away to war, and I left home before I could get word from him about his safety."

He watched her for a few moments. The tears began to drip down her face again. This time he was there to wipe them away.

"I could find out if he is safe or not for you."

"You can?" Princess Ellyria whispered, reaching out and touching his arm, as hope began to flow through her once more.

"I can scry and find out where he is, to make certain if he is alright or not," he offered, then stroked her hand gently and was surprised she had not tried to pull away.

"You would do that for me?"

"Of course. I would do anything for your happiness."

Ranulfr smiled at her and went to his cabinet to retrieve his scrying bowl. He poured water into it, then looked deeply.

"What do you see?" the Princess asked.

"I see a man with golden hair. He is bravely fighting against the enemy."

"He is alright then? Yes?"

The expression on the handsome man's face went pale. He looked up at her. He had only pity in his eyes.

"I am so sorry, Princess. He fought bravely, but could not best the ten or so men that had encircled him. He did not have a chance."

"No! You are lying!"

"No. I am sorry, but I am not. Look here, and you will see," Ranulfr stated, waving a hand over the water, to allow her to see what he saw.

Princess Ellyria peered into the water and saw the horrifying image of her love lying there in a pool of his blood. He was dead. How could this be? She flipped over the bowl and ran to her room.

Ranulfr could hear her screams from inside, then went to her. He barged into her room and pulled her into his arms.

"I am so sorry that you had to find out that way, but it is better that you know the truth now, before finding out later. Please Ellyria, you must calm down. It is not good for you. Here, drink this, it will calm your nerves."

She took the cup, and without even looking to see what it was, she swallowed it down. It was pleasant to the taste, and soothing going down. After a few moments of silence, she managed to dry her tears and calm down.

"Thank you."

"If there is anything I can do for you, anything at all, you have only but to ask, and I shall do it."

She nodded, then embraced him. He held her in his arms until she pulled away.

"I need some time to myself, if that is alright with you."

"Of course. Take all the time you need, but unfortunately, I have to leave again. I am not exactly sure when I will return this time. I will try to hurry though. I promise."

"What should I do while you are gone?"

He waved his hand over hers.

"A new spellbook for you," he said with a smile.

Princess Ellyria could not believe her eyes. He was incredibly talented.

"How did you do that?"

"If you study hard, you can do the same trick," he teased.

Princess Ellyria held the book to her bosom and kissed him on the cheek. "Thank you again. I would not know what I would have done without you being here with me just now."

"Think nothing more about it. I am here for you. You know that now, but alas, I must be going. I will return before you know it," he promised, before taking a chance and gently kissing her rosy lips.

Princess Ellyria did not push him away, nor did she return his kiss. She simply sat motionless with her eyes closed, until he pulled away from her. When she opened her eyes, he was gone...

Chapter 59

From out of the pool in the Underworld, Niflheimer opened, releasing Hrimthurs. Hella greeted him, as he emerged from his icy prison. He looked upon her and motioned for the others to join him.

"Why have you released us?"

"I released you from your prison to serve under the great wizard Raul. He has asked me to summon you to do his bidding."

"What is it that he asks of us?"

"To destroy our shared enemies in Valhalla."

"I will gladly go now to crush those who sent us to our frozen prison!" Hrimthurs said, flashing a wide grin.

"I am glad that you are willing to aid us in our mission, but you must wait until Raul gives us the signal to attack. Until then, we must be patient," the Queen advised.

Hrimthurs nodded before gathering his army to sit and wait for the signal from the wizard.

Hella sent word to Raul that she had opened the Niflheimer, that Hrimthurs' army was ready for the attack. Now, it was up to Raul to open the portal to the Jotunheimer...

Raul appeared in the Centre of the realm. He raised the earth to expose the portal underneath. A light glow from the darkness marked the entrance to the Jotunheimer. The ground beneath him began to shake, then the portal opened. He entered the darkness until he reached the otherworld. There, he observed his surroundings. Similar to his own realm, Raul searched for the leader of the Jotunn. He never would have guessed that he would live in what would appear to be a castle.

The castle was heavily guarded. Giants that stood like angry trees made their move to attack the wizard. With a flick of the wrist, majick proved stronger than muscle, and the giants were set on their arses. No one could stop this new invader.

Surte stood up from his fiery throne, sword drawn in hand.

"Who are you to enter my world human?"

Raul immediately bowed before him, to show respect.

"I am the wizard, Raul. I am the Goddess Hella's grandson. I have come to request your unique talents."

"What is it that you wish of me?"

"I need you to complete your destiny of course," Raul stated, flashing a perfect smile and laughing wickedly.

Surte thunderously made his way down from his throne to stand over Raul.

"You have yourself a deal, sire," he accepted, as his laughter bellowed throughout his chamber, then shook the wizard's tiny hand. "Tell me what you need me to do."

Raul looked up at the giant who was kneeling before him.

"Go to the Underworld and find Hella. She will then instruct you when to strike, but you must wait until I give the signal. You will follow her into Valhalla, and begin the war of Ragnarok," the wizard ordered.

Surte nodded his understanding and then left the wizard's side to gather his army, then Raul vanished once again...

Chapter 60

Princess Ellyria had spent the past two days working obsessively on the spells from the book Ranulfr gave to her. She tried desperately to get the images of Lord Brom out of her head. Every time she closed her eyes, she would see him covered in blood. If she was able to sleep, she was plagued by nightmares. Her only chance to avoid the dreaded dreams was to stay awake...

The Princess was now despondent. She no longer bothered to try and occupy herself with chores, or spells. Nothing helped to relieve the pain. She went to the mirror and almost did not recognize herself. Her hair was dull and lifeless from being unwashed. Her green eyes were puffy and swollen. The dark circles shadowed their former glimmer. With having thrown herself into her chores and spells, it left its marks by leaving bruises on her body. Disgusted by her image, she decided to try a hot bath. Maybe she would feel better, at least if she washed her hair that would help.

Princess Ellyria lugged several pitchers of heated water to the bath, then scented it with some rose oil she found in the cabinet. She slipped off her dress, letting it fall where she stood, before stepping into the water. The bath was perfect, and she laid her head against the back of the tub. Her eyelids became heavy, as she succumbed to her body's need to sleep.

The nightmares came back to haunt her. Lord Brom was slain again and again, before her very eyes. Blood seemed to be everywhere. She looked down at herself, and she too was covered in blood.

Princess Ellyria awakened to her own screams. Water had been splashed out of the bath, and she was brought to her senses by the soothing tone of a man's voice.

"Ellyria. Ellyria. Calm down. It is I, Ranulfr. I am here now. It is going to be alright."

She felt strong arms around her, with only a drying towel to cover her, but that meant he had to have seen her naked beforehand. Her cheeks burned not only from her tears, but also from the embarrassing state that she was in.

Princess Ellyria felt her tears being wiped from her face, then his mouth pressed to hers. What was she thinking? Suddenly she returned his kisses with such ardency, that she surprised herself. How was this even happening?

Ranulfr lifted her from the bath dripping wet and carried her to his bed. He set her down gently and removed his clothes. She looked up at his naked body. He was tall and slender, but very muscular. His black hair had come undone, and it fell over his broad shoulders.

Princess Ellyria welcomed him with fervent kisses and exploring hands. He too took his time in learning every curve on her body, trading out between hands and lips. She arched herself into his face the moment he buried his tongue inside her. She pulled his hair and wrapped her petite thighs around his head. He came up to place kisses along the insides of her thighs, as it was still pressed to his face. Soft moans escaped her lips, which were soon stifled by his probing tongue. They kissed passionately, caressing each other with curious hands, as if to memorize each other's bodies. He sucked in his breath when her small hand reached around for his throbbing member. She masterfully stroked him from root to tip, intensifying his desire. He then trapped one of her erect nipples in his mouth, gently suckling on it, while fondling her other breast. She writhed underneath him, trying to draw him closer to enter her.

Ranulfr did not want to take her just yet. He wanted her to be so ready for him that she practically begged him to take her. He made quick work with his fingers, plunging them deep inside her, as he continued his assault on her full breasts and hardened nipples. She grabbed his manhood again, urging him to take her. Her loins ached for him to enter her, and she almost whimpered in his ear. He felt as though he had kept her waiting long enough, then pushed his hard desire deep inside her. She met his thrust with eager anticipation, tilting her hips up to accept him further. They met each other's rhythm with vigorous strides, while their mouths searched with equal passion.

Princess Ellyria was flipped over, so she was now on top of Ranulfr. She rocked her hips over him in a fluid motion, while he placed his hands tightly on either side. He pulled her down onto him, so that he could penetrate her even deeper. Even he let out a moan of ecstasy, as he felt her wet haven wrapped tightly around him. She lost herself to the battle of her emotions finally letting herself go, allowing her body to take over. Her pleasure drenched his loins, exciting him all the more. Once she finished, he lifted her up and set her on all fours. She worried only for a moment, but did not give it a second thought when he took her from behind. He grabbed her hips, shoving himself deeper, and she moaned louder, as he thrust even harder and faster. He lost himself to the moments of pleasure, spilling his life deep within her, before falling over completely exhausted. She felt herself drawn into his arms again, now nestled tightly beside him. He kissed her softly, then brushed her hair from her face with his gentle fingers. Her sapphire eyes looked deep into his dark eyes, searching for anything to reassure her that she had done the right thing.

Princess Ellyria rolled over, and could not help but silently cry. Was it from guilt? Was it from loss? She finally closed her eyes, but the tears somehow still managed to escape…

Chapter 61

Weeks went by since Queen Anna had seen or heard from her daughter. She was held up in the castle with Isis for company, and needlepoint to occupy her time...

Queen Anna was sitting on her favorite chaise lounge keeping her hands busy, by making a new shawl for Ellyria. Isis was lying at her feet. The wolf raised up her head, alerted by something. She got up and began to whine.

"What is it, girl?"

"Hello, mother."

Queen Anna could not believe her ears and looked up. Her daughter was standing right in front of her.

"Ellyria! You have returned!" she exclaimed, rushing to her side to embrace her.

"I am afraid that I have come with terrible news," she stated, returning the gesture, but only briefly.

"What is it?" Queen Anna asked, then sat back down.

"Lord Brom is dead. He died in battle."

"Oh, Ellyria. Where did you hear that? I received a letter from him just a few weeks ago. It was addressed to you. He is safe, my dear," her mother assured her.

Ranulfr appeared carrying a piece of parchment.

"This letter?" he questioned, holding it up.

"How did you get that? Who are you? Ellyria, who is this man?"

Princess Ellyria walked over, kissed him full on the mouth, then took the letter from him.

"He is my new master, and I am his apprentice. This letter was sent before I had seen his death. Are there any more questions for me, mother?"

"No, I suppose not. Is he the reason that I have not heard from you?"

"I thought that you did not have any more questions?" Princess Ellyria retorted, as she sauntered across the floor. Her long, black satin dress was dragging behind her. "I have been obtaining more powers, so that I can defeat the wizard. Ranulfr has been a wonderful instructor," she added, seeing the worry in her mother's eyes.

"Ellyria. May we speak in private?"

"I suppose so."

They both walked into the King's study. Princess Ellyria closed the door, with a wave of her hand.

"What is it that you want, mother? No, wait. I shall bet I can read your thoughts, so you do not have to bother trying to lie to me."

"Wait, Ellyria."

"For what? Wait for what, mother? I know that you do not approve of him, but I did not come here seeking your approval."

"What did you come back for then?"

"I have come to take control of the kingdom. Face it mother, it is falling apart. Father is away with my brothers, taking care of Ian's kingdom. When he should be here taking care of this one!"

"Ellyria? Who are you? Why are you acting this way?"

"In what way, would that be?"

"Cold. You are acting cold-hearted. You are not my daughter! Now, where is she? Return her to me this instant!" Queen Anna shouted, then began to cry.

"Save your tears, mother!" Princess Ellyria advised, then flung open the door and stormed out.

"Ellyria! Wait! You must stop this madness. All this power has gone straight to your head!"

Princess Ellyria took a step closer to her mother and glared at her, her eyes showing a darker shade of green. She raised her hand, lifting her mother up off the floor. When she lowered her hand, Queen Anna fell back onto the floor.

"My power is all I have," Princess Ellyria declared, then motioned for the guards. "Take her to the dungeon."

"No! Ellyria, please! Stop this now before it is too late!" Queen Anna cried out, as she tried to fight them off, but there were too many.

"You are exactly right, mother. I am doing this for you, before it is too late. Grab the wolf too," the Princess ordered.

Ranulfr went to Princess Ellyria and kissed her passionately.

"You did well, my love. The throne is yours for the taking," he said, motioning to the throne. "You can be Queen, and I, your King. Together we will take back the kingdom."

"You are right, my King. We will rule together. Join the kingdoms once again. Then together we will destroy the wizard forever."

Princess Ellyria and Ranulfr walked hand in hand, then sat on her parent's thrones. Her old throne was empty; she looked longingly at it, as if looking back into her past.

"We could fill that empty throne someday, if you wish," he offered, noticing her steady stare.

"Do you mean, what I think you mean?"

"Yes, my love, an heir to your kingdom. Would you like that?"

Princess Ellyria smiled. She never really gave thought to a baby before, but now that she was nearing her fated destiny, by destroying the wizard once and for all; she could see having a child of her own.

"Yes. I can see us filling this empty throne one day."

The new couple held hands and looked forward to their future together, as the new King and Queen of the kingdom...

While on the way to the dungeon, the former Queen was thrown into a prison cell.

"Isis run! Go get help!"

Isis bit the man who had her by a rope. He yelled out and then tried to catch her, but Isis was too smart and fast for him. She got away, running back out of the dungeon as fast as her legs could carry her…

Chapter 62

A crisp chill lingered in the air. The trees had a rainbow of colors displayed on their branches. The daylight had grown shorter, but the days remained long to Prince Dakota. Weeks had gone by, yet he was still in Regnuom with his father and brothers. Progress had been made; the town was being reconstructed and the fall crops that were left were harvested. What mattered most, was seeing to it that families were reunited and their homes rebuilt...

Prince Dakota was out in the nearby field, when he spied something moving through the wheat. He walked hesitantly closer. The movement stopped, and so did he. When the wheat shook again, he followed the rustling in the field with his eyes, then it came close enough to see it was a large black object. Then two pointy ears popped out from the tall wheat stalks. Prince Dakota was stunned.

"Isis? Is that you girl?"

The black wolf leapt right over the stalks, almost on top of him, then he patted her head.

"What are you doing here, girl?"

She let out a howl and rubbed up against him, nearly knocking him down.

"I need to get you to father. He will know what to make of this."

Prince Dakota led Isis to his father. His brothers were completely surprised.

"Why do you think she is here, father?" Prince Dakota questioned.

King Jason rubbed his head, knowing what had to have happened.

"There is only one explanation for it. Something is amiss at home. Dakota, I want you to take her back home. Luna can fly you in the quietest. If you need help, send her back alone and I shall send help. Go, and report to me at once."

Prince Dakota left with Isis and called to his owl Luna. The giant, white owl screeched, as she landed before him. He placed Isis in the harness and leapt onto the owl's broad back.

"Take us home, Luna!"

King Jason watched his son take to the sky, then turned to his other son, Prince Anthony.

"Gather the men. Tell them to be prepared to leave, in case Dakota sends back word that he needs us."

"Yes, father."

"Sire! I just heard. What has happened? Is Ellyria alright? What of Queen Anna?" Lord Brom asked, as he hastily approached the King.

"I am not certain, Lord Brom. I sent Dakota to find out. He will send word, to what is going on."

Lord Brom watched as the King left to talk to his other sons, to fill them in on the matter at hand, then Rob the Red ran up to him.

"Brom, what is going on? I just heard the men are being prepared to go back to Toledya."

"I do not know, Rob." Lord Brom sighed, then walked away and went to gather his things. He was going to be ready when they were to depart for home…

Luna flew as fast as the wind back to Toledya. It did not take long to reach the kingdom. Prince Dakota was cautious and landed in the nearby field, to not alert anyone to his presence. He unhooked Isis from the harness, then she took off for the castle. He could barely keep up with her, as she led him to the dungeon.

Prince Dakota was surprised to see that the prison cells were not heavily guarded. Isis led him straight to his mother, who was lying on the cot. She was weak from starvation and dehydrated.

"Oh, mother. How long have you been down here?"

"Dakota, Isis came for you?" Queen Anna questioned, barely able to raise herself from the small cot she was on.

"Yes, mother. She did. Just in time too apparently."

Prince Dakota found the keys that were hanging on the wall and unlocked the cell door. He went in and helped his mother to her feet.

"I am going to get you out of here and take you to father, where you will be safe. Where is Ellyria?"

"She is the one who put me here."

"What? No. That can not be? I have got to get you out of here, before someone finds us."

Prince Dakota picked up his mother and he carried her out of the dungeon. Isis followed them to where Luna was waiting. He gave her some water from his pouch, after he had hoisted her up onto Luna's back. He then secured Isis in the harness, then together they took off to go back to Regnuom...

Luna flew across the plains, in the Centre of Ragnarok. It was then, Prince Dakota noticed the ground below. The ground had opened up; coming out from below the earth were giants. Armies of giants that were lining up by the hundreds. Falling in behind them, was the wizard's undead army.

Prince Dakota urged Luna to fly faster.

"We must get back to alert father and my brothers," he said to his mother.

The gathering storm had begun…

Prince Dakota landed Luna right in the middle of town. King Jason was alerted that his son had arrived. He was surprised to see that his wife was with Dakota. Queen Anna was assisted down from the large owl, but was too weak to stand.

"Let us get my wife inside, quickly."

King Jason followed Prince Dakota, who was carrying his mother into the castle. After the Queen was seated, her concerned husband embraced her.

"Oh, Jason," Queen Anna cried.

"What is it, my love? What has happened?" the King said, gently wiping away her tears.

"It is our daughter."

"What of her? Is she alright? Where is she? Why is she not here with you?"

Queen Anna grabbed her husband's arm, with desperation in her eyes.

"She has been taken over by something. A man. He was there with her. I think he was controlling her somehow."

"What man? The wizard?" the King asked.

"No. A younger man, she said that she was his apprentice," the Queen informed him.

"Alright. I shall send someone out to search for her. In the meantime, you need to rest."

Prince Dakota tapped his father's shoulder.

"We need to talk."

King Jason left his wife in the care of his son's scullery maid, then followed him, along with Lord Brom and his brothers.

"What is going on?" King Jason inquired.

"When I was returning here, I flew over the Centre of the realm and saw giants coming out from the ground. There were hundreds of them gathering together. I also saw the wizard's undead army falling in line behind them," Prince Dakota answered.

"Are you sure about this, brother?" asked Prince Anthony.

"Yes. I saw it with my own eyes."

King Jason went to the window and looked out at the darkening horizon.

"We shall set off for the Centre of Ragnarok at first light. Tonight, we must send messages to the surrounding kingdoms to gather together. It will be our only chance of winning this war," King Jason said, turning to the others. "We can not allow that bastard wizard to destroy our realm."

The messages were sent via pigeons, to the other kingdoms of Inamor and Narruc. The armies from Toledya were already together with the armies of Regnuom. Once the kingdoms were united, the battle would begin. The war for Ragnarok was coming…

Chapter 63

Arie flew high in the sky, against the strong winds, and time itself, headed for the Omr Mountains...

The dragon Nidhoggr was enjoying a lovely afternoon nap, until persistent pecking rudely interrupted it.

"Who goes there? Show yourself, before I have to eat you," he snarled.

Arie came out from behind him. She flapped her wings and screeched frantically.

"Alfodr sent me."

"How is it that you are making words, bird?"

"Alfodr had the Norns to bless me with speech. That is not important now. What is important is the message that I bear."

"What message is so important, that you deliberately interrupt my sleep?" Nidhoggr grumbled, slowly uncoiling himself, then sat up.

"Alfodr has requested you gather the other dragons, and assist Princess Ellyria in the coming war!" Arie exclaimed, perching herself on the branch of a nearby tree.

The dragon let out such a deep laugh, that the branch that Arie sat upon trembled underneath her.

"Does he now? Well, you can tell him that I refuse."

"It is not wise to rebel against him."

"What is he going to do? Banish me to the Underworld, so I have nothing else to do, but knar on the roots of that tree? I do not think so, bird," he growled, with smoke billowing out his nose.

"If you do not help the Princess, all will be lost."

"Does it look like I care? I stand corrected. I do care, about my nap that I am going to finish. Now, if you will excuse me, bird. I am going to have to decline Alfodr's kind invitation to war."

"There will not be any more peaceful naps for you if you let the wizard win. If you think that he will not come up here, and annihilate your entire race, then you are sadly mistaken. I am growing tired of trying to persuade you to fight for a good cause. I am just sorry that I have to go back to tell Alfodr, what a cowardly dragon that you have become in your old age," the bird warned.

Arie started to fly away, when Nidhoggr stretched out one of his massive wings.

"Wait."

Chapter 64

Dawn had arrived. Many soldiers stood in line, shoulder to shoulder. King Jason led his allies onto the battlefield. There were many enemies on the other side. The giants towered over them, and the undead minions were hard to kill. All the odds were stacked against them. The kingdoms were finally united together as one. They believed in one cause; that was their freedom from an eternity of the wizard's tyranny...

The war of Ragnarok began with music ringing through the air, while blades and bodies came together in battle. The giants and their undead allies attacked the King with full force. All the King's men fought alongside him fearlessly. It was a struggle against the giants. With their brute strength, they were able to pick up several men at a time and toss them aside like ants. The mortal soldiers slashed the giants' achilles heels, to make them fall. They took the opportunity, by jumping on top of them and slashing the giant's throats with their swords. Some of the men were not so lucky, as the giants crushed them in their strong hands. The sounds of screams, followed by the sound of cracking bones, were enough to challenge the will of any man to go forward in battle.

Blood spilled on the ground beneath their feet. The echoes of screams rang through the open field. The wizard's undead soldiers rose again, well after they were slain. This time, there was no way of killing them. They had become unstoppable. Even with all of the Prince's familiars fighting alongside them, they could not defeat their enemies alone.

Lord Brom had become separated during the battle. After being pushed from the King's side, he fought his way courageously through enemy lines. He was running purely on adrenaline, wielding his sword, with no hesitation to where he struck with his blade. He became surrounded by a few of the undead soldiers, but their heads fell to the ground by Lord Brom's swift skills with his weapon. The undead soldiers had been slain; before they were able to reanimate themselves, he picked up their severed heads, then scattered them across the battlefield.

Lord Brom made his way back to where the action was, but stopped dead in his tracks at the sight before him...

Ranulfr entered Ellyria's chamber hastily.

"I have news, my Queen. The great battle has begun, and the wizard himself is on the battlefield right now. If we go soon, we can catch him off guard."

Princess Ellyria waved her hand over her magic mirror. Images appeared to her of carnage and mayhem. She looked deeper into the glass. Surprised by what it revealed, she stood and walked away from the vanity.

"You told me that he was dead!"

"What? Whom are you referring to, my dear?"

"Lord Brom! I saw him fighting on the field. How do you

explain that?" she shouted, pointing to the image in the mirror.

"That is the wizard! He is using his image to lure you to him. I have not lied to you. I love you, and I could never hurt you," he professed, then turned her to face him. "Do you not trust me by now? After everything that I have taught you, and done for you. Are you going to let the wizard defeat you by doubting me?"

Princess Ellyria stood there silent. She should not have doubted him. She reached up to pull him towards her and kissed him intensely.

"Do you believe me now?"

"Yes. I am sorry that I ever doubted you."

"It is time to fulfill my destiny," Princess Ellyria declared, looking back at the mirror.

That was only moments before Princess Ellyria stared down her enemy on the battlefield…

"Ellyria?" Lord Brom could not believe his eyes. "Is that really you? Why are you looking at me like that?"

Princess Ellyria sent out bolts of energy from the palms of her hands at the undead soldiers, that were now circling over the wizard. They were probably trying to protect him from her. Why did he not try and use majick against her? Why was he just staring at her?

Ranulfr was right behind her urging her on...

"What are you waiting for? Kill him while his defenses are down. He must have been weakened during the battle. Act now, before he uses his majick against you!"

Princess Ellyria held her hands high in the air, absorbing the collective energies all around her until she had enough built up. She formed a huge anomaly between her hands, but held on to it for a moment.

"What are you waiting for? Strike the wizard now!"

"Ellyria, please! Do not do this! It is me, Brom! Remember!" Lord Brom swore, falling to his knees.

"Now, Ellyria! Do it now!"

She could not let the wizard win. Not this time.

Princess Ellyria hurled the energy ball at her longtime enemy...

The smoke cleared. The war raged on. The undead minions were still going strong. They should have died with the wizard. The heart. That is it. She must remove the wizard's heart to kill him. He must only be unconscious right now.

Princess Ellyria ran over to where the motionless body lay on the ground, but when she arrived he had not returned to his original form. His image was still that of Lord Brom's.

"Why has he not changed?"

"You must remove his heart first, then he should return to his original appearance," Ranulfr insisted, kneeling beside her.

Princess Ellyria looked up and saw Raven standing up ahead of her. Oh, what had she done? This was not the wizard at all. She looked back down at the man lying on the ground below her. Tears made their way down her cheeks, and anger flowed through her veins. What had she done? This man must be, Lord Brom. Raven would not be there to collect the wizard, but the warrior, he was. No! She fell on top of Lord Brom's body and began screaming.

"What have I done?"

"You were under a terrible spell. Do not place the blame on yourself," Raven advised, standing before Princess Ellyria.

"Can you bring him back?"

"No. I am afraid not."

"Are you going to take him to Valhalla now?"

"Yes, Ellyria. He was a great warrior, who fought bravely. He will be a great hero amongst our golden halls," Raven said softly.

Princess Ellyria kissed Lord Brom one last time, before Raven took him away...

Chapter 65

Valhalla was not immune to the plague of war. Even with centuries to prepare, they still could not foretell the coming events. Hella and the giant Surtr, brought an entire army of giants with them to exact revenge on the Gods of these ancient halls...

The giants were taken by surprise, as the great halls seemed empty. Then, from out of nowhere, they were attacked from behind. Alfodr delivered the first blow to Surtr, knocking him to the ground with his huge axe. Then Surtr rose back to his feet and raised his fiery sword to strike Alfodr.

Hella ran from the fight just as it had begun, trying to find a place to hide.

"Going somewhere, ugly?" Freyja asked, catching her just in time.

"Is that all you have to try to defeat me with? Crude remarks? I am not a child anymore, and throwing stones at me will get you nowhere," Hella replied, trying to pass Freyja.

"Not so fast, crone. I am not allowing you to leave."

Hella made a feeble attempt to push Freyja aside, then Freyja tripped her.

"You are pathetic. Go back to the pit where you belong," Freyja scoffed. She then laughed and shook her head. "You are not worth working up a sweat over," she added, then walked away.

Hella waited until Freyja rejoined the battle, before she scurried off to find her older brother, Fenrir.

Alfodr, and his son, Tyr, teamed up against the mighty giant Surtr. The giant's fiery sword easily cut down Tyr's sword, but Alfodr was able to set Surtr back with a bolt of lightning from his axe. Unfortunately, that did not keep the angry giant down for long. Surtr raised his sword to deliver a direct blow to Tyr, who was weaponless, Freyja snuck up behind Surtr, stabbing him with her spear. Surtr was unaffected by the splinter wedged in his leg. He pulled it out, broke it in half, and then backhanded Freyja. She was flung across the room into the wall and was left unconscious.

Alfodr, angered by what happened to Freyja, attacked Surtr with his axe; before the axe found its mark, the giant grabbed his attacker by his throat. Tyr picked up the broken piece of the spear and dove off the balcony onto Surtr, plunging the blade into the giant's neck. Surtr dropped Alfodr, then grabbed the parasite from his neck, flinging him across the room...

A deep growl echoed through the halls. Piercing, yellow eyes shined bright from the darkest hall. Alongside this beast was Hella, who had released her brother from bondage. She pointed to Alfodr, who was still lying on the floor.

"Here is your chance, dear brother, to have your revenge," Hella purred.

Surtr stepped aside, to allow the giant wolf his prize.

Fenrir licked his lips at the anticipation of his next meal. Alfodr had awakened to the sound of jaws snapping and snarling from the beast. He quickly jumped up and attempted to get his axe, but the wolf chased him and cornered him; just before Fenrir took his first bite, Tyr jumped in front of him. Fenrir bit off Tyr's hand, while trying to save his father's life. Fenrir swallowed Tyr's hand and tried to lunge for Alfodr once more.

Alfodr's other son, Vidar, then grabbed the giant wolf. Dragging Fenrir by his tail, Vidar yanked him back away from his father. Vidar grabbed the wolf by the top of his jaw, then stepped on the lower half with his foot. With his bare hands, Vidar ripped Fenrir's jaws right off his face, tearing the wolf literally in half. The remains of the wolf fell to the marbled floor.

Hella screamed over the loss of her brother and ran away once more from the bloody aftermath.

"Should I go after her, father?" Vidar asked.

"No, leave her be," Alfodr replied, before Surtr returned for another round.

Tyr had wrapped his bloody stump and returned to fight, with a new sword. He fought bravely against the other giants, but was taken down soon after.

Raven who had snuck past the giants, awakened Freyja.

"Are you alright?"

"Yes. I am fine. You must return to Earth. Bring back Princess Ellyria. We need her help to send back Hella and the giants. Now go."

Raven did as instructed. Freyja picked herself up and returned to the battle. There were too many of them and not enough warriors, that were ready to fight. This was not going to be the fated end of the Gods. Not if she could help it.

The wizard set this war in motion, way before its time. There was only one person who could change the fate of the realm…

Chapter 66

The war in Ragnarok raged on. The mortal men were losing the battle to the giants, and the wizard's undead minions. King Jason and his sons were trying to shout encouragement, to keep up the morale of their soldiers, but all hope had nearly been spent...

Prince Anthony and his brave horse Odin, trampled through their enemies, leaving severed heads in their wake. A mighty roar from the skies above distracted him. He looked up to the sky, then called to his father.

"Father, look!" he shouted, pointing to the sky. "The dragons have come to fight!"

King Jason let out a sigh of relief, that hope would finally be restored to his men. His men rejoiced at the sight in the skies above them and pushed on fighting against their enemies even harder.

Fire streaked across the sky in anticipation, as Nidhoggr led his dragon army into the battle below. The giants were the first to be assaulted. Some of the dragons worked in pairs, taking the giants into the air and ripping them in half. Other dragons simply set them on fire, roasting the giants until they turned to ash. The remaining giants gave up fighting the mortals, to fight off the dragons' attack on them. A few of the smaller dragons were too weak, against some of the largest of giants. They were quickly snatched from the air, as their wings were pulled from their sockets, then left to bleed out on the ground.

Nidhoggr wasted no time, picking off the undead minions and making a snack out of them. One of his favorite delicacies to eat was the dead. No matter how hard they struggled in his massive claws, they were soon shoved into a hungry mouth. He had settled down at the edge of the field, gobbling up the dead as they ran straight for him. There was no place for the undead soldiers to go, once the King's armies herded them to the dragon that blocked their path. King Jason's men were finally able to defeat the few giants that were left, pushing back the undead minions into the dragon's waiting mouth.

The war in Ragnarok was nearing its end. The dragons had helped save the mortal men from losing the realm. Although the battle against the wizard had yet to begin...

Chapter 67

Princess Ellyria had not moved from the place where she had struck Lord Brom down. Although she was far enough from the battle to not be harmed, all she could think about was the last few moments she had spent with her love, before Raven had taken him away...

The spell Ranulfr had her under had broken the moment she realized that she killed Lord Brom. Her eyes were now open to the fact that Ranulfr was the wizard Raul, this entire time. Princess Ellyria's stomach turned at the memory of the intimacy she had unknowingly shared with him. She turned and vomited. As she was wiping her mouth with the back of her hand, she looked up. Standing in front of her was the man she loathed the most. He began to approach her, as if nothing had happened. Did he think that she did not realize who he was by now?

Ranulfr knelt beside her, placing an arm around her, as if to comfort her.

"I tried to come back as soon as I could," he said, pulling a vial from his pouch. "Here, I brought you this. It will calm your nerves."

Rage boiled within Princess Ellyria. She smacked the potion

vile from his hands, and sent him flying when she stood up.

"Liar!" she screamed walking slowly towards him. "How dare you deceive me? I know who you truly are, wizard!"

Raul got back up on his feet immediately.

"Do you now? I suppose you knew that it was your true love that you killed, and not I," the wizard smirked. "I was surprised after all this time, with all your powers, that you still did not recognize me. It was very humorous on my part, but also very satisfying too, my dear," he added laughing.

Princess Ellyria wasted no time hurling an energy ball into him. Raul went flying back into a tree, but quickly rose back to his feet. He too sent a multitude of energy in a steady stream into the Princess. She fell to the ground and was unable to move. Raul walked over to her. He stood over her motionless body.

"You are making this way too easy for me, bitch," he said smiling, then picked her up off the ground. Her eyes rolled to the back of her head. "It is such a pity too. You were such a good lay," he added, pressing his lips to hers, before he tried reaching into her chest for her heart.

Princess Ellyria opened her green eyes and spat in his face.

"Not before I take yours first, wizard!" Princess Ellyria shouted, then punched through Raul's chest and ripped out his still beating heart. The wizard's lifeless body fell to the ground.

The Earth opened, and the wizard was returned to the Underworld. Princess Ellyria stepped back watching his body fall down into the darkness. Raul's heart was still beating in her hands. Now, she must destroy it. However, before she had the chance, the heart vanished into thin air…

Raven had returned to Earth, only to find Princess Ellyria on her knees. She reached up to Raven with blood-stained hands.

"I have failed. I took the wizard's life, and before I could destroy his heart, it disappeared," Princess Ellyria confessed, then started to weep. She rubbed her cheeks to remove her falling tears, but smeared the blood on her cheeks instead.

Raven took her hands and helped the Princess to her feet.

"You can not worry yourself with this now. Valhalla needs you."

In a flash of lightning, the two were gone…

Raven returned to Valhalla with Princess Ellyria nearly too late. Many warriors were slain; even the Gods themselves were nearing their final hours.

"Please, Ellyria. You must save them," Raven said.

Princess Ellyria took a deep breath, before walking right in as Surtr was raising his flaming sword to thrust into an unconscious Alfodr.

"Enough!" she screamed, raising her arms to either side of her. She sent the other giants flying across the room, all of them but one.

Surtr turned to face the tiny girl.

"What have we here? A new bug I can crush?"

"No, giant. You will not crush me!" Princess Ellyria said, sending the giant away to join the others.

He got up quickly, charging at the Princess. She held out her hand and stopped him dead in his tracks. Surtr could not move.

"What do you think you are doing? Do you really think that you can defeat me?" Surtr said.

Princess Ellyria threw back her head and laughed.

"I may not be able to defeat you physically, but I can

majickally!" she shouted, then clapped her hands together.

Surtr exploded, and the flames on his sword went out with him.

"And that's the end of him," she added, with a smile.

Freyja ran to the Princess.

"You must find Hella and send her back down to the Underworld, with the rest of the giants. It is the only way they can finally be defeated."

Princess Ellyria closed her eyes. If killing the wizard opened a portal to Niflheimr, then she could use the Amulet of Elements to will it open again. Now, she just had to find Hella. She used her powers to expose the crone's hiding place, then opened her eyes.

"I found her. Come with me. She is trying to escape."

Princess Ellyria led Freyja and Raven down the hall of Vidi. Why would she be hiding down Vidar's hall? She would soon find out...

Hella was standing over a water fountain, at the end of Vidi Hall. She was attempting to create a portal to return to her world when Princess Ellyria came up behind her.

"Going somewhere, Hella?"

The Goddess turned around slowly. She had no real powers outside her realm and stood waiting for the Princess to finally put an end to her misery.

"I was returning to where I belong," Hella said meekly.

"You were? How convenient, that saves me a lot of trouble now. Does it not?"

Hella backed up to grab the blade lying on the edge of the fountain. Once she had it, she lunged for Princess Ellyria's throat knowing that the Princess would have no choice but to kill her. Princess Ellyria then used the amulet to turn the knife into a flower.

"I am not going to help you take your own life, Hella."

Hella's shocked look on her face made Princess Ellyria want to enlighten her.

"I can read your thoughts up here. Apparently, my powers work better in Valhalla, than in the Underworld. Here, you are nearly a mortal with no powers. However, your thoughts and desires are no different than any other mortal, making it easier for me to hear. I do not wish to hurt you."

Hella's tears fell into the water of the fountain, opening a portal to her world. Once it was opened, she had the power to reopen the gate of Utgardar, the third world from the root of the Ash tree.

"Thank you, Princess Ellyria," Hella said, after sending back the sleeping giants.

"Thank me? For what?"

"For keeping the balance in the world. This war was not meant to have begun now. The Fates are never wrong, but my grandson tried to thwart them, and that is why I am thanking you, for stopping him."

Those were the final words the Goddess Hella spoke, before returning to her own realm…

Chapter 68

Standing tall before all of Valhalla, Alfodr called to Princess Ellyria to stand before him.

"Princess Ellyria Rose. You have fulfilled your destiny by saving my life and preventing the fall of Ragnarok. I thank you, as do all of my children."

"Alfodr, I have not fulfilled my destiny. The wizard's heart was never destroyed," Princess Ellyria confessed.

Alfodr looked down at the young woman standing before him and extended a hand to her.

"Come, my child."

Princess Ellyria took his hand and was led to the steps alongside him.

"Kneel," he said.

Princess Ellyria fell to her knees as instructed. Alfodr tapped his staff on the ground. It glowed brightly. He took the staff, then directed it towards the Princess.

"I grant you, Princess Ellyria Rose of Toledya, a single gift," Alfodr said, then touched the staff to her heart, and transferred the light into her. "I give to you the gift of immortality. You will never grow old, and you will never die. Only when you decide to return your gift, that you will return as you are now. Do you accept this gift?"

"I do, Alfodr."

"Do you swear that by accepting this gift, you will continue to search for the wizard Raul, in the event he is resurrected? To follow him to the ends of the earth, and through time itself, until he is destroyed once and for all?"

"Yes. I swear."

Lightning struck all around in the great hall.

"So be it," Alfodr said. "Rise, my child. You are one of my children now. You may now take your place within these great halls."

Princess Ellyria sat beside Alfodr, as a great feast was held in her honor. All of Asgard came to greet her, celebrating her triumph over the giants...

The littlest Asgardian came running into the great hall, eagerly waiting to meet her favorite princess. Heimdallr had hinted to her she was in Valhalla right at that very moment. Hnossa spotted her almost instantly and ran right up to her.

"Princess Ellyria!" Hnossa squealed in excitement.

Much to Princess Ellyria's surprise, this beautiful little cherub practically leapt into her lap.

"Hello, little one," Princess Ellyria said smiling.

"I am Hnossa. I have heard all your stories, from my friend Heimdallr. He told me that you were here, and I just had to meet the Chosen One," Hnossa said excitedly.

"It is nice to meet you too, Hnossa."

The look on her tiny face was priceless, as her mother Freyja came in and spoiled all of the girl's fun.

"Come, Hnossa. Let us leave the Princess alone."

"Ahh, but mother," the girl said pouting.

"Now, young lady. It is time for you to go to bed. Say goodnight to the Princess."

"Goodnight, Princess Ellyria," Hnossa sighed, choking back

her tears, then gave her new friend a quick hug and a kiss on the cheek.

Freyja helped her daughter from Princess Ellyria's lap, then took her by the hand to lead her to bed. Hnossa turned around and waved goodbye to the Princess, as tiny tears trickled down the little girl's round face.

Princess Ellyria had to wipe her cheeks, but was smiling a bittersweet smile. She would never know the love of a child, now that Lord Brom was gone. She dried her tears, as Raven walked up to her.

"Are you enjoying yourself?"

"Yes. I have had a wonderful time, thank you," Princess Ellyria said, then sighed. "I must be going back now. I still have family that will be worried about me."

Raven took Princess Ellyria's hand.

"Let us go then. Shall we?"

No one had noticed the Princess had left her own celebration. With the exception, of the one who sees all…

Chapter 69

The war of Ragnarok was finally over. King Jason, Queen Anna, and their sons were able to return home to Toledya. They had worried about the Princess and prayed to the Gods that she was unharmed, hoping that she would soon return to them...

The royal family settled in soon after they had arrived. The castle suffered much damage and the King ordered the repairs to be made immediately. With all the work that needed to be done, the castle was bustling about more than usual. Even with all the work going on, suddenly it came to a halt when the Princess appeared out of nowhere...

Queen Anna was the first to notice her daughter's return.

"Ellyria!" she shouted, running towards her daughter with open arms.

Princess Ellyria stood still, patiently waiting for her mother to embrace her. She too was happy to see her mother and returned her embrace.

"I have missed you too, mother."

King Jason caught on to all the excitement and joined them.

"Oh, Ellyria. I have been so worried about you," he declared, holding his daughter in his arms. "Apparently, your brothers are waiting in line for their hug as well," he added.

One by one, Princess Ellyria's brothers came to greet her. Prince Anthony picked her up and twirled her around. Prince Rowan looked her in the eyes for a moment, before he took her in his arms. King Ian grabbed her by the hips from behind, picking her up and setting her in front of him.

"Welcome home little sister," King Ian said proudly.

Prince Dakota, who came in with Isis, interrupted King Ian.

"I am so glad that you have returned to us," Prince Dakota stated affectionately.

"As have I," Princess Ellyria admitted, before Isis began to nuzzle her nose underneath her hand. She knelt down beside her wolf and petted her head.

"I am happy to have you home too," she heard Isis say.

"I am glad to be home too, girl," she said to her familiar.

King Jason helped Princess Ellyria to her feet. The look on his face expressed to her that he was going to tell her something she would not want to hear.

"Ellyria, darling. There is something that I need to tell you. We lost Lord Brom on the battlefield. During all the chaos, I lost track of him. We searched everywhere, but found only this," her father told her, pulling a ring from his pouch, then passing it to his daughter. "I think he meant it for you."

Princess Ellyria stared at the ring that was interwoven with silver and bronze, which spiraled up and around the garnet gemstone set in the center.

"Thank you, father."

"I am so sorry for your loss. I know how much he loved you," King Jason consoled her, before leaving his daughter's side.

Princess Ellyria grabbed his arm, then looked up at her father.

"Wait," she sighed, then paused for a moment. She had to tell him the truth. "I have a confession to make."

"Yes, my darling. What is it?" he asked puzzled.

"I am the one who killed Lord Brom."

About the time she made that announcement, her mother

and brothers walked in on the conversation.

"What? What do you mean you killed him?" Queen Anna questioned her daughter.

"I was under a deep spell, by the man that came here with me. I did not realize at the time that he was the wizard, Raul. He was giving me this tonic, which in actuality was a darkness potion."

"To turn you evil?"

"Yes, mother, and it had. It made me lock you up in the dungeon and blocked my powers so that I could not use them against him. He lied to me and told me that Lord Brom was dead. After that, I went into an even darker state of being. I only wanted revenge, and I craved more power. The more I craved, the more I drank of the tonic, until I was no longer myself," Princess Ellyria confessed, then began to cry. "After the battle started, I looked in my mirror and saw Lord Brom. That is when Ranulfr told me that he was the wizard in disguise. I did not believe him at first, but somehow, he made me believe that he was indeed the wizard. When I stood before Lord Brom and looked him in the eye, I could still not see who he truly was. I was blinded by the spell, and Ranulfr kept pushing me to kill him," Princess Ellyria continued, wiping the tears from her eyes and rubbing her arms. "I did not even think twice after that. I only thought about revenge and killing the wizard," she paused, then ran her fingers through her hair. "I came out of the spell after I had killed him. I knew then in my heart that it was him, but it was too late," she cried out, then wiped her eyes. "I truly loved him, mother," Ellyria whispered in her mother's ear.

"I know you did, dear. I know you did," Queen Anna whispered back, then embraced her daughter and held her in her arms until she finished crying.

King Jason could not take any more of the flowing tears, he thought now would be a good time to make his announcement.

"I hereby proclaim that we will have a ball, not only celebrate that the end of the world did not come to pass, but for us to celebrate family and love. It will be held tomorrow night. So let us prepare!" King Jason shouted, to all within earshot.

Queen Anna poked her husband and glared at him.

"What?" he asked.

"I love you."

"I love you too, dear," the King said smiling down at her, then kissed his wife affectionately on the forehead.

Queen Anna helped Princess Ellyria upstairs to her room, while the castle was being prepared for what the King announced to be the biggest ball since the Princess's sixteenth birthday celebration…

Chapter 70

The great ball was held under a full blue moon, just after Lammas. They celebrated the fall harvest and rejoiced over the end of the war. Many had gathered from all the kingdoms of Regnuom, including Narruc, Inamor, and some faeries came from the Black Forest. The King had even invited the dragons, but Nidhoggr sent a message saying that he was still too full to fly.

The entire crew of the Draki came along with Rob the Red, Lord Thomas, and Captain Jake with his family. Jake gave his regards to the Princess, and introduced her to the newest addition to their family. A little girl, much to Jake's surprise, who they had named Gwendolyn. Princess Ellyria had a difficult time explaining his brother's death, and left out the part where she had killed him.

Princess Ellyria sat next to her parents in the throne room, just as she had done all of those years ago during her first ball. She began to daydream, hardly paying attention to all the guests that were dancing, dining, and laughing all around her. Her thoughts returned to the very night that she had met Lord Brom. He was so handsome that night. She recalled him asking her to dance with him; he was so graceful on the dance floor. Then she recalled their moonlit walk through the gardens, and her brother Prince Dakota, interrupting the first time they had almost kissed. Princess Ellyria giggled to herself when she remembered sneaking back out into the garden, while everyone was having cake. The first time he had kissed her was more majickal to her, than all of her powers combined.

Princess Ellyria had made her excuses to her mother, then went to revisit the very place where Lord Brom and her had shared their first kiss. The moon was so beautiful tonight, just as it had been on the night they had first met and fell in love...

The Princess walked to the double-seated swing in the summerhouse. Without sitting down, she just pushed the swing, then watched as it swung back and forth. She was imagining herself and Lord Brom sitting there, secretly wishing that she could have had one last kiss with him. She let out a sigh and turned around, walking over to the remains of her favorite fountain. Her father promised its reconstruction, but other damages to the castle took priority.

Princess Ellyria sat down on the side that still stood unscathed. She looked up in the night sky and stared at the moon that outshined even the stars. The Princess turned back to the fountain, that was when she saw him. Was this a dream?

"Hello, Princess."

"Brom? Is it really you? Are you still…?"

"Yes. I am afraid so. Freyja and Raven snuck me out of Valhalla so that I could see you one last time."

"Oh, Brom. I am so sorry that I killed you. I never would have done so, without being under that spell. You know that right?" she cried out.

"Yes. I know that you did not mean to kill me. I know what you did felt right, and in the end, it was for all of Ragnarok. You are a hero in Valhalla, you know," Lord Brom said smiling.

Princess Ellyria stepped closer to him. She raised her hand to touch his cheek, but it went right through him. She lowered her face, then wiped an errant tear from her cheek.

"Do not be sad, Princess. Raven said that you could use the power of the amulet to make me whole again. Even if it was just for a little while," Lord Brom stated, lifting her chin to meet his gaze.

Princess Ellyria closed her eyes and held the amulet, imagining being able to touch Lord Brom, then she felt him take her hands into his.

"It worked," she said smiling.

Lord Brom wiped the tears from her face, then kissed her like he did that first time, all those years ago. When he pulled away, he noticed the ring on her finger.

"I see someone found the ring that I was going to propose with," he teased.

"Who said that you still could not?" Princess Ellyria offered, as she handed him the ring.

Lord Brom took the ring and knelt before her.

"Princess Ellyria Rose. I have loved you from the first day we met, here in this very garden. I have continued to love you, even when we have been apart, and I will still love you from right now until the end of eternity. Please do me this honor, in sharing this same love with me, from now until the end of our days on Earth, and to the end of time itself."

"Yes. I will. I love you, Brom. I will wait for you. I will give up my immortality to join you in the halls of Valhalla," she cried out, before thinking of her future, then sighed.

"What is the matter?"

"I have made a promise, that I will remain immortal until I finally destroy the wizard. There is no telling how long that will be," she confessed, unable to hold back her tears.

"I have an eternity to wait for you as well. I am not going anywhere either," Lord Brom declared, pulling her into his arms.

"Ellyria," he whispered, then raised her chin up to look him in the eyes. "I love you. I will always be here for you," he touched her chest, where her heart was. "In here, I will always be, if you let me," he added, placing her hand to where his heart was.

The fireworks were launched into the night sky, signally the witching hour.

"I am sorry, my love, but my time here is up," Lord Brom

said softly.

"No. You can not go, not yet. I need you here with me."

"Oh, how I wish I could," Lord Brom confessed, then kissed her passionately one last time before he began to fade.

"Brom, wait," she whispered. Princess Ellyria could almost feel him touch her cheek, before he began to fade away. "I love you," she called out to him, then he was gone…

CHAPTER 71

The portal opened and a funnel cloud of light took over the entire room. Darkness invaded the light and all was quiet. When Princess Ellyria woke up, she was lying in something she had never seen before. It was soft and warm. She pushed herself up off the ground, and the fine particles of the foreign substance fell out of her hair. Her feet sunk into the strange ground, that seemed very unstable. It reminded her of the ash at the Omr Mountains. She walked through the vast nothingness until she had to remove her shoes to pour out the tiny, warm grains that had collected between her toes. The golden wasteland seemed to go on for miles.

Princess Ellyria continued to trudge onward. She found herself at what seemed to be a large hill, so she began to climb it. It was so steep, that she had to crawl on all fours just to keep her balance. The ground underneath her moved, as she pushed herself up. She lost her footing and her grip, then found herself sliding back down the hill. Instead of giving up, she dug into the moving ground a little deeper, then pushed herself higher with her feet. The sun beat down on her face and back, her skin burned, and never had any of the hottest summers at home compared to this heat. She was without water, her mouth began to dry out, then she began to see things, hallucinating in the heat. The Amulet of Elements would have been a great help, had she had it on her neck. She did not remember what had happened to it, other than the fact that she was not wearing it. Finally, she reached the top of the hill.

Princess Ellyria looked up as she got to her feet. It was

the most magnificent sight to behold. Large golden stones were assembled on top of each other. Some had the shapes of animals carved into them. Slowly she walked toward the giant triangles, fascinated by the massive size of them the closer she came. She lost her footing for a moment, and before she could regain her balance, she realized it was not her clumsiness. The ground was beginning to swallow her. She tried to fight it, but before she knew it, she was choking, her eyes were burning, and she could not breathe. Then she was gone...

Princess Ellyria woke up to find herself in the face of a mountain that seemed to sparkle in the sunbeams, as they penetrated through the cracks. She knew this was not the dragon mountain. Where was she? Her curiosity got the better of her, so she decided to further investigate her surroundings. The cave was cool, much nicer without the hot sun beating down on her. The light barely shined through, and it was getting darker the further she went into the cavern. She found herself completely shrouded in darkness and tripped on something. When she got back onto her feet, large golden eyes illuminated in the darkness. She did not bother to stand around to be something's next meal. Princess Ellyria ran back out the way she came. Overhead, something flew by her at an alarming speed. Once her vision settled in front of her again, she stopped dead in her tracks. Never before had she seen such a creature. She did not mean to stare and had apparently offended it somehow, as it came closer to her.

"Come to steal my gold, have you?"

"You can speak?"

"Yes. Why are you here?"

"I do not know. However, I can assure you that I am not after your gold."

"Then you should leave."

"I, unlike you, can not fly. I do not know how I am supposed to leave," Princess Ellyria stated, while looking down over the edge.

"That is not my dilemma, now is it?" the monster informed her, before he laid down.

"No. Perhaps you could help me to get down?"

"The question is not in getting down. The question is, can you go up?"

"What is that supposed to mean?"

"It is a riddle of course. Do you like riddles?"

"I suppose so. I have never really heard one before. I have only read about them in books," the Princess replied, rubbing her forehead.

"I will give you the answer to the first question, but you must answer this riddle first."

"What if I get it right?"

"Then I will answer the first question."

"And if I get it wrong?"

"Then I get to eat you, my dear. I usually only eat the one-eyed men always after my gold. For you, I will make an exception. I will bet that you taste as sweet as you smell."

"What is your riddle?"

"What has eyes that can see a great distance, can fly from the earth to the sun, mates for life, and can answer the most obscure of questions? What is it?"

Princess Ellyria pondered the question for a few moments. She began to fret. She did not know the answer, but she was going to give it her best guess.

"An eagle."

"Is this your answer?"

"Yes," she said, after taking a deep breath.

"Although I find your confidence amusing, your answer is incorrect."

"What? That has to be right."

"An eagle can not fly to the sun, nor speak, let alone answer questions."

"Does that mean you plan to eat me? Can we not talk about this?"

"I shall even give you a sporting chance. I enjoy the hunt

most of all," the creature offered, while sharpening its large claws on the rocks.

"A head start? There is nowhere else to go but down!" she exclaimed. Then she remembered his first riddle. She could climb up! Quickly, and without a moment to spare, she went to the outside of the mountain and began to climb up. She heard laughter echoing from the cave.

Princess Ellyria was now too busy trying to hold onto the side of the mountain to be distracted. That was until she saw the monster's head emerge from inside the cave. She tried to hurry, gripping the crevices with her fingertips, then finding open cracks to push up with her toes. Time was not on her side, when she heard the creature's wings flapping behind her. She felt her back burn and the warm blood tickled as it went down her side. She lost her grip. Her feet came out from under her; she was holding onto the rock with only one hand. Princess Ellyria tried to grab hold again with her right hand, but the creature's talons struck her again. The wind whirled her hair all around her; her body went almost in shock as it went down...

Princess Ellyria sat straight up. Her heart felt as if it were going to burst right out of her chest. She tried to catch her breath, but it was all that she could do to not pass out. The new surroundings were strange. She was in a tent, alone. When she went to stand up, the sheet that was covering her fell to the ground. She looked down at herself. She was completely naked. Grabbing the sheet again, she wrapped it around her, so she could take a peek outside. There were men in strange attire, who were armed, their horses tied to posts. Then she heard a man's voice from behind her.

"Are you going somewhere? I do believe that you are not in the proper attire for an outing," enquired the naked man behind her.

"Where am I? Please forgive me, but I seem to have forgotten your name," Princess Ellyria asked, thinking the man looked confused.

"We are on an island off the Aegean Sea. I had been captured by a band of pirates. I have paid their ransom, but as a bonus, they traded you to me. Right before I slit their throats. Any more questions, girl?"

"No. I do not think so."

How did she become a pirate's bounty? And then she was traded to him? Why was she naked? Why was he naked? Princess Ellyria's cheeks grew hot.

"Are you alright? You look unwell. Here, come and sit. Let me pour you some tea."

"No. Thank you. I shall pass. Where are my clothes?"

"I have not released you yet."

Princess Ellyria glared at the man.

"I am a Princess where I come from. I was obviously kidnapped by those pirates and have no recollection of you. So, if you will excuse me, I shall be leaving now. With, or without my clothes."

"Very well then. You are on your own."

Princess Ellyria watched the man put on his clothing, not much different from the sheet she was covering herself with, then tossed her clothes to her.

"Here, you will need these, and do not forget to coil that hair up under your turban. You need to go out, the same way you were brought in."

Princess Ellyria picked up the clothes, then put them on. They were very loose-fitting, and the head wrap kept falling into her eyes. She stepped out the backside of the tent, where he told her to go, but not more than a few feet from the tent, another man grabbed her.

"Where do you think that you are going? Get back to work."

Princess Ellyria was pushed in a new direction and fell into a line with some young boys. Did she really look like a boy? She looked down at her attire. Baggy pants, a tunic, a pair of sandals, and a head wrap. Yes. She did look like all the other boys made to walk in line, but to what destination, she did not know. Soon

Princess Ellyria found herself amongst the other strapping lads, on a ship out at sea. There was nowhere she could sneak off to use the amulet's power, without knowing where she was or even who she was supposed to be. Princess Ellyria could not use majick, she could not risk the exposure, or risk changing her history. The ship finally docked. When she stepped off the ship with the others, she slowly broke away from the herd...

Princess Ellyria had no idea where she was. The landscape was breathtakingly green and lush. She walked around for what seemed to be hours. Nothing but green grasses, ancient trees, and an abundance of clover covering rolling hills. It looked similar to her lands, but was a lot greener. She felt as if she was never going to find the end of the rainbow, that arched brilliantly in the sky and soon faded with the setting sun off in the distance…

A full moon now lit up the darkened sky. Princess Ellyria came upon another strange place. Torches were lit in a circle, from what she could tell, there were people clad in long robes. The two people in front appeared to be the leaders. One of them had a full headpiece made of horns from a stag. The other wore a wreath of some kind. The distance between her and the group made it difficult to see the fine details. She decided to step closer, so she could see what was going on. The closer she crept, the more curious she became. While she was steadily watching what was going on in front of her, someone grabbed her from behind. She tried to scream, but a hand held her mouth tightly closed, then she was thrown to the ground. Part of her hair had come out of her headcloth and gave away her secret. She was being pointed at. They were speaking in a strange tongue. They began to remove her clothes, until she was stripped to bare flesh. She was carried to a long flat rock and then tied down. This could not be happening to her. Princess Ellyria looked to her left, and then to her right. Columns of large stones that stood like trees surrounded her. She thought that being tied to this rock naked was bad enough. Then she changed her mind, when the person wearing the horns was wielding a huge athame, and the one wearing the wreath was chanting. When she heard the chanting, she knew what was about to happen next. She saw the horned man hold the athame above her, then she heard the group start to chant in unison. Princess Ellyria could not break free from her bonds. Her majick was not working in this strange place. It was as if she was blocked somehow. The chanting became louder. She saw blood splatter on the robed man. Her blood…

Princess Ellyria sat up awakened by her own screams. She looked around in the darkness. This was her room. Was she home? Isis let out a whimper, then she knew that she was definitely at home, and safe in her chambers. She could not remember anything after the ball, or remember how she made it to her room…

Chapter 72

The next morning came, and Princess Ellyria had awakened with the sunrise. She remembered the dream from the night before. What an incredible journey she had. She could not shake the feeling though, that she was in for many more adventures. After all, she did have to find the wizard.

Princess Ellyria walked to her vanity and sat down on the cushioned bench. She began brushing out her long black hair. Her hand began to shake, so she set the brush down. She then cupped her face in her hands and sobbed. She missed him.

Isis placed a paw in her human's lap and began to whine. Princess Ellyria looked at her and saw one of her favorite books from her childhood in her wolf's mouth.

"Isis, thank you. Where did you find this? That is very sweet of you, girl."

The wolf wagged her tail and laid down at her feet.

The Princess looked over the book. It was worn, the cover was faded, and the pages were still folded over to her favorite stories. She tried to recall the last time she had seen her book. It was several years before. It was also after her first adventure. Princess Ellyria wiped the tears from her eyes. That was after she had met Lord Brom. Even after Liza had kidnapped her, a few times she mused, but in the end, she triumphed. When she went looking for the Amulet of Elements and was kidnapped by Vikings, she at least got away. She received three new powers and had mastered them all. The Black Forest was saved from the evil Seither, Vala. She had two wonderful mentors, Vadoma and Mala, who lost their lives for her, and whom she missed dearly. Princess Ellyria began to think of the two greatest loves of her life, Alfar, the brave Halfling, and Lord Brom, who she would never stop loving. In all these years she had tried to destroy the wizard, he had always been one step ahead of her. He killed the people that she loved and cared for, as well as many other innocent lives. She must stop him once and for all, or the loved ones that she had lost would have been in vain.

Princess Ellyria could not only think of all the bane in her life. She had to admit some good had come from all the despair. The kingdoms had been reunited. Lord Thomas and her caregiver Nan, found new love with each other during the ball last night. She did save Valhalla from total destruction, was gifted with immortality, and she saved the entire realm of Ragnarok from extinction. It was bittersweet. Why should she feel guilty for her anger? Princess Ellyria slammed her book onto the vanity, while looking at her reflection in the mirror. Her eyes were green. It was always so amusing to her, how her eye would color change with her moods, blue like the color of sapphires if she were happy, and green like the color of emeralds if she were angry. As she was right now...

Princess Ellyria picked up the book again. No matter how hard she wanted to believe it, there were no happy endings. Even though she was indeed a Princess, it did not mean that she would have a happily ever after. Her life was not like that of a fairytale...

EPILOGUE

Little Hnossa was running through Asgard shouting for Heimdallr. She found him, where he always was watching over the bridge. He turned toward her and smiled at the happiest vision that he saw every day.

"Heimdallr! Heimdallr!" Hnossa squealed excitedly out of breath.

"Yes, my child. What is all the fuss about?"

"You never got to finish your story about the Princess."

Heimdallr tossed back his head and laughed.

"You are right, little one. I did not. Where did we leave off?"

"Tell me what happened to the Princess after I met her."

"After having saved Valhalla and her realm in Ragnarok, Princess Ellyria went back to Earth to be with her family. She was very brave, but lost the man that she loved in the process."

"That is sad." Hnossa began to cry.

"Do not cry, little one. It will be alright."

"What will happen to the Princess next?"

"That is a tale, for another time."

Hnossa stuck out her bottom lip and began to pout.

"Now, go home to your mother. She worries if you are gone too long."

"Yes, Heimdallr," Hnossa replied, then ran back home to her mother, reciting the stories aloud as she went.

Heimdallr looked out to the sky beyond the Rainbow Bridge. He watched as a shooting star took flight heading for Earth. As the seer of all, it was his duty to always watch over the Princess...

About the Author

Rose Marie Machario is an author, actress, model, filmmaker, and producer at Machario Productions, to include films Give My Love To Rose, An Affair To Remember, and An Affair To Forget.

Rose has worked in several principal roles, and has been featured in various television shows such as Ozark, The Originals, Nashville, Homicide Hunter, Killer Couples, Murder Chose Me, Murder Comes to Town, Snapped, #Murder, Justice by Any Means, Notorious, Fatal Attraction, Murder Mystery, Murder Decoded, American Nightmare, and Mark of a Killer. Her movie credits include Tag, Super Fly, The Road Less Traveled, and The Last Movie Star.

Then from onscreen to print, Rose can be seen on the cover of a few online magazines such as February 2016 issue of Hell on Heelz Magazine, and March 2017 issue of Electric Pinup Magazine, and also featured in several other national and international online magazines as an alternative, pinup, and tattooed model.

Rose is also a published author of her debut fantasy novel, The Amulet of Elements, the first novel in the Majick Of The Chosen Ones series. She also writes screenplays, and also in the romance, and horror genres, and her column called Always Dream Big.

In her spare time she enjoys a daily routine of yoga, loves to cook, and cuddling up with her fur-babies while binge watching her favorite television shows, and movies.

.

www.ingramcontent.com/pod-product-compliance
Lightning Source LLC
Chambersburg PA
CBHW030846030726
47495CB00005B/1400

* 9 7 9 8 9 8 6 1 1 8 5 1 2 *